By Alex Creen

Meeting

It was a snowy winter solstice. For Dublin that is unusual. It generally doesn't snow until January. However every now and again something special happens and it can put one in the mood for, well something else special to happen. Unusually it was the second occurrence of snow in Dublin that season, the pre-Christmas season and a festive spirit pervaded throughout the city. Strangers made eye contact and even a brief hint of a smile could occur. At the bars punters jostled merrily, not aggressively for over-priced, watered down beverages, whose cost increased by the hour every hour until closing time. For once it didn't matter. There were no Nite Link buses operating and the normal Dublin Bus service was to finish at 9 pm. That was ok too, it was snowing, the evening was freezing but it was crisp. For once there was no damp, no soft day to frizz even the straightest of straight hair. That's all Dubliners wanted, a change, when everything from the economy to the average car colour was grey a bit of white was light, bright, taking the grey out of sight.

Ok, so it was kind of romantic, she was out with two work colleagues. She had as she did every few months, organised a cultural event and this time it was a walking tour of Georgian Dublin. The main point was to be colour and its significance in each of the beautiful ornate doors of the Georgian Houses. Grey was not her favourite

1

colour. She had selected three Georgian Squares and they were all going to have a whistle stop walk through them and then have a Christmas lunch. However it was only Don and Stephen who had turned up. Both had heard the tour before. Stephen was very encouraging with Ciara and her research, Don reminded her that he had heard the tour before!

They abandoned the tour due to the blizzards and lack of numbers and had a boozy lunch. The only colour they could see outside was white which Ciara construed as purity and perfection. Ciara often took the cultural high ground feigning interests in Opera, esoteric books and artistic exhibitions. However since the cultural high ground ebbed and flowed like the tides of the river Liffey, she found herself caught out, stranded like a traffic cone at low tide, somewhere in between Heuston Station and the Four Courts.

They went to a micro-brew bar after lunch to sample a range of whiskies, gold was another good colour and whiskey bonders aimed at 40 shades of gold. Truly the sampling was to ascertain which particular flavour more particularly accompanied the range of stouts brewed in the four neighbouring counties. It was a perfectionist thing. Palates had been sullied and so refreshing and re-tasting was required to relieve the uncertainty which remained with the threesome. Don had a hankering for the highlands and after two beers would generally switch to scotch. Ciara and Stephen didn't wish to disoblige so switched as well but also drank beer so the whiskey would go down a bit slower. Well that was the theory at least.

'Here's to customer dis-service' Don toasted his fine scotch whiskey. These days everything seemed to be about service, good service, poor service, prompt service, slow service. Client services, that was their area of work but Ciara thought that this was a slightly inappropriate term. She thought it was similar to services of the corporal rather than the corporate kind so she called their work the complaints department. It was really a call centre in a nice big building, new and bright with lots of windows. Don had found her comment on customer dis-service funny and mentioned it at every work outing toasting it with mischievous mirth, the joke had worn thin for her and Stephen as they heard it at every work outings toast. Today they saw themselves as the core of the office social club.

'Tell me Don, why is it that the more you drink the more expensive the whiskey becomes' asked Stephen? Ciara looked at Don then looked at the change in her hand then looked up at the 12 year old Glenfiddich, yes the last one had only been five years old.

'The more I drink the stronger the taste needs to be as my taste buds get a bit muted,' said Don.

'Oh,' said Ciara, 'could you not go onto the really harsh and cheap stuff then?' They say the change is in your pocket but hers' rarely got that far.

'I could but my body couldn't. The hangover from poor whiskey is rough.'

'Oh' said Ciara again, 'screaming tots and all that.'

3

'Yes my children are naughty only when I can't handle it. They seem to sense my weakness,' said Don.

'Is it the blood shot eyes, or the box of painkillers?' asked Ciara.

'Poor you,' Stephen nodded not knowing exactly what to say. Don was the only one with children.

Right so we are all post-modern, health-conscious, well-informed people and no one smokes anymore or anything but two out of the three had to pop out for a quick weather update. As updates have to be updated every thirty minutes or so a little nicotine was inhaled along with the crisp fresh air.

Ciara was out inhaling this air and thought back on the day. It had been most enjoyable, it was fun pushing Stephen's wheelchair through the snow over the cobbles of Temple Bar and onto the restaurant. He normally had a super duper electric chair but had left it at home this day given that there was snow on the ground. The weight became too much for Ciara to push so Don needed to take over especially when the breeze blew snow flurries into eyes, nose and mouth. Her arms felt as if they were going to fall out of their sockets any minute and even her hand bag was too heavy to carry.

Don had enjoyed displaying his male strength and Ciara had unhelpfully remarked, 'it takes a lot of snowing to make snow.'

'Yep, you're observant,' Don said. 'It had only been snowing for the past three days.'

'No I mean there is less than a foot of snow yet it had been snowing for three days non-stop,' replied Ciara. She had a feeling that she would lose this argument if she persisted.

'You probably knew the exact moment the snow would begin you weather channel addict,' said Don.

'It's true I do like watching the weather at work but only when things are quiet.' Ciara was a bit taken aback by the statement but since weather was her favourite subject she was happy to elaborate. 'This storm was interesting though there were live stream feeds of the snow clouds descending from the north. It was very exciting.'

'Can we go in somewhere' said Stephen, he had forgotten his gloves and his hands were turning a deep shade of blue. Ciara took off her gloves and rubbed his two hands in hers. 'I can't feel anything' he said worryingly. So they had decided on the micro-brew or more specifically a brew house as they brewed more than microscopic quantities of beer. Thankfully!

She was tired at this stage of the evening and realised after a myriad of texts from loved ones that the weather was worsening and getting home to the outer suburbs, let's face it almost Galway, was going to be arduous unless decisive action was taken. So decisive action was taken and they left the bar. Stephen decided to walk out instead of taking to his chair and toppled over in the snow knocking Ciara over. The knock made her realise as she was chin deep in cold, dirty snow that she had forgotten her cap. It was freezing, she was tipsy and she looked ever so slightly inelegant with her bottom in the air. So she ran back in to get her cap, retrieved it from under a bar stool and she whisked out the door to say goodbye to the two boys. Somebody held the door open for her but she was so distracted that she forgot to say thank you or even look at him. How rude.

Then she proceeded to light a cigarette, return the first missed call and walk up to the bus stop on the Quays. Wonderful multi-tasking she thought to herself. She didn't hear footsteps behind her as the sound was muffled, and she was a bit preoccupied by doing more than one thing at a time. So when a rather tall man stopped her, whilst carrying a lot of bags she got a bit of a fright. "He must be a tourist" she mused as he was far too good looking to be Irish.

'Hello' he had a decidedly Irish accent. She was confused. 'I just saw you in the bar, in fact you just left the bar and,' "he talks too, this must be an apparition." Most men in Dublin looked as if they were about to pop out twins any minute and were so proud of their paunches that they fed them regularly on stout and Supermac's. This is the Irish version of east meets west as Guinness comes from Dublin and Supermac's from Galway. These fine specimens of the Irish male could often tell you the cost they had incurred gaining the curvature and the years and dedication it had taken, the gut was one of the serious pastimes the Irish male began in college. So she ignored the apparition, walked on and continued her phone conversation.

'Am, would you like to get a drink with me?' he persisted. There was a politeness to his tone which made her think he had been educated beyond primary school.

'Sorry, just a second I am on the phone' she returned to her phone conversation, "Yep sure, I am at the bus stop now so will get the next bus." Returning to the tall stranger in front of her, thinking there definitely was too much whiskey in her line of vision, she really didn't think imaginary visions were this big! 'Yes that would be lovely. Where did you have in mind?'

'Karl is my name, by the way.'

'Hello, I'm Ciara, if I were Italian my name would rhyme with tiara, but I'm not so it doesn't.'

'No it doesn't,' he sagely observed.

Well that witticism fell flat, as flat his stomach, well actually she could not be absolutely sure given the necessary layering affect of the cold and current fashions if his tum was truly tight. It definitely did not have a pregnant look to it.

'What about here?' she suggested. They were standing outside a hotel which had a nice bar and it also was just beside the all important transport link. Really what on earth was she doing consenting to go for a drink with a complete stranger when there was about a ten minute window until the last bus left? Taxis were always an option but there had been rumours throughout the day that less and less were available and since she lived on a steep hill they would not take her to her door.

'Great, handy' and he held the door open for her, again; this was good as her arms were weary from pushing Stephen around all day.

They sat Karl and Ciara, the two names had a nice sound, the K was strong then softened through the words, they chatted, drank and were merry all thoughts of the homeward journey were banished and phenomenology reigned supreme. She was completely in the moment, alert, responsive and alive. The lethargy of a long day out was shaken off, energy coursed through her veins and she felt vital, appreciated as a person rather than just a person of production, a unit of labour facilitating profits for the large corporation to which she had bonded herself. Mortgage repayment and base rate trackers were gone, European Central Bank bailouts were ignored and for the moment she could just be. He didn't know or maybe not even care for anything about her life and it felt wonderful. No information was imparted on either side except for light fun stories of travel and adventure. No specific destinations were mentioned and the talk was a vague yet vibrant whirl of colour, sights, sounds and smells.

'I'm out this evening as I have just got a promotion,' Karl announced. Ciara was a bit annoyed as she had wanted not to talk of work or anything boring like that. 'I feel a bit guilty getting moved up in a firm when many people are being moved out.'

He was celebrating more than the weather and the festive spirit and yet it was probably difficult to tell people that sort of good news. She wondered what reaction he was getting from the recently redundant punters who were drinking their redundancy pay rather than buying Christmas pressies for their children or making lump sum payments off their mortgages. They might be, she didn't know! No that was silly she shouldn't assume such things and she tried to concentrate again on this vision of a male specimen in front of her. That sounded clinical, as if he were a white mouse in a lab, "focus Ciara" she said. He was right to celebrate his achievement she concluded mentally after a long internal dialogue, in which her eyes had moved slightly from left to right like an old fashioned type writer.

'Yes I am beginning to suffer from survivors' syndrome myself. What area do you work in?' she asked.

'Right here in Temple Bar,' he smiled.

'Ah that's handy,' she said a bit confused.

'Ooh I see you mean which discipline, architecture.' He was quite specific she noticed.

'Cool, that's kinda interesting,' she wanted to be a bit encouraging but she didn't want to enter a long monologue of how he got into it. 'So how did you get into it?' Oops, she could blame the booze. Best get the boring bits out of the way.

'My grandfather is Norwegian and he builds wooden houses by hand. I use to help him as a boy. I was fascinated each log cut to an exact angle to fit into the next one, wooden pegs hammered into place with the skill and precision of a diamond cutter. It was great fun, in his spare time he builds boats and I also help with the building to this day.'

'So this is where the pale hair comes from.'

'Yes my father is from there and my Mum from here. What about you?'

'I'm all Irish,' she said, 'unfortunately,' she added.

'Unfortunate is an unusual term.'

'Maybe, but it isn't exotic like Italian or Greek. I have the big hair but not the even glossy complexion of a Mediterranean.'

'I would never say pale and interesting in your context, you have the whitest skin, with a hint of a freckle or two on your forehead. You have a strong contrast with your features.'

Wow, she was underwhelmed! Or then again was it that he didn't want to say too much as she may think him a bit creepy? 'We should try to get home.'

He gave her a half smile, was this smile of lust or just mischief? Could he mean he wanted go to back with her? After ages of celibacy could she consent to this? No she would not even consider it, well not seriously anyway. When break ups are bad, as her previous one had been it can often leave one in a state of inertia. Ciara was enjoying the flotation process especially as it was filled with the black stout of amniotic fluid which could be a life blood or at least a good substitute for a relationship.

Then clarified his half smile 'no of course I wasn't suggesting together,' Karl was confirming, drat!

'Of course not,' she said with a little giggle. Her defences were up again but maybe there was a hint of disappointment. He could have tried.

They left the bar and she decided to freshen up in the fancy powder room, was there any lipstick left on her lips? Were her cheeks overly ruddy from the affects of alcohol? She should leave him with an attractive memory.

She powdered and returned but there was no sign of him. Ah well maybe he was just an apparition after all. He had paid the bill so a decidedly friendly ghost. Then he waved to her from outside and grinned sheepishly, he was smoking. However as she came close to him she noticed he was smoking a very light cigarette so that would mean he was not a committed smoker, an intermittent smoker hopefully. That would be good as if she were to see someone it would not be a good idea for that person to be a smoker, it would mean an intermittent bad habit would turn into a regular occurrence.

'Hello again,' he smiled, 'which way are you going?'

How not to be rude but to give away absolutely no information in case he turned into a scary stalker? 'Well actually I was going to get a bus on the Quays.'

'So you live on the West side then.' How did he know that? She could have crossed over the river and got a bus to any other destination in Dublin. Was he smart or did he realise she was lazy?

'Yes and you?' she enquired.

'I live in Kildare,' he was also being a bit cautious. She could well seem like an unhinged female who would take to camping on his balcony or his front garden for no particular reason except to annoy and embarrass him in front of his neighbours, friends and family.

'Oh that's unusual, I never knew anyone who lives at my side of the town.'

'Well now you do. Am, may I kiss you?'

"That's weird", she thought "do people ask to kiss these days". Does it spoil the natural flow of events to truncate by questions? Maybe it would not be polite to ask if there had been a break in the conversation a silence.

'Well actually I have boozy breath, my friends and I was busy all afternoon, sampling whiskey you see. Also I have sneaked a few sly Marlboros and I am probably like a fire breathing dragon.'

'Ah, don't worry I won't notice. I have had a drink or two myself,' he wasn't to be discouraged that easily.

So he moved a bit closer, shuffled his Christmas presents somewhere out of the way and kissed her. She leaned her head back, even closed her eyes, felt a bit dizzy and touched his arm to stabilise herself. It felt so exciting to touch him even if it was just his winter coat, she felt a bit forward but what the hell. It, this was special, the kiss was beautiful. He pressed his lips more firmly against hers and she felt a wave of desire coursing through her whole body.

He took her cap, that old blue peaked cap in his hand and gently pulled it from her head. Her hair was free and unruly and blew in the sharp wind. He withdrew appraised her and said 'how can all that hair be caught up in this cap?'

'Crazy huh!'

'I am going away tomorrow.'

'For Christmas' she asked hopefully. How he had deflated her hyperbolized and blown up fantasy of boats, made by his grandfather, snow and Fjords this time next year. Or maybe that was it, the moment was as fleeting as a melting snowflake, he would be gone on the Emigrants flight fleeing the depression and lack of prospects that Dublin had to offer. No, that wouldn't make sense he had just been promoted so he would be around for another month or two yet. "Breath Ciara, it helps you stand up."

'Yes two weeks to see my family they live in Norway.'

'That's nice I hope you have a great time.' "Phew, I can cope with that. Not that I am looking for anyone or anything but it would be nice to see him again." She didn't want to ask where in Norway as this may be too inquisitive. Nor did she wish to know how far from the airport they lived, or why his father and mother had not been mentioned, as it was really none of her business and it was damn cold out now. The kiss was over and he made to hail a taxi.

'You'll be back' she stated, not out of desperation but certainty, he was only going for a short time. He would be back, but whether he would be back to her was debatable.

It seems that he thought for some reason she had said "no strings attached!" He murmured it echoing her statement. It was a constant occupation of his in the texts he would send. How Freudian of him, a slip of the ears or winds carrying ones thoughts to their brain. There are strings, there are always strings attached.

So forever in her memory that corner of Wellington Quay and Parliament St would be sacred, would have an indelible memory of a kiss which seared through the shard of ice which had consumed her heart, her feelings, it had melted her frozen will not to be open to anyone. Well except for the non-threatening variety of cute small children and charming little old ladies, it was safe to be open to them.

A taxi stopped, miracle and she reluctantly climbed in, and this moment was over never to return. It was like a death. Maybe she should be getting out more. He hopped in too, aha, a man of action!

They chatted as the taxi drove a kilometre a minute down the snowy Quays past the Four Courts, along Usher Quay and out to Heuston Station. There were deep drifts on the road and the driver was being particularly cautious. She was glad that it was safe and warm in the car but she did feel a large hand land on her leg. Better not to say anything, it was a confined space and he was doing the confining.

'I have my hand on your leg' he stated.

'Yes but I can barely feel it through this heavy skirt.' She felt he didn't need encouraging. So he pressed harder. 'Yes I can definitely feel that. Ouch, it's a bit sore.'

He smiled and kissed her again. More confidently this time, they touched tongues and everything. It was as if he knew she wasn't going to hop out of the car on the Chapelizod by-pass and could explore a little more. She was his for this journey and this journey was quite long. So she changed the subject. 'So what did you buy for your family?'

'I got flannel pyjamas for my sister. It gets quite cold there so they could be useful at this time of year.'

'That is thoughtful. I love fleecy things at night in bed.' Woops should not be encouraging those sorts of thoughts when he was consuming all the available space. "Think I will get out on the motorway so as not to have the driver get stuck on the steep hill to my house and so they don't take too long a detour."

'So if you had a choice which era would you live in,' he asked. He had not taken up the fleecy theme for night time apparel thankfully.

She thought for a moment as history had always been her favourite subject.

'If you lived in the past would you not be dead already?' she asked.

'I don't know, maybe there are parallel times or something. So hypothetically speaking would you?'

'The idea of living in the past has always interested me, the romanticism of it, the costumes, the sights, different sounds such as carriages instead of cars. However as a woman I think today is really the best time to live'.

'Well as a man maybe I may be better off in another era, yet it is true that society was a lot less equal. Hopefully I could have be the lucky 1% One of those aristocratic families who owned most of the land. I could have a great big townhouse a wife half my age and several mistresses.'

Her eyes widened, he was joking she could tell but by how much it was hard to ascertain, as he was new to her, after all.

'I jest, today is pretty good.'

She appraised him, his scarf was tied in a Chelsea knot. His hair was wispy, his long neck narrow and elegant.

'Could you be a tall Napoleon? You have a Romantic look about you of the early nineteenth century'. She could imagine him out on the tundra striding for no particular reason but to be active. In the command of large forces and being decisive, that was how she saw him. She wasn't sure if Napoleon had ever been to Norway but she certainly hadn't.

'Someone with ambition bigger than even my own!'

She really wasn't sure what he meant, was ambition meant to impress her? Conversely was he trying to say he had things he wanted to do but wasn't a megalomaniac. He was hard to read so she said nothing. He was complex or was she being overly analytical.

'So what is your telephone number?' he asked and she thought this was a positive move. He keyed in the number and dialled it. "Does he think I would give him the wrong number I wonder?" Her phone rang and she said 'so that's you!'

'What is your first memory?' Ciara thought she would see what sort of depth he had.

He thought and he moved his eyes from left to right to mimic hers when she had been deciding what to speak about in the bar.

She hit her hand onto his to show she could see this as the light brightened and dimmed with each passing lamppost.

'It was my grandfather creating' he said at last. 'He was, is, he is still alive, so creative. The main fruit of his labour is of the wooden boat variety, but he built wooden cabins for my father, his brothers and just about anyone who asked for it. I always remember wanting to be able to create too, to help him, to learn and have something to show for my efforts.'

'That's nice' Ciara now felt a bit challenged in her first memory, as it had been quite destructive.

'And yours?'

'My grandmother dying.'

'Oh I'm sorry.' Maybe that dampened his ardour somewhat.

'No, it wasn't sad at all. She was a really old lady and had a long healthy and hopefully happy life. She had a brain haemorrhage when I was very little. She died really quickly with all her family about her, her eyes were open so we put pennies on them as we laid her out on her bed. Then we ran in and out every few minutes, all my sisters, brothers and cousins, to her bed. We were checking when she would turn cold.' She had only one brother she wasn't sure why she was feigning a large family, maybe it was his look, scared.

His eyes were staring at her with incredulity.

'I was never frightened of a dead body after that, I was curious as she was still my Granny, I wanted to know what rigour mortis was and understood it from an early age. It sounds odd, but it was a very happy time for all of us children and it was lovely for my granny not to die alone.'

His eyes were at the most extreme point of opening, she thought his balls might fall out of their sockets. Had she lost him before he was won? Maybe death wasn't the best subject for a first meeting.

'Oh' was all he could add.

She directed the taxi driver as to where to stop and she hopped out. 'Lovely to meet you' she bellowed. Life, death and taxis, the three certainties of Dublin life in the recession.

He smiled at her as the car pulled away and then was gone.

There was suddenly a cold shiver which passed through her. It was not just the biting cold but a sense of loss. "Ciara be practical, it was a lovely and unexpected meeting. That is all, he won't call and realistically you don't want him to." None the less she floated up and over the bridge humming out of tune, a very old song, "Dancing Cheek to Cheek". It was a lovely feeling and she would enjoy it and not expect more. Maybe she should not have said so much.

Nice Texts

She walked in the door kicked off her boots the house was cold yet she felt exhilarated. She had a hot feeling inside, boozy maybe but a thoroughly satisfied and complete sensation. The day and night had been wonderful, she had the sort of feeling that if she were to die right now it wouldn't be such a bad thing. The pagans of old had shuffled off the dark cold winter through festivities and so had she. She could feel a link right back to New-Grange and the Neolithic peoples who had built it. Wow what a lineage further back than those title seeking Normans! The phone buzzed with a text tone. "Who could this be" she thought to herself, it was a bit late.

'Hope you got home ok, this is my own number. The other phone is my work phone.' He had sent a text already!

"Oh my goodness, that's somewhat keen, scary stalker in the making. I will ignore the text, no maybe I should answer so he doesn't think I have fallen over and frozen to death in the snow. Ciara don't be so dramatic, he wouldn't be thinking that, he could just be feeling bad about me hopping out at the side of the road. Ah," she re-read the text, "actually it is to say that he had his work phone out and he must be bringing his personal phone on hols so no point in leaving messages on a phone which most likely won't be used." All was rationalised and deemed to be perfectly fine and within usual dating practices.

"I will leave it until tomorrow so he won't think I am desperate. Because I am not, really I am Not looking for anyone, independent, single and strong, without a man is that wrong!" Maybe she was protesting too much. She repeated the mantra she had written to herself aged 19.

"He will be gone tomorrow", she had not asked him his flight number so maybe tonight was better. Texting was hard when one eye had to be closed. Maybe she should get a new phone, a voice operated one for times of extreme merriment.

'Yes back in one piece, have a great trip,' she texted twenty minutes later. She thought this was simple, a succinct response and no sign off was necessary. Before sending it she changed her mind "great to meet you" no maybe "can't wait to see you again". She had already mentioned that meeting him would be good so why reiterate it. Just an acknowledgement on the new number that he got the right number that was all. Typing with unruly thumbs which are determined to hit words such as "love" "adore" and "worship" can be trying, there also seemed to be about eight keypads, so the original text was sent, eventually. Where there was a will she would find a way to work her phone, however slowly and get it to stay still.

"Also", she continued in her internal monologue, "he wouldn't have to feel responsible for me trundling up the slippery slope from the motorway, alone, in the middle of the night, in the cold." She didn't know whether he had noticed her unsteady foot work, he may have just sat back, dosed off and thought of how to pack all the presents he was carrying into 12 kg of cabin baggage.

****
****

Work was finished early for Christmas as most people could not make it into the city. So Ciara spent the next day productively in bed, watching old films and feeling festive. She downloaded a few black and white oldies to feel romantic, especially the musical variety, which assisted her mood making. There was a definite Fred and Ginger theme since she had been singing "Heaven" or "Dancing Cheek to Cheek" on her way home and the song was still playing in her head. Actually it was getting a bit annoying now, she really wanted it to stop and listen to another song on the self-play loop that was her brain. She adored the 1930 glamour of Ginger Rogers's wardrobe, the Art Deco features displayed in cars, architecture and the bold writing on signs. It was a different era, when the entire world was starving through the Great Depression the people had an escape from their worries and cares through cinema. The plots were paper thin, songs and dance routines were spectacular and things always worked out in the end for the hero and heroine. Maybe there should be some reality TV talent show and the winners would remake modern day versions of Fred and Ginger musicals. It seemed the depression was being relieved here and now so why not have the escapism to match it?

There was one film that took her fancy. It was the film where "Heaven" was sung. She played it and was lost in the era as always happened when she began one of these films. It was called the "Gay Divorcee", and Ginger had been married to an old man. A geologist in fact and she wanted to divorce him. There were some lovely dance routines especially a beach scene in Brighton which made her think of sun and holidays on this cold duvet day.

The closing scene ran and The End was clearly displayed on the screen. Her escapism had come to an end and she had to get on with the day. She lay in bed a while longer and shook the coffee pot, it was empty. Sugar she had no longer an excuse to lounge, her hangover was nearly gone and she had things to do.

She made her Christmas list and now that it was the afternoon she headed to the local mall to buy all her presents in one fell swoop. It took a while to get there as the roads were still snowy. There were only two other people in the mall, both with the same idea. What a result, this was ideal shopping weather, no queuing no jostling just choosing and buying. The shops were so quiet that they were even gift wrapping, fantastic she really disliked wrapping presents. Ciara had never been this organised in her life. It was only the 22nd and she had purchased all her Christmas gifts, what would she do for the next two days? All the jovial happy eye contact of the day before on the streets was lost on those two shoppers in mall-land and they were serious about their acquisitions. They had their heads down, arms out, purchase, wrap, pack and out of the retail units as fast as their laden down frames could carry them. Shopping was such a chore. Also they wished to be home before sunset and the roads refreezing. She drove back home jubilant at threeish, less than an hours' work. What a productive day!

That evening as she finished another Fred and Ginger film she received a text.

'Greetings from Norway, it is freezing here -12 and there is 6 feet of snow. A winter wonderland,' said Karl.

"Hmm, he is thinking of me," she thought. "Wow, maybe he is real after all. Oh, what should I do? It's so exciting I thought he would be busy building boats or striding the tundra, or something. And I have barely thought about him all day" she lied to herself. She had not been imagining that she was Ginger and he was Fred and they had been dancing and skating and driving and picnicking in her fantasy 1930's land all day, honestly! "Anyway my era of fantasy with him is going to be the beginning of the nineteenth century." He was the tall Napoleon after all.

'Lovely, the snow is here too but we can't compete with 6 feet.' A bit of a rhyme, quite lame in fact but she didn't want to seem as if she was contriving too hard on the text-talk. She had left it a few hours before returning the text. She didn't want to seem too impulsive and also wished to look occupied. "I wonder which part of Norway he is visiting, I could look it up on the atlas or the app- less, no that would be silly, what do I care where he is, I don't know him and chances are I won't get to know him. Don't waste your energy on a random run-in, let him prove himself before you dedicate any mental energy to him." Her thoughts were oscillating between seeing him all the time and never speaking to him again.

It was a lovely evening, no one called and she called no one. Bliss, she was lost in her head and her head was a very happy place at the moment. She had to prepare herself for the onslaught of Christmas with family, neighbours and random small children. It was going to be as arduous as ever this year as she had nothing, well very little in common with people who were married with small children. What did she know about interrupted sleep patterns, solid food and inoculation? She was considering getting the flu jab if that counted. It was an alien yet parallel life to hers which she neither understood nor was interested in. Children were cool but babies she didn't get.

The two days passed blissfully but far too quickly, it was her first time being off in ages, and on Christmas Eve she was about to head to her parents house relaxed and contented when he texted.

'Kisses from Norway on this snowy Christmas Eve,' he said. Wow, great, cool. She was falling hook line and sinker and she didn't even go fly fishing or whatever this phrase referred to.

Nice, not too soon, not too late, not too lecherous but cutting the cold with a hint of warmth. 'Many Happy Returns from frozen Dublin.'

'If a face could launch a thousand ships then your eyes could call them back' he texted. She wondered if he was being a bit Troy, epic and maybe a tad general. She was getting confused with all the fantasy worlds, the early 19th Century, the 1930s and now ancient Greece. Was he sincere or strategic? Sometimes guys text more than they mean to generate a bit of interest, get the lady hooked so to speak, is this more fishing? It was amazing how suggestible some ladies could be in the early days which could lead to falling for the guy, missing him and falling hard. Ouch, was that a knee or an elbow which was hit by the bow of one of those returning 1000 ships? Obviously Ciara was not that susceptible. Obviously!

Of course Ciara was different, she was smarter, more cynical, a tough cookie! She would be no fool, not after the last time, she had forgotten all about that romanticism stuff. How eloquent males could be in the wooing process, 'my love is like a red, red rose' or 'like the sweet magnolia tree, my love blossomed tenderly'. Did they say these things just for effect or were they true, how could one tell? Could one enjoy the ride and not be affected by the circumstances? That was like asking could a scientist not affect the experiment, was it possible. Merely by being there affected the outcome. The objective here would be to keep fatalities to a minimum. She was still on the phenomenology buzz, being in the moment and all that. Pity she had only tuned into Heidegger when at college, she may have had a more balanced psychological outlook. In other words she would only think of him when she was actually sending or receiving a text. If that is what the theory meant!!

Should she respond to this compliment, or could she pretend that she hadn't seen it? Nope there were delivery reports these days, silly technology! She felt embarrassed when she was complimented as she didn't feel worthy of receiving something well so wordy! So massively involving events like the Trojan Wars were above her, she was no Helen. Ciara, clear, plain and simple, not the Italian Chiara, that was much more exotic. How could he think that of her?

'Is there a horse outside?' she joked reminiscent of the U-Tube hit a while back. The typical Irish response to emotion was to rebuff it with humour.

So how could one, an individual who was a stranger become another's someone and then become that someone's one and only? This was another Fred Astaire song from his Broadway Days. Was this a truism that existed only on Broadway shows and Fred and Ginger movies? She was going to have to broaden her range of downloads if she wanted to get balance. Maybe she should see some boy films with lots of guns and car chases. "It must be true though," she thought again about the concept of true love, her father loved her mother, it wasn't just dependency right?

She should really be heading out the door but she stayed a while longer, thinking and rethinking what boys wanted. A friend of hers who had lots of brothers told her that a boy decides one day that he wants a girlfriend, but before that day there is absolutely nothing a gal can do to persuade him! It could be a brief interlude but it would not develop into a real relationship. "So love is a decision!" she concluded. "I wonder what Mae West would say to that?"

She packed up her very nicely wrapped presents and loaded them into the boot of the car. The roads were slippery now that the sun had set the snow was turning to ice so she debated whether to drive or take a taxi. She returned to the living room and again her thoughts returned to this concept of what would make a guy fall for a lady.

Another friend had informed her that her brothers said a guy always goes for a 'nice' girl, the type of girl who doesn't get drunk and has a sleep-over the first time she meets a guy. The girl who speaks well, but is not too challenging, who listens lots doesn't talk too much. To Ciara's mind this was a bit of an act, a ruse, pretending to be something she was not. That someone was definitely not her. Could a boy not like her as she was? It wasn't as if the boy was putting on an act pretending to care about what she was interested in or worrying about what she had to say. Or maybe it was just a method of getting what he wanted.

'Yep this horse is outside, in the cold' Karl responded to her line of humour. He took up the baton so to speak and was able to run to the next person on the relay of texts. So was she merely the next person on a relay of texts? Or was there a destination, a finishing line on the race?

"Should you take a ride" she thought of sending, or no that was actually a bit lame, err! "Head out for a gallop" that was even worse. "With legs as long as yours your walking stride could be a canter." She didn't want to over compliment him, she would have to think on it. "Be wary of Greeks bearing gifts as they may freeze en-route to

Norway." Save the text to drafts, that was the best thing. "Oh my goodness" her drafts box had so many half finished texts it was almost full. She had forgotten press send and so her thoughts to friends were as yet unsent. It was no wonder people hadn't responded to her! The key to texting is to press the send button.

So back to the Horse Outside, would he canter or would he gallop, maybe she should lose the legs part of the text and just say stride.

'Am I out in the cold with you?' he sent after ages whilst Ciara had been day dreaming about the ideal relationship on this dark, cold evening. She had not realised that time was passing. Had he wanted her to be outside with him, or was he implying that she was taking too long to respond.

She sent, 'beware of Greeks bearing horses as gifts because they'll freeze outside in Norway.'

'I'll remember that as this half Norse is wholly frozen waiting out here for you!'

She left the texting at that and so did he for the moment. She had very important stuff to do, like get out the door and not start another Fred and Ginger film. This was her imperative as she was about two hours late. Should she call her Dad to pick her up, but he may have had a few mulled wines and been over the limit. She would drive she had good tyres and hardly ever used her car so she would be fine. She would go really slowly.

'Horse where's your stable?' she sent as she just set out on her journey.

She drove the ten minute journey to the other side of the village, the old village as some liked to refer to it as. She heard the buzz of a text but had to ignore it in these challenging driving conditions. She felt very relieved to reach her parents home and stable there until clement weather conditions returned. It was almost like the Holy Family, away in a manger as there was a garage for her and everything.

'Celbridge but I'm only renting' he justified. That was confusing. He must have been referring to Dublin as she didn't think there was a Celbridge in Norway.

"Like OMG, I didn't realise we lived so close!" 'So near but currently so far,' she texted in was a very corny line but inspiration was limited after concentrating.

'Well it's only for two weeks Ciara.'

'Is it a good heated horse box? The one in Norway I mean,' she asked.

'Yes, we have a nice dry horse box or stable.'

'You would need a good blast of heat in that cold Mr. Horse.'

'We do' replied the stealthy steed.

She was still sitting in her car, engine off the temperature was rapidly decreasing, it was she who was the horse outside now it seemed.

'I'm going into the parent's stable; the car is too cold in icy weather! Happy Christmas again.'

Christmas was conducted, with family and friends the weather was still cold and this was the first white Christmas Ciara had ever experienced which made the experience, well a special experience. There had been one time in the Noughties where there was a snow flurry on Christmas Day but it wasn't the same as having laying snow several feet deep, well about a foot and a half. The back garden actually looked pristine, the empty flower pots were filled with white fluff so it appeared that there had been some form of gardening conducted in the house in the years that she had lived there. Her Mum was not a keen gardener. Then it was over and she was back to work.

Thinking about Texts

So texting had not really been Ciara's preferred means of communication. She was thinking of them on the bus home from work as recently she had received and sent more texts than she had ever done since she got a mobile phone. She always liked to get a call from a guy. Now it seemed, dating protocol had changed and she had to change with the times. They, texts are an efficient means of getting one's point across with minimal impact on or to oneself. There is a record of an encounter or conversation, however truncated or short, which can be kept or discarded according to the person's wishes. Does it replace the love letter? The three lines of sentiment poured over by lovers and poets of old. Or is it a new-ish form of communication with its own language. It included such poignant and meaningful scripts as "RUup4it?"

Do people consider form and composition in a text as a letter would have demanded? Or is it expedient, quick or even perfunctory. Can they be judged by the same measure? Which has more weight? In response, the letter one supposes would have more weight as it is tangible; trees have had to die for the sender to be able to hold the paper in hand and for the thoughts to be captured.

The next year would be the twentieth anniversary of the first text. In technology terms this made it an ancient form of communication. Would it survive the next twenty? It is very popular with the males of our specious, much quicker than a phone call and then, whatever supposed duty required a text would be expedited and they could move onto something else.

There are no technical supports for developing text writing skills such as there were for honing letter writing skills in the days of old. With the advent of the Industrial Revolution letter writing output must have increased with trains and steam ships taking letters further faster. The penny black must have been a veritable communication revolution. Who she wondered received the first letter by penny black? Could it have been Queen Victoria? The system began in 1840 and the first letter sent was to Miss Jones, it was sent just before the stamp was introduced so the receiver had to pay for the postage.

Then later still with pylons and cables the telegram came along, maybe telegrams were the original texts. They were succinct, purposeful and not usually romantic. Were there telegram writing courses such as there are for internet marketing? Did people ever propose by telegram, or divorce? They certainly did via text. If scientific development had happened in a different way how different would the world be. For example if the Romans had decided to free all their slaves maybe the industrial revolution would have happened ages ago. There is a certain amount of evidence that there was the capability for this type of development, they were great engineers on parallel with the Victorians. Would that mean that we would be at the other end of climate change? All the coal would have burned by the 5th century AD and then the atom may have been split to fuel the planet. The information highway may well have superseded the railway and the car. Would that mean scrap metal wouldn't be so expensive? Hey maybe the copper sculptures would be still intact. This was a long bus journey which Ciara was taking and her thoughts were on a ramble also. She generally let her mind unwind so that when she got home she would be out of work mode and into home spirits.

How had the text method of communication come about? It was from a computer to a phone but the phone did not have the capability to receive it and it was not until the next year, 1993 that Nokia brought out a texting phone. How had the world changed, it was reported that Irish people sent one of the greatest numbers of texts in Europe. With the advent of web access on phones however would they become redundant soon?

Yes, texts could well be the progeny of the redundant telegram, she was back onto the telegram theme again as she had watched a musical from the 1930 on the previous night. It may have been a Fred and Ginger, again, but she wasn't admitting to it, even to her own psyche. The telegram linked the world by wires and cables or was that radio waves and wireless? It was the smart technology of the day. Texts linked by really large pylons conducting satellite waves were the smart technology of the last decade. What would be next?

Emoticons! What did they mean, why did people use them, where was it best to use them, and who would you send them to without looking silly? Small children used them excessively; they loved symbols such as Santa and

Christmas Trees for festive times or bunnies for Easter. Were symbols the same as emoticons? Could they have the same significance as heraldic symbols of old? It was all a mystery really. EMOGI, it sounded like something from a science fiction film, how did that relate to anything? Ciara may need to look into terms a bit deeper.

All these thoughts were just idle musing, the subjunctive opportunities of technological discoveries through history such as a helicopter prototype being invented in the Renaissance then waiting 400 years before the design could be implemented. Would all of this fit into a text to Karl and if Ciara sent it, would he be interested?

She was, as a result of all these thoughts, going to find out how to be a competent texter and get with the new decade even if texts were nearly two decades old. She would draft up succinct, script, it could be sexy maybe saucy and she would keep the interesting ones proverbially up her sleeve but actually in the draft file as this guy, this Karl seemed a bit competitive. "Let the games begin."

No Text

The days succeeding Christmas were quiet, on the texting front that is, there wasn't a beep. No Text after all the sweet words of ships and horses in their stables or outside this was a bit of a change. At least there had been two days of work to keep her mind occupied. It was New Years Eve and Ciara thought it would be about the right time to hear from him. That there was no contact since Christmas Day was understandable he was with his family. "Should I text him at 11 pm as he is on CET or should I wait until midnight GMT? Maybe I should really wait until he texts me, as he may think I am clingy and cramping his style" she thought.

Then a while later when there was still nothing. She moaned a bit to herself and decided to visit her mother that always meant she was occupied. There was always Turkey to be used up and it would be nice in some of the 500 baked potatoes which still remained un-eaten since Christmas Day. It would while away time before the NYE party at Dons house and she wouldn't... she couldn't... what did she not want to do, premature-text maybe? "Well really boys should lead in the early stages of texting" Ciara decided in her ignorance of the world of text!

"So what am I mooching about? He has no tie to me, no obligation. He made me no promise to meet and maybe I was a bit dismissive when he said he was going away" she rationalised whilst driving over to her parents house. She was really trying not to think of him, but it just wouldn't work. "You'll be back eventually" may not have been the kindest statement when departing someone's company for the first time. It had merely been intended as a truism. The afternoon with her parents was busy and Ciara felt occupied and suitably distracted.

So the evening of New Years Eve arrived eventually, Ciara was stuffed, too many spuds. "Now focus Ciara, get ready for the party, first task is to finish the hair," she had to decide what to wear, "clothes boring, shoes fun, definitely exciting." Then decide on mode of transport "yes certainly driving not trusting public transport on a night like this." Especially when by car the party was 20 minutes away and an hour and a half by bus. Radial routes are not as developed in Dublin as larger cities due to the lower population density.

The party was great, small and intimate with loads of food but she wasn't in the mood, definitely too many spuds and she was text-less so preoccupied with a Quiet Norseman. There was sangria, yum. Ciara decided to water down her sangria with extra lemonade she really didn't want to be over the drink drive alcohol limit. Apparently it was a Scottish tradition, every year they had sangria not driving when booze was taken! Well in Don's household anyway, the wife was from the lowlands of Scotland and her accent was very light, as light as Ciara's drink, she was feeling excessively virtuous. Don the host, work colleague and friend seemed, externally anyway to be a very content person and a jovial spirit. He was perfectly affable, a great host and a devoted husband. As the company at which he and Ciara worked was creaking financially the office was beginning to resemble a ghost ship. So it was Don who would be called from the school when one of his children was sick. He was to all intent and purpose a "new man" metro-sexual, in touch with his family and Ciara suspected he had a skin care routine. She had a feeling he had more skin products in his bathroom cabinet than she did yes he had such good skin.

Everyone was drinking their sangrias, eating their finger food and trying not to talk about work, imminent redundancies and the weather. What else was there to talk about religion and politics?

'So Ciara, how has your Christmas been?' Don asked.

'Yes good so far, wasn't the snow amazing that night?'

'Wow it was so heavy, romantic almost and the fact that it stayed for Christmas, well it made Christmas for the children. Did I see some tall guy hurry out of the bar after you?'

'Well yes, actually you did. I think he may have been a vision though as I have not heard much from him since.'

Where was he from?'

'He's half Norwegian and half Irish.'

'That is a bit unusual.'

'Yes, he is, how can I put it, he's dynamic.'

'Is there a little sparkle?'

'You never know' said Ciara delighted to talk about her current favourite topic. She was about to be polite and ask Don how his Christmas had gone, then swing the conversation again to the tall handsome stranger, when..

'Honey' his wife interposed, 'could you check on the food you are so much better than me.'

'Must be all the practice I get' smiled Don. 'Excuse me a moment Ciara.'

'Of course, unless you need a hand,' but Don was already gone to the kitchen. He was a brilliant cook. Ciara smiled at the wife, what on earth was her name again. Sugar they had met at least ten times. 'Can I help you with anything?' she asked the wife.

'Ah no Ciara, it's fine' and they smiled at each other. She went off to talk to some of her friends and left Ciara to daydream a bit before she decided who to talk to next.

Don often talked about his children in the office and enjoyed looking at baby snaps when ladies returned from maternity leave. He could add 'when my Derrick was that age,' and other useful phrases. Ciara couldn't stand being subjected to baby-books and photos considering it the most boring thing ever. Babies to her were similar to old men, toothless with beer bellies sorry milk tummies. The only children she could bear were nieces and nephews and in small doses.

Maybe it was because Don had two of his own that he was interested in children. Or maybe it was a substitute for work. Ciara really admired that his wife was so high powered Ciara would never have dedicated so much energy into making someone else rich. How the wife handled the stress, the pressure was beyond Ciara.

There remained a very faint, tiny niggle that Don might have his robust and well adjusted male ego a tiny bit dented. Yes it was logical for the highest earner, to be allowed earn, but did men not like being the main bread winner? Did he go to bed at night after cleansing, toning and moisturising his good skin, and his soft freshly ironed PJs, probably by himself, completely content with himself? Ah what did Ciara know? Most lightly she was wrong.

Ciara looked about the room and was more than a little surprised to see her boss was at the party. "What a lick Don is!" She looked at Anna, her boss and was put out by her presence, not that Ciara was drinking. No it was more that Ciara would have to be polite and nice when she wanted to be natural and not so polite.

Anna saw her looking in her direction and made her way over. 'Lovely party' she said. 'I can't believe I can eat so much food after gorging myself at Christmas.'

Ciara's gaped incredulously, she could never imagine Anna doing anything which wasn't perfect. She was a good boss but was perfect, too perfect to be actually human and be on Ciara's slovenly level.

'Apparently Don gets a lot of practice at cooking!' she said.

'Ciara you are bad. Síle is a lucky woman.'

That was her name, Síle, Don's Síle. There were so many scarily bright and competent women at this party Ciara felt really inadequate, Anna, Síle and of course Aoife her non-date-date or plus one or whatever.

Ciara thought back to when she had first met Anna she had been in awe of her. It was at a graduate recruitment fair and even though Ciara was of the "because I'm worth it" generation, she had never really felt "worth it." Should she be changing her hair product? However Anna had told her to send in a CV to the MNC which she, Anna had set up the Irish or EMMA, or was that EMEA or some other anachronism which Ciara didn't know or understand or really care about.

She had sent in her CV and was really surprised to be called to interview. Anna interviewed her even though she was really senior and way above Ciara. However Ciara was warmed by Anna's approachable nature, her care and her humanity. For some reason unknown to Ciara she liked her enough to give Ciara the job. Anna was a cool boss and Ciara respected her for it but was a bit fearful of her also.

'Is your husband here tonight?'

'Yes, Adam, you remember him,' Anna was clarifying as she knew Ciara was hopeless on names.

'I do, yes he is talking to my friend Aoife.' Of course Ciara remembered him; she had been on Anna's hen night and at the wedding. Adam was a nice guy, tall and chatty. He seemed quite easy going which was good as Anna was a whirlwind of energy. "Delighted for the name prompt" thought Ciara. 'How are you getting home?' she asked.

'I'm not sure yet, the roads are still slippery and we forgot to take a dip as to whose driving so we both started.'

'Woops, but sometimes it is good to let go.'

'Exactly,' agreed Anna.

11 pm came with no text, then it was midnight and still nothing, no buzz, her phone must be on silent, no it was just silent. There was the countdown and everyone began hugging and dancing around in a circle to a song which didn't make sense but Ciara felt alone. It was a strange feeling to be alone when she was surrounded by her friends. She could not shake herself out of this distraction and connect with the celebrations. By 1 am she was bored and sober and everyone else was decidedly merry. She was as sober as all the traffic police she would meet along the M50 and just as happy! She decided to go home with her plus one good friend, Aoife. They could compensate with a Prosecco breakfast after an abstemious evening.

Aoife was also ready to go which was convenient as they were the only plus ones at the party a non-couple. 'Are they not the most functional family you have ever met?' asked Aoife as they donned their coats. Whilst the snow had stopped the cold had not, it was the coldest December on record according to the Weather channel. Well technically it was now January.

'Yes obviously we don't know the ins and outs of their lives but they seem a happy couple' Ciara felt a bit guilty about her previous thoughts, these were Don's emasculation in marriage but well, is not everyone entitled to their internal thoughts. It is only when internal thoughts are shared that the problems start.

'If I ever get married again it will be to someone who has an outlook like Don,' continued Aoife as she hopped into Ciara's very cold car. Aoife had been married to Ciara's ex-boyfriend's good friend. They had often been a foursome and polite grown-up-style dinners, it didn't suit them. He the ex-husband, had not been worthy of Aoife in Ciara's opinion, he was a nice guy but Aoife was a very successful, motivated and beautiful lady and she had traded down in order to be a bride in her twenties. Well Ciara would think this as Aoife was her best friend and had a definite halo in Ciara's eyes.

Ciara turned on the engine and the heat to blast the ice from the windscreen and stop their toes from freezing like the windscreen wipers currently were. 'Just the cooking side would do me' she said. 'Do you know Don made all of that food and it was from scratch not a pre-made party-pack?'

'My ex liked to cook BBQ stuff, you know Irish style.'

Ciara smiled, 'yes where all the cooking actually happens in the garage.'

'Exactly, to keep the food dry as the rain will always fall on BBQ day. The other Irish phenomenon is that I would do all the marinating, usually the meat but sometimes also vegetables, buy all the food, bake the spuds halfway before wrapping them in tin foil ready for the thirty minutes on the BBQ. Finally I would make the desserts and the salads and he would take all the credit.'

'That's sort of why I don't like BBQs,' said Ciara. 'Anyway, Happy New Year, may the road rise before you and all your troubles be light.' Since she was on the Irish-ness theme she may as well get a complete plastic Paddy blessing in there too.

'Thanks Ciara, on rare occasions you say some very nice things.'

The next morning a great boozy breakfast ensued with lots of gory gossip of recent antics. Obviously they were not dissecting the merry men they had encountered during the winter holidays. No they were comparing and contrasting the guys they had met since the summer as unfortunately pickings were slim in Dublin. Thus at least six months was needed in order to get enough meat for the proverbial BBQ.

'Still no text from the Norwegian?' Aoife asked eventually. 'Ah well he has obviously met an attractive milk maid with wonderfully formed pouring utensils otherwise described as jugs in lads mags and flaxen hair I would assume.'

'Thanks, will I see you off now then?' Ciara joked feeling a bit hurt by glaring reality. 'I think his grandparents live somewhere really rural, so possibly there is no coverage'.

'Anything is possible. I told you I met a guy and he is a lawyer. He took me to a very swish Christmas party.'

'Oh yes, tell me some more' said Ciara, lying, she had no interest in talking about some other guy until Aoife endlessly discussed Karl. That was never going to happen, so Ciara tuned into reality and out of fantasy.

'Well he must be doing well as most of the associates were not allowed bring their partners. He was a bit dull though.'

'That's a pity, but I suppose you can't have it all.'

'Much as I try' said Aoife.

'Yes' mused Ciara. She really should try, maybe go out with more than just Don and Stephen. She could possibly chat to boys and see what they were like, but they were not all Norwegian Gods who looked as handsome as Karl. Actually what did Norwegian Gods look like? Bearded, probably maybe like Vikings, she would have to research them when there was nothing fun happening on the weather channel.

'You look like you are busy.'

'Sorry I'm just thinking.'

'Well stop it, it's bad for you.' Aoife smiled. 'I had best go anyway as I have to get ready for work tomorrow' said Aoife.

'Sure, of course. I will see you soon. Actually do you want me to call you taxi?' Ciara didn't want to lose her driver's licence on the first day of the New Year after being so abstemious last night.

'No I feel like walking, it's only twenty minutes. Bye and Happy New Year.'

'Bye and see you soon.'

****
****

By the second of January, in other words the next day, she thought it would be ok to send a jokey style text. She was back in work and sitting at her desk. All the news had been exchanged around the office and Ciara was a bit bored, 'hope you have not been borrowing your sisters' Pj's to ward off the cold weather,' she sent. No response ensued. It was a good half an hour later when she decided, "So that was it, a truncated snowy story." A good fifteen minutes later she further decided to cut him out of her life. It had been an agonising two weeks or so and so she deleted his first text to her. Then after lunch she deleted the missed call he had made to her in the taxi, in the next hour another text and one more the hour after that. This direct action was empowering. By the late afternoon she decided to delete his work number. Then on the bus home she deleted another text. The 'kisses from Norway' text, she had read and re-read each brief message he had sent. That text she could not delete. It was unhealthy this text thing and she needed to move on.

Two days later there was still nothing, she no longer felt empowered, she was sitting at her desk and there was very little work to do. The weather wasn't helping her as it had reverted to the soft variety, grey dark and like the rest of Dublin her finances were stony and broke. She really needed a pick me up and something tall, blond and intelligent would have been nice. On the 5th of January she sent a one-liner...

'Back? Meet? Drink?' It was three words of desperation, ever so slightly short of "please call me" or "I can't believe you don't want to know me." She was about to delete his number and that would be the end of it when...

'Had a bit of phone trouble, Happy New Year, how are you?' That was his response! Wow she was deflated. She sat grinning into her blank work screen none the less.

Then another one came through, just afterwards, 'oh just received your texts now! No didn't need to borrow my sisters pj's as the houses are hot. What I wear in bed is a secret, but don't worry I'll let you into my secret!! Outside was freezing so did wear thermals.'

'Good to hear from you.' "Phew" she thought. 'Like long johns,' she sent. "Woops, why did I send that?"

'You like long johns too! Well I have a range of colours, black, white and orange. Do you have a colour preference?'

'Black for formal wear and white for more informal occasions!' she send, "what am I saying? Really I can't believe I am having texts about long johns, but they do remind me of cabins and the Wild West, pioneers, wagons and adventure." Anything would seem romantic on a day as grey as that.

'I will bear that in mind for when we meet,' he said and that sounded hopeful. Yes maybe he did have phone trouble. She was ready to swallow a brick as January wasn't the most inspiring time of the year. She had heard this was the most likely time for people to break up, especially marriages, could she buck the trend? Start a relationship at the start of the year, when all was dark except the large red credit card bill, rapidly approaching like a juggernaut with faulty brakes.

Actually this was going to be a diversion, well that was what she attempted to rationalise as the start had been so shaky. She sat on the back seat of the bus later that day and read back those texts, both sent and received. It was like reading gold, her heart was gladdened and her mood lifted. This was nice, it was fun. It was harmless as all was at arm's length. She need never meet him if she didn't want to. Texting was safe.

Text Again

She was sitting on the top deck of a Dublin Bus when it happened. She had heard that there was to be a lunar eclipse that evening and so she was scanning the horizon for it. Well actually she had been scanning the weather site all day at work. 'Did you see it?' she texted Karl.

'See what?' he mustn't watch the weather channel at work, maybe he was busy in his new position. Karl had been back in contact with Ciara for a good three days now and she felt he was a permanent texter. In other words, he was keen.

They had been talking of nothing else and on the weather site and showing lots of examples of what eclipses' would look like. Ciara had been hooked and had done a good five minutes work all day, luckily things were quiet. How could Karl be so out of the metrological loop?

'The lunar eclipse,' why on Earth would he know, what she was thinking about? She hadn't explained it.

She went on to describe at great length the lunar eclipse 'the sun was a fiery ball illuminating the sky and then nothing as it was taken over by the small moon from our planet. Darkness reigned immediately turning our world from day to night with no twilight. It was spectacular I was engulfed by nature. It overtook me and I was left feeling tiny and insignificant. The force of nature is separate and independent from me and every human on Earth.' She was thinking of perspective and how something so much smaller can eclipse something so much bigger just by the angle you view if from. She used as many big words as were in her vocabulary. And at least three texts, she was flamboyant.

'It was nothing like the "total eclipse of my heart" on the winter solstice' he responded, likening this beautiful meteorological phenomenon to a 1980s' song. Was it a bit cliché or was he just not that into the weather. Or then again maybe it was merely a loose word association, pedalled out for affect.

'Interesting,' she replied.

Then a few moments later, 'you were illuminating, I mean the bar in the Hotel ignited by your presence.'

A compliment confused Ciara and sent her brain into illogical thought processes. What did he want? Where was he leading her? He was leading up to something surely? He was an architect after all, building layer upon layer of flattery to achieve some goal. What was that goal she wondered? There must be some objective here? It wasn't as if he was texting out of the kindness of his thumbs.

'More interesting' she replied trying not to be too excited.

Comparing this lunar eclipse to Bonny Tyler, yes that was the 1980s' singer, was a bit odd but maybe it was the only song he could think of at short notice.

'Don't get too carried away Ciara!' sent Karl a moment later. It was as if he could read her pretexts.

'You were not too bad yourself, on the night in question' she texted in reply to his "ignited" observation. She was not certain of what to respond, so she didn't know what to do. She could wait, or ignore the comment or else gush that she felt exactly the same. Generally on the rare occasions when she received them, compliments that is, she would make a weak attempt at humour to divert the sender from her unfamiliarity with the situation.

'Cool Ciara, you really push the boat out on your compliments.' Was that cool as in popular cool? Or cool like a cool day which was really cold but you didn't want to seem like a weakling? Yes she had been expected to return the compliment.

Was there something fundamental nay elemental about meeting at the shortest day of the year, with snow, when things couldn't get any worse weather wise? Then with the next sign, the lunar eclipse, could this be significant? How the setting sun burned the sky was beautiful then it was gone. It was a blazing fire, all engrossing, then leaving a dark sky, a void of nothingness until dawn. Only a long dark ribbon of a cloud filling night sky remained. Remarkably the sky had been completely clear, well apart from this solo cloud, so the affect was apparent and visible to the eye. If there had been the expected cloud blanketing which the weather site had predicted the effect would have been lost.

Was this how she saw Karl in her fertile fantasy-land of a head? Was he so bright that she was eclipsed in his presence?

'I can but try, hee hee' she was not going to say more than she meant at this early stage and that he was not too bad was about as much as she knew. This was the formal stage and if they were living in France they would probably still be using "vous" instead of the informal "tu". He was Napoleon in her fantasyland after all.

'I like you, so now you know.' He said.

Yep she was grasping at straws trying to make something like the lunar eclipse a herald of some great Grecian style love affair. He was a guy and he had said he liked her, that was good but it was a regular everyday occurrence. There was nothing metaphorical about his statement. She read the text again. She dismissed it.

'Well I had said "back, meet, drink" so would you like any of these?' She un-dismissed the text, there was something there after all, she grasped at the single straw of hope.

'All three please,' said Karl.

'Now I may be a bit over whelmed if we did all three at the same time!!' she was attempting humour again. It was falling as flat as his tummy, maybe she hadn't admitted it but she had had a quick finger inspection in the taxi and the tum was indeed truly taut.

'What I would like is another Kiss' he texted back.

Wow he wanted a repeat performance and she wondered if she was up for it. Could a second kiss live up to the first, the Waterloo moment on Wellington Quay?

'Have you any other Quays in mind?' she asked. Ok he wasn't to know what thoughts were in her head, so he would not necessarily know that she associated their first and to date only kiss at Wellington Quay. However since it was the place if she were special to him then the place might be too.

'Inns Quay?' he could have remembered that they kissed on the Quays.

The not knowing, the maybe, not quite is far more enticing and dream making than the hum drum, every day of going to the supermarket on a Saturday. The imagined man does not snore, the distant one does not nag, doesn't feel the stubble of an unshaven leg and comment. The remote guy can't bore you with his computer games or his sloppy friends drinking beer and eating take-away food while watching sports in your living room all weekend. This would make him unavailable to go to the newly opened Museum in town or fun exhibition in one of the galleries, but conveniently being available to his friends. Obviously Ciara wasn't admitting that this had ever happened her, no it was just a supposition.

Then he hastily responded with, 'do I have to kiss you on a Quay again?'

'Depends.'

She thought about Inns Quay, kissing outside the four courts, would everybody think they had just got off a crime?

'Do you want to kiss me again?' she asked.

'Depends!'

Then a few moments later, 'what about Wolfe Tone Quay, its less legal than Inns Quay and more of the era' he suggested, yes he had remembered the significance of the Quays.

Did he remember the tall Napoleon reference which she had been reliving in her head? Was it a compliment to refer to a guy as Napoleon?

'Well you have got the era right anyway,' she smiled as she sent.

'Yes I remember the location maybe a bit unsafe but definitely of the Napoleonic era.' This Quay had been noted for its' ladies of the Night, some years ago.

He remembered her likening him to a tall Napoleon that was amazing. If nothing else happened for the whole year that fact would keep her warm. Would Napoleon have worn five inch clogs to enhance his stature? Had Josephine fanned herself demurely in masked face yet obscenely low dress? Post French revolution ladies dresses became so low they were virtually topless everything was for sale then for the cost of a slice of bread. Ciara was trying to inhabit the era, smelling the face powder, feeling the draft and the pinch of uncomfortable wooden clogs!

Of course the dream guy, Karl, would find this irrelevant information relevant, no dazzling, exciting and fun. Well obviously he is a direct personification of her imagination.

'The Collins Barracks has a large cafe, with lots of military history. Maybe we could meet there as I may get arrested for street walking if you were late,' Ciara finally replied to the potential meeting place. Was the area still known for prostitution she wondered?

'Your skirt need not be that short' Karl cheekily responded.

'Ok I will wear a burka!'

She wasn't sure whether she sought perfection in a relationship, but she certainly didn't want to settle for something that wasn't special. Ciara was realistic enough to realise that relationships were not special and fantastic all the time but there needed to be elements of this sparkle to retain her interest. She was a broad minded person with lots of interests, not many of which she pursued but they were there ready to be taken up again, any moment now, when the spring sun began to shine she would go out hill walking again. Or when the evenings were brighter she would definitely return to the swimming pool. "Come on Karl, text back".

Therefore she wanted someone broadminded with lots of interests to do fun stuff with. And if he were into BBQs he should know how to marinate his own meat! Just like Don did but Aoife's ex didn't. He, the ideal male, would be a new-man in the full sense of domestic capabilities. She concluded her internal dialogue when he finally responded a good 5 minutes later. This was five minutes of torture as her internal monologue was getting a bit silly at this stage.

'You needn't go that far, just wear a long coat!' said Karl.

'Is Croppies Acre ever open?' the site in front of Collins Barracks had a sad tale. Supporters of Wolfe Tone, the Quay, fought in a rebellion back in 1798 and were executed there. It was named Croppy as the young men cropped their hair to be like Napoleon, the rebels!

The Ideal Texter

What is it about humans that the wishing is better than the having? Is growing up when you have what you want and you are not bored?

'Hello my alluring Josephine!' pinged Karl the next morning. He had not texted back on the bus ride home, nor during that evening, so she assumed that was it, over, forever, the end.

'Greetings tall Napoleon,' so he still wanted to be there, that was a relief. Her inner fantasy world would live to consume her thoughts another day.

He had said "your eyes would call back 1000 ships," when he was in Norway. So was she or maybe he hoping for a Grecian style fantasy after all? Not Napoleon and Josephine ok strictly speaking, it, the reference had been Trojan, just like a computer virus but with a horse and it was just fantasy. Maybe somewhere there was a place that Paris and Helen would be real even though they were mythical. She thought about fashion in Grecian terms. Could size zero be a result of seeking perfection because in Greek numbering only nothing can merge with infinity and therefore it is perfect it is the only sort of perfection on earth. Size one, was skinny yes but still there, you were close to infinity but not yet merged with it. She could go onto trees falling in the forest in the French existentialist sense and debate if you were a size zero well you were not really there at all. So how could you know whether a tree had fallen or not? Ciara had unfortunately missed that class in college in her vox-pop module of psychology so couldn't rightly conclude this stream of consciousness.

"OK Ciara that is way out there, he will be back in five. So switch on the monitor, stop thinking it is a Minotaur and relax. You're over-thinking, he didn't mean anything Grecian or the Trojan Wars by saying you had nice eyes. It was a convoluted compliment." She definitely did have a thing for Italy though and Venice so any chance to romanticise about it was taken and was all engrossing.

She was still thinking of the complements and they gave her a little confidence boost. Her boss was walking by, so luckily her monitor was illuminated. Could she see what Ciara was typing? Hopefully not.

'Hey, I'm playing the Emperors' Suite very low on my computer' it was Karl a while later.

To delve into the known, to get more, make excitement out of the hum-drum, day to day. To enjoy oneself in a DIY home store, to go in wishing to buy a lamp shade and come out with a complete kitchen, which you can't afford and may not even like. This was a true gift but she couldn't get excited about that. Maybe Karl would be as his was a practical world of the built environment. Ciara did not like practical things, she preferred things she could think about and then the problem would be, well thought about. Decisions were not Ciara's forte. Where were these thoughts coming from? Was she thinking of setting up home with him even before they had a first date?

In fairness though Karl was not a builder so he may have no knowledge or interest in practical domestic things. All he had admitted to was helping his grandfather make boats so why would she think he would be able to put up wallpaper for her. Was she fantasying about the ideal life with Karl.

'As long as you steer clear of the 1812 Overture' she cheekily replied to his Emperors Suite text. She didn't want him to get too big for his boots or 5" wooden clogs!

'Don't worry I won't imagine the fall before I have the assent,' he texted back in a moment.

'That is understandable, what was the result of your Croppies Acre search?' the short haired revolutionaries interested Ciara they the fashion victim of their day, 2000 or so had been massacred on the site.

'I think it is only open for special occasions, but I will check it out. I like your idea of the military history' texted Karl, he had waited a long while to return this answer. Was he trying to leave her dangling? Would this mean he were in conquest mode?

'Cool' Ciara texted.

'Before I set a date I will check the weather forecast for more lunar activity and any planetary movements. Talk soon.'

'Cool' she repeated, "cold" she thought. He wasn't setting a date that was a pity. She would have to be patient which was not one of her strong points. Patience was a card game not a dating tactic.

'So Ciara have you any metrological updates?' Don asked walking by and spotting the weather channel open once again.

'Not today, but some planetary ones, I believe Venus has collided with Mars!' now she was really getting her metaphorical references mixed up. Venus and Mars were from ancient Rome! Why did the Romans have to change everything and insert testosterone in their Gods? All the lovely whimsical Grecian ideas, well according to Ciara were, well far off and ideal as indicated by "ph" in all the spelling. The Romans seemed to humanise everything by changing the "ph" to "f", you see the "effing" Romans!

'I often collide with my Venus, she can be such a fiery planet that I feel like charred debris in her wake,' said Don after a moment's thought.

'Sounds like Síle is a planetary ball breaker,' said Ciara impressed by his reply.

'No way, she is great.' Don seemed to be backtracking.

'Yes smaller in size but great in lunar terms and very warm,' was her scramble back to polite work talk.

'That's a bit of a step down Ciara, but she is the best. I would be lost without her,' said Don.

Ciara smiled, he looked embarrassed after saying so much.

Later that day she was on a particularly full bus and Ciara was very lucky to get a seat. She had begun scouring the seats for signs of Karl, a large hand, a leg which refused to fit into a seat. Even a forgotten glove left by a toddler would have been enough to get Ciara excited. It was possible that he would take the same bus home and he lived along a similar route. She thought about the attributes which would make Karl an ideal texter. Response time, this was the most important thing. Ciara wanted a quick response time.

'Where was your favourite holiday?' she texted to get the thumbs tingling again.

'It was Corsica of course,' he replied in a flash. Was work slowing down for the day and he was slightly bored sitting at his desk or maybe he was on another bus coming home from work, or was it just easy to talk about Napoleon she wondered? This was good response time.

'Must say I preferred Sardinia' she mischievously replied as in truth she had never been to Corsica. The Emerald Coastline was really beautiful, maybe there was a spot like that in Corsica. Her feelings however, were that Corsica was a bit corrupt and had scary undercurrents like some other Mediterranean states. Maybe she was being a bit pedantic disagreeing when she had no empirical evidence, just received opinion from Corsicans she had met abroad.

'It is true that Sardinia is beautiful, but I thought this was a French fantasy rather than Italian idyll' he observed.

'Thought Corsicans were different from either French or Italians,' she was in a bit of a stirring mood this evening.

'Ah but it's the fighting spirit that interests me,' he skilfully negotiated the multi pronged trap that she had set. 'And maybe us both' he added.

"Strangers in the night" she hummed to herself as it was being used in some advertising campaign or other. "Texters at first sight," she improvised, hoping not to disturb the person sitting next to her "thumbing together..." she could go on but maybe she should respond to the text in hand. 'I prefer the fun to the fight.'

'Well maybe there is fun in the fight,' he replied.

'The jostling, cajoling and riling up of the troops is fun, but the actual battle with blood, sabres and cannons is a bit too involved for me.' The next rule in the ideal texter is to have a sense of fun, tick Karl definitely had that.

'But maybe when the blood rises and adrenaline is flowing are we truly alive.' Wow maybe he was a bit of a thrill seeker. He was definitely alive and could take up a concept and run with it. Third tick he had a strong sense of fantasy and could work outlandish concepts into a coherent stream of texts.

'You could always join the army, is there still National Service in Norway?' she said then added. 'Have you any holiday plans' this may have seemed like a rather skewed sentence but she wanted to lighten the mood.

'Actually I'm going to an architect's conference soon.' He had again been polite and not reacted to her jibes.

'Ah nice,' she replied 'are you speaking, exhibiting or participating in any other way?'

'Yes' he continued, 'one of our buildings is up for a design award for some of its conceptual elements.'

'Which award is that, not that I know anything about architectural awards?'

'It is an international award held in New York, I won't bore you with the details but I am pretty excited about it.'

'Well good luck with that,' she said. "He is only just in his new position and he is getting an award. He must need a strong conceptual brain to imagine up a whole building, I wonder does he play show house at work during the quiet times. He could move the walls about and change their colour. He could put in furniture with some design program on his computer and make lots of areas to have coffee?"

'Thank you, I'm keeping my fingers crossed,' he pinged back.

She felt close to him now and she thought about him that whole evening. He had shared something with her which was real. He was allowing her a glimpse of his life; his dreams and his aspirations and that made him more tangible, less remote to her. This was something actually happening, in the present, rather than a continued imaginary fantasy from 200 odd years ago. If she were reflective she may have noted that he did not ask of her holiday plans. He did not enquire how her day to day life was. She ignored this point. She just wanted to be happy, maybe this was what every human wanted. It is amazing how mood can change ones behaviour, if she had gone out with friends that evening she would have thought nothing of spending a few hundred Euro. However when she was sad she used up the soap until the very end of the bar.

The forth golden rule of the ideal texter was to give her a glimpse into his inner world. He had just done this, he was not closed with her and spent a long time constructing replies which were interesting, humorous and developed the themes which she proposed be it Corsica, Napoleon or even the Trojan Wars. Yes she was defiantly dropping Troy and Greek numbers and her fantasy world was getting a bit crowded.

Work Friends

Ciara's best friend at work was Stephen. He was the most positive person she knew. He had cerebral palsy due to the lack of oxygen to his brain at birth. This resulted in mobility issues but he was alive and he let everyone know he was. Alive and kicking! He had a towering stature of 5' 2" but a personality at least a foot higher! His vibrant personality allowed everyone to forget anything of the physical difficulties he experienced. He could walk, with assistance and climb stairs, which was fortunate during fire drills as their workspace was on the 6th floor. Although he could have complained constantly of his situation he never did. He was never "that fun guy in a wheelchair" but "that fun guy."

He had a great love for life, with a mischievous streak to match Ciara's. Some disabled people seem to remind one of their disability in subtle ways, to make one feel guilty for being able bodied, but Stephen never did. The only thing he reminded Ciara of was St Stephen's Green which was actually his own private park and he was munificent enough to allow all Dubliners access. The feast of Stephens' was obviously his day and he had his own private shopping gallery, the Arcade. Yes, he had a lust for life; if he ever met Iggy Pop surely the aging pop star would completely be won over.

He had begun work at the company at about the same time Ciara had, both were recently out of college and it was their first real job. Stephen took the job seriously, Ciara didn't. He genuinely gave customer service and Ciara didn't. She was genuinely bored from the moment she began up until seven years later, which was about the time of this tale.

There was a multi-lingual section to the customer services function. Ciara encouraged this branch to come along to the social nights which she organised. Stephen was the regular at these events but numbers fluctuated greatly. Ciara encouraged as many people as possible to come and as the internationals were new to Dublin the turnout was greater than in the main body of the company. Or in other words, the internationals didn't have many mates in Dublin so would go out to work events.

Ciara had wanted work colleagues to appreciate Dublin the way she did, this was why she had organised a Georgian doors tour. She compared modern or contemporary architecture to classical in forms of style and structure. She also organised paintballing when everyone complained of over culture. She really enjoyed the organising and every few months she would come up with a new hare-brained idea. Then it was up to Stephen to put the idea into some semblance of and outing. He enjoyed doing this as he liked to be involved in making fun for the whole company.

On one of these evenings a very attractive French lady caught Stephen's eye. She was long, in fact everything about her was long; her hair, her arms and her lithe legs were long. She was so long that she was a good seven inches taller than Stephen. He was a terrier though, a big dog trapped in a small body.

Her name was Sophie and Stephen became determined to improve his school level French beyond the ability to order frogs legs in an attempt to win her attentions. Ciara helped him, encouraged him in these pursuits and even went to conversational French classes with him for moral support.

'Are you just going for her as her name starts with S?' asked Ciara on a grey day in February three weeks into their French classes. They sat quite close at work so could gossip and giggle when there was not much work to be done. This seemed the situation most of the time with less and less clients renewing their contracts.

'Of course not,' said Stephen.

'I think you are copying my alliteration with Karl and Ciara. Could you not go for someone whose name began with T?'

'Why' and then he got the weak joke. 'Ciara you are supposed to be caring not making silly cyclical remedy jokes!'

'Whist, she coming! I will pretend to be working but if you need any help on the colours or the days of the week I'm your woman.' The lithe Sophie was striding through their floor and was about to pass Stephens' desk.

'Je m'appelle Stephen,' was his approach after these weeks of French language classes.

'Je m'appelle Sophie,' she replied. 'I speak quite a bit of English but if you wish to practice your French with me you are welcome,' she fluently conversed with just a light accent.

'Oui' with a great sigh was as much as Stephen could get out. Then after a moment he said, 'would you be going to the next social outing? It is this Friday coming.'

Ciara edged back to her desk slowly, she didn't want to be too obvious about her ear wigging.

'Yes, I think so. I am only a few months in Dublin and it is difficult to make friends who are not French. It seems that your culture is very pub based, so if you don't drink alcohol so much it's hard to meet people.' Yep her English was a lot more fluent than the colours and days of the week.

Stephen considered this not drinking business, well supposedly only at very expensive French restaurants and with very good wines. Also, her grasp of the English language made him decide to converse in English. He gave her a lesson in Irish social history instead. Ciara hoped this speech wouldn't turn into a lecture.

'You see Sophie, in Ireland long ago people lived on the land and would go into a pub at the end of the day to have company. Stories were shared and information about cattle and crop prices exchanged. A pub was not just a place to get alcohol but it was a shop, sometimes a post office and later on also a petrol station. It became a one stop shop. So, it is true that many people drank but often it was tea. So, this is how it developed. Dublin has some of the oldest museums and galleries in the world. If you would like me to show you around sometime, it would be my pleasure.'

Ciara was now sitting at her cubicle at the centre of the office with her head lowered staring at a blank screen, pretending not to listen. She was smiling so widely though, that if Stephen had cast his eye in her direction he would have known the truth.

'That would be great' smiled Sophie. 'I would love to do something cultural.'

'As its' work time now maybe we could talk about this on Friday,' Stephen smiled back.

'Great again,' Sophie confirmed and walked off.

On Friday Stephen, who was normally a stylish dresser was extra groomed. Ciara whose brain didn't function before 11 am was generally slovenly dressed. The contrast was heightened when Ciara actually thought of the ease with which she dressed and the difficulty which Stephen faced on a daily basis.

Ciara chided herself sometimes when she complained of things which she took for granted but which were really difficult for Stephen, activities such as climbing the stairs or dancing. Stephen had had three leg operations yet still had restricted mobility. Ciara, when she considered it cursed 1980s birthing practices, to leave a for baby thirty minutes without oxygen and a life time of suffering was inhumane.

Ciara decided to distract herself and think of a nice subject, shoes, she was interested in shoes. It was a lazy type of shopping as you had just to remove your other pair of shoes rather than everything you were wearing. Stephen could only wear one pair specially made for him at a hospital so he focused his shoe creativity into Ciara's purchases. He would accompany her on many foot-wear forages. In these recessionary times, there were always sales and Ciara never liked to pay full price for anything. Not that she would boast but the fashion had changed from how much something cost to how little you could purchase the item for. Even people who didn't have to be frugal were embracing the frugality band wagon and shopping at inexpensive stores.

****

'The top brands cannot afford to have sales outside the two designated sales seasons as it dilutes the brand value,' Ciara explained to Stephen 'and the perception of quality which each brand attempts to exude in order to justify the monumental pricing,' she and Stephen, were out that lunchtime scanning Grafton Street.

'Oh I see,' Stephen replied politely without the remotest bit of interest in trying to see at all. He had wanted to get out and about that day so as not to seem lurking with the intention of running into Sophie. He was also going to see what was in for men this season just in case Sophie was fashion conscious.

On Friday morning Stephen was looking especially dapper with his thick brown hair gleaming through shampoo and male hair products which Ciara didn't know or understand. He smiled over at her. It could have been Brill cream which gave off that lustrous sheen, or maybe wax or even hair oil. She thought she had better ask as he had gone to so much effort.

'Hey handsome, why all the effort?' Ciara smiled back.

'I'm going to the dogs!!'

'Nah you're already there! Just like myself, so what has your hair so gleamy?' she asked.

'It's Clean and Neat,' he replied. 'Designed to make the hair glossy instead of greasy, do you like it?' Had he memorised the label or made up the jingle himself?

'Impressive, I approve,' she replied with a smile. Her frizzy hair was always messy and only got straightened when she visited her mother. Her mother was unfortunate to have the same hair type and hate it, so she didn't wish to see her hair mirrored in her daughter. Ciara would root out the hair dryer from the back of a wardrobe and "do it" to save her mother the reality check.

'So Stevo, what are you wearing?' she enquired.

He was still in his wheel chair as he had not managed to get to his desk yet. The rumours of Stephens' fast approaching date had spread rapidly among this idle bunch of co-workers. And the story had inflated in the telling. Everyone had either seen or heard of Stephen talking to Sophie. They all concluded that they were a firm item and that Sophie was a lucky lady to be the object of Stephens' affections. Stephen was very popular in the office for his charm, chat and general good humour so all and sundry wished him well. Stephen was in his element, it had been two years since his last relationship and he loved being the centre of attention. Consequently, that morning he had still not reached his desk due to the chatting and wishes of good luck for the night ahead.

It was a great opportunity for all bored employees to be involved in something, since there had been redundancies and pay cuts the morale had lowered significantly. With little to look forward to, many had become disengaged with work. This was another reason why Stephen was greeted and stopped at each work station. Yes, he was in his element but he was almost talked out and this was only the start of the day. How was he to keep his jovial debonair mood up all day and still have enough energy for the excitement of the night ahead?

Luckily the day passed quickly and the evening arrived. The entertainment was greyhound racing at Shelbourne Park only a few minutes from the office. The crew had been complaining of over culture so this was Ciara's concession, dog racing. Dog racing was an urban version of horse racing only much cheaper.

Fortunately the evening was mild as the race track was outside. It was still February but Spring was in the air and the days were beginning to lengthen. Most of the work party headed to the bar to order drinks and examine their race cards the decide who to bet on. The dogs were beautiful, scrawny admittedly but sleek agile and lively. Stephen stayed outside with Sophie and they admired the dogs in the line-up. They then went to place a bet on the first race basing their decision partly on the look of the dog and partially on the name. Obviously, they were professionals in the betting arena.

Ciara admired them discreetly through the glass Stephen and Sophie were almost a couple and seemed so natural together, as if they already knew each other well. Ethically Ciara had issues with greyhound racing as the dog were often abandoned after about four years and found their way into pounds. Ciara was considering lobbying the race track to set up a fund for retired dogs as there used be in bygone days for retired soldiers. They may already have one for all she knew. It was on her to do list to check. Her colleagues though, enjoyed this outing as it was very convenient, near to the office and a change from the pub. Essentially it was the same function, boozing but with a different name. She popped over the bar to give Stephen space with Sophie and chatted with everyone. Everyone was mature, for a change, 'let love germinate' one of them said. It almost killed Ciara not to pop outside and observe, but she restrained herself, with great difficulty.

She peeped through the windows after five minutes though as surreptitiously as possible and all was proceeding well. She would get all the ska the next day.

New Phone

The next Monday Stephen didn't get a moments' peace. Everyone crowded about his desk to see how the evening had gone. Stephen had slipped off with Sophie before the dog races had finished so no one had been able to see how things were progressing. Whether there had been whispers of sweet nothings, or hand holding or even just a win on one of the races. Ciara couldn't believe how grown-up everyone was pretending to be that night, but they were all certainly making up for it today.

Stephen was giving them blow by blow accounts of every breath, sigh and slight mispronunciation which he found particularly endearing. It was nearly 11 am by the time everyone settled into their own work space and it was only because there were rumours of Anna passing.

Ciara figured that Stephen wouldn't be up to the same onslaught at lunch time, even if he loved the attention so she decided to do something with him. She already knew the gory details as she had called Stephen at 8.30 am on Saturday morning. He had never sounded happier in his life.

A decision was made and decisions were not a regular occurrence in Ciara's daily life. So, this was almost an event. As lunch time drew near Ciara edged towards Stephens' desk. 'Fancy coming for a spin?'

'What are you up to Missy?'

'I am finally entering the twenty first century and getting a smart phone.'

'Sure, I will come with you if you like. It will make a change from shoe shopping.'

'Ah Stevo I'm not that bad, am I?'

'No, of course not,' he lied 'what had you in mind?'

'I want something simple, easy to use that I won't end up calling Australia by accident.'

'Have you still not deleted Sean's number' he joked but realised he was right when he saw Ciara's reaction. Her ex was an undeleted, so in the nether regions of status in her emotions. It was a bit like draft texts, thought about, considered ideas framed but not sent.

'I have intended to, maybe if this relationship goes well then I will. Ok!' said Ciara.

'Ciara that is a pity, right Grafton St. it is.' Stephen had heard the ins and outs of Ciara's previous relationship and had concluded she was not in a healthy, happy place. He did feel sorry for her but also felt it was time to move on, Sean had been years ago. He pulled his crutches out from under his desk while Ciara turned on his electric chair which was sitting over at the wall. It was quite a difficult chair to operate so she had to sit on it in order to direct it to go straight. It was very powerful and lurched forward almost knocking into several desks.

'Why can't I operate this machine and you have no problem,' she complained?

'It just takes a bit of getting used to. Anyway, I have to be able to operate it or it would take me twenty minutes to get to work from the Dart.'

Ciara looked at Stephen and felt a bit guilty for complaining that she was useless at everything when she could walk freely and operate both hands. Stephen only had the power of one, the right hand and lucky for him he was right handed.

So, they whizzed out and Ciara had to put on her runners to keep up with Stephen, he enjoyed being her keep fit guy. It was so freeing not to have to walk slowly for Ciara as generally when she went to a Mall with her Mum everyone else seemed to shuffle so slowly that they barely appeared to move. Then she stopped herself in her tracks; that was another inadvertent mean thought. Stephen was so quick on the chair and not so quick on his feet but that was good, it meant Ciara had to exercise her very inactive patience gene and if it didn't get exercised it would go away just like her arm muscles had a while back. She really should get in the pool her arm muscles were wasting away.

They went into the first phone shop and were overwhelmed with the array of devices now called hand-sets instead of phones. 'Why are they called hand-sets?' she asked Stephen.

'Maybe because they have more functions than just a phone.' He was so clued in, why had she been oblivious

76

to these technological advances? Was it a fascination with the past?

'I see, well I have better get some assistance as I don't need a service just yet!!' She was returning to their well aired joke about customer service, like a NCT or MOT. It sounded a bit more involved than merely describing a phone, explaining the features and benefits and closing the sale. Or, maybe that was what sales were, it was all very confusing to Ciara.

'Tell them you want an easy one as I don't want to have to work out how to use it!' called Stephen.

'Right boss,' this new assertiveness of Stephen was good, since he had been seeing Sophie a good three days and so far, so good, he was beginning to be independent of Ciara. She realised he wouldn't be available to power walk with her every lunch if this relationship developed. He may well have other plans, something better to do, with Sophie. That was good in lots of ways, she was glad for him but definitely she would miss his company. Was she prematurely missing him, forecasting outcomes before they were actually decided?

They got a Samsung! The deciding factor had been pocketing, or which phone fitted into Ciara's pocket. This was the only one which did. So, she pocketed it. Apparently, it was so easy to work.

Back in the office she discovered that there were no instructions with the phone, 'woops!' the key selling point had been its size and she was so bamboozled by the range that she had felt intimidated and wanted to run.

But she was determined to buy something, she needed a phone, her old handset was half a decade old! A dinosaur in today's terms. Why was it that the velocity of obsolescence was verging on three months! This was a recession; things had to slow down technologically. Not everyone was an oligarch. Even if they were, conspicuous consumption was decidedly out of fashion.

Don walked past and helpfully noted, 'Ciara you will never work that thing.'

'Thanks, my partner in wine!! I will just have to go to tech support and simper for a day or two until they help me.'

'You will need to get out of those trackie bottoms, wear a skirt if you want the techs to help.'

'Don that is not nice, I only ask the techies for help when I can return the favour,' she lied blatantly. She could never help the technical support she didn't know how much cables even weighted.

'That's right Ciara.' Don was persisting. The big meanie.

"Ouch, that was a bit unkind. Where did that thought come from? Don is my friend, right? We're the dis-servicers, like the three amigos or the musketeers." She sighed deeply before going down to the technical support guys on the floor below. It was just guys as the only lady-technical support person had recently left the company. Ciara's computer was on, she had left in such haste she forgot to close down the text file. This was the one with the recent text which she had sent to Karl.

Anna was in the area and noticed the unusually illuminated screen. She leaned forward and began to read. Ciara had opened a text file. It was all her texted messages, both sent and received to Karl, she had copied out every word he had sent. After initial false starts with Trojan horses and the Quays of Dublin, Karl and Ciara had settled down to Napoleon and Josephine fantasies. There were daily texts, sometimes many were sent in the space of hours, it depended on how their ideas sparked.

Stephen looked up but said nothing. Anna was seriously scary. Stephen would have texted Ciara but he knew she wouldn't be able to work her phone.

Stephen was getting worried. He shifted uncomfortably at his work station as Anna was still there, reading and reading and then reading some more. What had she seen? How would this affect Ciara? Would she get fired? He decided to do something productive and help Ciara with her phone quandary. He opened the Samsung website to download instructions for the phone.

Anna stayed a while longer reading then walked away looking and maybe feeling a bit guilty for invading Ciara's intellectual property! She had a half smile on her face which was unreadable to Steven.

'Here you go tech-less,' said Stephen handing Ciara the instructions when she finally returned.

'Thanks mate, you're a star.'

'Ciara, Anna was looking at your computer.'

'Oh no, how long was she there?'

'Quite a while. She was reading something.'

'Oh no!' Ciara said again.

Anna walked by so they all tried to look busy, 'what are you doing Ciara, you are very quiet?'

"Uh oh!" 'I got a new phone at lunch-time and I'm just getting using to it.' Ciara scanned Anna's eyes for signs of guilt or contrition. She could see none. Either Anna was a professional and could hide her thoughts somewhere other than her face or maybe she felt no remorse. Ciara was going to have to be more careful, what she was writing on work time was seriously unprofessional. So she would have to hide it better, or close the file when she left her desk. A second decision of the day, this day was really productive!

'Right, may I see it?' said Anna.

'Of course,' she had seen everything else today so why not show her the phone?

'Ah this looks nice and simple, maybe I should get one for my Mum' she handed the phone back to Ciara.

When she was gone Stephen came back for a quick chat, 'it's cool there is a voice operation function.' He wanted to change the subject quickly so Ciara wouldn't dwell on the matter.

'Yep that would be handy for you.'

'Maybe.'

If only there could be seminars for the technologically inept, everyone could meet on a Monday night and have a little group meeting and then in a non-threatening environment discuss their phone fears. They would be like minded people, possibly older than Ciara, but she wouldn't know anyone so she could unburden herself of her phone-woes! At the end of a six-month session she would be able to use her phone. Then the whole cycle would begin again when she got her upgrade! The distraction allayed her fears of Anna and the text file. She, Ciara must be more careful in future.

Ciara was fiddling with her phone on the long bus journey and she was too afraid to press any of the buttons in case she did something wrong and wouldn't be able to undo it. The helpful sales assistant had transferred all her numbers onto the new phone and she was almost going to risk a text to Karl as an experiment. She was a bit worried though, she may send it to her Mum by accident. She put the shiny, pocket sized phone back in its box and prayed no one called as she was only now reading the instructions. "Getting home with your phone" that is what she would call the seminars or group meetings. It would be a bit like training adults need when they get a new puppy.

Web Texting

Recently she had discovered web texting well yesterday. This could have been something to do with her new phone and playing with it on her long day of low productivity. 500 texts a month, free, well inclusive, amazing what you can learn when you are surfing on the job! Yep if she was honest she had got more into the internet at work these days, things were quieter than last year and the weather had been perpetually grey and damp. So, the weather site was a bit boring. Ciara had thought that there were 250 texts provided free, as that is what according to her service provider was available, but there on the screen, in blue and white were 500 texts. She intended to use them all, and use them every month. She would be able to text her friends all over the globe as everyone was now scattered about the continents with this economic depression. No wonder she was into the 1930's, she was living it! She would scatter these inclusive texts globally to reinforce their depression! Ah no, she had got that the wrong way around, to lift the mood, raise their spirits, that was her objective!

Why had she waited so long to work this free service out when it had been available for yonks? Was it that she hadn't been hard up enough to have to seek out alternative means of paying for texts? Perhaps she had not needed to send so many in the past. With the arrival of the texter she needed to have enough ammunition – credit wise to be able to blow him back to the tundra!

Is web texting just an e-mail to a phone or does it have its own distinct place in the texting hierarchy? Is there a textual hierarchy? If so where is each component placed? Why was she curious and why did it matter? Yes. It mattered to her as it was an indication that Ciara was not fulfilled in her work and had too much spare time to think then over think small things which didn't really matter. Anyway, she would be texting Karl on web, free, every day whether he wanted to hear from her or not. No, he wanted to hear from her, but maybe not all the time.

It was true to say that she was interested in form, how a document looked after it was produced. So, would the means by which it was produced affect the form of the finished document? She was taking the view that a document was not just an eight-paged report, which was formal, had paragraphs, full stops and headings. A text was also a document, it was shorter and less formal but it was still a form of communication. For heaven's sake even scraps of the bible which comprised less than a few words were considered documents, so why not a text. It was a testament to what someone wished to say, a message, the word was made text and sent amongst us!

There was a new thought sprouting in her fertile tech-brain, do we think differently when we use all our fingers on a laptop or tablet which makes the output less thumb and more fingers? In other words when we use our thumbs are our texts more awkward? Does a touch-tone smart-phone change the speed and therefore the style of the text? "Waiting for him to text is like waiting for pears to ripen," she practiced her web text functionality. "Days pass and they are as hard as rocks. Then all of a sudden they all ripen at once." She could have added and go off before there is time to eat them all, but that was enough for now. She would save it to drafts. Then she thought who could she send this to? She had to use up all these 500 texts each month, it was a challenge and she would rise to it. She also had a new draft file which was important for composition. It was much larger than her previous draft file.

If the voice recognition button is used are texts different again as there is no blockage between the head and hand? Does the text begin to read like a dictated letter typed by a secretary through an old-style Dictaphone, "The major will direct his troops at 0500 hours to rise and make their beds, then breakfast at 5.15 after an ice-cold shower Etcetera," she tried it; "Ciara" came out as Keira – not too bad, then she tired her name again and "cara," then "k rock, f". These were interesting results.

"Dear Karl" became "care.com." "Do you fancy taking a Gondola ride?" turned into "teen fancy taking up and arrived" very odd indeed. One would never know what they were getting.

'Ciara are you playing with your phone again?' asked one of the lads. She was at her desk at work, playing with her phone.

'Yes, well I'm trying to see how this voice activation thing actually works.'

'Well say something interesting please as I have to listen to you.'

'Sorry! So, you don't fancy taking a gondola ride then?'

'Ciara!'

Voice recognition would be good for Stephen but it would help to be sighted using voice recognition as those of visual impairment could really be caught out! The idea was good but the application needed very clear diction for the correct words to appear. So, speaking one's native tongue would be imperative. There were also difficulties however for deaf people as, if they had never heard a word sounded it was unlikely that they would input the word clearly enough for the monitor to record it. Ciara wanted to be inclusive in her thoughts.

It was fair to say that Ciara was a bit of a late adaptor to technology, it was not necessarily gender stereotypical fear of gadgets. It was really more a lack of interest in playing around with stuff indoors when she could be out doing, well outdoor stuff. However now that she had finally got to 'home with her phone' she wanted to play with it, maybe she didn't need the phone group seminar after all. Her phone was fun especially as she had someone to play with. Karl did respond and with wit, enthusiasm and suitable Napoleon references. She was in a playful mood and thing were going to be different this year, better, more active and all the usual New Years intentions. This was March but anyway intentions were supposed to last all year, right. Was it the Karl hour yet? When was his usual texting time?

She was a bit put out when the mobile phone companies stopped access to the web-texting bit of their web site from mobiles. This prohibition lasted only for a short while but it took Ciara ages to realise that she could once again web-text from her phone. These mobile communicating devices are otherwise known as smart-ish phones to those who used less than 1% of their capacity. It was not that the phone was not smart but really the user's ability to use the handset which was the difficulty.

'So, I got a new phone, half way towards a tablet and it's great for quick responses,' Karl texted optimistically one morning. 'I can use it as a weapon, just as the pen could be used as a sword, this tablet can be a blunt yet strong instrument to defend myself from muggers!' He sounded like he was in good form today, sometimes gadgets can humour guys.

"I bet he didn't have any problems working out how to use it'" Ciara thought. "Cool Karl and his cryptic gadgets, why is life so unfair?" So, he wouldn't need the getting to home with your phone either. Ciara stopped feeling sorry for herself she had mastered the phone and forgotten what the instructions had said.

'Yes, a tablet to make, a tablet to take and a tablet to break,' she sent a bit cryptically back. Was she being a bit cocky or even kooky?

'Maybe Moses used his tablets as weapons too and broke some of the commandments. Was it the Egyptians he would have been fighting?' said Karl. Well he was certainly trying to get into her line of thinking, no matter how kooky.

'I defer to your superior knowledge but were the tablets not written documents rather than pieces of writing etched onto stone?'

Some moments of silence whilst the tablets tabulated! 'Sorry I am thinking on the tablets to make and wondering about that origin will have to look it up later. Yes it was the Egyptians as he -Moses parted the Red Sea as fable/the bible says. For now though, as I have you all to myself, I want to chat. I want to know the Ciara Creed.' He was in a Biblical mood, hum.

'Oh, am I now a doctrine? Maybe I want to know why you're a cool Karl.'

'No, you're not doctrinal or even a doctrine well I hope you're not! Thanks for the compliment, always appreciated. What is your driver?'

'My Audi alteram partem you mean?' she tartly responded. "I know he wants to delve but I want to play!"

'Now don't get Latino on me! Can I glean from this you drive an Audi, let me guess an A 3?'

'Pass, I would drive a Bugatti if it were not for my environmental sensibilities'. "Where did the A3 conclusion come from you brainy boy, how could you know? That car, the Bugatti is also too rich for my economic sensibilities other-wise known as budget". She knew he really meant what was driving as in what motivated her but she didn't really wish to answer him so she said added, in a new text, 'you are a great big black hole to me, so I don't want to disclose too much until I get a bit from you first'. "Don't send that bit or he will think I am too keen. Really though she didn't answer as she didn't know what was her driver. 'You are as nebulous as the Dublin skyline atmospheric references relate to my wish to understand you and maybe know you a little more.' She sent after considering the best response. She had his ear but wanted his eye.

'Well Ciara, I like rowing among other sports, hopefully or preferably under a bright Dublin sky. Generally, I row on my own so that I can feel the wind in my hair, regulate the speed to my liking and feel the splash of the water as the oars make contact with the water.'

Then a moment later he sent an addition, could he have also been web-texting? 'I like working up a sweat and burning off the alcohol from the night before. I like gaining an appetite for a big breakfast, no not with fish, in case you think all Norwegians have fish for breakfast. I like a bit of everything, eggs Florentine, a bowl of fruit salad, on the side, some rashers or sausages and a fresh Danish pastry while I'm waiting for my order.'

Wow, she had an in, he was telling her what he had for breakfast! 'So do you row during the week? Maybe before work?' Ciara asked. This could have been a reason for not seeing him on the bus.

'Usually try to once or twice during the week, generally mornings and then at the weekend either Sat or Sun, maybe both if I have no plans. So now lady of mystery, your turn, what's your thing?'

'Unf I don't have 1 thing, I like swimming, cycling, hill walking but I'm a bit of a hedgehog. I hibernate, activity wise over the winter. I admire you getting up and at it even on dark cold days.' She was trying to write text speech but then reverted to long hand as the abbreviations didn't make sense to her.

'Does that mean you get bristly in the winter?' Karl asked.

'Ha, ha, no, normally I take holidays in the winter to get a bit of sunlight. I'm into light and sit near the window at work. So I do the swimming, hill walking and cycling in the 3 weeks of holidays. Rest of winter is spent at plays, cinema and friend's houses. I do walk for nearly an hour each day over lunch, sometimes with a friend but often alone.'

She thought for a moment and her only aim at work was to get to the light, the floor to ceiling windows and she wanted a window seat. That was her one driver for the year. Well at least it was simple.

She continued her power walking theme in a new text, well she had plenty to spare, let's not spare them!

'I suppose it is a bit like your rowing rhythm, the pounding of feet, the swinging of arms, it is hypnotic. Almost like a march.'

'Hmm I see what you mean. The march of Napoleons troupes to Spain or Switzerland' said Karl.

This was the exact moment Ciara discovered that the mean phone companies had stopped web text on her mobile. Maybe it was the beginning of a series of cost saving initiatives but the timing was terrible. She didn't realise that this application could be set up on her work computer. These things were still new to her and presumably Karl was waiting for his breakfast, lunch or whatever meals went into feeding his giant of a frame. She couldn't respond! Drat a normal pay text from her mobile phone was necessary.

It was working so well, this text conversation and she was getting somewhere. She copied and pasted the text into a normal text. It didn't send. What to do, she only had 5 Cent Credit. She would have to wait until her lunch break, Anna was on the prowl. If only she had the top up on phone option set up. How would she do it, this was far too early in the day to learn anything. However the timing would be lost, forever. She would never get back that conversation.

Sophie, her only French connection would call the device a portable and it sounded so sweet from her lips. Actually portable was a more correct term as the person was mobile rather than the phone. A phone could only walk in adverts.

The next blow to her intellectual, well phone usage advancements happened when she discovered that she could not send international web texts. It truly was a nuisance as having changed from bill to pay as you go, her phone costs were finally manageable and she was keeping in regular touch with her overseas friends and ex-boyfriend. She wanted to be with them but could not afford to leave her home, so regular virtual contact was important for her. Web texting had meant that she didn't have to worry about time zones or disturbing people, as she could schedule a text. Nor did it mean trying to get them at home as mobile calls were beyond the beyond financially.

However when she was out, socialising and a moment would remind her of a friend and something that had been shared. She would be compelled to share it, she would ring, no wonder she had 5 Cent credit this Monday morning.

She did look into other means of communication, such as Viber, Skype, Bbm but that was just for Blackberries which Ciara had called blueberries for ages and What's App, she liked this one for the symbols. However you can de-text the gal however you can't take the texter out of her.

 Luckily the Web text prohibition it was just a temporary adjustment as many customers voted with their thumbs and changed providers.

She went down to the techie department after lunch and they told her how to access her own web text page from her work computer. This would look as if she were working, great she was back in business a glorious afternoon of texting lay ahead. "Come on Karl I'm ready for you!"

Then she had a blank, she could think of nothing to say to Karl. She read and re-read the Biblical references. They were funny but noting came to her. So, she left it. She had to leave it as the response had to be witty.

'What colour is your car?' she texted towards the end of the day. Inspiration had not returned.

'Red' good he had a car.

'As red as a Ferrari?' asked Ciara.

'Slightly more muted.'

'Have you got any pics?'

'Loads'

'When I work out the camera bit on this phone you can send them over.'

'Have you a new phone too?' asked Karl.

'Yes....I do....it's really cool! It's red.'

Teasing Texts

She got some inspiration after a few days and developed the biblical theme of tablets and the Red Sea, but maybe the trail had gone cold.

'If there is a Ciara creed surely there is Karl credence!' It may have been a bit lame, a desperate play on alliteration but she want didn't ask him what car he drove. He had already spoken at length about what motivated him so what else was there to ask? She was being a bit tough on herself, sure if he liked her would it really matter what she said?

He didn't respond so she waited a while. It was really annoying though as she still had nearly 300 texts to use and the month was drawing to a close. These texts would run out and never be returned, what a tragedy. Sugar, maybe it did matter what she said!

'Bored with the Bible, wondering what colour your little car is' he pinged later in the day.

'It's racing green, but with all the speed restrictions in suburban Dublin I don't get to do much racing.'

'I don't get to do much driving in Dublin never mind racing' replied Karl.

'I know the feeling! Have you been using your tablet to defend yourself recently?' She asked thinking a change of topics might be helpful.

He gave no response, how frustrating. He must really be looking for lively texts.

'Maybe I will use it to get into the car park at the supermarket, there is so little parking that the spots are fought over as much as the Trojan Walls were defended.' He remembered, that's good! The text was sent at about 7 pm maybe he had been in a long meeting. Then he continued, 'I would extend my tablet like a shield out of the drivers' window, but it would be turned into a weapon, an attack rather than a defence. I would shriek my special Celbridge war cry so fiercely that it would make the babes in their back-seat-toddler-chairs wail with fear and dread. Then I would deftly manoeuvre into the yummy-mummy spot and ignore all complaints to the contrary. The Norseman has come!!'

'Wow, I didn't know parking was so aggressive in Celbridge, or maybe I'm not a Norsewoman.'

So the texting was going well even if it wasn't the most inspiring however Ciara fancied an old fashioned telephone call. Was this asking too much?

Then that was it, nothing that day, nor the next so she sent him a silly one liner. 'Maybe you should shop in Liffey Valley!! The car parks don't resemble battlefields.'

Then all went cold in the Norwegian air was it due to embarrassment about the victims of Karl's car park rage? The days passed incredibly slowly and Ciara's only relief was to read and re-read her text file. She also drafted up some texts on the Napoleon theme to be prepared. This suspension of text, was similar to the events after Christmas, lots of chat about the horse outside being Greek or Trojan or something from the Republic of Telly, now the same blank textless nothingness. Ciara thought back to the first blank and considered maybe he had been busy with his family. Days had passed when there were no texts, Christmas Day, St Stephens, significant and meaningful time which could have been spent away from family, doing romantic type things such as texting her, had been wasted and now it was happening again. Finally when New Year's Eve had come and gone marked primarily by Ciara checking mobile every five minutes, she had despaired. And she was despairing again, all was quiet once more. What had happened? Had she seemed too needy? There had been a few nice texts, well lots and lots of them and then he was almost a text-ex! "Ciara pull yourself together. This is ridiculous! Enjoy your life, be with your friends not mulling and dreaming in your head."

Some people say time is relative and the relativity factor for Ciara was the frequency with which she checked her phone. If she had a good day she would only check it about 19 times and then two days of an interlude between Karl's texts would seem like two weeks. However on bad days she may check her phone about 200 times and so two days without texts from him seemed like two months. Was she addicted to her new fone? Oh, sorry she had gone Roman, phone, back to the perfect Greek since she was not having texts she was text celibate.

One rainy evening when there was nothing on the telly and still nothing from Karl, she decided to call him. They had never spoken on the phone. People didn't seem to these days. So she thought she would change the means of communication and get talking. She wanted to hear his voice again, but it was a bit scary picking up the phone. She stared at the lovely, shiny perfectly formed Korean device and willed it to do something. "Ring, do for me. Oh Samsung, my Samsung perform." Nothing happened, well except that she lost her nerve.

Then she couldn't not call, she had to know. This was definitely a time for external bolstering; Dutch courage was not strong enough. Russian was needed, a bit of Boris Good-enough by Shostakovich and she had just the thing in a Russian Standard, 40% proof from St Petersburg, or vodka to the less initiated. Even in her own mind Ciara could not be honest enough to say, "I need a drink before I call Karl" yet that was all it was.

There was a huge fear factor as so much time had passed since they first met and they had lapsed into the normality of texting. They had not met again. In old fashioned dating, before the advent of texting, it was the boy who made the first call. She may have been over thinking the Russian affect, as one brand of vodka had the same effect as the next, but it was a necessary motivational thing. One very strong measure and lots of derogatory hip hop music with a particularly violent undertone fortified her to pick up the phone. That was important, to have rap or hip hop playing gave external atmosphere, she could pretend to be out in a bar. She pressed play. She dialled the number and let it ring three times, but her courage failed her and she hung up. She was annoyed with herself and frustrated with him. "Well that was great," she flung her phone onto the sofa and brooded. What could she do? Dance? around the living room, at Seven-ish mid-week? Yes, her neighbours knew she was kooky buy they may be committing her to the local lunatic asylum if they saw her! She sat and drank her second vodka whilst rooting for her phone under one of the cushions.

"Maybe a bath was in order"; she would be more relaxed rather than geed up.

She ran a rather hot bath with lots of bubbles and essential oils, if she smelled good maybe she would feel good enough to call. "Serious lack of self-esteem Ciara" she chided. Of course she was good enough, she was drinking Boris after all, or was that Vladimir? Any Russian name would do as she had been reading about Napoleon's long walk back after the Muscovites burned Moscow. She wanted to share this with Karl whether he wanted to hear it or not. "Anatoly, I think that is my favourite Russian name" she smiled, War and Peace had taken her an age to read.

Aoife called her so she splashed and chatted and sipped her Boris. 'Hey, how are you?' asked Ciara.

'Good, are you in the bath?'

'Yep, how can you tell?'

'There is an echo behind the Lil Kim,' said Aoife.

'I'm in the bath, chilling, drinking and singing history, really out of tune.'

'Why?'

'Well I'm just feeling frustrated about Karl' said Ciara.

'Ciara, I am sick of this to-ing and fro-ing he is a tease and the sooner you get him out of your mind the better.'

'Yep Aoife, you're right, you're so right.'

'I can hear a "but" in there, Ciara what are you not telling me?'

'Did I tell you how dashing he is, like a strong silent type in a novel from the early nineteenth century, he could be

Keats or Shelly if they had such flaxen hair.' Or maybe a silent movie since they never talked!

You've mentioned he is cute yes, but what else?'

'Well I tried to call him.'

'You did not, you mad thing.'

'I did' said Ciara.

'And what happened?'

'I lost my nerve and I am having a measure of vodka in the bath to pluck up the courage to do it again.'

'Try again if you really must, but he seems a bit like that film.'

'Which film?' asked Ciara.

'It's called "he's just not that into you" we saw it together.'

'Oh,' said Ciara.

'Karl is emotionally unavailable.' Aoife was not mincing her words.

'Don't say that! At this time of the year I really need something a bit fluffy, even if it is total fantasy. Also I need a bit of moral support from you.' At least Ciara realised she was onto a detached male even if she wished she weren't. She would prefer if the character were blond and maybe out of True Blood as the Vampires didn't tend to be emotionally available. So that was normal. The good-looking one was even a Viking, how fitting.

'Ciara don't waste so much mental energy on him.'

'I don't, I only think of him at down times such as on the bus, in the supermarket, at my desk, only joking.' She could hear Aoife inhale deeply with concern. 'By the way, how is that solicitor of yours?'

'He was just too boring for words, I dumped him. So it's New Year, new man!' It was March but anyway.

'Fair enough,' wow Aoife was a strong character. 'Right I am going, the bath is getting cold.'

Her friend encouraged her to try again, well not really encourage, but she knew what Ciara was like when she got idea in her head. Aoife had suffered the inane prattle of Ciara's doubts, fears and anxieties concerning this texting contact. She wanted to see some results be it a meeting or a parting. Ciara hopped out of the bath shivering and bid her friend goodbye. She poured herself one more vodka with the nice, actually really nice orange juice that you only buy when feeling particularly flahulach, or to anyone who didn't follow the Facebook page, extravagant orange juice with the bits in it. "The bits are the best" she thought.

Now was the time and she rang Karl's number again. This time though she let the phone ring this time until it rang out. No answer. So that was it, it was at an end.

Then a text arrived about ten minutes later 'Who is this?'

What to do? He had deleted her number, how rude! Why would he do that? Or maybe he was just pretending. She nearly threw the phone out her bedroom window. However she had finally mastered the functionalities of it so she stopped herself.

She wanted to make a strong statement, a retort almost, to this insult to her identity. It was worse than identity theft it was identity deletion, it must be a criminal activity. It may have been a good idea at this stage for Ciara to cut communications with someone who was feigning knowledge of her but she would persist. If she were wise she would not have already been drawn in, but there was such a rush texting him. That rush was not achieved in any other part of her life and so she craved it, longed for the ping, no matter what time of the day or night it arrived. Her phone was always on, waiting, hoping, longing.

Maybe if she didn't have so much time on her hands things could have seemed different. Then this interaction or exchange of texts would be docked here, at this juncture, like the truncated tail of a dog. She was so angry she couldn't leave it. Yet she knew it wasn't sensible to continue. She locked herself in the bathroom and had a little anger attack it is what she had always done when Sean lived there. This was a really sensible thing to do as she was living alone.

'Are you the tall Napoleonic stranger I met in the snow?' she texted after some thought.

'I fear your eyes are looking for something different from his?' He replied a bit mystically but he hadn't forgotten her! He had lied.

That wasn't the response she was hoping for. This would take a little bit more thought and a lot more vodka. So she thought hard and rationality left her.

'If I was to name your tablet it would be The Napoleon 1812 model' serves him right she smiled to herself.

'That's good would yours be "Josephine the wistful"?'

'Well it wouldn't be "The Austrian" anyway' she smiled then she thought it was an Austrian princess that Napoleon married, wasn't it? She should look up the history again and get her facts right.

'Ah, you do make me smile Ciara! Are you suggesting I meet someone new?'

'Karl, considering we have never met and you don't even want to chat on the phone it's immaterial.'

It may not have been the best reply as he had warmed up a little, maybe she could have been a little gentler. She didn't hear anything from him that night and well that was okay because it was really late but he did text the next morning.

'So Ciara have you a fluffy pink case for your new-ish phone?' Karl texted before 7 am! Ciara read it and rolled over, she had already had a bath so she could laze in bed until about 8, yeah.

"A cover, never even thought of one. It could be a good thing though if I fancy flinging my phone about and pretending it is a self-defence weapon." She slept on and replied to Karl when she was on the bus.

'Not a huge fan of pink, but a good idea I should get a gel cover, thanks' that was nicer!

'I read War and Peace a few years back and I remember the bit about Moscow burning. I would like to Conquer Russia, but do it in the Summer!' he was being communicative.

'Yeah there is a lot of snow in the winter.'

'There is, you know when the rivers froze they used to travel on the ice in sleighs, it was much faster than on normal roads.'

'I didn't know that' said Ciara. 'Quite interesting actually' a bit of encouragement was good.

'So are we attacking Russia in the Spring?'

'Maybe, Josephine never followed Napoleon to Russia' she said.

'To be away from Josephine may have been a good thing. However I seem to have lost without her!'

That was a bit of encouragement here. 'No Josephine and lots of snow. It doesn't sound like a happy campaign.'

'No, I'm not a happy campaigner today' said Karl.

'Did something happen?' Gosh he had changed his tune a bit.

'The Russians burned all the fields and when we retreated we starved' he sent.

'Is your day actually that bad or just your characters'?'

'Would you like me to be,' he asked? He didn't explain.

'That would depend on you and your actions Karl,' she thought he could elaborate. What type of bad did Karl mean?

'Or maybe your reactions my lady without strings,' he continued. Well that was different but he wasn't answering the question.

'Josephine could never play Napoleon if she were without strings. Could the strings be your heart strings? Could it be that I pluck them?'

'Is that a threat?'

'Maybe, hopefully not,' Ciara back tracked a little, she wasn't sure where he was going. 'I won't be plucking your purse strings anyway as this is not direct contact!'

'Yes, we have indirect contact,' he went on.

'Is that indirect or infrequent contact?'

"Both, either or neither if you wish,' he sent.

'If you're bored just go.' She was about to send this, but then she figured he would, his mood was running cool to cold in this exchange and she decided to make a scramble.

'Maybe there is a place for an online coffee. Or is there a virtual internet cafe?' Why had she said this? Admittedly it was a concession as he seemed bored, but she didn't want a virtual coffee she wanted a real one, with a real life Karl sitting in front of her looking at her, talking. She wanted to see his lips move, and his arms gesticulate as if he were stealing a car parking space from a yummy mummy and her screaming tots. Morals of conquest aside she just wanted to see him, was this too much to ask?

'Yep it's called your living room and mine,' Karl replied.

'Hope you have a good coffee brewer,' Ciara decided to go for something cool rather than hot as her brain was overheating with the politeness. Her army was not advancing, she felt like the Russian generals sitting watching Napoleon march away letting the cold and snow ravage them rather than attacking to win victory.

'I do, while I wait for my brew to stew, later, can I seek the eyes of Josephine, green and on fire' he was advancing now. Was his living room safe ground?

'Are my eyes on fire' asked Ciara boldly?

'They were that night, melting the snow around Wellington Quay' he said.

Hmm that was nice but this conversation was not how she had planned it. She had wanted him to pop over for a coffee, later. Her brewer was fixed by her helpful brother and she could share the freshly ground, rich roast blend with him. Or if he wanted neutral ground they could go to a cafe somewhere between Lucan and Celbridge.

The upshot was that they were still at square one, how annoying; the Wellington moment was brilliant but was it their defeat. Could it be that the tall Napoleon was content to text? Where was the advance?

This Karl was like the Peninsular War Napoleon, too busy with other aspects of his life to dedicate time to meeting her. He was focusing North whist she was being set adrift somewhere in the Med. Her hopes of meeting seemed to be floating away on a piece timber blasted from an exploded ship after the Battle of Trafalgar. The explosions were happening elsewhere and she was just getting the debris. He was alive, she was sure of that but her ability to move forward with him was about as likely at the rebuilding of Pillar of Lord Nelson on O'Connell St. Her current Napoleonic reading material was focused on the sea battles and it was really fun stuff. Ciara could imagine herself as the live figurehead leading the large boats to victory, particularly in the warm Mediterranean Sea rather than the frozen Baltic.

Later on she was home, showered and still thinking, was just being dramatic, he wanted to text and she wanted to meet clean and simple. How was she going to clear this impasse and find a route through the Straits of Gibraltar? Sail out to the open seas of coffee shops or even park benches, where they could chat make eye contact and she could ascertain whether she liked him or not. Life was a mystery especially when Ciara lived in history, it seemed that the present was just fantasy. Or maybe the almost present could be somebody's fantasy. She should get out of her bathrobe and put on her electric blanket so as not to die of hyperthermia and get back to reality.

'May consider MEETING you for that coffee with no euphemisms attached' she responded when suitably reheated and attired and tucked up in her warm bed.

'A latte with lots of steam,' was he texting dirty or maybe she was reading into this reply a bit too deeply?

'I hope you have a steamer attachment on your cool coffee machine.'

'Well I do, I can make lots and lots of steam!!!' Was he making euphemisms with his coffee machine?

"Really" Ciara thought "where is he going with this line of thinking?"

'Yes I have attachments to my coffee machine which I doubt you have.' "Yucky" he was heading south like the Mediterranean wars. Maybe he was into this part of Napoleon too.

'No I don't like complicated gadgets' she said.

Could the s of sex elide and merge with text to form stext? Could you have stexts she mused not quite knowing what to do. He was responding which was good, but not the way she wanted. Whilst fantasies were comforting on grey dark days, to encounter reality in such a head on steamy fashion was a bit affronting. She didn't really feel ready for the nice the fantasy to be over?

Maybe she would need to seek some subtle references which would help slow him down.

Ciara googled stext and was very disappointed to hear it was the art of dirty talk via text! Karl must have visited the website already as he seemed well practiced. Ciara had never even thought about this concept before. It was interesting if it was art, if it was a concept maybe, but she was not really sure she was ready to engage in it just yet. He would have to take things slower, one text at a time.

She had been thinking French for a while, thanks to Napoleon and French classes with Stephen so when she turned on the radio instead of the TV she listened to the old tale of Roxanne. It was a bit of a coincidence and she was very happy. The radio play was Cyrano de Bergerac and the words took her to another level. They were romantic rather than raunchy. It was beautiful, Cyrano was wordy but Christian the handsome suitor was well worthy.

She was going to have to think about this one as she had just cleared her fantasies of Troy and Greek sagas and was trying to introduce the sexy Nordic weather god Thor. Should she be introducing a new theme to confuse the idealised cocktail? Thor was hot though, he had Thursday dedicated to him, definitely one of the best days of the week.

She would think on it and she was going to sleep. For the first time in a long time she turned off her phone. Ah the head space was novel and well deserved.

Fin Amour / Sophie's Special

Ciara pulled off the six year old football posters from her living room wall. They were faded tatty and worst of all none of the players were hot. There was blue tack all over the walls and as she tried to pick it off she removed a lot of paint. She opened the curtains to see what she was doing and realized that the areas covered had not faded the same way as the rest of the walls, why had she not painted everything white? Her mother had convinced her to go for a cream substitute which was a sort of mix between duck egg or egg shells and mushrooms. Yes the colour was off cream. Sugar she was going to have to paint her living room. It was one of the two rooms she used so she may as well have it right. These texts were going in circles and they had her considering redecoration again! Things were getting serious.

'Sophie?' a bright spark of inspiration hit Ciara and she called for some help, the phone was dialling before Ciara had considered what she wanted to say. Sophie would be the ideal candidate, being French she must know about art, interiors and everything visual. How to ask for help without seeming rude was always a challenge.

'Hi Ciara, how are you?'

'Yes I am very good, but I have a little problem' Ciara realised she hadn't greeted Sophie and she thought she had better as she wanted a favour. 'By the way how are you?'

'Yes, well thanks so what is your problem?'

'It isn't a big problem, it is just that I need to get some art for my walls and you are about the most artistic person I know. So I wondered if you would like to join me on an art hunt in the City.' Recover the walls with paintings would be easier than actually painting herself.

'I would like to where did you have in mind?'

'I was thinking of Merrion Square. There are paintings there every Sunday so some sunny Sunday we could go.'

'If you like, it would be happy to help.'

That would be great.'

'You are the weather-woman Ciara, so you will know the best day!' Sophie was getting into the office colloquial obviously.

'Actually this Sunday looks as if it will be bright I don't know whether you are free,' it was Thor's-day evening yes she was relating the handsome Nordic God to his designated day and this should be enough notice for Sophie. Ciara didn't want to seem too forceful to Sophie as she didn't really know her as an entity yet, she was more an appendage of Stephen. Ciara didn't want this she wanted to know Sophie as a person in order not to feel so protective about Stephen in a clucky mother hen manner. This was actually a good way to chat and become friends as Sophie seemed as if she wanted to be here to stay.

'That is fine Ciara, it is good even, I have never been to this artists fare and I hear that it is quite popular.'

'Not to mention there are great bargains to be had!'

'Bargain! This is the word of the moment in Dublin' said Sophie.

'Yes apart from a few years of abandon it was always a word to describe Dublin,' agreed Ciara the formidable bargain hunter.

'It is different for us, in France we buy a few good quality items and they last for a very long time.'

'No we do the exact opposite, buy loads and loads of bargains and throw them out after a very short time!'

'So Sunday, maybe about 1 pm?' asked Sophie.

Ciara would have liked later preferably pushing for 4 ish when the artists would reduce their prices to an affordable level but she was asking a favour so she couldn't quibble. 'Perfect and the coffee is on me.'

'Great see you there.'

One of the lovely things about going into town on a Sunday is that you can drive, yes, it is true that the terminus of the three buses available to Ciara are on Merrion Square but she had decided that large pieces of art were to be acquired and so her boot would be necessary. Who ever dreamt of carrying paintings home on the bus? Chances are that she would rip the canvass, she was a bit of a swan out of water, no matter how hard she tried to glide she always bumped into things. Maybe gilding was only possible in water when one is 1/6 of their body weight.

Ciara had no trouble parking on the Square that Sunday and as the day was glorious she was able to leave her jacket and jumper in the car.

Sophie was there already and smiled as Ciara came up. 'This is lovely Ciara, I had no idea there were so many exhibitors here selling their works.'

'I'm glad you like it, sometimes I used to come here to get away from my ex and his x-box! It is vibrant but you can be alone here without being lonely.'

'Yes I can see that, many people are deep in thought, so have you a painter in mind?'

'Not particularly, I thought we could wander and see what caught our eye. Then you could tell me if my choice was completely terrible and I could admire yours,' Ciara's confidence was still at a low ebb. She had tried to make the content with Karl more-subtle over the last few days but the texts were silly, feigned aggression and retraction, attacking Continents and retreating. He was constantly pushing the boundaries of propriety and she was well outside her comfort zone. It had been about three in the morning when she finally gave up last night after her predictive phone began thinking for itself, there were too many grammatical errors and enough double entendres to make any 1980's stand-up comic proud.

Now she was even thinking this way!! It was so frustrating.

So they browsed chatted and drank take away coffees in the square. Ciara decided to talk about Stephen, anything to get her mind off Karl, 'so let's talk boy stuff!'

'You mean Stephen?' responded Sophie quickly. 'All this artistic flattery has an objective!'

'I'm only flaky on a Friday' Ciara joked. 'Really though what do you see in him?'

'Do you really wish to know?'

'Yes of course, unless I am being too intrusive,' said Ciara.

'No it's ok Ciara, I know you are protecting your friend. I see in Stephen someone who could be my best friend as well as my boyfriend. He is centred and completely happy in his own skin. In fact I see him like a chevalier of old on a Knights Errant.'

'Except his steed is faster!' said Ciara and Sophie smiled. Then she regrouped her thoughts, 'you are right, this is why I feel so close to him. However he is not as strong as he seems, he is quite fragile in many ways.'

'All men are, everyone is, but he is true. I think you are looking for this also.'

'What do you mean Sophie?'

'This fin d'amour it is the perfect love and almost a removed love. I have the fresh new romance where things are new and exciting. We meet, at work or do things together but your love is distant. You imagine yourself as a lady locked in a tower needing to be saved from a bad witch.'

'Like a pre Raphaelite painting?' Ciara was listening but she hadn't forgotten the task in hand. Maybe Sophie was getting a bit close to a truth which Ciara had not realised or ignored even and definitely was not admitting it to herself.

'No much further back. Back to the middle ages, there was life before Napoleon!' wow Ciara really was that transparent.

Ciara sat still and was silent letting Sophie's words drift on the air like the gentle steam coming from the coffee cups.

'It was a time when maidens were beautiful and Knights were brave' Sophie continued. 'When men wrote poetry to their ladies and posted it on the tree near her house.'

'Really I can't imagine Karl doing that,' said Ciara. 'I don't think I want him to.'

'You do, each text is like a love letter, full of romance and far off times. He is happy to play Napoleon as then he has a reason to be away from you. He has wars to fight, Europe to conquer and laws to enact. It is a dance of desire from a distance so he can conquer you and your heart when he is ready.'

'Wow Sophie, you have thought about this.' Ciara felt a bit taken aback by these words.

'We are not very busy in the multi-lingual section either and you are a constant preoccupation of Stephen's.'

Ciara thought and was silent and wondered if there was any truth in it. It gave her hope and she would text Karl this evening with lots of French references, Roxanne probably and maybe on a theme of milk as Roxanne had said "you give me milk when I want cream" he had expressed an interest in lattes, well seam in coffee makers so surely this was the same thing.

They walked about Merrion square again but Ciara was not in the mood to purchase art as she already had enough beauty in her head. Her thoughts were inflamed with horses outside but just after a jousting match rather than being fed on half a bag of yokes like Shergar the stolen horse of the Rubberbandits eulogies.

'You give me skim milk when I want cream', she texted when she got home.

'No I like regular milk in my coffee' he replied swiftly without a clue what she meant.

Was he being pedantic or had he not been moved by Cyrano de Bergerac on the radio? How could he not know that the lovely Roxanne claimed when Christian spoke his own words they were not as rich as Cyrano's, they were diluted into 0% fat milk? She had loved Christians face but Cyrano's words. Maybe she should explain what she was thinking.

'In the radio play of Cyrano de Bergerac Roxanne rates the words from full fat cream down to 0% fat milk. The more beautiful the words the higher the cream content,' she sent. 'It was on the radio this week.'

'Ok cryptic Ciara, let me look it up and I will come back with a suitably creamy content!'

'Now how can you embroider cream?' he asked after an hour. That was a good response time.

'Churn it into butter maybe?' she suggested.

'Not that I am deft with a sewing needle but still butter is a semi-liquid and they didn't have fridges so I don't see how it is possible.' Could a boy be bright and creamy, well dishy would be more apt?

Karl had a point you could embroider but not with butter, maybe with icing sugar or rather spurt it onto a cake and use a fork to make a nice snow scene and it would harden to stay in shape. Yes but butter that was a tough one.

'It could be metaphorical, the more meaningful the words the more viscous. So words that resonate would hang in the mouth of Roxanne and the more fluid would be swallowed down and quickly forgotten.' Ciara wasn't exactly sure where she was going with this but she was trying to say she wanted some memorable words which she could repeat when she finished her Napoleon book or had tired of singing Fred Astaire songs for the morning.

'So are you into oral?' He enquired. Wow he was a bit weird or maybe he just liked his hot milk as frothy as a cappuccino. Could he really be referring to the beauty of words or was this is what all boys thought but were a bit too polite or inhibited to say so. Texting in Ciara's expansive experience is such a removed art form; there is separateness to it as the receiver is remote and unseen. One could potentially forget that the receiver was human at all but just a response mechanism to humour one at idle moments through the day.

'Yep I talk a lot!' She thought this may add a bit of humour and deflect from the overtly sexual and explicit nature. She did think of talking more about dairy products, maybe cheese, as in he could spend his cheddar taking her to dinner. "I have lots of cheddar but we could spend yours together" in the eloquent words of J Lo, or something like that.

However he wasn't biting. Maybe he wasn't into rapper references, she really didn't know, but she always found them funny. Bread had been the usual term for money but it had gone up market as rappers got richer, so now cheddar was the new word for money.

What about dental products, Oral is as oral be, or B, prevents more than just a tooth ache, it can relieve a pain in the whole head. Or maybe more than a toothbrush, it could be a means of improving conversation. Well clean breath reduces the chances of the other person retching when talking face to face obviously. Would this improve the chances of him biting? She was digressing, she would have to see what he came back with.

'Dodger' he replied. Could this dodger be artful? The conclusion Ciara came to was that Karl wanted stext or text dirty or whatever he was currently doing and there was no stopping him.

'I will think of you when I brush my teeth tonight!!! I will slowly squeeze out the paste and rub the brush hard against my teeth.' "Haa haa" she was happy enough with that one.

'I will also think of you when I brush my teeth' said Karl. He was such a copy cat, or maybe he had zoned out.

So it seemed best to leave the conversation for a while, she was feeling annoyed. The text could get a bit sleazy and she didn't want this. Then, well later that evening, she brushed her teeth as it was bed time. She thought of him, but not the oral type manner that he may have been hoping for. She imagined he had really good teeth, American white teeth, really straight and perfectly proportioned and he was smiling. He was smiling at her. His head was looking back at her through the bathroom mirror and it felt good. Just as she was about to fall asleep with lots of happy thoughts about teeth the wand of mischief waved.

'R u into anal?' he asked.

Like OMG! "Are you just anal Karl?" She thought to herself in a somewhat affronted and quite sleepy manner. That is a bit beyond the beyond! It was beyond the Pale even though they were still in it. Or maybe it was he who was into it, could suffer from hard...., no she didn't want to go there, not even in her own brain. Yes he was being weird. Was he a complete dirt-bag? How inappropriate for someone she had only met once. She pondered great and deep issues such as are women more likely to be friendly via text communication? They may send kisses and smiley to people with whom they would not likely shake hands face to face. "He needs his nappy changed!" Yes she was awake now!

Are men more likely to be more sexual when they don't have to see the facial reaction and most likely not have to deal with any real-life consequences? Actually this question was a bit last millennium, dating back sometime in the 1980s with the advent of home computers. Do we have to be braver in real life than virtual life! Is that why internet dating is popular?

'I fear sweet breathed Napoleon you have taken matters too far south' she texted with one eye open. 'Remember the Egyptian defeats.'

'Fear feeds my fantasy,' he said.

"Go on ya good thing, was it not you who started the fear," she was getting cranky now. 'Karl I was drifting off to sleep dreaming of your really clean teeth and fresh breath only to be rudely affronted by a stale garlic after-taste. Now your imagination will have to wash that vision away with your pink sponge and your lily of the garden soap!!!'

'I'm a boy so I wear boy soap, like eau do Rambo or the sweat of Napoleon!'

'Maybe your Overtext!' She had had enough.

She wanted to play with the term to get him thinking in a different way. She had no intention of objectivising herself for his distant gratification. Well not much anyway.

'It's good to have a lively text life!' He responded several hours later he really was a topper. Those grey cells must have been working overtime as the text time was close to 3 am.

'It depends on what you're into, a full inbox, group text, predictive texts x' He was on a roll and followed up first thing in the morning with this one liner. She did have to smile.

'I have a small memory mobile, so full inboxes are easily forgettable, delete-able and achievable... Group texting is confusing Karl or is that Hans'. She sent but maybe she should have considered deeper and changed the tone or at least toned it down. No of course not, she fancied a bit of humour, this was Ciara and she had too little activity and stimulation of her grey matter. She needed some inspiration. She thought of other terms to relate to a full inbox come soon or happen easily, maybe come early, but she discounted them. They were not subtle enough for her delicate sensibilities. Well at least she thought she was delicate even if no one else did!

She considered sending something for the predictive such as, "you never know what you're getting with predictive. You start with Anna and finish with Boob!" This was actually true, she had nearly sent a text like this to Stephen until she read what she had typed. For some reason though he seemed to receive it, maybe at a later date, maybe she had been cleaning out her drafts and sent it by accident. Whoops!

'Whose Hans?' he enquired, was he interested or confused?

'Exactly my sentiments,' she quipped.

'Now I'm confused.' He continued.

That was a good days work for the thumbs she thought and it was only 10 am.

A good friend

It had been a while since the ill-fated phone call attempt, then there were all of these sexual undertones like overtext, and group-texts and it was all getting too much for Ciara. She needed some sound advice and who better to call than Aoife.

Every heroine needs a good friend and Ciara was lucky to have a number of very close friends. Aoife was probably the closest friend she had, but Ciara felt it unfair to classify her as her best friend. This may have been because she was only her best friend sometimes. Aoife was a complex character with lots of blind spots which she really didn't like being reminded of. Ciara also had blind spots but wanted to be at least aware of them. They were extremely similar in outlook, humour and taste so often had fallings out even though they were supposed to be grown-ups. Maybe Aoife didn't like seeing a lot of her own personality mirrored in Ciara especially those areas which she didn't like about herself. It upset Ciara that Aoife seemed to be able to make critical remarks about her but, when the return was enacted long silences and unreturned texts would be the result.

Aoife always tried to do the right thing but somehow or other it always turned out wrong. Her choice of men was disastrous and her choice of holiday destinations seemed doomed to failure. Yet in spite of this she was a good friend to Ciara, true and trusting, maybe too trusting. She worked for a social networking site or search engine company, Ciara wasn't sure what the difference was and in spite of herself Aoife was hugely successful at work. She was constantly planning to dump in the day job and work with the poor in India or Africa or somewhere else worthy to prove to herself that she was a good person.

'I'm still thinking about that poor lawyer you dumped,' texted Ciara on the bus into work.

'Why is that?' replied Aoife already at her desk.

She always over worked to compensate for her self-doubt and was sure she would be fired soon. This assumed lack of her abilities did not work so well on the romantic front and unfortunately her marriage had failed within the first year. She had tried so hard at the courting stage to be perfect that when she finally relaxed on the day after the wedding her new husband didn't actually know her. When he got to know her after a few months he didn't like what he saw and the divorce proceedings took much longer than the courtship unfortunately.

'I don't think you gave him a chance,' said Ciara referring to the lawyer-guy rather than the soon to be ex-husband.

There was a bit of silence as Aoife's feathers had been ruffled then she responded, 'am I too harsh?'

Aoife's outlook on life was still romantic though and she wanted everything to be perfect. She didn't want to hear about anything negative. In other words she was setting herself up for failure. Ciara had been bridesmaid and whilst appreciating the honour had felt that the groom was below Aoife in more ways than one. He had been a regular guy whilst Aoife was dynamic and brilliant, well at least in Ciara's eyes.

'Yes sometimes you are a bit severe, once someone is in under your barrier you are super-nice, but before that you have a bullet proof protective layer.' Maybe Ciara was saying too much but she really wanted Aoife to achieve some sort of middle ground with boys.

His name the nearly ex-husband, had been Brian and he was content working, meeting friends for a few pints in the pub and watching telly. In fact he had got on quite well with Sean, Ciara's ex-boyfriend. Sean had been distraught when the marriage broke up and had tried to help, tried to patch things up. He couldn't understand Ciara's ambivalence and thought her cold. Sean could not see how miss-matched a pair they actually were. It was only when he finally realised this did he recognise how little he and Ciara had in common. Once the realisation dawned he began to look for an exit strategy and stopped trying to make things work. Luckily for Ciara, she had not bothered analysing her own life as she was too busy with everyone else's. So maybe Ciara had more blind spots than she thought!

'Do you really think that Ciara' texted Aoife.

'Do you think that maybe you are being overly harsh on the lawyer-guy to compensate for being overly lax with Brian?' Ciara was on a roll with the directness and just couldn't resist pressing send in spite of the consequences. She had more or less reiterated her thoughts from the previous text. There was no response for quite a while, when would Ciara ever learn?

Aoife and Ciara had wild nights out even when Aoife was married. Aoife never sought but always generated lots of attention. She was dazzling not just her looks but her intelligence was brilliant, constantly shining through. Ciara was always overshadowed by her beauty but she didn't mind, it meant she never had to do the leg work. Aoife always landed the pro-offered drinks.

Unfortunately Aoife could never see what she had, accepting when a bit merry, whatever fell on her lap gratefully rather than realising she deserved so much more. Yet when sober, at work say no man ever had an in, she was imperious. Brian had assumed she would be there and would always be there, until he finally became intimidated by her ability to cope with any situation which arose. It seemed to Ciara that guys would throw themselves into Aoife's path then denigrate her worth to reassert their sense of value and improve their own self-esteem. Brian had not appreciated that she was a gemstone, rare, beautiful but quite fragile. It seemed that the cycle would continue until Aoife worked out what she actually wanted and went out to get it herself.

'Yep I did try a bit too hard with Brian,' Aoife finally responded just as Ciara was coming through the doors of her office. This was a great advancement in the friendship. Aoife must be in a good mood.

Ciara really enjoyed having her about and always sought advice from her. The advice was sound, measured and well balanced, well most of the time anyway. She thought she shouldn't investigate into the lawyer guy too much as maybe it wasn't as straight forward as Aoife made out. Really it was none of Ciara business and if Aoife opened up great. It was funny or curious rather that Aoife could give expert advice to Ciara, insightful, considered and generate a range of options as solutions but could not turn the analytical prism to her own life and relationship issues.

'Hi Ciara, how is life?' Aoife was texting at about noon a few days after the near break-up of the friendship through Ciara's clumsy texting. Aoife must have put away her sensitivities as she seemed to be genuinely worried about how the evasive but quite persuasive Karl was affecting Ciara's equanimity.

'All good, had some texts from Karl but nothing tangible.'

'Oh, texts are always intangible as the techies wouldn't print them out for you!! Only messing, good or bad sub-text? Actually don't answer that lets meet for lunch and you can tell me all.' The olive branch was being thrown Ciara's way and she took it up with relief.

'Sure, I'd love to' replied Ciara. Even Aoife was joking about her need to technologically outsource, she was going to start those phone fear seminars, she would set up a meet-up group it would be a very secretive group. 'Would about 1 pm suit you to meet?'

Ciara always looked forward to a nice lunch with Aoife. It was lively, informative and generally Ciara would be completely up to date with current affairs, the state of the government and the world economy, so much so that she didn't have to watch the news when she got home at night. Often times she would be able to avoid the media for the whole rest of the week. Ciara was not a huge fan of current affairs she much preferred the world inside her head to that outside. It was a much happier place.

'Sounds wonderful.' This was Aoife's standard response to even the most mundane of texts.

'I think it is my treat this time as I will be expecting some sound advice,' asserted Ciara.

They met in their usual place which did an all day breakfast. Ciara was addicted to eggs Florentine, not just as she wished to get away from the French theme which pervaded with that Napoleon Guy but she actually had convinced herself that spinach would counteract the effect of over egging her diet. The coffee was also good there and sometimes Aoife and Ciara would have Vodka-tines not necessarily later in the week but usually later in the day than lunch.

The sometimes habit of Marlboros was extending to a greater part of the week as anxiety was extending to a greater part of Ciara's life. So luckily there was a nice smoking area outside which would receive the full beam of the sun's rays should it ever choose to shine on this rain drenched Island.

'Hey Aoife, great to see you,' Ciara chirped when they met she was in need of refuge today.

'Yes and you Ciara, how are you?'

'Great,' she blatantly lied. She read the disbelief on Aoife's face. 'Ok going up the walls but I want to hear how you are first before I launch into me as this will take all our lunch.'

'Right me first!' said Aoife. 'You know Brian agreed to the divorce?'

'No, really!'

'Yes, really.'

'I thought he was being really obstinate,' said Ciara.

'Yes, well he had been. It has taken ages for him to agree.' Aoife smiled.

'Why does that not surprise me?'

'Well in the end it came down to money,' said Aoife ignoring Ciara's last comment.

Ciara smiled and said nothing. So, he was taking her to the cleaners! They say that the law is always on the side of the weaker party and Aoife was definitely not the weaker party when she decided on something.

'Do you know how long a divorce takes in Ireland?' Aoife continued.

Ciara didn't get a chance to respond as Aoife knew she wouldn't know. Divorce was a relatively new occurrence in the Republic and Aoife was going to relish every moment.

'And it has taken the maximum amount of time, four years. Can you believe it, four years! So I am now a free woman! Well nearly, the terms have to be perused by our solicitors which will probably only take a few weeks.'

'Congratulations, again, maybe we need a vodka-tini after all!' Ciara should really try to get into the spirit of things and what better way than Vodka? Yes she definitely preferred it to Whiskey. She wondered though could Brian still squirm his way out. She wasn't going to say as Aoife's face read relief and she didn't want to dissipate that sense of joy.

'Maybe we do have to celebrate but I have a heavy afternoon. Actually we are celebrating right now,' said Aoife being responsible as it was daylight.

'What about later?' Ciara suggested. 'A mid-week night out is always more illicitly sweet.'

'Yes that would be great, this is definitely something to take us out on a work night. I can't do a 6 am though.' This was the usual time they would return home if the evening was successful. Ciara generally lost all concept of time after two drinks and Aoife was able to forget her unusually keen sense of responsibility when socialising with her.

'One drink at a time sweet Jesus,' Ciara changed the not drinking song to suit her own requirements and then felt a bit bad. 'So when will you sign the papers?'

'I don't know yet, the terms were agreed in my solicitors' office yesterday and I think the contract has to be examined with a fine tooth comb by both sides before we can sign. I know it's not completed by any means but I am euphoric. Wow Ciara, the freedom is something wonderful. I am no longer tied to anyone, well nearly. You wouldn't understand as you were never married.'

'Ah no I was seriously relieved when the ex moved out and happier when he emigrated to Australia. I get what you are saying though I was never legally tied to the ex, he was only my common-law husband, hee hee.' Relieved but lost ever since he had moved out if she were truly honest.

Ciara restrained the "I told you never to marry him" line in reference to Brian, as similar sayings had so seriously frayed their friendship in the past. She was learning, however slowly that people do not wish to be reminded of their mistakes. Her great mistake was Sean, even the mention of his name sent darting pains of fear and regret throughout her body. Hopefully Aoife had not known the extent of it.

'Yes you know how I feel, that is good. So tell all about this crazy Karl?'

'Apart from the fact that my visual memory of him is hazy I am getting a sense of his drivers,' Ciara replied using very Karl like words. She was really enjoying the virtual as in removed sense of this intercourse! This was removed and she was safe from hurt but not frustration.

'And what might these be?' enquired Aoife.

'The good thing, you know knowledge in the virtual sense but not the virtuous one and maybe knowledge in the biblical sense'.

'Ah, he wants salacious texts. That is strange as you never did that with you know who.'

'Exactly,' how did Aoife know that thought Ciara?

'Is this a bit of a racy renaissance for you?' asked Aoife.

'Pardon, I'm strictly in the Napoleonic era?'

'I mean you have been so closed since Sean-'

'Don't say that name!' Ciara defensively interrupted.

'As I was saying, you have been slightly tetchy and closed and it seems these texts are opening you up.'

'Maybe' considered Ciara, she wondered whether there was any truth.

'Just use them for an opening and don't consider Karl as a closing in the Fred and Ginger happy ever after silver screen type closing. Ok?'

'Ok, but he does want me for my texts.'

'Is that ALL he wants?' asked Aoife rather pointedly.

'Well, I don't really know. He is so complementary most of the time and then gets a bit forward and after that stops texting completely for a while. Whilst it can be a little annoying he never enters my personal space, which I really like.'

'Why do you think this is so?' Aoife delved.

'Which aspect do you mean maybe the stop start nature of the texting?' Ciara was worried about the personal space nature of texting more than the stop start style of communication. Karl was invading her head space with a strategy Napoleon would be proud of.

'Yes, that one,' said Aoife.

'Coz he's a boy!'

'Oh, ok.'

Aoife knew Ciara was not happy with the situation but she had as many prickly hairs as the hedgehog of her exercise routine which was hibernating for the winter, every winter. She would broach the issue after Ciara had a few drinks. Some say in vino veritas but Aoife knew once Ciara started drinking she completely lost touch with reality. It wasn't that she lied but she could not see a question actually relating to her so she would be creative in her replies. It was so fun to watch. The more questions asked of Ciara the more embellished her answers would become. It was particularly amusing when the same person asked the same question over and over again, each and every time a different answer would be returned. It was a fact that her fantasy life was being lived in the bar, restaurant or pub and her fantasies were vivid.

To prepay or not

-I've no credit- web texts one teen to the next. It is a constant complaint of the youth and the doler's otherwise known as people on social welfare. It was the most common opener on any phone call or text conversation on the bus. It excused a multitude, the reason for not calling, the reason for being late and the reason for not turning up. It was pertinent to Ciara as she was thinking of leaving a pay as you go package and entering the grown up world of bill pay.

To be tied and constrained by one service provider. It seems like as much commitment as a marriage. Potentially a phone contract can last longer than a modern Irish marriage does. Also they seem more difficult to extricate oneself from, a phone contract that is. It potentially could become more expensive than a divorce to terminate prematurely. At least with a marriage you can say you were insane at the time of the wedding as love is a state of temporary insanity, from which we hopefully recover. Or drunk on love, as love is a drug apparently which is an excuse for all sorts of odd behaviour. But phone companies don't assess the sanity of the customer before signing the up to contract. Ciara's thoughts of getting a bill pay phone were plaguing her as the array of options were as vast as the rainbow appearing before her on the top deck of the bus and to understand them was as likely as reaching the end of the rainbow and retrieving the crock of gold. The features of each plan were confusing and the benefits seemed not to be useful to her.

'Fancy some fun?' texted Karl, phew she could give her brain a break with a bit of text candy.

It would depend on what type of fun Karl wanted really, good clean fun like freshly brushed teeth to give a nice, white dental advert smile. Or maybe something not quite so clean, teeth stained after a night on the tiles by many deep and meaningful smoky chats with random strangers. No she would think about phones a while longer.

'Can you see the rainbow, Mr eau de Rambo?' ok she had not been very successful with the eclipse but why not try again on the weather front? Also she was bored of phone options.

'Eau de Rambo? You want to know what I wear in bed, you already know what I have for breakfast and now you want to know what I smell like. Whose getting personal now Ciara?'

'Errr' she blushed.

'So you're phishing now?' ah rats, she must have sent him her Greek and Roman theory about ph.'s changing to f's when the Romans came along. Was there any region of her overheated brain safe from him?

'Anyway can you see the rainbow?'

'No I'm at work, slacker I bet you are still on your way in!!'

'Slacker, or maybe I'm highly efficient and organised!!!! Hee hee' gosh he was committed to his work.

Phone contracts, she would go back to the task in hand and calm down a bit. It would seem that phone contracts are as tying as Microsoft Outlook; only one provider can be used just as only one PC can be used for Outlook, how old hat. Any other e-mail account can be accessed from any computer but outlook requires the user to be shackled to generally their work PC or MAC. It is true that phones have slightly more flexibility, one can take a sim card out and use it in another phone, but this phone has to be unlocked. The power these companies wield.

'Is it nice? The rainbow,' said Karl.

'Beautiful, the rain is clearing east and the sun is shining to the west I can almost see the whole arc.'

'You must be only as far as Liffey Valley if you can see that wide an arc!'

'Excuse me! I am on the Quays and the sun is behind, the rainbow is ahead. You must only have a ground floor office.' She was lying though she was only at Liffey Valley, the breadbasket of west Dublin and now the Mall-basket of west Dublin.

'Cheeky, first floor actually where is yours? The penthouse?' Karl asked.

'Not quite but a good few floors up. So do you consider phone packages to be fun?' she said.

"Pay as one goes is like dating, changing partners as a better offer comes along," she thought. Serial monogamy or potentially duality happens when one has a chip for holidays or cheaper long distance texts as there is a shift in tides of deals with varying service providers. Opportunistic text users can be hoppers, there is the freedom to accept offers as and when they arise. If there is no reason to change they sit it out and wait, conserving their credit for a rainy day. Is this American style dating as there are not usually that many people in Dublin who one would wish to date?

'Could be,' said Karl.

Yes Ciara was still thinking about her price plan and the array of choices were mind bending. Maybe she would just stay put, sit on the fence a bit longer until something that she understood finally came along.

'How?'

'Well I have a large phone package!' He would wouldn't he, such a bragger.

There was now even a package which you sign up to for a month that was cool. Yes she would ignore Karl for a while. Every little chance to help make a cent as the slogan of the price-plan could be construed. One could top up on a monthly basis at a very low introductory rate and then... Well then you can top up again.

'Good for you, do your texts get sore when they are all bundled together?'

'Like tight undies,' you had to give it to him Karl was quite focused.

'So do you think pay as you go is like dating?'

'Ciara I had never thought of it in those terms. You are very phone focused today. Well now that you have moved on from the weather, maybe I should revert to the weather.'

'So now you are....thinking in phone terms, do you?'

'How phones are like dating... well you can change partners or packages as a new and better offer comes along. I suppose.'

'Exactly,' said Ciara. 'So if you have a phone plan it is like serial monogamy.'

'Maybe, except these days a service provider will buy you out of one price plan if you are a big spender.' Karl was being helpful, what was happening. 'So there is still flexibility to browse' he continued.

'An exit clause could be likened to seeing a pretty lady in a bar,' said Ciara.

'Nope I prefer when they are face down in dirty snow myself. It's a great way to check out the rear view!'

'I didn't know you had seen me fall over, now that is embarrassing.'

'Why else do you think I asked you out?'

'Now I am feeling really disillusioned, I had thought you had liked all my clashing colours.' She was going to send him a pouty faced emoticon; yes this was the time for an emoticon. However she couldn't work out how to do it. Her pout was really large and she was frowning.

'To be fair all I could see were your long black leather boots and you had nice patterned tights on. My though you have a grand arse on you girl.' Karl was not even a bit contrite.

She pouted some more and fiddled with her phone to work how to send a grumpy face this time. This thingy wouldn't work, she was feeling quite frustrated.

'When you finally stood up and your lovely bouncy hair bounced back into place, then you put on a hat and covered it all up. I saw how tall you were and I was chasing you, phone conversation to your Mum and all.' Was this a slight compliment? He was still at it though she was confused as well as frustrated; so much for the safe, removed art of texting.

'How did you know I was on to my Mum?' she asked.

'It's a tone of voice thing, we are the most impatient with our parents. Maybe because we know they will take it!'

'Yep, you are right, terrible really but true. Right this is my stop, talk to ya!' She hopped up and scrambled her way down the bouncy bus, the driver must have been racing to the garage to get her tea as the large double Decker was reaching break neck speeds. Ciara tried not to fall again, one embarrassment a day was enough for her even if the first was historical.

'There must have been REALLY heavy traffic this morning!' yes he knew she was lying, he texted her at about the same point on her bus journey most days.

'Incredible!!!'

'I may text you later' he sent but he didn't. Not that she was checking her phone even carrying it into the washroom just in case, nope Ciara would never admit to an interest this interesting.

Aoife & Ciara

Aoife and Ciara were out, they were celebrating, it was Aoife's soon to be divorce and Ciara's desire to get out and they were doing it a few days after their luncheon.

Ciara was sitting in a quite empty club looking at all the people who were on their phones. 'I thought the whole point of going out was to talk to the people around you.'

'No, the reason to go out is to inform everyone sitting at home where they are,' replied Aoife.

'Oh that is strange, I am obviously not up with the times.'

'You don't have Facebook' said Aoife.

'No, I don't.'

They were walking out of the nightclub a few hours later and a rather handsome man came over to Aoife. Ciara didn't necessarily see anything unusual in this, Aoife was often chatted-to by handsome men. The unusual factor was that he had been looking over all night and his expression had not been happy, it would be more accurately described as quizzical rather than awed by Aoife's beauty. Even more unusual was the fact that he had not approached her all evening. When he called Aoife's name she also started frowning, blimey what was going on?

'Aoife' he said as he came close to her.

'Oh hi' said Aoife, 'I didn't see you there.' Ciara suspected this to be a lie.

'When are you going to stop texting me?'

'Sorry I drunk text by accident sometimes,' said Aoife.

'There are not too many men in Dublin called Evan. Please, ten texts a day is a bit excessive. I know it didn't work out but have some dignity.'

'Ouch, Mr. That is a bit harsh,' said Ciara defending Aoife's honour. 'Let's get this taxi here.' They hopped in and were away from the scene or what could have developed into a scene in a flash.

Ciara looked hard at Aoife through her vodka goggles, 'so what was that all about.'

'That was the lawyer guy,' Aoife looked down at her hands and played with her rings.

'I thought you dumped his rear months ago.'

'Well it was really he who did the leaving,' confessed Aoife.

'I am sorry,' said Ciara, 'why didn't you tell me?'

'I don't know why I lied but I just really liked him. I just had to keep texting him. I just thought if I tell him this he will like me or if I explain that he will give it another go.'

'So he got in' clarified Ciara. Aoife had never used so many "justs" in one sentence so she must be upset.

'Yes.'

'That's a terrible feeling, when you want someone and there is nothing you can say or do which will make someone change their mind. When they decide that it, then that's.'

'Unfortunately yes and maybe he will block me from his call list.'

'Well maybe you could delete his number from your phone, if you have to key in the digits it will make you go slower.'

'I did delete him and most people don't remember mobile numbers but his was a really easy one with lots of eights and twos so I can type it in really fast' said Aoife.

'Oh' Ciara though it would be a good time to be practical or caring but her head felt a bit fuzzy. She tried to think. 'How long were you seeing him?' this was the best she could come up with.

'About a month.'

'Early days when feelings run high, so what did he say when he broke up?'

'Something about me being a ball breaker and not having much in common,' said Aoife.

'That sounds a bit damning.'

'Thanks Ciara.'

'Sorry,' she was trying but this was a hard subject. It was hard to face reality especially a friend's reality when she had been having fantasy with Karl for three months or so. In many respects it was nice not to have issues. The most serious was when he got over-familiar and if she was honest she didn't mind it too much. Obviously she didn't want Karl to know this.

'I don't understand Aoife, you are beating off guys with a hurling stick, why turn into a mental case with this lawyer guy?'

'Great I'm a mental case.'

'Sorry Aoife but I just don't understand' Ciara repeated.

'As you said he got in.'

'Oh,' then in a moment 'after you broke up when did you first text him?' Ciara was trying to move the subject along. She was hoping not to cause Aoife too much aggravation after her previous statement.

'In the taxi home.'

'That soon! Sorry and what did you say?'

'You are making a big mistake.'

'Oh' said Ciara again. 'Did he reply?'

'Yes, a day or so later he said that I had just confirmed his instinct about me being a ball breaker.'

'Ah,' she was trying to vary her responses.

'Then I was out the following Friday and I sent the woeful "I miss you" text,' said Aoife.

'Did he reply?'

'Yes straight away he sent "I'm not surprised" that was embarrassing and I vowed not to text him again' said Aoife.

'You did though,' said Ciara.

'I did, over the weekend I texted him to see if he wanted to meet up for a chat. He did respond that he would think about it. A week later he said that he didn't want to meet.'

'That is tough, rejection is the hardest thing. So what happened then?' asked Ciara.

'I just kept texting and it got a bit out of hand sometimes ten other times fifteen texts a day. I couldn't stop myself.'

'I'm sorry Aoife, I know how terrible it is to feel hurt.'

'So anyway I stopped as he blocked my number and he stopped replying but to see him tonight was cutting.'

'Yes Aoife, it is awful. Texting can be dangerous. It is so quick to do and once sent there is no chance to take it back.' The knowledge had been hard leaned by Ciara.

'I am an excessive texter!'

'Maybe leave your phone at home on a night out.'

'I am over sending him texts,' said Aoife.

'I said to Karl that he was "overtext"!'

'That is a good one, what did he say in reply, as I know he always has a reply?'

'It's good to have a healthy text life.'

'Ha ha' Aoife laughed, 'I suppose mine was a bit unhealthy' and she was serious again.

'Don't worry, NEXT, is that not your motto.'

'It is' said Aoife, 'you are right.'

Trying Texts

"Who is this" she asked herself, after receiving the tinker bell toned text. She had popped down to the techie guys to find out how to attach emoticons and they had changed her text notification tone to tinker bell from Peter Pan as it was a nice sound. They also wanted to confuse her. This sound was similar to a wand and alerted her to a new text it took her a while to recognise the sound as her own. So she had set text notification volume very loudly so she could hear it when she was out shoe shopping or on the bus.

'Tis I, the tempting texter,' he said. The sound did have mischievous undertones.

She looked at the number and didn't recognise it. It is true to say she had considered deleting his number but she didn't think she had gone the whole way to actually deleting it. Now that she was —home with her phone- she couldn't have deleted it by accident. She had admittedly at the very beginning of the year deleted his work number and felt the empowerment of deleting one text at a time from his personal number. That was ages ago. Yes it was true in many ways they were still at the beginning, but in other ways there was a connection with Karl, they spoke many mornings, he was her bus companion. He was there for her often, even though he really wasn't there at all.

'You forgot to add hopefully!!'

This time Karl had not only changed his number but changed phone companies. He must have got a better offer in his large text bundle. She discovered this, the service plan that is, as the cost of returning his texts greatly increased; she had no Wi-Fi on the bus, this was the time before free Dublin Bus Wi-Fi, so she couldn't web-text. He may well have been going for one of those cheap options as his formally cool number changed to something unmemorable and clunky.

'Hopefully!'

"What is he tempting? My patience!" she thought. She would ignore him, yes, definitely. Her thumbs had an auto-pilot and unfortunately had sent her thought before she had fully formed it. Sugar she had double-text! He was supposed to say something else first.

As far as Ciara could see he was not prepared to put in as much effort as she was. Chancer was the phrase that sprung to Ciara's mind with reference to the last texting banter but then he could say such nice things. He was a mystery. She was oscillating.

'Tempting fate, in order to continue this most pure contact.' He must have a different concept of purity to her.

She was proud of her burgeoning technology skills, she could delete texts. However deleting her web-texts she had found more difficult to work out. To delete the web texts meant merely putting them in a holding file, she had persevered. She had succeeded in working out how to totally delete this holding file. It was very empowering and gave Ciara a semblance of control. The trials of texting were so trying though; she was drained with mental exhaustion.

'Yes pure contact but not pure content' she replied. Now he was back again after over a week of absence, with a new number. He must be in sync with the Irish Construction Industry; a hive of activity in the Noughties then nothing, the industry inactivity gave him lots of free time to text.

'Was fate pretty?' she was worried that she would send him off again so she texted something sweeter.

What did his voice sound like? Was it deep or hollow? Did it boom or resonate? What kind of words would he use to cheer her up if she were down? "Your eyes could call back 1000 ships" now that was a reassuring line.

'Pardon?' he asked.

'Well if fate is always tempting she must be something.'

'Oh, I see, well she may have a beautiful dowry,' said Karl.

'I thought I was supposed to be Eve?' when in doubt a religious reference would do. Her knowledge of other gods was a bit hazy, she would have to look up Fate and see if she were nice. See if she were Greek or Roman but Ciara was going for Roman Catholic here.

Ciara started feeling sorry for herself, she hadn't met anyone when out with Aoife a few days ago so she was more critical of Karl. It was text now then text again in a month well generally more frequently but it felt like a month's gap sometimes. He only ever contacted her when it suited him. He never apologised for non-communication. Did he see himself as a carrot or maybe an ice-cream, a bit more enticing, to be waved about in her inbox whenever it took his fancy? What was he exactly trying to tempt, he wasn't offering her anything. Maybe fate was male after all, you could never tell with these ancient gods. In fact it didn't matter because he was wasting her time and emotional energy, tying it up so she couldn't get enthusiastic enough to go out and look for someone else.

"He is tempting my sanity to leave me" she concluded looking back to his opening text of the day. She wanted someone real, or really him to be real. The crux was he was her type, the sort of guy that, if she were actually looking, he actually would be. There was however no actuality about this circumstance, it was only virtual.

'In this day and age not everyone is a creationist, with equal opportunities men can be tempters too!' said Karl. Sugar he was beginning to think like her, he must be fate.

A few cyber offers may have been tempting but lead to nothing and did not a relationship make. It was impossible to be seeing someone if you were not actually meeting them. She was not dating so what was she doing? Having texts she had amused herself with this turn of phrase previously, now however the joke had worn thin, as had her patience. What was this thing? There must be something there as he kept coming back. She didn't get it, there must be an objective, but what was it? Could chemistry exist and be enhanced by text? It wasn't as if it was awkward to meet, he lived just over the road from her house, well very close and worked within a mile of her office. So it should be easy to meet, things should be carefree and simple. Sans Strings, since she was unattached and he appeared to be, they should be "fancy free, and free for anything fancy" as Fred Astaire had so gaily stated.

'Did the Creationists base their dating of the World on a theory developed by a man who studied at Trinity?' maybe a bit of cerebral stimulation would help.

Maybe he was a perfectionist, wanting to have the great job, the big car and the huge deposit before he entered the proverbial marriage market. Well at least before they met, chatted and got to know each other a bit. He would have enough to offer on the material side not to be refused. However he didn't know Ciara, she was 'independent, single and strong' as she kept telling herself. So she didn't need any financial stimulants but, well, maybe, a subsidy could help her mortgage repayments from time to time. If she were to be with someone she would like to build things together, she would even let him do the designing if he wished. Was that what he was saying about a beautiful dowry? Would she try to entice him by her material charms? The thought stung in Ciara's brain. No, she didn't want either of those options she wanted something they could develop together. Not to have everything preformed and perfected was her goal, like a steel rod in a slab of concrete already supporting the ideal building. That was her vision of their life or a perfect life and a building they would construct together would not just be their home but a place for ideas, a place for dreams, a place for hopes and what's more for the fun they would have working all of it out. She would like input, choices and the ability to make mistakes and joke about them together, with that somebody who she would be with, in that ideal world.

'I was thinking of creation of a different kind!!! X' Karl said. Yes he must also be thinking of constructing a beautiful building together!!

Or on the other hand, maybe he wasn't into her, there were many chick flicks on this subject and he was contacting her only when he was bored or in between dates to get into mischief from afar. Aoife has said it to her, and the concept stung her as it rang true. It may not even be the case that she was more into him; it was just that she had a lot more free time than him so she willed herself into an admiration of him. He was the perfect male because he was removed.

'To whom are you tempting?' she asked, she thought going back to the start would dampen his ardour. Maybe he would regress if he had to return to the opening text and have him text in circles, may confuse him into being nice if that were possible.

'To Eve or Fate whichever you wish to be,' he replied.

'Maybe the texter tempts himself. Maybe you are the serpent.' Ha she thought see what he comes back with. She considered "are you group texting all your female contacts to assess the response rate?" but thought better not. He may think she was a bit sour. Or "a closed evaluation group" but that sounded odd and a bit market research like.

'Could I tempt you to an apple or rather a coffee?' he enquired.

Were there to be euphemisms attached to this coffee she wondered? For once, he had actually said what she wanted to hear. So maybe she should be nice to him. He also used her words which was complimentary it showed he had been listening and paying attention to what she had said. Was not mimicry the highest form of flattery? Admittedly the adage mentioned imitation but mimicry was the apt term as he had an objective to achieve. But what was it?

'After all the compacted ice which has formed on those old coffees from the last time, we would need a bit of global warming to defrost them.' Her dreams of coffee were as frozen as her dreams of Norway. He had her going around in circles, how many times did it take for him to discuss a coffee before it happened? She was getting dizzy from repeating the same metaphors.

'Even with global warming, Dublin would never be as hot as the Garden of Eden. Tell you what... I'll buy you a fresh cup!!!!'

She waited a short while, at least two minutes before replying, 'is it an espresso you're after?' She did have to smile though. Really she could have said -fresh is better than frozen-, but she had pre-texted or texted before she had considered.

On the other hand she wanted to reduce the blow that if they arranged to meet and he actually turned up, that she would be emotionally prepared for the eventuality that he may leave after five minutes. She wondered why she was being so defensive.

'Could be an allongé as we are in France metaphorically,' he conversationally added. He was being nice, friendly and open-to something neutral, wow it was almost a beige day if they decided to go for lattes! She was not into interior design and she didn't like the colour beige at all, but this line of texting sounded like progress. Beige in her mind, was roughly the mid-point between black and white when she avoided grey.

'Well for once the sun is shining we could almost stretch to an iced coffee! Is that cafe glacé?' She was in work at this stage and thoughts were beginning to race ahead to lunch already. An iced coffee on a sunny day could be bliss. Ciara smiled to herself, this felt nice.

'I must defer to your superior knowledge of the French coffee terms, being more Nordic and therefore beer focused.' He was attempting a compliment, 'but it sounds good to me.'

Progress was being made, definitely, should she set the time, either lunch or just after work. Or maybe she should allow him to be manly and make the decision. She leaned forward at her desk and fiddled with the mouse only to realise the computer was not turned on. The time was almost ten thirty, woops! How easy it was to get distracted by anything other than work. It was true that business was not good at the moment and the work phones were quiet but this was ridiculous. "Cop on Ciara" she chastised herself as she quietly and discretely turned on her PC. She opened her inbox of e-mails and there were actually tasks which needed to be attended to before lunch. She got busy and forgot to text back until nearly lunch time.

'Would you like to meet for a late coffee or an early coffee?' she enquired when she got back into text stream.

'I had been thinking lunch time but since you didn't get back maybe we can do it later,' was his slightly despondent reply.

'What time do you take lunch?' she asked

'I am already there, sorry. I will see how things are panning out and let you know late afternoon.'

She was devastated as it was he who had suggested a meeting and if he had really wanted to meet her at lunch, maybe he could have said so a bit earlier.

He didn't come back to her that afternoon, she was really disappointed. Another empty promise, so she waited until the next day and sent 'a new number, are you dodging someone?' She was not going to put up with this sort of behaviour again.

'Got a new phone, how are you today? X' He had sent an X, did this mean a kiss, or was she was his ex, no that couldn't be right, she couldn't be an ex until after she met him for coffee. To be a text ex may not even necessitate a coffee though.

'Good thanks, a bit tied up at the mo but could meet you at lunch if you like.'

'Thought you were the lady sans-strings!' he was attempting humour, however lame.

'Funny!' she sent, "I knew you'd be back, Mr Strings attached!!" she said to herself, she would have sent this thought but she was not brave enough.

'What about just after work?' she texted after a moment or two. She was thinking of maybe a vodka espresso or was that a vodka-tini hankering for? Would this be a bit of a mixed message though, a coffee and an alcoholic drink? Or would it be seen in a positive light of two dating steps in one? Maybe she would hold that thought and see what he said. The time was well after lunch and heading for mid-afternoon when he finally got back to her. She had not been able to concentrate on anything all day.

'A work thing can't be rearranged. Tomorrow?' he said.

"Grrr" she thought.

She left her reply at least an hour well an hour and one minute, it was a struggle but she did it. 'Right let's see how tomorrow pans out.' It wasn't as if she had anything on but she didn't want to seem too eager or desperate. The ball was in his court now.

'The day is busier than I thought' began his text the next day. She felt her wellbeing fade and annoyance rise. 'It will have to be another time' he continued.

'It would seem you are attempting to cut your strings!' she considered this to be an appropriate reply as he really was strings attached, work strings at that. She was going to give up on him, "Mr. Tied up in himself." First there was considerate Karl, then cringe Karl and could this be Cruel Karl? With all his teasing texts he was trying her patience!

'Are you going Belgian on me?' she double-text incredulously after he had not replied to her first text within the hour.

'Napoleon was from Corsica,' he assured her. Yes he studies windows but closes doors! Of course Napoleon was from Corsica but Waterloo is in Belgium as everyone knows, ninny.

So she sent him a racy picture of an oriental pose, in front of a baroque door with the caption "pity" just to assure him that the door was now closed! No response came; maybe she had fired the cannons too soon. She had installed, well one of the techie people had installed what's app for her. She didn't know how to use it but she was going to work out how. She went through the camera to this picture, the only brave photo she had in her on-phone-album. She had two very long almost sheer scarves tied about her in place of a top. She clicked on the image and there was a share option, "wow share myself, that's an odd concept." She did though, share her image at least when she pressed the what's app choice. Karl's number did appear under her contacts. How had that got there, never let a phone think for itself they are too smart by half. So this was how she did it. She sent a photo to Karl all by herself. She was very proud of her technological advances.

She typed and saved to drafts, "I am not the personification of your ego gratification!! And I know you still fancy me," well she actually knew nothing of the sort but really hoped he still did even though there was no way she was ever going to meet him, or consent to meet him now. Honestly.

Her photograph was in the style of "I dream of genie in London" and she was standing in front of a large Georgian door in Mayfair wearing pale fitted trousers and scarves wrapped provocatively in lieu of a top. Her hands were in an oriental pose with alluring smile and far away gaze. She had developed a taste for Arabia. She had the slightest hint of a tan, so she didn't look too pasty. For once Ciara was doing the legwork on drink outsourcing. It was a contrast to normal as Aoife always got the attention when she was out with Ciara, without ever trying. So when Ciara dressed daringly she was unused to the results and unsure of what to do exactly. Aoife had said 'smile and have fun.' It had been an interesting experience but was not repeated.

"Never again," she wasn't going to try to meet Karl. "You are ex-texted!" she thought. Or maybe he was the text-ex. She felt he would think of her with loss, maybe, hopefully. She really didn't know.

We send texts and we receive them and when we have received them they are in our inbox then we have them. We have texts, but to have texts sounds so euphemistic with only a gossamer thin layer between perfectly acceptable behaviour and nasty talk. He was a text tease!

As he had changed his number he seemed to be avoiding or hiding something. He had said he got a new phone he didn't acknowledge the new number and rarely wished to contradict her. "Not a good policy to contradict a stranger, especially a lady whose favours are uncertain." It was a new number though she had almost learned the old one by heart since she looked at it so much. It had been a cool number with lots of sixes and nines in it. It had been very easy to remember. Was she turning into Aoife and having excessive texts. Maybe she was a text addict? Was that a bad thing? Would she need a class in her phone seminars about over-texting? Yes it would be an important point in the 'getting to home with your phone' class. She looked at her phone again the cost was not just emotional as the price of each text was greater now. She had checked her balance this morning and added up that the morning bus texts were higher. Who was he trying to avoid, her or someone else?

Maybe it was the work phone he was using for the last few days that must be it. Probably it was the case that his phone was in for repairs, that was it, definitely. Not one niggle of doubt remained in her carefree little head.

To bar or block a number

Ciara was frustrated. One minute he was discussing the finer points of coffee and whether to have French, Italian or Corsican. Corsican sounded a bit explosive with lots of codified undertones and tastes. The next minute he was ignoring her, well maybe Corsican coffee was too strong. It was all too much! Also, Ciara was finding the content of some texts teasing and mean she decided to do something about it. Context was the word which sprang to mind, as in the texts were a con really due to the fact that the content was misleading and sometimes annoying and delivered at arm's length so not affecting the sender. He did not have to see her reaction and more importantly not have to deal with any consequences of his actions. All was contained and distant, perfect for him. However it was upsetting for her. Did she really wish to cut ties though as he had sent some really nice texts also? It was a bit of a quandary. The most upsetting sequence was the previous few days when he had nearly met her a few times. Maybe he was very busy and important but really the property market was in NAMA, she had heard a development was nothing unless it was in NAMA. Or maybe that was the developer, anyway he was telling her great big porkies. He could meet her it didn't have to be a three hour long lunch. Just a coffee would have done, but no, it hadn't happened and now it wasn't going to. Even though she may act it, she was no fool.

She web-texted her service provider to see about barring his number, "I am being harassed by a serial texter" after three days there was no answer. So she tried again maybe they didn't get the context of serial texter. "I am being harassed by text can you block the number?" Still no answer, Customer Care seemed a contradiction between terms and activities maybe customer care was a passive thing and customer service was active. "Am I supposed to call them?" she asked herself.

ABOUT A WEEK LATER she got a response, but not the type of response she expected.

"Thanks for your email.

"I am sorry to hear that you have been experiencing nuisance calls / texts.

"Unfortunately we do not have the facility to view the details of received calls while you are in Ireland (where else would she be?) and we cannot block any incoming calls from your phone. If you wish to take action on such calls you must make a formal report to your local Garda station. The Gardai will then investigate this appropriately. If you are receiving nuisance or malicious texts you can avail of our "Block It" service which will stop these texts being received by your phone.

"Click here for more information on this service."

So she clicked, "**information;**"

"For Help and support type in this number"

So she clicked, "**help;**"

There was a complicated message about how to block a number and then a five digit number to call. So Ciara copied and pasted the number into her web-text file and pressed send.

It failed. So she did again and pressed send but the web-text failed! Again she tried it with the 01 Dublin prefix, yet again failed. So if one is being harassed, virtually stalked one has to text the old fashioned way not via the web, Ciara concluded. "Is this an ethical company!" exclaimed Ciara. "You have to pay to bar a number. This should be an inclusive service, no?" However it wasn't, she would have to send an old-fashioned text.

If she were a teenager in school or college would she wish to go to the Police if she were being harassed? Probably not, she would be worried what people would say, the stress of going to the police station to make a statement. People would find out, ridicule her. She would have to explain to her parents that people were picking on her and she was not able to handle it anymore. So this was how she equated having to text the phone company and would have the record of the text on her phone. No wonder shy, thoughtful young people were suffering depression and contemplating suicide with arms length bullying. Ciara on the other hand was, well in terms of years anyway a grown up. She was less ruled by fear and a bit more by a sledge hammer or maybe a machete. Obviously she would never hurt Karl, but she would like to hunt him down and embarrass him in front of his neighbours, family and friends. So maybe it was better for him that she blocked his number.

A few days after this there was a customer service text ascertaining whether quality had been delivered! "Can you answer these 4 questions and it's free? Could you rate between 1 and 10 the following questions? How do you find our CS? Did we help you? Would you recommend us?" After not doing anything right why would they ask to be recommended?

One would say the Gaul but there was none of the Napoleonic efficiency at this company!

She had a bit of time in work so, she logged onto the service providers website to see was there any other way. She looked up the service mentioned, it was called "Block It?" According to the phone company "Block It is a free service that allows you to block certain numbers from texting you. This also means you won't be able to send any messages to this number."

'Aye there's the rub," Ciara exclaimed with the only Shakespeare quote she knew. Don and Stephen looked over at the same time. Ciara did not look up as she really didn't want to discuss what she was up to. A gal has to have one secret in her life. "That will be the end I can't hassle him if I am feeling bored...Well there is always what's app!" she said to herself. It wasn't the same, what's app, Karl hadn't been using it much so she couldn't play with it.

Ultimately she did not bother to block or bar or inhibit communication at all by crazy Karl. It was not actually the 7 cent it would cost to send a text but more the fact that Karl had and could again change his number and she would know it was him. She would only have to open the text.

"Is there a difference between blocking and barring?" Ciara thought, she hadn't shut down the website yet so she was thought she could differentiate between the terminologies. "Is one term like building a wall and the other heating up an element?" It seemed that they were interchangeable words used without great consideration given to their meaning. This was good food for bus musing, it would take her a whole journey home to work out.

Later that day she discovered on her mobile that there was a Call and SMS blocker! It was part of a security package she had inadvertently downloaded while fiddling with her phone. She examined the "app" to ascertain whether there were any benefits to her. 'Click' she did and entered the blocking zone then, "purchase your annual subscription." 'Pardon!' she only wanted to block one number not subscribe to a year. How many crazy guys were they expecting her to encounter over the next 12 months? These security companies thrived on calamities or the fear of one occurring. Ciara was not a victim, not of Karl nor of security companies trying to steal her shoe strings! Well shoe money really as she didn't have too many laced up shoes.

Military Texts

'Hey, it's been a while, I'm that Napoleon guy,' he was back.

She was bored, idle and maybe feeling a little mischievous. The texts were gone flat, as in flat line, no contact. It was time to get them vertical, ram-rod straight and alive.

'I can't remember you clearly. Are you small from Corsica' —woops she just pressed send. The game was on again and she could be bothered as it was too much fun to ignore. This was it though, if he didn't meet her after this round of texts she would either delete his number or faint outside his office from exhaustion the 19th Century term for Bi-polar.

'....And about to invade Russia,' she continued her thought stream into another text. Again there had been a long silence, like an army waiting for months to fight, marauding about in distant villages, out of sight. As if they didn't exist to their opponent except in her imagination.

'Well your focus is correct but your handle on size is not quite big enough. You need to enlarge it much more' He replied —OK so he was tall!!

What do you say to that, "Is it your ego that big?" No he was an architect so should say something work like "are you redesigning Russia?" No that sounded terrible.

"Better human rights than military wrongs" no that is a bit too worthy. She had started this line of chat so she would have to embroider it. Something light and amusing decidedly non-committal as she didn't want to give the wrong impression after the toothbrush affair, with his perfect white teeth and penchant for oral stuff, like smiling, hopefully. It was going to be good this time.

'**So what is your strategy?**' she sent. This statement was way too direct, very committal and maybe even a bit forward but nothing else would come to mind.

'**I was thinking, start with a peace agreement, then, line my troops up and take the country by force, fixed bayonets at dawn.**' He was in character. Was he researching the Napoleonic Wars also or was this reference to something later in the nineteenth century?

"From bodice ripping page turner this is now a Russian novel! Are we in for a long hard winter?" Wait had the peace treaty not been with Austria, oh yes and Russia changed sides, so confusing. Did she want to encourage salacious over tones? She would have to snog someone else to clear her head! Maybe she could then be restrained and make Karl wait for a response. What to do.

She would keep the statement in her arsenal or to any normal texter her draft files. It may be necessary to review that file at some stage as her work computer was creaking on opening full of her texting fluff. To Ciara this set of files was not a memory but a living, breathing series of her conscious thoughts. It also represented the future as some of these texts were as yet unsent. They still had the potential to make him do something.

Whatever that something consisted of she was as yet unsure. Hopefully not get her fired as she suspected Anna was prowling about and reading it from time to time.

'Are you thinking of the Italian Campaigns, or is this a Russian affair?' he had not specified Russia so this would be suitably historical question to give him pause, hopefully.

'Italian definitely, I like that level of booty acquisition!' So was he thinking of the ransom of Milan or just all the plunder that was sent back to France? It seemed like he was on the offensive, battle stations were readying. Or maybe he had only begun to swat up on his Napoleonic History and hadn't got to the Russian bit yet. No he had said that he read War and Peace, did that count?

'And so?' she enquired.

'Well show me a picture so I can focus on my target!' he was getting hopeful. Had he not checked his whats app recently, she had certainly sent an eyeful. However it could well have been to the wrong number, his old number. Texting trials!

Hmm, what did he think she was pop porn? Or even historical pop-porn. **'My décolletage does not quite fit the Empire Line, as demonstrated by the lovely Josephine. What sort of picture did you have in mind, Caravaggio, Raphael or some other object of artistic merit?'** Ciara was trying to convey that these were the types of pictures plundered for the galleries of Paris but also hopefully to raise these somewhat sordid texts to an artistic standard. Was booty better than quarry?

'More the former than the latter, just it has been such a long time. It would be nice to refresh my memory of you.' Had he forgotten how she looked? It was true that her scarves photo had been quite out of focus so even if he had received it he could not see her face when he zoomed in. Yep she must have sent it to the wrong number. He could see every undulation of her form apart from her face. She could remember every contour of his face, each feature etched out for eternity in her memory. Or rather it was the idealised Karl who was there in her hard drive along with the make-believe personality she had constructed for him, the jokes they would exchange over the frozen coffees which would be heated up, again. Yes she had a strong imagination and her sense of an imaginary life was much more fun than the reality of text teasing.

She took a photograph of her face and tried to send it. There was a problem. Her shiny new phone had a systems error so was gone into the mobile phone hospital and so, she was using quite an antiquated version in other words her old handset. The picture would not send. Drat, she tried again, double drat. From her technological triumphs of whats app to her old but usual phone, she seemed a defeated techie.

'It won't send, have you a full inbox?' she joked, referring back to one of his lines about having a lively text life. This old phone of hers seemed to run on WAP which was extinct to her mind.

'**Infantry primed and awaiting orders,**' he sent hopefully, ignoring her humour. He might not have thought it humorous.

When there was nothing from her he continued in an encouraging tone '**there is serious unrest amongst the rank and file.**'

'**I'm afraid that my IT skills are as outmoded as swords and cannons. I have not been motivated or inclined to update to heat seeking missiles,**' she sent after several hours of attempts with the same system failure.

'**E-mail me here as there is a suitably large memory for all your visual exploits.**' He must have been feeling optimistic. She looked at the e-mail address, karl_other@xx.ie. He didn't give his surname, wow he was cagey. She wouldn't be able to Google him or check out his Facebook page. "He must think I'm a potential stalker. Silly boy, I wouldn't have the capacity to find out where he lived." She tried Facebook just on the off chance that "Other" was his surname. It wasn't!

'**Why don't you send me one to see if it works?**' she wanted to see what sort of content he was expecting! So he tried to text an image to her brick of a handset.

'**Did you get it?**' he asked hopefully a few minutes later.

'**No sorry do you want to try and e-mail me?**' She was now at home and looking at the web cam at the top of her green net book. Every time she took a photo on it the image was terrible. Her face looked elongated and emaciated. It must have been designed for round faces to make them look angular as hers looked as if it were drawn out like a single file row of troops stretched along the horizon to infinity. The flash was so bright that any colour in her complexion was washed away, like a bridge dynamited in the pouring rain. Ah no, that invention was a bit late nineteenth century so cannon balled away. Generally she didn't look her age, well hopefully, but in this light she actually looked a lot older, it was so unfair that the flash was so harsh.

Karl at Bathroom Cabinet

He sent his submission. Apparently it was where boys spent most of their time, looking in the mirror so often they send pictures from here. He held his very large telephone in his rather large hand. The left arm is poised at quite an awkward angle as he wished to portray the extent of his expanse. His arms were held high to accentuate the muscular frame of his upper body.

His head was forward and his hair still wet. The steam from the recent shower was still apparent regressing under the mechanical extractor fan just visible to the top right of the photograph.

His eyes were bright and shining with mirth, twinkling like the moon on a cold clear night. His mouth had a composed closure, concentrating on getting the angle just right. Ciara thought this shot may not have been his first attempt.

His skin displayed an Irish paleness rather than a Nordic sallowness and there were some spots, small red dots clear on his shoulders. "Unclearasoled" thought Ciara as she gazed at this composition. The aspect which stood out most clearly was not the beige wall tiles and probably matching floor. Nor was it the newish sanitary ware about the sink but the large colourful shower curtain.

"Am I just cannon fodder" she thought to herself as she looked through his photograph of himself then closed down the net book and sat on her couch. She didn't like what she saw. It was too much reality clashing with her perfect fantasy. Could he possibly be vain? From his poise in this picture it would appear that this was the case. Then Ciara thought to herself "he isn't so well practised in self imaging. The first rule of the 'selfie' is not to see the phone." She hoped or maybe assumed this was the first time he had ever done this!

Ciara's Contribution

She trawled through her holiday snaps in 'my pictures' like who else's pictures would they be if they were on her files? Eventually she found a suitable one. She wanted to allure but not reveal too much. She couldn't send the scarves shot again could she? He said he liked her eyes so that was what he was getting and all that he was getting. Her eyes! She was standing in front of the Atlas Mountains. She was in a green Jellaba, Moroccan for Burka, but not as extreme. The Jellaba had a long hood which when worn up generally resulted in better prices when haggling for trinkets in bazaars. Well at least she thought so.

She was trying to convey an image of otherness and allure. There was nothing of her on display except light green eyes, was this the antithesis to what he expected or maybe hoped for from her image? She wanted to show that he needed to try harder if she were to meet him. However whether she knew it or not he was ever so slightly drawn in. Jellaba vaguely rhymes with pyjama, only a bit lazier. One doesn't have to get dressed with either but with a jellaba you don't even have to do your hair. This is how to embrace a culture and your own natural lazy culture in one fell swoop.

The mountains were to represent the divide between Karl and her as there was a tall wide gap of knowledge which only time would reduce. Whilst geographically they lived quite close to each other it felt that there was a huge mountain between them. It was called the N4. Could they surmount it, this mountain of a dual-carriage way she hoped it was possible? Like a good Muslim woman her fate was not in her own hands, it was controlled by someone she barely knew, but hoped to know better.

Initially she had thought to send an Egyptian image when considering Africa in the Napoleon context. This would most represent Napoleon's oriental pursuits, but she liked the look of this photo. It was a good start to the image exchange she had thought and she hoped there would be numerous exchanges.

On reflection his was not exactly a Napoleonic submission either, it was not as if Napoleon would have had a smart phone to snap his posterior. Even if he did, his frame was so diminutive that it would be unlikely that it would be his back that he would snap. It would be some tall, broad general.

Napoleon was no Cromwell in his "warts and all" outlook to his effigy or image, his were always rather contrived pictures. Most lightly if he lived today, he would have photo shopped his image to improve it, perfecting it into the deity he thought he was. He would be aiming for the image of the Imperial Emperor and maybe the average French person would not have recognised the man after the image-enhancement techniques had been completed.

Driving

She had tried to analyse Karl, the strong silent type he was not. Verbally reticent it was true to say as he would not call her or take her calls, but virtually he was fluent and expansively so. His cadence was almost poetic, racy in parts it was true, but there was a beautiful use of words, which inspired and encouraged her to respond in greater detail, emboldening her to delve into her psyche to see what she dreamed of, fantasised about and as he was a stranger, not to be met there was no sense of repercussion. She had a flash of his spotty shoulders and pale skin from the picture. She went a little pale. It was as if she were taking the photograph but she was blinded by the cameras' flash.

She didn't know what was inside her as it was as frozen as Norway in winter. She let loose, for the first time in a long time, she was allowing her fantasy life to delve beyond Fred and Ginger and Georgian Architecture. She imagined what she could be or more pointedly what they could be. She created parallel lives where they knew each other in a biblical way.

Was he just seeking a cheap thrill? Was he merely wanting all of the fun and none of the fuss? Or did he want to bring her to a crescendo so that when they met, eventually, it would be wonderful, spectacular and unforgettable. Or was he wiling and idling away the time as Ciara often did. Was he a bit bored maybe, possessing the ability to do a more fulfilling career but not the ability to change position in these recessionary times, economically grey like the most popular car colour? Could he have been telling fibs about that promotion? It was a mystery.

He contrived some very interesting scenarios and utilising such a wide vocabulary, Ciara was impressed. Had she met her intellectual match she wondered. Everything she read of his was brimming with ideas. His thoughts were so different from hers, that she opened each of his submissions with excitement and trepidation. Or maybe it was the halo affect!

She imagined that they are driving along the Strawberry beds on a sunny Spring afternoon the hood is down even though there is a chill in the air. The wind is in their hair and they are counting the speed bumps all twenty odd of them. The Liffey is high even though there has not been much rain that day, the leaves are in bud and she feels alive. The year is just beginning and hope is certainly in the air. The road winds and twists as the car speeds ahead before having to brake sharply before the next sleeping police man or speed bump. The music is blaring and all the windows are open to enhance the sensation of the outdoors and movement of the car through the bare roof. The music is lively and the conversation is being shouted at full hilt.

She turns and realises it is her friend who is driving and he is but a fantasy. Her lovely warm, familiar even feeling is gone and she is jogged back to reality, how annoying.

Aoife – 'so what were you thinking?'

Ciara – 'why do you ask?'

Aoife- 'there was an internal glow to that smile.'

The dappled light fades as the trees turn to woods. The ramps jar the car which is not a convertible and does not even have a sunroof. The windows are down though allowing the fresh river smell to permeate through the air. 'Shall we count the speed bumps?' Ciara suggests.

Aoife- 'why not, there are so many on the Strawberry beds.'

Ciara- 'we have had five already. Oh I love this song!' she exclaims as the music changes on the radio. It is the PCDs, buttons. 'Yes, I know it's crass but it is fun.'

Aoife- 'direct, like to the point.' The Pussy Cat Dolls are great dancers, some of them can even sing, Ciara likes their forthright sexuality as it is on the polar opposite scale to hers. They are so liberated, however Aoife is not of the same viewpoint.

Ciara drifts off again but as much as she attempts to re-evoke the fantasy it doesn't work. She can't re-visualise a sporty convertible or sense Karl in the car, his great expanse sucking all the space out of the somewhat confined interior has disappeared. It is now replaced by Aoife's form. She is in the moment and this moment is good. Driving home with your good friend on a sunny day is as equally a good moment as being with your dream Viking, No? Aoife is smaller than Karl but she is decidedly not svelte, she is a sizeable size. Very curvy and the look works, that look always works. She works on it, works out and dines out on it, sculpted to perfection. She has perfect proportions or would have been, had they been living in the 1950s before match-stick figures became de rigueur or popular to everyone living outside French fantasy land. It is indicative of Aoife that she is perfect in everything she does and is, her life is such a challenge.

It is so nice for Ciara not to be a CIE VIP today. To have an offer of a lift, a willing offer at that is so much more pleasant than the bus. Aoife is youthful, good company and fun with a carefree outlook. An ideal travelling companion and Ciara had been delighted when she had suggested the rural route as opposed to the traffic laden motor-way. "He just wants me for my texts" she giggled to herself.

Then she is back in her fantasy car, it is a deep red colour. It is like an old French wine colour, definitely not Ferrari red with that harsh glare and conspicuous consumption connotations. Ok maybe that comment is a bit of a hang-over from the heady days of Celtic success and maybe a deep red colour was a bit girlie and too feminine for Karl. However it is only an illusion, not fully coloured in. The seats are heated and the roof fully open and the seats are made of kid leather. The interior is small and Karl's long legs have forced his seat back to touch the row behind. His knees are splayed rubbing against the door at one side and the gear box on the other. He exhales softly and smiles. The same song is playing.

Karl- 'I can't believe you like the PCD's. You look so contained. Not quite conservative but on the reserved side' he observes. She is getting stick for her music taste even in her fantasies, there is something not right there, she can visualise criticism but not the exact red colour of the car! She can't even tell if it is an Austen Martin or a Bugatti.

Ciara- 'hmm, that's interesting. I didn't think I came across as reserved at all,' she considers.

Karl- 'maybe I just want to bring out the wild side in you!'

175

Ciara- 'is that your agenda for the day?' She is slightly concerned by what exactly he means by "bringing out her wild side."

Karl- 'fun, that is all that's on the agenda, sun and fun.' He reaches over a hand to touch her and it falls on her leg just as it had in the taxi home then another of the thirty or so speed bumps comes upon them suddenly. 'Sorry I didn't mean to crush you' he smiles only semi-contrite.

Ciara- 'keep your eyes on the road, your hand upon the wheel' she states in a weak attempt to retrieve her music credibility. She is pinned to her seat, anxiety levels running high, excitement racing, just to be there. The feeling is so intense. She can think of absolutely nothing witty to say, so silence will suffice until something comes to mind. Actually all she wants is for him to be there, smile and saying nothing. The picture is complete.

Aoife- 'are you thinking of your trying texter?' Reality jolts Ciara again, like a bump on this almost rural road within the M50 corridor.

Ciara- 'yes, I don't get him, he is very complimentary, texts regularly, you could be corny and say we have regular texts. He has even slipped the odd hint of meeting. However the issue is − let's not talk about problems before I even know him. Actually the problem is whenever we arrange to meet he cancels.'

Aoife- 'maybe he has a girlfriend?'

Ciara- 'it is possible that this is the case and usually the obvious solution is the most likely. Although I feel he is a bit of a perfectionist and wants to be at a certain position in a job, with a car and property before he lets himself become serious with somebody. I could be completely wrong.'

Aoife- 'you are easily deluded, maybe his girlfriend is boring, or travels with work and he is alone a lot.'

Ciara – 'maybe.' Ouch Aoife could cut her dreams into tiny ribbons with one scissors.

Aoife – are you sure you are not getting obsessed about him?'

Ciara – 'It may be the case.' Ok it definitely is the case but Ciara has to retain some semblance of pride from her perfect and nearly best friend.

Aoife – 'We should get out and see what's out there.'

Ciara – 'Yes it would be good to have a night out and a Friday this time, midweek is more studenty. I have cleared my credit card bill, so I won't feel guilty about spending what I don't have.' That is a complete lie, Ciara has a huge credit card bill and its colour is Ferrari red! She is acquiring shoes at a rate that Napoleon acquired principalities across Europe.

Aoife – 'You clear your Visa bill! Somehow I don't believe it, but you live in West Dublin where there are lots of large industries. Why don't you rent out a room or two to help with your crippling mortgage? Surely there would be many people interested.'

Ciara – 'I have enjoyed having the place to myself since the ex-left, so much so that I would feel it would be taking a step backwards to have a housemate.'

Aoife – 'Maybe backwards in a lifestyle sense but for financial planning it would be a great leap forward. Sean was not just emotionally immature he was financially

177

irresponsible, leaving you in that way after he was the one who wanted such a big house. What was he thinking of really?'

Ciara – 'Yes he was a bit of a cad, but even though I am paying all the bills, I am really glad that he is gone and I don't want to see hide nor hair of him again. I am delighted he chose non-enforced transportation to Australia. Actually Oz seems to me like the Irish debtors-prisons from the eighteenth century'.

Aoife – 'that is an interesting analogy, enforced transportation in the financial sense.'

Ciara –'You're agreeing with me.'

The speed bumps have ended and they pass the boundary walls of Luttrellstown Castle on the right. The road continues to bend and the river is high, engorged with rains from a few days ago which are only now reaching here. It seems to flow as quickly as the car but is flowing in the opposite direction. The branches hang low over the water and the road in need of a spring trim. All of nature is primed for action, a new season is underway full of activity and Ciara decides she should get back to life to nature and increase her outdoor pursuits now that the winter was well and truly over. Maybe a new sport, hill walking on fleeting sunny days such as this day could be lovely.

Ciara - 'This is lovely we should do it more often.'

Aoife -'Yes, especially in summer.'

Ciara- 'If we get a summer.'

Aoife smiles- 'We could have something to eat in one of the river pubs on a nice or a not so nice evening.'

Ciara – 'Yes we should.' Ciara smiled she meant should in a non-conditional sense because saying shall sounds much too formal.

Aoife drops Ciara to her door, declines the offer of a cup of tea and is off in her busy way.

Lets' talk about texts

Ok maybe the adjectivization (whatever the word is for making an adjective out of a verb?) of text is being overdone, but Ciara had to get the message across. "Should there be a filtering feature on phones designed for the under 18's? Or maybe the vulnerable over 30's who text the emotionally unavailable?"

'Did you get my picture?' asked Karl a few days after sending it?'

'Yep, get mine?' she wondered what he thought, also she figured that Karl would not want a filter, or maybe he could do with a soft light filter to cover the spots!

'Wasn't sure who it was from...;) (wink)'

'I certainly knew you. But did you like my eyes?'

'Ahhh couldn't quite see them under the hoodie!'

'Anyway, Karl is a bit bob the same as bit buzz?' Ciara texted a few hours later, she was at work, bored as she had finished all her tasks for the day by ten thirty. All the guys were joking about this phrase "bit bob" and she hadn't a clue what it meant. It most likely had rude connotations though as they were really laughing, it was that type of hearty-naughty laugh which gave away the pointed undertones. She felt out of the joke.

She was thinking still, about the ethics of texting and wondered whether it was ethically responsible for a phone company to screen texts in a potentially bullying context? There have been many examples of bullying by text, one or two even ending in suicide for the recipient. If this were to happen, the phone companies' screening, would there be a short time delay where the company would have an automatic screening process of the text for content and the use of key words? What would these key words be? Language is so subtle and a bullying text is not obvious, it might refer to a previous conversation at school, college or in the work place. Would it be detectable or would it be in invasion of privacy?

Could this screening be an invasion of intellectual property and freedom of speech? Maybe there could be two packages one for adults and one for teens, well, come to think of it a pre-teens package may also be necessary for primary school children. Do you know baby goats are being called children as our young have stolen the name kid! Slightly odd but true, Ciara was tired of kids, kids-zone, cool for kids, kid's stuff. They were children and maybe, if goats have feelings or intellect they may be annoyed that their name has been stolen by marketing, advertisers and the lazy of speech. Why was she thinking of this? Was it that she was bleating like a kid every time that she got a text from Karl? The late primary schoolers are rampant texters, their fingers are nice and small so they don't have to turn their mummy's smart phone to landscape to type in a message.

'I don't think so Ciara, I'm not too well up on my West of Ireland colloquialisms, but I think a bit bob is a bit like your toothbrush fascination!' said Karl eventually.

"So bit buzz is free time and bit bob is definitely bad! Is my terrible texter a group terrible texter not even my exclusive texter? He could be bit buzzing loads of people. How can I know he is texting me exclusively?" She wasn't sure what to think anymore everything had sexual undertones. The problem was she saw them everywhere, these undertones, and he was provoking them, he was responsible. Then she thought she was a grown woman who made her own choices, she could choose not to and never to respond to him. She could also decide to close her eyes when she brushed her teeth and not think of him. She had actually tried this but her nice electric toothbrush kept banging up against her gums and this was a bit sore. She also didn't want her gums to recede as then maybe her teeth would fall out.

'Thanks Karl' she texted at least two seconds later.

So were the younger males incapable of a telephone call? Was it something to do with the sexual revolution which hit Ireland in the late 1980s? The art of conversation need not be cultivated as women were willing to comply from then on. Maybe this is why songs lost some of their lyrical dynamisms guys didn't have to do so much wooing so they didn't have to use the lyrical side of their brains. What do they use their brains for now? Hurling? Did they have a slither in the uterus these days? That was the true definition of a sporting Mum!

'Any time (smiley face)' she was right though if anyone knew what a dirty word would mean, then Karl was your man. The guys on her floor were really taking the toothpaste, they knew she was never up to date on anything except maybe history, which was am... in the past. Also shoes, shoes were her forte and they were not into footwear, except to wear it, so gave her free reign. How had this crucial phrase, bit bob, got past her?

'Karl, I will think of you tonight when I brush my teeth. I will squeeze the long tube of toothpaste hard. Then I will ...maybe I told you this already!'

Everything was texted, from your Dr's Appointment to house directions for a party. You didn't even need to use your car GPS anymore as the what's app message would include the map with the invite. It is undeniably an efficient means of information transfer but it is quite cold and direct. If the message is one line there is very little context in which to interpret it. Texts can be taken up the wrong way. On a phone call one can contextualise slightly by non-verbal hints such as sighs, voice intonation and the rapidity of deliverance of the message. However this is not the case with a text. If there are a stream of messages one after the other then maybe a fuller picture can be drawn but it still does not have the complete feel which a phone call does. Maybe people complained about phones in such a manner in the nineteenth century.

'Thanks for that Ciara, you are so thoughtful!' Then a moment later, 'I have not forgotten my research project for you.'

"That must be coffee" thought Ciara. At least he had mentioned it, so he had not totally abandoned the possibility of meeting.

The text is expedient, it can end marriages, and records can be kept by phone companies of the numeracy and frequency if not the actual content. They are very useful when one is busy but are they the best grounds for building a relationship? Ciara supposed boys don't have to talk about fluffy stuff such as feelings at all in a message.

'Thanks I know you are good at laying out the ground work. Do the beans or ground coffee make better foundations?' Ciara hoped he didn't thinking she was too silly likening coffee to concrete and screed.

Maybe Karl was feeling jokey too as he sent 'x smiley face whole bean coffee x.'

A charity or two were becoming aware of the perils of the text with '2in2u.ie' using text speak to attract and retain the attention of younger people. This charity aimed to prevent domestic violence in a text format.

Were texts becoming redundant now though with applications such as 'what's app' which were free. They were quicker than a text and the treads were easier to see. Did one express themselves in even briefer terms with this mode of communication? One friend had mentioned the length of time Ciara took to type out her thoughts as she had not got used to her predictive function on the phone. She tried to send invigilate and got invite. Smart phones shouldn't be allowed to think for themselves.

Ciara sent back '> <' she was feeling proud! It almost looked like a face. This evening the texts were going to read, "come hell, Fred and Ginger films or excessive teeth brushing, we will meet." She was going to make a statement, an assertion even, there would be certainty. Would she send this text though? Was she really brave enough to take a "sorry Ciara I have a hot date with my toothbrush" type of rejection? His toothbrush may vibrate! Did he even know who Fred and Ginger were? If so did he care? Well she did, she was happy the morning was passing well and it was only 30 minutes to lunch. Yes she was thinking of "I'm dancing and I can't be bothered now!" This was her favourite Fred song, it picked her up on a windy wait for the bus, or a particularly bad song playing on the I-pod next to her. She started humming and she thought she was humming to herself.

'Bad news, go away, call around some day, in March or May, I can't be bothered now!'

'Is that you trying to sing?' Don asked her.

'My bonds and shares may fall downstairs, who cares, who cares. I can't be bothered now!' Oops, she may as well sing out loud now since everyone in the office could already hear her.

'Do you know any songs from this millennium?'

'The thirties are being lived right here, right now in grey old Dublin and the only way to elevate the mood is to watch their films,' asserted Ciara.

'You can always cook your way out of a crisis,' said Don helpfully. Why was he so food focused, show off!!

'No I prefer Fred, he is my one stop feel good hop! So is Ginger, she is so modern.'

'Yes as modern as Art deco.'

'Yes it would be my favourite artistic movement.' Ciara's mood was not going to be dampened, Karl was going to find the perfect coffee spot and they would meet. That was certain.

'Is that your version of a smiley face?' asked Karl cheekily. Ciara ignored him.

Lunch with the Boss

In the beginning there was Adam and he was a nice guy who was married to her boss. Yes Ciara had been to their wedding but she had no idea about her or him, Anna and Adam, or whether they were real people at all. They were just so competent, a perfect couple, her boss and her bosses husband. Did they have the same texting issues way back in distant past when they weren't perfect! Anna was passing with her competent yet content happy face, "I bet she got the hang of emoticons straight away" thought Ciara to herself.

Today was a power walking day, she would forget about the terrors of texting for lunch-hour as the sun was up, the temperature was above 12° C and she was beginning the routine which would become a habit. Power walking day had nothing to do with being bored of going to the staff canteen nearly every day. It also had nothing to do with Don and his home made couscous salads or even his home made sushi, Ciara did not feel in any way inadequate about this. At least Stephen had nice normal lunches, ham and cheese sandwiches on fluffy white bread and most of the time he bought his sandwich in the shops like a regular office worker. He did that is, until Sophie began making him lunch with lots of complicated French stuff like sauces on her salad and different coloured lettuce. Why did life have to be so competitive?

It was a good habit to start; this power walking twice a week was going to be her new lifestyle habit. It would be a change from boozing and smoking. Exercise, this was something from which she would get fit and not feel like her body was turning into one big yucky cigarette, it would be a positive change. Cigarettes made her hair smell like a night club at 4 am before the smoking ban. The runners had been donned and Ciara was just about to head out the door when Anna stopped her.

'Ciara, do you fancy having lunch with me? It will be on me,' Anna asked.

Anna was being really nice to Ciara at the moment so she thought she had better consent. Also Anna had offered to pay. This was not a moral dilemma more it was a case of a work issue. Would Don and Stephen think she was being favoured? She really didn't want to put anyone's nose out of joint. However she really liked Anna so she wasn't being a lick going was she? Of course not, it would be fun and she could go walking tomorrow. Yes tomorrow, hail rain or shine her runners would be out on her high speed walk and pavements would be pounded.

'Where would you like to go Anna?' she asked.

'I don't mind you choose,' said Anna.

'There is a new Italian cafe nearby and they do lovely sandwiches. All the food is from Italy and it is really good!'

'Sounds good, is it far?'

'No not at all. Anna, do you know what it has?' Ciara was smiling as if she were seven she had a not so secret, secret. It was fizzy lemon, not the clear white lemonade stuff, but the very yellow, the highly coloured, the highly sugared, the highly flavoured fizzy lemon. The thought of fizzy lemon always made her feel like this, seven years old.

'Tell me as I haven't a clue what you are thinking.'

'It has posh fizzy lemon, the Italian one with bits and everything.'

'Actually I did suspect you had a bit of a weakness for this and sometimes when you consume it by the gallon I think your teeth will rot in your head.'

'That is generally only after a night on the tiles with Aoife,' fizzy lemon was her hang over cure. Even if it didn't cure anything it was much more palatable than food on a delicate stomach.

'Well we will have to try some,' said Anna. She then slightly devilish added 'does Karl like it?'

Was this a half admission of snooping? Ciara didn't exactly wish to confront her on the issue but she was still feeling embarrassed about her boss seeing her text file and just about every thought she had relating to Karl the King of texts.

'I don't know. I think it is one of the few things I have not asked him. I will do on the bus home.'

Anna could see that anything relating to Karl was taken extremely seriously, there was no lightness to Ciara's touch. 'Shall we take a window seat?' she asked after their short stroll along the Liffey.

There were enough people in the cafe to create a buzz but not too much to distract conversation. The window seat view was quite similar to the one from their office but a few blocks west heading towards the City. There was a very lovely outlook on a tall ship and sometimes on a grey day Ciara would imagine sailing away to somewhere less grey.

They sat down and admired the ship for a while. Then had a look at the lunch specials and ordered the first on the list. They sat for a moment or so in silence and Ciara decided to pluck up the courage to ask Anna something which had been mildly preoccupying her for some years now.

'Anna?'

'Yes Ciara.'

'How did you meet Adam?'

'Ah, I was wondering when you would ask me and then I thought you never would as it is such a long time ago,' she stopped a moment and smiled a very warm open and brighten up everyone in the cafe's day type of smile. It was infectious and Ciara wanted to smile too but she didn't know what it was about.

'Go on Anna.'

'I met Adam the same day I met you.'

Ciara had to think back for a moment as she wondered when she had first seen Anna. Then it came to her. She had interviewed her. She had been the only one to interview her, this was back in a time of unprecedented prosperity.

'Really, you met him at the graduate recruitment fair? That is curious.'

'Yes it was, seven and a bit years ago. You had just left the stall with an interview date and he came over, he may have even been standing behind you waiting to speak to me.'

'No way, was he a student?'

'Nooo he was an exhibitor and was bored there. He had said the standard of applicants was very low, they were arrogant and the skill sets were a miss-match for his organisation.'

Ciara flicked her hair to re-enact the advert which epitomised her generation, there had been so many jobs people had stopped trying so hard and felt they should get the plumb positions merely because the economy was prospering. 'Go on' she said when her messy mop ended up in her lemonade.

'So this is probably why I like you.'

'So you think I brought you luck. That's cool I'm so much bad luck to myself it would be great to pass on some good.'

'Yes that and your Karl file,' said Anna ever so slowly in a mouse like squeak, finally there was an admission of the snooping.

Ciara felt her face was going very red she would have blamed pepperoni in her dish but unfortunately it had yet to arrive. 'Yes Stephen told me you read it,' there was no point in pretending it didn't happen.

'Yes I was sure he would. I wish there was enough work in the office to inspire you to that level of creativity. It is quite funny though, I knew it was wrong but I was laughing so hard I couldn't stop. Karl is a devil, charming, sharp but Ciara he has a nasty streak in him. Do be careful, he could really hurt you.' That was ok then. Anna was human after all, not some scary-perfect-boss who never admitted to weakness.

'Anna, thank you for caring, no I mean that as it has come out of my lips with an "I know better" but you are right. There is a level of arrogance to him and a large ego which is constantly gratified and that is worrying. However the problem is I am a fish in the Liffey with a hook in my back, no matter how hard I try to swim away he can just reel me in whenever he likes.'

'You know what I used do when a guy got to me?'

'Knee him in the goolies' woops she had just said that to her boss, why was it that when she relaxed all of her barriers came down and formality was chucked into the river? Sugar!

'That is always an option' said Anna, 'but what is most effective is to meet someone else. At least it will put Karl in context.'

'Do you know I NEVER thought I would hear this from you. NEVER EVER, but then again I never thought I would be in a cool cafe with my boss, maybe I am beginning to grow up.'

Anna smiled, this smile was the sort which read "Ciara is my new project" if this was the case what was in store for Ciara's dull but very relaxed work life?

'It is my friend Aoife's birthday soon so you never know, maybe I can have one of her cast offs!!'

'Apart from that your texts to Karl are a source of interest to you and whilst it has absolutely nothing to do with work your morale is higher than most of your colleagues. I don't know maybe you are spreading a bit of fun and lightness. Now I am not advocating spending most of your work day setting up a file and retyping all your texts and thoughts about this guy as it is highly unprofessional and unproductive.'

Ciara looked at Anna's face and it was clear that Anna didn't mean any of this, she had liked the texts and maybe this meant she liked Ciara more too and this may give her a bit more slack. Result!!

The other guy

She removed her nail varnish with the vigour and effort of one assenting Mount Everest. Her toes shuddered and shook under the force applied. Why was she so angry? Was it to do with the other guy? The distraction that she sought from the Napoleon guy had been attained.

Ciara had been out at what she thought was Aoife's birthday party and met someone. She was in Google land. The location would not have been her choice as she found the bars and restaurants slightly contrived and catering to a corporate market. The prices were inflated to keep the local residents away. And the local residents only lived a street away. It was a convenient spot for her though as her office was nearby and the drinks reception began at clocking-out time. She was at the bar ordering the 'birthday girl' a cocktail when someone offered to pick up the tab. What a nice gesture she looked at him and he said, 'I work here so I get staff rates.'

'Oh thank you' she wasn't exactly sure what to say. It would be rude to decline and maybe a bit forward to accept but she hadn't been dating so long she didn't know what to do? She examined him as he wore a defeated look of one who had given up the fight. His large eyes were pools of sadness, or maybe it was his eye colour slate blue, hard and worn down. She wasn't sure if he was already unhappy or was looking for someone to do it for him. Yet he did not look old. It looked more of a mileage than age phenomenon, was that from Indiana Jones? 'What do you do here?' she asked aware that she had been staring.

'I am a chef or chief chip maker' he replied self-deprecating.

'A very useful skill to wow women with!' this was her personal www alliteration line which she wheeled out from time to time.

'So it is said' he could have added that he was being wowed by Ciara but that could have been too predictive and shallow. Or that whatever diets women were on, they always seemed to include chips, but instead he was honest.

'It is ironic, I have had stomach problems all my life, I am a shrunken twig yet my job is filling the paunch' he continued.

Yes he was slight of frame but tall enough to compensate. 'Hmm an interesting turn of events, or maybe it was genetic prediction, a predestined gene which made you choose food. The fact that you couldn't satisfy your tummy made you satisfy others.'

'That's an unusual take young lady, but no. I was an accountant until I nearly died of boredom and decided to do something active instead.'

'Ah good,' she said.

'Yes cooking is quite physical.'

'Do you like it?'

'I would if there was more variety to the menu. But as you know ideal jobs are as elusive as the Dublin sun.' Was he into the weather? There may be a connection. Had he wished to be a meteorologist from the age of eight also? Ciara's thoughts were racing ahead, imaging they would be texting each other weather channel updates on a daily basis. If it got serious maybe they could have hourly updates!

He had an original turn of phrase, she decided to revert to reality for once, it was necessary. 'I must return to the birthday party, but join us later if you would like. Thank you for the drinks.'

'I would like that,' he smiled.

Ciara returned to Aoife who was in flying form, she was fanned by her work colleagues and friends most of whom were male. The scene reminded Ciara of a Nicorette advert where the lady walks to the bar and ten guys offer her a light for a cigarette. Ciara was definitely showing her age the smoking ban was introduced over a decade ago.

Aoife was wittily explaining an incident which would normally be embarrassing but she told it with humour she amused the audience and lightly glided over any awkwardness to make it a very funny tale.

'Ah, Ciara, thank you for the drinks, you know Joe, John, Jeff my 3 J's they manage to sort out all the work issues. I call them just in time, just a minute and just about to.'

'Do you mind the cloning?' asked Ciara to none of them in particular.

'Not at all,' two out of three chimed. 'She is just so lively it is always a pleasure to be around Aoife,' the third continued, the one who had not spoken. They were in unison, how could Aoife bear that level of adulation, being the centre of attention generally unnerved Ciara.

'Here is your Birthday present.' It was a bound, special edition of three books in the series of Jeeves & Wooster by P G Wodehouse. It was one of Ciara's favourite writers and she hoped that Aoife would like them.

'You know it isn't my Birthday for another two weeks' said Aoife. 'But thank you, it is a cool present.'

Ciara blushed and said nothing for a moment.

'Oh so what are we celebrating?' Sugar Ciara was so Karl-ified that she had forgotten the date of her almost-best-friend's Birthday.

'My divorce,' said Aoife.

'Did we not celebrate that recently? I almost remember that boozy night out. You ran into that "lovely" lawyer guy again.'

'We did and we didn't' said Aoife. There wasn't even a hint of "don't remind me" in Aoife's tone, she was in her confident mode and nothing was going to knock her.

Ciara was confused and couldn't ask whether the night had happened or not in front of Aoife's fan club. It had happened though Aoife had a hint of frailty just like Ciara.

'Well as you know Brian had accepted the terms and both solicitors reviewed the papers.'

'Yes I remember that was the next phase in the process.'

'So this morning the papers were biked over to me to sign. Which I did, I almost biked them to Brian's solicitor myself I was so happy.'

'Really, congratulations that is the best celebration reason ever. Twice! When will it happen?' It wasn't that Ciara felt guilty, but Aoife now knew that she had forgotten the actual date of her Birthday. Hopefully she was too distracted to say anything. Life was just so confusing, she was going to have to learn how to use her phone diary it was an imperative.

'So you are now a free woman! How does it feel?'

'Brilliant, I feel brilliant, now there is no chance he will squirm out of it. On the other hand though, I feel as if I have lost four years of my life. It was a stupid decision to conform, everyone else was marrying so I had to also. Now I have finished my sentence and I have been released from jail.'

'Gosh is marriage really like that?' asked Ciara. She was having mild weather fantasies of traipsing up the aisle in wellies and an oversized yellow rain coat whilst Mr. Chipman was waiting at the far end in his swimming trunks, flip-flops and large aviator style sunglasses.

'Only when things begin to unravel, it is great when you are deluding yourself that things are perfect.'

'Ah, I see,' Ciara was trying to concentrate on reality but she was in such good form it tended to elude her. 'Well done, again, do I need to give you a second present for your Birthday?' Ciara was only half joking, the gift had been more than she was able to afford.

'One present will do for the two events. It is lovely and I will enjoy reading them' said Aoife.

So conversation and cocktails flowed and fun was being had by all. Ciara regularly glanced over to the off duty Mr. Chippy to see if he was looking over. She had a really embarrassing moment when she was caught checking him out. He looked up and she had been staring at him. "Woops" she tried to say under her breath, a daze, maybe it was a daze as she was zoning out from the conversation. The rate of exchange of ideas, witticisms and work-stuff in this conversation was slightly too rapid after a day of brain doldrums and it was taking her a lot of effort to keep up.

He smiled.

She smiled back. And that was it, there was another guy. Someone else was there to fill her head with apart from Mr. Norway. Someone new to think about, she wondered what it had been like to work as an accountant, had he made his fortune as a "Celtic Cub" and now could do what he wanted to do. Or had he gone travelling and spent everything he owned each year as was the norm in Dublin back in the day.

He came over to be introduced, he made conversation she could hear him breathing and see his chest go up and down. She almost wanted to put her ear to his chest just to be absolutely certain but considered that might be a bit weird. She could smell his hair, it was a nice scent. No, she had no memory of this with Karl. Karl was fantasy. Karl at this stage had accumulated attributes which he would never have in reality. He was not standing in front of her, it was someone else. This guy was real and he was there, she could touch him if she wished, should she go for it? Was it being disloyal to her perfect picture of the ideal male? She would never be hurt with Karl as he would never be there.

They had a very interesting conversation, she and the 'other guy' Ciara didn't want to name him just yet, in case it didn't work out. In case he didn't compare to an ideal and all of those protection issues one has were borne out. He moved closer and actually asked for her number, she assented but wished she hadn't, it was too quick. Almost business like, with a 'can I get your number and we can meet for lunch?' It was like an American film, once they exchanged numbers she was taken aback somewhat. He wanted to know her, barriers were rapidly being raised. He wanted to meet, gentle alarm bells were beginning to ring like those of Christchurch Cathedral. It was a bit overwhelming, it should have been normal but Ciara had become so guarded that even this early stage was unchartered territory.

'You look worried,' said Mr. Chipman.

'Oh' and she was, she knew somehow that this was going to be real life not fantasy weather channel. Did she want this?

The next day he called her he didn't text. She almost fell off her chair when it was him. It was so nice to speak to someone. They arranged to meet for a coffee at his short break the following day and Ciara took a late lunch to accommodate. There was a 'someone' who wanted to be there, he wanted her to be there, fantastic. He was deep, contemplative and expressive even if he was a bit wizened. Her hands were shaking and her knees felt wobbly, maybe she should cancel, he was only going to let her down, that is what happened in her life. A meeting, a very important meeting was coming up. That would be her excuse.

'Good luck today,' Aoife texted.

'Pardon?'

'Your date!! With Mr. Chippy.'

'How did you know I had a date?'

'He told me he would meet you.'

'I don't know if I'm going,' said Ciara.

'Do it, he is nice, he is gentle and sometimes you have to leave your cave-like comfort zone.'

'Yes bossy!!' said Ciara.

Coffee went well and he was alive, real and not in her imagination. That was a big plus. It may not sound like a lot but to Ciara it was everything. They chatted about art, culture and how he loved poetry. Ciara wondered if he may be a bit too in touch with his feminine side.

'My parents were deeply involved in the poetry societies up and down the south coast. We children (there were loads of us) were trotted out to recite at every opportunity. There wasn't a choice,' he said and his lips moved in sync with the words coming out. She was amazed.

He had attended so many poetry recitals as a child and competed in so many competitions that he couldn't remember the television ever being switched on in the front room. They were like a performing group of minstrels. Hers was not a deep love of poetry but she appreciated his passion for the subject even if it had been received from his parents. His parents did sound a bit pushy coaching, chiding and then dragging their children around the flas and feis of Ireland to recite Austin Clarke, Patrick Kavanagh or any other depressed, drunk or otherwise non-functioning poet. No she shouldn't be too harsh, there was beauty in the bottom of a pint glass, it just took a while to get there. Poetry spoke to many people and maybe she was a bit too prosaic for her own good. Her humour was too similar to advertising slogans.

'What was your favourite poet?'

'Seamus Heaney,' he said.

'He is one of our four Nobel Laureates for literature.' She had to prove she knew one thing.

'Yes but growing up Heaney inspired me.'

'What about Yeats, did he not do it for you.'

'Yes he was brilliant. We often had to recite him.'

'Did that put you off?'

'No not at all.' He smiled, Ciara could see a glint of a half-truth, some piece that was a dastard to remember then he continued. 'Have you ever been to the Yeats exposition in the National Library? He asked.

'Actually no I haven't. Have you?'

'Yes but only once and I was a bit hung over so I didn't really take it all in. Would you like to go?' he asked.

'Ah....yeah,' she said slightly unsure. 'That would be nice.'

'Good.'

They met a few times and he drank, and he drank and they had fun. He didn't try to flatter her, he didn't cajole he just amused and charmed as if she were Queen holding her court. It was nice to feel that her opinion mattered. Whilst this was interesting, complementary and different, she was not entirely comfortable with it. Ciara was not used to and didn't like being the focus of someone's attention.

He was very open as if there was no barrier between the inner life and the facade which we portray. He told her everything, the boredom at work, the feeling on the sun rising on "the Rock" in the middle of Australia, the fights he had with his siblings growing up. Everything was there, whereas she was the opposite, her inner life was contained within her frame. She had wanted an in with Karl but she was so far in here with Mr Chippy that she could see how his internal organs worked. It was too much.

'Do you always verbalise your thoughts in such a revealing way?' she asked.

'I have about as much to hide as you.' How did he know that? Ciara was very deep, way deeper than the shallow end of a swimming pool.

'It is refreshing,' she said but she wasn't sure if they were getting to know each other too quickly. She felt like she was de-briefing him in a scene from a spy film. She wasn't used to opening up so rapidly. She wanted to take her time about it, peel the layers of experience back like taking the feathers out of a pillow one at a time rather than walloping them at him so hard that the pillow burst. She could see white feathers everywhere. Was this a sign of defeat or victory?

Maybe it was a family thing, he had siblings, lots of them, and they talked about feelings. She had one sibling they talked about not about feeling but subjects, history, documentaries, travel plans. Activities that's was what had occupied the supper table growing up and her ex, well if the subject wasn't about football or rugby he didn't know or want to know.

Was she afraid to open up as she was saving some of her special stories for Karl? Or it could have been that she was a little out of practice on the dating scene. She had never been speed dating or internet dating. Or maybe she was just a private person who needed time to be comfortable with someone before she let him in.

So the spotlight shifted from her to all the other patrons of the bars in Dublin. Initially it was a relief. He played the jester to everyone, ebullient and uplifting as if it were his personal responsibility that everyone in the bar had a good night.

'Do you have shares in this place,' she asked one evening when they were out together and he was talking to some random person he had met once in the bar he worked at. It was as if he could only live if he were in someone else's reflection; or maybe the spotlight would be too bright and he needed someone to shield it for him.

She was thinking, for a change of her on the bus home. It wasn't that she needed someone it was just nice to know that someone wanted to be with her for her. Ok it is fair to say he had been light and bright, but maybe not Mr. Right. But he had been Mr. Right now, as romantic comedy films often describe the filler guy as. He had been diverting, if not fun, he had been solace in the absence of sunlight.

Hope is what remains when everything else is gone. Well some call it hope, others call it lunacy, deluding oneself to believe in something when all evidence is to the contrary. Maybe Karl was an addiction.

'Hi, it's Ciara' she was calling Aoife.

'I know it's you, your number comes up. So what's the story?'

'That guy he is the story. He dumped me.'

'Oh' Aoife was a little surprised.

'What is most annoying is that he dumped me by text,' Ciara continued. How apt she thought to herself after all the texts she had exchanged with the Napoleon guy it was now her mode of communication. She had even been texting Mr. Chippy instead of calling him. It was such a habit now.

'Ah Ciara, that is terrible. What a twenty-minute egg!' said Aoife. She must have been reading the P G Wodehouse books which Ciara had bought. They were so lovely with attractive Art Deco covers Ciara had nearly kept them for herself. 'How rude, I am shocked,' said Aoife.

'He is a rotter, I know that the time spent with him was not long nor was the relationship serious and we had not argued so why could he not have picked up the phone or arranged to meet me for a coffee and told me to my face. Am I an ogre, or something else scary?'

'No you are not, but his lack of respect for you and his casual means of ending things shows you his lack of care for you and backbone in his spine.'

'Wow, go you, no wonder they are in awe of you.' Ciara now felt even lower about herself.

'What in heavens' name are you doing with someone so obviously beneath you?' Aoife was asking. She was a harsh judge of men now that she was being protective of Ciara. She had initially liked the Other Guy but had gone off him when they met again.

The heaven reference reminded Ciara of the parable of Jesus talking to the Pharisees or some other ancient group of Israelites. "Take out the log in your own eye so you can see the speck in your neighbours" or something like that. Ciara thought it rich that Aoife would be so dismissive of someone when her husband had not been the most dynamic human on the planet, amoebas could be considered more dynamic than him. Or maybe it was that Aoife had taken out her ex-husband aka "log" out of her eyes and could see the truth.

'Yes he was a nice guy but he dumped me. Apparently I wasn't enough into poetry for him.'

'Well you are better off' confirmed Aoife.

'I know, but well, at least he was real, he called me. As in he actually picked up the phone. We had met, several times, chatted and got to know each other a bit; he was real even if he wasn't the real deal.'

'Yes, I know what you mean but really he wasn't for you. He acted like he was a host on a reality TV show.'

'Ah yeah, like come dine with me. There is an opposite point to indifference and it seems to be trying way too hard. That is him. At least I am not totally unattractive to the male race and maybe someone else will come along in the next decade or so.'

It was fairly clear that Ciara didn't watch much reality TV as she had absolutely no idea who Aoife was referring to, or which show he was on. Aoife didn't correct her as she wished to stay on the subject.

'You never know, there is an outside chance you could meet someone else' Aoife joked back about meeting someone interesting. She was of the same mind as Ciara which was good but it still hurt to be dumped by someone you were not interested in. Ah well such is life.

Could Aoife have had higher expectations for Ciara and her ability to meet a nice guy than Ciara had for herself? As Aoife was so bright intellectually and so confident in her ability to meet and retain the attentions of Dublin dudes that maybe she projected this onto Ciara. Ciara on the other hand was not in the least bit confident. If a guy tried to talk to her she would automatically assume he meant the person next to her.

'Well at least he was better than the terrible texter,' said Ciara.

'No this Karl is cruel, but he got you interested. He was what you want in a man.'

'Yes it is true that he was manly in his ways and so forth but I have just wasted too much time on him. I want someone who wants to meet me.'

'Not time, it is more a case of mental energy you have wasted. You have not had the time to spend out meeting and getting to know someone else.' Aoife was confusing, one minute she was hailing Karl as the ideal male then she was telling Ciara that she was putting all her eggs in one basket when the basket wouldn't even stay still.

'Maybe,' Ciara wasn't sure it was all too much effort! What was Ciara to do? "I'm putting all my eggs in one basket" she hummed yes you guessed it a Fred song. "I'm betting everything I got on you, I'm giving all my love to one baby, heaven help me if my baby don't come through."

'Are you humming Fred Astaire again?' asked Aoife.

'I might be,' sighed Ciara.

'Anyway back to this vain Karl, what do you mean maybe, it isn't going anywhere? There is no relationship to go anywhere with. How many times have you deleted his number? Or nearly went for a coffee, Karl is a big tease in the ego sense. You are fanning his feathers for him.'

'Maybe it is so.' Rock and speck thought Ciara and her biblical parable, but on the other hand Aoife was being a friend and friends look out for each other. "Heaven help me if my baby don't come through" a bit of fantasy to bat away reality.

'You called him and he didn't pick up the phone, then he texted to ask who was calling,' said Aoife. There was nothing wrong with her memory unfortunately.

'You may have a point.'

'May have?! He is playing you.'

'Ah really? And I thought wedding bells in frozen Norway next year' said Ciara messing.

'Wedding what do you mean?'

'I am not serious but your clarity, the way you can express yourself, how you can get to the point without rambling around the garden for half a day like I do is something special. It is remarkable almost.'

'Thanks Ciara.'

'At least you are three months older than me so I can put your wisdom down to those extra few weeks on this earth' joked Ciara.

'Thanks again!' said Aoife.

'You know I am only messing.'

'I know you are only half messing but I will take the compliment of wisdom at face value. You are my friend and I am glad that you appreciate me.'

'Right, we have to plan our night!! The Real Birthday Night! No ex-accountants, no arrogant lawyers and no fictional architects. This night will be real life, real fun but with slightly less vodka.'

'It's a deal, by the way it's today.'

'Ha ha ha, you know I know this!' how many times in a month could Ciara forget Aoife's Birthday? She would be the ideal friend if they were in their forties when all Birthdays wish to be forgotten, but for now she was going to put everyone's Birthday's into her phone calendar or reminder, or whatever it was. Definitely!

Playful Texts

'Hello my charming Ciara.'

He was back and Ciara was glad to hear from him after the disaster of reality she was happy to have a bit of make believe again. She had felt she had put herself out there on the dating scene with the other guy. She had actually tried. It had been three harrowing weeks of reality but Ciara was a trooper she had borne it with the strength of Job, she had only complained to Anna, Don, Stephen, Aoife and all the guys in the techie department when trying to install Twitter. Apparently this app was great for calling Australia free; obviously she wasn't aware of the functionality of this App. Also she wasn't Aoife, overtexting the lawyer, no she just ever so often liked to hear Sean's voice on his answer machine. Especially now that friends of friends said he had a girlfriend. It would really get him in trouble. Yes she was totally over him, but she really liked annoying him!!

'I'm extremely busy Karl' she responded seven minutes later.

'It's 1.30 am Ciara!'

'I'm out' Aoife had called Ciara to say she was in the taxi on her way over to Ciara's house. Ciara, of course wasn't ready so had to do her make-up on the way. Now she was sitting with dodgy make-up and glupy eye lashes all stuck together. A thought struck her, "I definitely prefer doing my make-up on the bus."

'Why are you replying then?'

'Everyone in the club is on Facebook so I wanted to twiddle my thumbs while the DJs switch' said Ciara. It was true, everyone was playing with their phones just like the last club and they may as well have been in their own living rooms. Clubs were virtual these days when most people were chatting with people who were not in the room.

'I think it is hilarious that people set their location on Facebook so that the robbers know they have a three hour window to burgle their house.'

Now Karl was texting again she must have a thing about remote guys. Maybe they were really just remote access units. Maybe she was just following the trend, texting was contagious.

'Karl the anti-creationist!' she replied. She didn't know how to set up Facebook on her phone and as she had a grand total of 11 contacts she wouldn't have need to do in the foreseeable future.

'Are you Bibling me again?'

'No, why, would you like me to?' asked Ciara.

'New topic, where are you?'

'Can you not tell? I have my GPS on, hee hee.' They were in a Georgian Town house and the whole house had been set up as a club, piano bar, terrace and canoodling area. If one got bored they merely had to wander around to get a new view or experience. It was cool.

'I'm no hacker Ciara, has the new DJ started?'

'Nearly, she is supposed to be great. She is setting up now!'

'Is there free Wi-Fi?'

'Yes' said Ciara. 'Do you think clubs shouldn't have Wi-Fi?'

'It depends on the company you keep I suppose, but I notice you always text me more when you have it!!'

'As you do you, I still have a good 200 texts to use by Tuesday so I will keep your ears buzzing and your thumbs twitching!!' asserted Ciara confidently. '198 now!!'

'No if you remember I have a large text bundle.'

'Yes I remember.'

'Anyone more attractive than myself?'

'Cheeky Mr. Sore bundles!!' said Ciara then she thought "is he snooping?"

'I take good care of my texts.'

'I bet you do,' she said. Then in a new text 'gotta run' she didn't want to be too available to Karl.

'Bye!'

****

'Good night?' texted Karl at about noon the next day.

'Great' said Ciara then she thought, "is he worried that he won't have my undivided texts?" She thought some more "should I mention this or is it just in my imagination?"

'Anything fun happen?'

"Nope it is not in my imagination, there is a niggle of jealousy here. Yeah!!!"

'We went to a cool after party.'

'Really?'

'It was in a penthouse of a hotel,' she actually wasn't lying. The part she wasn't telling Karl was that the person giving it had been older than her parents and was a Meteorologist for an American TV channel. He was a terribly nice guy with three children about Ciara's age. He had been her idol since she was three and she bombarded him with questions like the usual wind direction of a cyclone in the eye of the storm.

Nothing.

Karl was thinking. Well maybe he was thinking as Ciara rolled over in her bed and fell back asleep.

When she woke up again Ciara felt a bit mean. 'So what's new with you?' she asked.

'Lots, went rowing this morning and at work I am finishing up this current project and then finally going to a new site' said Karl.

'Phew, you really sounded bored on this project! This is Saturday,' it was more a question than a statement as she was still in her leaba.

'I know Ciara! Some people are committed to work.'

'Well its better than an asylum,' she was joking but she thought she had best backtrack. 'I had a full inbox from your previous project, hee hee,' Ciara couldn't stop she was feeling a bit cheeky. There was probably more vodka than blood in her system at the moment.

'Well there will be a long time lag before the next project begins, so expect some more!'

'I will, I'm all thumbs!!'

'Do you not use all your fingers?' asked Karl.

'What's a secretary for?'

'Ciara!'

'Karl?'

'Oh I see you get your letters typed up for you,' clarified Karl.

'Yes, I keep my thumbs clean!!' she said. Karl must have been thinking of secretaries in a 1950s manner.

'As I do my breath!'

'Have you given up smoking?' she knew he meant their silly toothbrush thing.

'Only in the snow with mystery ladies who have long black boots,' said Karl.

'Quiet days at the offie?' she texted, he had been unusually communicative recently.

She referred to his office as an offie as they were always boozing in it, well in Karl's imagination anyway. Always the ping pong table and the fuse ball which was intended to inspire creativity but these activities were just used as an excuse to save electricity in the employees own home. It sounded a bit like a crèche for adults to her. Keep them off the streets and out of trouble until at least 6 pm.

'We do work hard here Ciara.'

'Of course you do.' Blank she didn't hear anything from him, unusual! It was fair to say in the time that she had been seeing the other guy her response times to Karl had greatly reduced and she didn't put in her usual effort. Now though now that she was single again it wasn't fair that Karl had blanked her for something so minimal.

A few weeks later he was back. Maybe he had been insulted by her "offie office" comment, or busy with the ping pong and plonk.

'Hey, how are you? It that Napoleon guy again' he was getting into the 19th Century character with ease these days.

'Which one as there have been so many battles in the interim,' she tartly replied. It was enough of a gap for Ciara to display that she wasn't hanging on every word Karl sent. He had to work a bit for her attentions as she didn't give her texts away freely these days. Also he had dropped her for nearly two weeks; it had been an unbearable time where she had wondered should she try to fix things with the other guy. He was a real person, the one whose chest moved when he breathed the one whose mouth opened when he talked.

'Clue, the Norwegian Napoleon,' he replied.

'Ah you were building a boat to escape the Irish weather.'

'Yes that one, how are you?'

'Life is good I can see blue sky for a change.'

'It must be my eyes' he asserted.

"How presumptuous of him" she thought to herself but then smiled remembering her imagined arctic blue colour she had imagined for his eyes.

'Only joking' he rapidly re-texted, it seemed he didn't want to push things too far. 'I'm between projects so I have some head space.' So he was quiet at work and was sick of bluffing that he was busy!

'Good for grifting.' He was the most organised person she almost knew so it seemed he would never waste his time. Well, except maybe on other peoples' time. She did actually know some other very organised people, work motivated and all that and they were called Aoife and Anna. She had also just seen "the Grifters" film the night before and was taken with the term even if she didn't know how to use it correctly.

'Not entirely positive connotations madam,' this was as impolite well apart from the s-texts as he had been so far.

'No pejorative connotations intended only the freedom of not knowing,' was her scramble to not offend, too much. Maybe it was a bad word like "waster" good, he needed a bit of gentle insulting and she could feign ignorance as it was the truth.

'Nothing pejorative taken,' "phew", why was she feeling so uptight? He was the one coming back and she had the upper hand, "relax Ciara, he is back" she said self-motivationally.

Her work in customer (every now and again) service for a MNC was a bit dull, every month there was less and less work to do. It really didn't stimulate Ciara the way she needed. So she "grifted" in to work every day and drifted out again at close of business. Her cubicle was in a large open plan room, no ping pong but a good canteen and a view, had she mentioned the view; it was essentially the only reason she turned up for work. Every time someone left the company she edged a bit further to the window, she would pack her things and make a quick dash towards the light one desk at a time. As each person left there was more and more space around each desk. This was lucky as each empty desk reminded Ciara of the recently departed. It was a very sad situation, so many nearly friends but more than co-workers were gone.

On a happier note the view was becoming clearer with less people about and the windows were glazed from floor to ceiling with a light green tint. Within a month or two she may well have a window desk and would see the river with no visual obstructions. Environmental scanning was very important for focusing on boring customer issues. With less and less calls to the business, she would scan the horizon more and more the closer she got.

She was trying to get past the annoying unnecessary blocks on social networking sites with Anna, her direct line manager. Ciara had stated the level of customer service issues could be raised on open forum. She wanted to tweet ideas, 'these are a good forum for motivational and team building sessions' she confidently informed Anna.

'I'm not so sure about that Ciara, you just want to twiddle your thumbs with your friends. Or worse stalk Karl on Facebook.'

'On the contrary Anna, it is a good medium for giving back to the customer and an opportunity for them to buy more. Of course I'm not going to socialise virtually, I wouldn't dream of it'. However after working such a long time with someone Anna knew exactly what she was up to! She had seen exactly what Ciara was up to when she read her texts file, unfortunately.

'Are you trying to say you don't know Karl's surname?'

'Yep! Seriously though Anna it could be a good thing using social media sites' Ciara continued.

'I will consult the powers that be' this was Anna's standard answer as most control was situated outside the tiny windswept island of Eire.

The view of the New Bridge the Samuel Beckett Bridge was lovely especially in the rain but to think Samuel Beckett hauled a harp around with him in a knapsack while being homeless across Europe seems a bit of a stretch of the imagination. If he were musical at all would a mouth organ or a pair of spoons not be more portable?

It was a majestic bridge with the elongated harp positioned on its side. It was not quite the Brian Boru harp or the Guinness harp, which was actually the same thing but the opposite direction. It was more like the Ryanair harp but not quite so fast. It was like waiting for Godot as the bridge opened infrequently maybe once a year. It opened for large ships but it didn't require that the ships steam through as impatient bridge operatives read airport ground staff, tapped their fingers and encouraged passengers to run as our sometimes national carrier did after charging them for not putting their handbag into their luggage!

'So crazy Karl, are your projects as big as your ego?'

Yes the harp and not the shamrock was the national emblem. How many people played this complicated instrument? It was so difficult to master yet the sound was so very beautiful when the instrument was eventually understood and played the way it should. That must be the reward, the playing.

Yes the days dragged by.

Procedural Texts

Each morning the sun rose a little bit earlier and the bus was at a nearer point from home. In the depths of winter the bus was at O'Connell Bridge by the time the dawn broke. Then it was a Quay closer to home, Ormond Quay then gasp Wolfe Tone Quay and Collins Barracks was illuminated in a dawn burst.

'Yes I work on massive projects,' said Karl a few days later and so his reply was quite out of context. Ciara couldn't really complain as she often sent him streams of her conscious thoughts with very little explanation. Karl would then have to work out what she was talking about and revert to texts of the previous few weeks to understand the context.

Every evening the lights were switched on a minute or two later, the days definitely were lengthening and soon it would be equinox. A quarter of the year had passed and she had not set eyes on this interminable and intermittent texter. Really she couldn't really remember what he looked like, he was tall with blond hair and that's about it. She may not actually fancy him at all should they ever meet! His face was like a child's sketch, a shock of blond hair she could not remember how it sat. Then there was a gash of blue for the eyes with a non-descript nose and mouth. She couldn't even draw a smiley face for his mouth, just a line as she could not remember him laughing.

'I hope you don't get vertigo looking down from your eyrie like ego!' she pinged back a while later. Just as the phone rang in work.

What would it be to meet him again after all this effort and find zero attraction, to realise that it had be the Scotch and not his charms which had enticed her. That it was merely the romance of snow and pre-Christmas rush which had her thumbs worn numb from over activity these past few months.

She gazed out the oblique view of window at work, after a particularly dis-serviced customer had let off steam and burned her inner ear. She saw a sea gull gliding, nay hovering in mid-air, being aired up by a current Ciara couldn't see. Her ear would cool down with that lovely fresh sea air coming in from Dublin Bay. The sea gull was very close to the window so there may have been an air conditioning outlet or vent, she wasn't sure. Since it was so close she could see the bird's feathers ruffling in the wind. Its position seemed effortless, almost graceful for what was normally such an ungainly bird. It was free and Ciara in contrast seemed chained to her desk. It was true to say that she was in a warm dry room and it had a bird brain and was out in the cold. Yet at what cost had Ciara paid for her warmth.

The bird was free and doing exactly what it wanted and she was not. "I have so many bills," she reasoned as she gazed intently at this common or garden bird. "I couldn't just leave and build a nest on the eves of my office block. After all where would I wash? The Liffey is a bit grimy and

I would have to make a shoe shack!" She made light of this but the thought grated with her, she felt trapped.

'Well they say size is important, but I think verticality is also up there.' Karl was texting back about whether his projects or his ego were larger. Where was his thought process going? He probably wasn't serious.

She looked a little longer and the gamely gull seemed to turn its head to her, maybe she had stared too long like looking at a painting in a gallery and you think the eyes are beginning to follow you, but she had a moment when they locked eyes. Ciara and the seagull were connected. For that moment all of Ciara's worries and cares seemed to blow up under those feathers on the other side of the glass, flap for an instant and were gone. "Wow" thought Ciara and she felt as light as the feathers and then the bird was gone. "This is why I need a window seat!"

What else is there to say about the view, it was of the Liffey, meandering and narrow, a stream to some tourists widening at the mouth near Google-ghetto. The only decent span of the river begins about here, starting with the pedestrian bridge. Resembling in no small amount a foot bridge in London, spanning the Thames from the City to Tate Modern, except the British one was more wobbly and a bit higher up!

'Well my view is bird's eye. I have just locked eyes with a seagull!' would he be impressed? She ignored his ego and focused on the eyrie.

The widest bridge is the East Link; almost American sized more or less spanning the sea with the brackish waters flowing beneath. It is the only toll bridge now on the Liffey, well apart from the West Link over the Strawberry Beds but the Liffey Bridge was once a toll bridge. The Liffey Bridge is the most photographed bridge in Dublin but it is better known as the cost of the toll. The toll had lasted for a hundred years and was a Ha'penny. It, the Ha'penny Bridge was constructed to celebrate the Battle of Waterloo, Napoleons final defeat. The toll was lifted ages ago but the name of the bridge is still the cost of the toll. Would it now be the ten cent bridge, or the euro bridge with current rates of inflation? Karl worked near there. Was he facing his Waterloo without having spent his ½ pence?

'Could you not have chosen a more beautiful bird?' he asked.

'Well obviously I am a gamely bird myself but if you send me an exotic bird to flap its wings outside my window that would be nice.'

'I will do my best my fair and fine feathered maiden!'

Later on in the day he used the bird theme again. He seemed to be developing her thoughts into some semblance of sense.

'Are you free to discuss how Napoleon and Josephine sent letters? We could pretend we were beneath the Wellington Monument and modern modes of communication like the carrier pigeon or special seagulls could carry our messages.' He was attempting to be a bit humorous but she was confused. Why would they need to send letters if they were beside each other and why would Napoleon wish to stand beneath the symbol of his defeat?

'I thought your research was going to be on Wolfe Tone Quay and Croppies Acre?' she wanted to be gentle with him.

'Ah yes, my special research project! Still awaiting information, pity' was he actually trying? It seemed that only drug users used the park so maybe it wouldn't be the most romantic location to meet.

'Yes pity' she texted in agreement.

'What did you have in mind?'

'Maybe we could send messages between the Ha'penny Bridge and the Wellington Monument,' this was silly but she was bored so she played along.

'I could walk down to Temple Bar Square, catch one flee ridden pigeon, tie a note to its leg and send it to your window,' he suggested.

'Good idea,' she texted. Then she thought, he had wanted a really beautiful bird. 'Could you borrow a pretty bird from the zoo?'

'It looks like rain' Karl continued. 'The birds would be more reliable in the fine weather.'

'Wow you're brave,' she was underwhelmed.

He wasn't going to do it, 'well hypothetically speaking, if you were going to send a message what would it be?' she asked.

'"From Karl"'

'Inspiring!'

'Well if I told you, then it wouldn't be a surprise.' There was a point there.

She left it a few hours and on the bus home she got the thumb tingles.

'Yes the Wellington Monument is in a very open spot. If you didn't die in the downpour, you would be blown away in the wind gusts. There were strong today.'

'You're right Ciara' he liked bus texts. He knew she had already left work.

'If you were to send a message to my office and the pigeon actually found me, it would probably break its beak trying to tap its way through our triple glazed windows. Nice thought though!'

'Maybe something else then,'

'Maybe.'

A few days later he was back with his idea.

'What about a daylight campaign, it could be interesting, in the vein of Napoleon and Josephine,' his thoughts were rambling, definite sign of boredom. Oh hopefully it not a reflection of Ciara's disparate thoughts as this would mean he was becoming overtext through her excessive texts.

'Well give me a line of your poetry to see,' said Ciara. She knew he would have something prepared.

'"Whilst surveying their northern territories, Norway obviously being the most important, they are heading north and the days are lengthening towards the summer solstice." There is some symmetry to this and maybe even significance as we met at the winter solstice. Imagine daylight throughout the night! Imagine how far you can travel when it is always day.'

He had reverted to the seasons, which was as good as the weather to Ciara, or maybe he was in season. Anything which referred to signs of things improving or planetary alignment with the sun worked for Ciara. How had he worked that one out so quickly?

'We have a bit to go yet until June,' she texted then continued 'did Napoleon conquer Norway?'

'I will find out by the solstice.'

'You are right though we will have to meet on the 21st of June,' this was an imperative.

'If not before,' Karl responded.

Whilst Ciara knew he didn't mean it she did still believe that he wanted to meet. If he didn't intend to meet, then what would the purpose of texting actually be? On the other hand did this sound like something he had said before? Or was he trying to re-stress his sentiments.

'So are you requiring Napoleons Brandy for some inspiration?' she enquired.

'Yes, we need fuel for the fanfare; I have many brothers to install in pocket dictatorships so a bit of French inspiration could assist the cause.'

Yes Napoleon had a large family, she wondered about Karl. Had he many siblings, did they live in Norway or Ireland or somewhere else. It was true that she knew what he ate for breakfast but little else. They had never texted about their families not for any particular reason on her part, except well currently she didn't really care about Karl's sisters or brothers she just wanted to see him. She wanted to hear his voice and see his chest rise and fall with each inhalation and exhalation of breath.

Where would she meet him in a cafe or maybe a cinema, no that would be way too dark he would probably start groping her! A lunch-time meeting in a nice bright restaurant now that would be ideal. A fitted dress which could almost be construed as work wear but with a bit of analysis was actually too smart to be realistic in this casual wear your PJs everywhere type of work style. Something a bit demure a cross-over type dress DVF (Diane Von Furstenberg) as opposed to DVT (deep vein thrombosis). Or in other words a wrap without the food connotations which could add some allure. Make him want her but know it's not going to happen right now! Enough of a barrier material wise, to make him want to listen to her conversation, yes that is really what guys do! Maybe he could even contribute to it. He did seem able to talk the first time so why not again? In the main his texts had been conversational and complementary so hopefully it would remain so in round one, the first session.

So what would she say to him when they met? "Hey cool Karl, what's been keeping you?" Or would she be coy rather than direct. "Is this your usual lunching venue" nah sounds like "do you come here often?" "Is it nice to get out of the offie for lunch, or have you told your boss you are entertaining potential clients?" "Hey Karl, or is that Hans" a group text joke, maybe she had overdone this line too much. Actually that was a point, she hadn't been joking about what he looked like she really couldn't remember. Ok she had an image of him, his back, but the focus was not his face, would she recognise him. As so much time had passed would it be like a blind date but with someone she knew? It was odd situation.

Would he say "Ciara, it is a pleasure to see you again?" No a bit slimy maybe "do you want to play house in my show house?" Or maybe the practical "Nice to see you again, it's been a long time."

What she did receive, by e-mail though was this composition.

'It is good to take a lunch the day can be so long and monotonous when luncheon is always taken in the office. Coffee always tastes better when served in a china cup, especially when it is poured from a long-necked pot. Then it is drunk at a relaxed pace in an inspiring environment. Conversation sparks when the time is taken, almost stolen out of the work day. We are entitled to a lunch hour, but we never take it. So taking two lunch hours at one time is fair and equitable, a just exchange for all the days when we have no lunch. We can relax into the time and enjoy getting acquainted a little bit. Enjoy the furtive eye contact and the hidden messages given by our body language. The mutual appraisal and survey to give the encounter interview language. I remember the curl of your hair, the flash of your eyes, so light they are almost yellow.' He had thought about this a bit, maybe on his long bus journeys home when he had listened to all his downloaded music or his kindle battery had died. Could he be slightly too close to his feminine side, Ciara was worried.

'Yes my eyes have been known to scare small children in direct sunlight,' she said. 'Your eyes are remarkable though, such light blue that there is more than a hint of the Arian in you. Your straight blond hair is a refreshing contrast to my dark gruaig. One is attracted to the other, the opposite would you not agree?' She hoped she had his attributes correct, she was making it up.

'One is attracted first and analyses why later' he wisely observed, again by e-mail. 'If the looks work it is the general overview which is the draw. Details taken at random can detract from the impression of the whole. However there are safe areas which one can comment upon such as eyes. This will always be acceptable in polite society and true.'

He was obviously not a woman who took every detail and analysed it down to microscopic levels. For example the texture of the hair, if it were fine, would it bald and by what age. From which direction would the balding begin, the crown, the temples and would it merely recede like the tide or be completely washed away with the violence of a tsunami. If the hair were to be all gone how would he look, was his skin tone deep enough to be able to carry off the hairless look in a cool manner or would he get melanomas on his crown and die of skin cancer early and so leave her.

"Ciara, don't be silly, this is a coffee date, euphemisms are being implied but marriage certainly isn't."

'Interesting' she replied.

He waited a few days then e-mailed again, his creative output must have been spent on his relatively long composition. 'Hey Ciara, do you know any bar/cafe/hotel type place/' he pinged over. This seemed like he was trying to cover all options. In other words he wanted the option of getting a room without the expense of actually paying for it until he gauged how the encounter was going. Something safe until he decided whether a full frontal onslaught would be appropriate, she decided her full battle gear would be required. That is high heels, short skirt and full make-up. Hang the demure she was getting one shot like an interview to get free chocolate for the rest of her life. Should she shave her legs on the off chance that she felt in the mood? Was it presumptuous of him or was he being practical with the broad range of locational meetings?

'I have vouchers,' he hopefully added.

"Cheap skate!!" She almost believed it, he wanted to meet. She did want to meet him too but it was a bit sordid meeting in the afternoon that was what he intended with his daylight campaign she presumed. For booty, this was probably the purpose and not much else, daylight booty at that. This seemed like too much history with little chance of a future and absolutely no present or presents. "Hey who needs chemistry when we got history," she thought inverting the old pun.

'He is more like the pirate of Milan than the Emperor himself!' she exclaimed loudly at her work computer. Both Don and Stephen jumped.

'Ciara, are you alright?' asked Stephen.

'He is keeping his options open,' she said.

'Ciara, what do you mean?' Stephen delved.

'Nothing Stephen, but Karl has asked to meet.'

'It that not good?'

'Yes, but, well I don't like the terms,' she huffed and puffed and stared at the screen. Nothing was on the table but maybe all could be in house! Was he being slimy, sleazy, or calculating a maximum return for minimum investment, could he have some banking genes in him? The costs to him was firstly, outgoing texts, about 5 cents a pop or free if he was web-texting, e-mails free, but maybe a roaming charge, which seemed appropriate given his behaviour and suggestions. Secondly and finally his time, did architects calculate their time at the same rate as lawyers and bankers? Billable hours, he seemed to give it freely, willingly even. Excitedly, almost, yet demanding more of her time and effort as he had not suggested a location.

'I am sorry Ciara, but if you are not happy leave it a few days and then get back to him.'

'Stephen you are a man of sense,' she smiled.

She waited until the next day then sent Karl a link to a boutique hotel, quite expensive as she wanted to ascertain what she was worth to him! It had full room occupancy for the foreseeable future so that closed of the room option and foiled his sleazy plot. The destination had lots of individual areas for a quiet coffee or maybe even a light lunch. Alternatively there was a bar and restaurant for a full lunch this should cover all options. There was even a nice smoking area, if the mood took them.

'Take that Northern Napoleon!' she had pressed send.

'I may need to take out a mortgage to cover the outgoings' he texted back. So he was looking for a cheap date, maybe he used his show-houses for this purpose usually!

It seemed probable that just one encounter was his aim and all that texting was an attempt to build up to a crescendo, maybe to save the pocket from wining and dining. Or maybe it was to save the time and effort of dating. The objective was to make her comfortable with him, make her feel that she knew him, but make her a physical stranger to him, maybe to heighten excitement for when or even if, they ever committed the ACT. Make it more exciting and enticing. Was it that? Was that all he wanted? Why are boys so predictable? He probably wanted to rent a room in a hotel to keep things distant from his real life! She wondered if he really was emotionally unavailable, could he be dedicated to something like his work. What did it matter anyway it wasn't as if things were actually leading anywhere, crescendo, diminuendo or even innuendo.

'Thought you had vouchers, Napoleon? Was it a lean bonus then?' So was he measuring her worth or her value? These terms are often interchangeable or used for the same reason even though fundamentally they have different meanings. Worth is – according to the Ciara world view, what something is worth or means to you the individual. A ring given by her grandmother was worth a lot to her because it meant something to her different to the intrinsic value. She loved it as it retained a link now that her grandmother was no longer with her. Whether it would have a high market value was debatable. To her value was a price realised when the ring was brought to the market, an open, general concept of what a willing buyer was prepared to pay for the item. Whereas worth was an individual personal concept or what it meant to her.

'Yes I do but they were not to that value!' said Karl.

So he wanted to see her, but how much, was he putting a price on his affection or potential affections. Was he hoping to have maximum return for minimal outlay? Was he hoping for more than one usage? Not necessarily, but he was attempting to imply a meeting or maybe more than one meeting without actually promising anything.

'Maybe we could commence with something small,' she suggested cautiously. She wanted to see what he would come back with. She could have added she was worth that level of outlay, but she didn't.

'Could there be somewhere closer, maybe in Dublin 2?' he questioned. Was he getting lazy, or maybe he was just busy at the moment in work, making permissible uses for the site he was working on and maybe her? The less effort he put in at the beginning would be multiplied exponentially later on, if there was a later on in their relationship.

'I thought you were the properties expert,' she stated. 'Maybe I should defer to your superior knowledge.' A bit of flattery may encourage him to do some research. Also it would be interesting to see what if anything he came up with. Maybe a hotel in Temple Bar, it would probably be somewhere cheap and easy for him.

Whoosh, a veritable wind tunnel of inactivity and cold air ensued. There was no response, days passed and nothing, still nothing. So he wasn't prepared to invest anything! Or maybe   something   else   had   come   up.

The Wedding

'I'm in Temple Bar for a meeting today and we can meet.' Ciara was taking no more, shoe fashion victim maybe, a sucker for rap and the thirties definitely but errant texters were not going to get the better of her. Period or full stop or whatever was not related to the female cycle but referred to one textee's determination to meet the other, no matter what came between them, come fuse-ball machines, carrier pigeons or play writer, mouth organ toting Nobel Laureates. It was June. Her statement was not a "can we meet" nor was it "I would love to meet" but a "we can meet" as we live in a tiny City that would really be a town if it were in any other country.

'I'm going to Norway today for a family wedding.'

'Cool do you want me to be flower girl?' said Ciara, she was going to take no negatives, no way, this meeting was happening even for five minutes.

'I'm sure you would look very fetching with flowers in your hair, but I'm short on time today.'

'So what time is your flight?' Ciara asked.

'Maybe peacock feathers would be more you!' he quickly typed and they cross texted.

'3 pm when is your meeting?' he got back on track.

She was going to have to think of a reasonable time. 'It starts at 1.40 so I could meet you for a quick coffee in Cha.' Cha is Dublin for tea.

'Ok, you're on, but it will have to be quick as I need to get to the airport.'

'I talk a lot faster than I type!!' Wow, now she had it, a chance to meet him. The Joy of Cha was a great place to get gun-powder green tea, so strong that it, well it caused the Chinese to invent gunpowder one supposes. 'So that is 1 pm Yes?' she confirmed in a moment of fear that he would turn up at 1.35 pm for just five minutes.

'Yep, 1 pm' he reassured her.

She got there early to cool down, it was an unusually warm day and her power-walking was at a rather brisk pace due to the nervous tension which made her entire body twitch with anxiety. Would he show? Would he fancy her? More importantly would she fancy him?

She had a large bottle of bubbly water drunk within the first five seconds of seating and also ordered an iced tea and more water. She considered venturing out to the smoking area at the back but wanted to have fresh breath after all the toothpaste references. Also she might miss him; he could be thinking she would not turn up as much as she thought he wouldn't.

She took off her runners and put on ridiculously high heels, she had patterned tights on too as he had mentioned that he liked the ones he saw. She had a suitably low top which she only ever wore clubbing but he had said he looked at the whole picture rather than the minute detail which she obsessed about. She checked to see whether her face was dewy or shiny one was apparently a natural glow and the other was hot and bothered. She even put on a bit of lip gloss was she going over the top? This may be the only meeting or the start of something special so she should try not to blow it, act cool. Try not to act Ciara, be more like Aoife really as she was really cool.

'Uh Oh!'

There he was so tall he almost had to bend his head to step through the frame of the front door, he stood on the threshold sucking up all the light and he seemed to absorb the entire space of the tea shop by his presence.

She had an uncontrollable urge to duck, to just pretend that the table was a pond and quickly but deftly put her head under it. She began the manoeuvre but his eyes were adjusting to the light and he shouted out, 'Ciara!' There was such joy in his exclamation that she stopped her movement and pretended that she was picking up a napkin.

'Ciara, I really didn't think you would show' said Karl. He had a huge smile and he almost ran over to her.

She was going to play it cool and say "I knew you were" when he was already on top of her. She stood up to greet him and was thankful of her heels and their fingers touched. Her eyes could meet his with her elevated position. An electric current coursed through her body and he jumped back.

'Ouch!!' he exclaimed.

'Ouch back' she confirmed and they were only going shaking hands. It was real, it was mutual it was super-duper scary.

'Would you like to sit down' she asked as Karl looked a tad pale? Her voice was barely audible more of a squeak than a sentence.

'Maybe before I fall down, Ciara, it's you. It is really you. Why has it taken so long?'

'Maybe we were both a bit afraid. Self-protective or something, can I get you some tea, or maybe a glass of water,' she felt her face flush Ferrari red and her voice would not keep an even tone. Why does our body never obey orders at crucial moments? Her eyes gazed longingly at him like a young doe in love and her torso was pointed directly towards him. He sat down into the tiny space available opposite her at the table and she felt very close to him. She was very close to him it was a narrow table and it seemed unreal, dreamlike almost.

'No its fine I will get it,' by getting it he meant raising his very long muscular arm in his grey short sleeved polo shirt. Ciara breathed deeply, she was going to faint at the sight of his biceps, was that sad or what?

The person behind the counter came over to take Karl's order very quickly yes it was a really small tea house.

'So a family wedding, not yours I hope.'

'No of course not' Karl laughed nervously. 'I would need a mortgage before my marriage.' Was he saying something which Ciara had thought? He seemed to be like the Karl she thought she knew.

'They can sometimes be mutually exclusive' said Ciara finally speaking normally.

'I am straight forward Ciara, mortgage, marriage and then munchkins.' Ciara laughed, Karl was many things but straight forward he was not.

'I should hope that your children would be better looking than munchkins Karl' she joked. 'You have increased your gene pool by at least 5 million with your Norse blood.'

'No Ciara; that honour would go to you.'

'Pardon' said Ciara not quite following.

Karl looked at her.

'Yuck,' she had grasped it, 'now don't be giving me any corny lines, you have written them all before and sent them to me.'

He smiled, 'No I still have a few more munitions in my arsenal. The odd time you inspire me!'

'I say I pretty much evenly inspire you as it only an odd time when you don't come back to me.' Ciara was going to ask why but she didn't want to break the spell just yet. Magic was wafting about the room like the smell of baking bread at 5 am when Eddie Rockets is closed.

'Ciara, I am serious in life, I have still a long way to go in my career before I think about settling down and if we can electrocute each other by touching fingers I couldn't think it could be with someone other than you.'

Ciara took a deep drink of her bubby water, was he really real or was this just another of her waking fantasies? Was he repeating what he thought she had said to herself or what she wanted to hear? She looked at his grey polo shirt which was open at the neck, she could just about discern some chest hairs poking out the top. He had a large watch on his left wrist which she thought unusual but didn't wish to ask why. It had a very shiny face and looked quite expensive, like an overindulgent Christmas present.

'Well hey then get a move on with your life plan, I'm pushing 22 and I wanna be married by 30!!'

He smiled, 'if only,' then stopped. 'No I like you the age you are, you never told me but mystery is good. You have an element of fragility to your very complex personality which is endearing but sometimes too enticing not to take advantage of. You are full of contradictions and you have a strength and determination which I find irresistible. If we had met when you were younger I would have not recognised that contradiction as it would not be fully formed.'

Ciara considered this, was this a moment for revelations as in her age as she was already showing enough of her physical form, or did he prefer as he had said a woman of mystery. He was certainly mysterious. 'I really don't get you, definitely you are one big mystery to me.' She couldn't think of any witty analogies or wisecracks.

'You know me, maybe more than anyone else knows me. I am focused and ambitious.'

'Yes, so you say, but everything you say cannot be contextualised. I have no points of reference with you' said Ciara. How could he say she knew him, he was a void to her, a voice crying in the Ethernet.

'I have told you of my inner life, you know what makes me tick.'

'Do I, I mean have you? You have shown me only parts of yourself which you think will entice me, hopefully, but not the real you.'

He leaned forward but didn't need to go far as he was sitting opposite her scarily close already. He took her hand and she hoped there were no electrical devices in the area which could short fuse. She felt it again, raw desire and attraction. He moved her hand to his face and rubbed it gently against his cheek. Her arm was limp and he seemed to take control of it, she could not move her fingers. Why was she happy to abdicate control, she was a self-reliant young, well youthful lady living her own life. Yet it felt so natural she couldn't resist even if she tried. He was physically more powerful than her, probably not brighter, hopefully, there in this area they were very much even. Yet she still wanted to hand over the reins of herself, her life, everything to him. Now that was a frightening thought, if he had asked for anything then, at that moment she would have said yes, yes and probably another yes just for good measure.

'Ciara, what do you want from life?'

'Nothing,'

'Really, well you will always be happy,' he smiled and she could feel his cheek go taut under her fingers. 'What do you seek then?'

'I have a romantic view of life, so I want to be happy with someone special.'

'Could the special someone be me?' Karl asked.

'I don't know we would have to see. You know it can be difficult to change fantasy into reality.'

'Can we not have both?'

'Like being an old married couple who write letters to each other each morning?' Ciara asked.

'Well by the time we are old even texting will be redundant, like your cannons and messenger pigeons.' Karl smiled. 'Oh and I do love your IT skills, they are hilarious.'

'What are you smiling about, I am really improving and I know a cute guy in the IT department who has given me really useful tip on my smart phone?' Ciara had to let him know.

'Do you have to go on a date with him for each IT favour he grants you?'

Ciara's eyes narrowed, was there a hint of jealousy or the stag marking his territory with his scent? No he was probably just seeing how resourceful she was. 'I am an outsourcer and hopefully a resourceful one at that!'

'Kiss me then my Ciara outsourcer, my tauntress and my tempting textee.' He didn't ask this time, he told, should Ciara be getting scared? Would she find that he would become as forceful as Sean, the ex and the constant sleeveen?

She stiffened a little but he moved even closer and kissed her, quickly enough that she didn't have enough time to think and cogitate all the permutations and combinations of kissing her remote ideal texter. Was it she who was afraid of changing to reality. He had begun kissing her very gently at first and she thought she would be embarrassed by other people sitting at tables nearby. However they vanished from view and all she could see was him. Karl was her line of vision and she was a little afraid to kiss back just in case it was not as great as the first Wellington moment. This time was lovely, she felt close to him closer than she had ever felt to anyone in her whole life and so incredibly vulnerable as if should he let go of her she would disintegrate into tiny pieces of gun powder tea. She kissed back and pressed her lips to his. They were warm and firm and she opened her eyes for a quick peek, his eyes were closed. Then he opened his left eye and they both smiled moved apart and giggled.

'Ciara, you are the one for me.'

'Karl, please don't say this if you don't mean it.'

'I mean it!!' said Karl.

He smiled and then he had to go. He had not even taken a sip out of his tea, like dinner in an American movie where all the actors were on a diet, or maybe the makeup artists were really expensive. She obviously had to run too, to her fictitious meeting so she didn't get a chance to say he was the one for her in that romantic vision that there is only one person in the whole wide world that will ever make you happy. She didn't say it also because she wasn't sure it was the right time, like saying "I love you" just because the other person had just said it.

She looked up and he was gone, she hadn't even waved, time was swirling like a purple haze and she was caught in the middle, she couldn't see the people around her, the table, the front door no all she could see was the purple changing to black and the void where he had sat.

A bit of analysis was required, what had happened? What had he said or she said. Had they said too much, she felt overcome but wow he was over-exposed. Or had his reaction absolutely nothing to do with his feelings? No that couldn't be right, he had said "you're the one for me" now that was a strong statement. It was a very certain action to which she was certainly reacting.

'Ahhhh' she texted to Aoife a few minutes after he left and the tea house was reality again.

'Hey u, that sounds baaaaad. R u OK?' was Aoife's reply a micro-second later.

'Ah, don't know. I met Karl.'

'Really met, like in real life you had a conversation?'

This was going to be a to and fro texting conversation so she called instead. 'No, I mean we met for tea and he has just left. My legs are shaking so much I can't stand up.'

'Good shaking or bad shaking?' asked Aoife.

I'm so shaky I might need a glass of vino to calm down,' Ciara was sick, love sick.

'Wow, that's intense! Can you restrain yourself?' asked Aoife. 'I mean it's only lunch time! So how did it feel meeting the cold Karl?'

'He's not cold Aoife! He's hot' Ciara had to fan herself whilst making this assertion.

Aoife was glad Ciara had called as she was impatient with Ciara's slow typing. 'What do you mean he is hot? You have already told me again and again how gorgeous he is.'

'It's not just his looks Aoife, he is warm right through to his soul!'

'What do you mean?' asked Aoife.

'I mean he told me I was the one for him and he would wait until I was ready. Or maybe it was until he was ready? I'm confused now as I'm so excited.'

'Ciara that is great to hear but if he is lying I will string him up by his orange long johns!!' Ciara had told her about every text no matter how boring it was for Aoife to hear.

'He looked into my eyes and told me, so I know he is not lying.'

'Right my place later, lots of booze and we will get at the truth of what he was really saying.'

'He was really saying this is special, we almost shorted the circuits in this tea shop, and everyone is still gawking at me after our passionate kiss.'

'Well at least he's a better kisser than that useless creation of the other guy.'

'Ah, you could say that. Can't wait to see you later!' said Ciara.

'Let's say seven.'

'Perfect.'

Ciara left and just as she went out the door she realised she had forgotten to pay, she turned around and went back to the counter. 'That giant paid for it' was the reply she received.

'Heaven, I'm in heaven and my heart beats so that I can hardly speak. And I seem to find the happiness I seek, when we're out together dancing cheek to cheek.' She was off on an elated Fred and Ginger moment. She didn't care how loudly she sung as she toppled along the cobbles of Temple Bar, she had forgotten to change into her runners but there was no such thing as sore feet or out of tune singing in a moment such as this.

Text Talk

Now that Karl was in the bag Ciara could sit back and contemplate texts and their language. She was reviewing her text file at work later that day. She was making a list of short texts.

'L8r sums'

One of the techie guys called her summer and he got to be winter as they were both terrible at remembering names. He might have had a soft spot for Ciara as he was helpful when she had technical issues. He showed her how to abbreviate, for example summer became sums. Was she a hard sum, more than two plus two, or was he just lazy with his speech?

'Jst in da door!'

What fine examples of English literature these texts were. Many great minds had discussed the denigration of the English language since the advent of texting. Ciara did not include hers among them. Had people not bemoaned this dissolution of pure English since the advent of language, some people were always looking back. Was it not for the very fact that nobility spoke French at the time of the Normans that English became such a diverse language? How many other languages have the concept of house and home? Probably lots but it was a good idea. However text "speak" or "talk" simplified language to the core of the message. It was a reduction to the most basic, fundamental level and using the least number of words to save words and keep everything, the message in the one text. It also saved time, this brevity, especially in the rain. This is probably why it was so popular in Dublin.

'Im on de bus'

There was no need for annotations or for correct grammar, punctuation or contextual syntax it was a message plain and simple. Probably people thought telex language was defiling the English language in its day. Who knows? It was however an interesting study in communication.

'Ya im dare'

Karl used full sentences and quite complex ones at that, he had not given himself over to text talk. His grammar and syntax were perfect. Maybe he was older than he seemed! Could he have been lying about his age and actually be older than her, obviously she would never reveal her age and no, she wasn't considering doing it about an hour ago, but he was 33 if whiskey memory served her right. Why would he lie? Or possibly could the length of his text display his independence of thought and freedom from the short text fashions. He may well have a complex telephone package with lots of bundles of texts. He was a large text bundle boaster after all. Now do bundling texts together not sound a bit cruel, would one's thoughts get tangled in all the ether like socks in the washing machine?

'Tanx do'

When friends short thumbed her, Ciara was fine with it as she knew they were warm to her and just short on time. However if Karl had done this she would think he was being well, short. "Ur de 1" if he were sending her his commitment to her by text would it be this? No it would be "my contradicting crazy but sometimes cool Ciara, you are the ONE!!!" Yes, he would definitely expand things, he was expansive after all. She would give him family time now in Norway, he would need space just in case he had over-committed. Maybe she should have gushed back "u r 2," why do we have 20: 20 hindsight? She had finally met him after half a year and all she could say was "you short the electricity" and maybe she hadn't even said that, only thought it afterwards and really, really wished she had been able to find some semblance of humour.

'I'm putting all my eggs in one basket' she hummed as quietly as possible as she didn't want to get any more stick from Don. 'I'm betting everything I have on you.'

Don looked up from his screen, smiled and looked down again.

'I'm giving all my love to one baby' Ms Fred Astaire or rather Adele Astaire but a good octave lower continued. 'Heaven help me if my baby don't come through!'

Back to thinking about how people abbreviated thoughts to save credit, 'telegram for Mr Astaire, I'm dancing, I'm dancing and I can't be bothered now!'

'Can you at least stick to the one song you 1930s DJ you!' said Don but by his tone Ciara could tell he was as bored as her and enjoying the distraction.

'I don't need a MPC player as I have a music mixer in my head.'

'Yes Miss vinyl, it is MP3 player.'

'It could be MP57 for all I care, I like my gadgets pre-loaded' replied Ciara.

'Well if you buy one my two children will up load all the Fred and Ginger songs you want, then I will do the rap. I don't like them listening to your 50 Cent or Lil Kim.'

'Thanks Don that would be cool! I may get friendlier looks from the other passengers on the bus!'

For some reason there was a little chuckle from more than one work station as everyone imagined Ciara singing, "isn't it a lovely day to be caught in the rain?" The sodden stony faces of the other passengers would turn slate grey rather than car colour grey which was supposed to be silver. There was nothing lovely about being caught in the rain unless one lived in the desert. She was so happy at that moment that nothing could get her down; not the rain, not the waiting times of Dublin Bus or the lack of activity in the office.

'No way,' piped up Stephen. 'Can you imagine Ciara, she would be singing out loud on a bus and not realising. Those poor passengers, what they would have to listen to!'

Then everyone began to laugh, 'yep Ciara you would be throttled on the 66X !!' one of the other guys said verbalising their internal thoughts.

How did they know she sang that song nearly every rainy morning and remembered the scene where Fred had said thunder was when one great big cloud banged into a small fluffy one? Why was she so transparent? That dance scene was her favourite it was in a band stand in a Hollywood version of Hyde Park.

'If you are not careful Stevo I will tell Sophie you sing that song with me every time we go out in the rain.' Said Ciara, she almost said "so there" but she was pretending to be a bit more grown up than seven today. Everyone else could tease her but Stephen had to stand up for her that was the rule.

Ciara went back to her text file and analysis of text talk. 'Cool call over' – no that was a boring text there wasn't even any abbreviation.

How many texts does it take to become a serial-texter? Probably it was to do with the space in time in which they were sent. In other words when Aoife had sent about 300 texts in the space of a few weeks to one guy that was bad. Ciara had sent about 1000 texts in the space of about six months to someone who did respond. That was good, in-fact it was totally normal. She had met him, yes after a space of about six months, but some people have busy lives. Consequently it wasn't as if she was texting a total stranger, he was Karl, the unknown but not unknowable. Maybe they would get to know each other, who knows? "How long is he in Norway for?" she wondered. "Should I send him a quick line 'U r 1' no that would mean he was either size 1 or you are out there on your own." Abbreviation was not Ciara's forte. Maybe if she used "Ur de 1" that could be slightly better.

'C u l8tr'

At an earlier stage in her life boys were like a stream of buses, one coming along every five to ten minutes. If boys were like buses though, could you choose your destination or destiny according to the bus number? 46A would be a posh south side lad and 49 would be a Tallafornia fella with lots of muscles.

'C u s'

'See u soon,' or if even more time constrained 'Cus' that was a brilliant way of saying to someone that you were stuck at a red light. Not that Ciara advocated texting in the driving seat but maybe, just maybe if you knew the lights would be read for ages could it be ok? It almost looked like the polite American way of saying curse. "She liked to cus" or however those Southern States people spoke.

'Mornin'

How romantic from the guy of your dreams, his emphatic yet succinct morning greeting. She would be over whelmed if she received such an enthusiastic text.

'Cool'

'Cool!'

'Cool?'

'Kool'

There were so many ways of expressing one word.

'L8 as usual'

It may be a good idea to keep a text short if one were actually in the process of getting somewhere.

'Dunno'

I don't know, you don't know, he doesn't know, she doesn't know.

'I'm gud'

Well it was definitely better than saying "I'm god," hasty typing could sometimes have negative effects. Did some people keep these sorts of texts in their drafts to send expediently at short notice? Would there be a market for "clubbing and just met X"? or "having posh nosh in Y"? Maybe not, if someone were gloating they would like to spend a bit of time on it. Maybe it was like someone on Facebook putting in a locator to say they had just landed in New York, or type "just been upgraded to business class on my way to Tokyo." Now that was gloating if she ever heard it, it probably meant that everyone in the Business Class Lounge was too busy doing business to bother talking to the Facebooker.

Images

The first novel in the world, well the first known to Ciara had pictures; it was about the inner lives of people viewed through the lifted roof of their house. History books often have pictures in the middle of them so maybe Ciara needed the visual also. Ciara had exchanged images with Karl and these captured a sense of what she was craving. Well Karl certainly gave her an eyeful! If it was good enough for the Japanese with their novel it was good enough for her. Ciara saw the picture novel when playing gooseberry to Stephen and Sophie they had taken a trip to the Chester Beatty library. On the guided tour whilst there were many beautiful things on display yet the Japanese novel struck Ciara. To be able to see into someone else's life was tantalising. Could she lift the roof of Karl's house and see how he lived? See what he did when he wasn't texting her and she thought back to the shower room shot.

Everything since that first novel had become visual from tiny pencil sketches to cartoon images where the text was smaller than the image. The scale developed slowly for the first several hundred years but with the advent of email and photo-messaging the pace rapidly increased. When Ciara and Karl were exchanging most of their images Ciara's phone was broken so she used e-mail as the means of transmission. She wanted to relate her images to the development of the Napoleonic theme. He was not necessarily that focused, or rather his images focused on the development of his muscles rather than Napoleons' epic story, so was Karl the brawn of conquest rather than the strategist?

Rowing

There was an e-mail from Karl and she opened it excitedly hoping for some inspiration. The journey home had been really long as there had been an accident on the motorway. In her living room the netbook seemed to take forever to open up, maybe the attachment was too large. Then when it finally downloaded it was of Karl, rowing on the Liffey in clinging lycra. The rowing image sent had significant timing for Ciara the traffic had been at a standstill on the river part of the journey. She would have been quicker rowing home than bussing it. She looked closer at Karl, rowing and it was a definite and unadulterated MIL or man in lycra moment (thanks Mr Brockmyre.) Technically it was better than MAMIL or middle-aged man in lycra, but only marginally. Too much information displayed, yuck. He was attempting to display his virility through an activity. Maybe get her thinking about him in a physical way; well it was causing physical affects, she felt nauseous!

She knew he liked rowing, he had told her, many times. He was proud of his physique he had told her and shown her. She did like that fact that he was disciplined in his routine and he would arise early in the day to row hail, rain or shine. He was hardy, she was not. She liked that he cared about his health and maybe wellbeing but didn't wish to see the results quite so clearly. Yes he was a poser.

She remembered the very long arm reaching up in a very small tea house to catch the attention of a waiter. He was real. He was in Norway but he would be back. Then as time went by, especially as she was on the bus when she passed by his rowing club she would look at the image. She saved the image into "My Photos" so she could ogle it on her phone. The initial gloating of his face and the arrogance of his posture were softened and were replaced with a wistful hope that she would see him again soon. See him when he was rowing or see him when he hopped back on a bus that she would be on so they could have an impromptu meeting. She need not force him to meet this time, it would be natural. They would just casually run into each other. How would she find out which the time he rowed? Maybe there was a timetable at his club?

He would be alert, hopping onto the bus, cheeks reddened and rosy by the wind and cold, eyes shining and mouth smiling in a warm excitement at meeting her. She would have her makeup routine completed at this point and would be looking fresh and awake from her gentle wake up on the bus. Her hair nearly dry as the journey would be three quarters completed and the wet would have transferred into condensation and lodged gracefully onto the windows of the upper salon.

They would smile at each other, he would sit beside her they would chat and then go for breakfast. This was her fleeting yet recurrent dream every time she passed this rowing club.

Yachting.

He is leaning against someone else's boat with a smirk. Not quite carrying off the 'welcome to my crib on waves' look. He was obviously on holidays and on dry land standing beside a berthed boat. Was he trying to be a cling-on or portray an air of wealth and sophistication? It looked like he wanted the bling without the bucks! Also the yacht was a bit yuck. Not her style at all. If he were to have impressed her he should have chosen a schooner or some sort of elegant wooden boat, with a high mast and polished deck rather than a white plastic floating male-member extension!

It was odd as what attracted Ciara was the handmade boat he was crafting with his grandfather and not a white prefabricated floating bar in some dodgy dock which was highly priced but lowly inhabited. That is the natives could not afford to live there since God created woman. Yes Napoleon was from the Med but he was more a land than a sea animal.

Skiing.

He was cross country skiing, in contrast to having a lot on show in the bathroom image, he decided to do a Ciara and show only around his eyes. He was in an all-white ski suit which made him look like a baby seal. Ciara enquired as to his colour of long johns and thermals. He demurred but said he always liked to match! At least he did have a sense of humour.

The background caught Ciara's attention, as it was not as barren as she had expected. There were depths to the white and there were trees to be seen surrounding cute wooden houses. It was a perfect Christmas scene. She was really grateful to receive this image although she did not tell him, as she had always wondered what lots and lots of snow really looked like. And now she knew. It was not as if Ciara were not well travelled, the case really was that she sought heat rather than cold. So this outlook represented the opposite, the other, winter when she was summer.

There, in the background was what looked like a Fjord. The sea was frozen, or maybe it was fresh water from a river which was flowing into it. It had been stopped mid-flow and there, far into the horizon was an old man and a wooden boat. She wondered was this Karl's grandfather, was this one of the boats which they had built together. It was the best image he sent as it gave Ciara a view of what she wanted. She wanted to see the other, the rural, the rustic and maybe even the cold. It was in keeping with her internal life.

There was snow dappling every branch of the pine trees, more than dappling it was covering and obscuring their shape. The weight of the snow on some branches was so heavy that they were bent down. They were almost reaching the ground, bowing to the winter master. Behind them, a long way off were mountains. There was snow on every peak, the sky was so clear and fresh that each undulation was visible and as she magnified the mountains she could see log cabins, winter homes, weekend retreats clustered on many plateaus. She could not quite see the roads as her screen went a bit fuzzy when she zoomed in too much but she imagined them there. She imagined all the people who lived in those houses, who existed in that winter world. How cool! How interesting it would be to be able to ski from your very own front door. More than interesting, exciting, fairy-tale like, it was perfect.

'Northern Conquests indeed!' she said on receipt of this.

'Dominate the indomitable,' was his reply. She was not so sure. How could one dominate frozen water? When one touched it then it would melt? Maybe active men needed to think like this, she truly hoped he didn't think like this about relationships.

Her inside an engine.

She was sitting inside an airplane engine somewhere hot in peach and grey uniform with silly head set. The plane had stopped, the front of the engine had a cool swirly bit and her friend knew the pilot. The picture is happy she was with friends out and about and doing something silly. It was a bit of a fantasy shot as she was wearing air-hostesses' clothes, she had borrowed her friends' costume which had a pill box hat and a veil of sorts. They were on the tarmac somewhere warm and exotic while the plane was being refuelled. They had decided to take some fun pictures to mark the day.

One of her friends had been a stewardess or flight attendant she wasn't sure which term was less derogatory and more PC. Due to her crippling mortgage repayments her ability to travel had been severely reduced. Her friend was able to offer her reduced-price tickets and Ciara was very happy to accept. So her friend had facilitated her wings. It had meant that she could get the all-important winter light, sunshine during dark winter days in Dublin. Her friend had been a flight attendant for some years and they had travelled together to many places, hot, exotic, sometimes politically unstable but always bright. Ciara was a good travelling companion in that she didn't mind where she went as long as it was warm. This was why she had no concept of cold, no feeling for snow until Karl froze her in her tracks.

Lost in India.

And there were loads of people around, smells, heat, spices the many colours. Was she trying to look vulnerable, needy and seeking a white knight take-over? This was one of the overwhelming and unforgettable memories of India, there were hoards of people, everywhere. Every space was populated. People slept in the train stations, sides of the roads, washed in rivers, walked with sandals along streets barely wide enough to carry two vehicles at a time. She had been overwhelmed. Fortunately her friend was about to keep her grounded.

She thought the sense of exotic would intrigue him. He was in contact so he was still interested. Ciara also felt India was fitting as it was the ultimate destination of Napoleon. His advancement to Egypt and Syria had merely been a preamble in order to acquire the valuable land of spices, the land which was later described by the British as the jewel in the crown. What would he have thought when Queen Victoria was eventually crowned Empress of India? If he had lived he may well have seethed at the idea.

Maybe she should have taken the dates off the pictures as it gave away her age. Although Josephine had been older than Napoleon and had children from her first marriage so maybe the analogy would follow through, in that he liked slightly older ladies. She doubted this though when he commented on the date!

Egypt

She was sitting on a Camel in front of the Giza Pyramids, her friend was sitting on a donkey so she thought it best to photo shop her out of it. The nice guy in the techie department, who called her summer, did it for her as she could not get the rat to stay still long enough. She knew it was called a mouse but it was so clunky that it moved more like a rat. Rats! Anyway the donkey's bottom looked big! On reflection Ciara wished to contextualise or rather help Karl visualise some of Napoleons journeys and adventures. Many of Karl's references had been to places Ciara had not visited so they made her feel even more distant from him than before, this however was somewhere she could relate to. On Napoleons trip to the Orient there had been a myriad of experts, mathematicians, orientalists and botanists. The journey was to be cultural as well as military. This was going to spark an interest in all things eastern and it is fair to say, well in Ciara's world view anyway, that the Grand Tour extended to Egypt after knowledge of the Pyramids and all that they contained was proliferated around Europe.

Her friend remained loyal with cheap flights and had felt for her plight, the desertion by Sean landed Ciara in the financial desert of debt and the lack of ability to pay her way annoyed her. So it was an interesting choice to land in the Sahara Desert! Her friend had taken her to somewhere she had always wanted to go, Cairo. It was the home of the Egyptian Museum and was full of Egyptology. They had no desire to cruise the Nile for fear of catching some water borne disease. All they wished for was to see the city of Cairo and it had been Ciara who organised the trip to Alexandria. The Museum was the high point of the trip and they had spent three out of the seven days there. They had both loved it, the wealth of artefacts on display had almost overwhelmed them but they soon became familiar with the terms, lineage of rulers and Ciara was sure if her friend had stayed any longer she would have begun to learn hieroglyphics. Yes she was very capable. In reference to the photograph Ciara had enjoyed the camel ride, but she was highly insulted when her friend was only offered 500 camels. As a few years previously she had been offered 2000 for her friend in Morocco. Maybe it was the price of her friends' blond hair, the cabin crew lady. Her friend was blond, naturally. She had fared well in the Middle East and she had met a handsome banker, they moved to Canada and were expecting their first child. Who says air miles don't pay?

E-mails

Back when the military was in style Ciara and Karl first started e-mailing. He wanted to see what he was aiming for. Maybe a solders cap, flag and not much else, she was contemplating what picture to send, to get the correct tone and so hopefully encourage him without playing the sex object. She really wanted to see him in a military style. Maybe it could have been Karl dressing up in a uniform from early nineteenth century, shiny boots, slim fitting breeches and cropped hair. Then she realised her new phone was broken and she had to resort to other means of visual communication otherwise known as the e-mail. On her old phone the pictures didn't send anymore and she had to use 3000 words of prose to make the picture. She encouraged him to send an image first. This was the shower image she was disappointed this was not in the military style. Then she considered a retaliation, another bath image of herself with bubbles and a 1950s style shower hat but had discounted it as she wanted to be 'clean' in the metaphorical rather than just the physical sense. Anyway who would she get to take the picture? Aoife would laugh at her. Selfies were out of the question, Ciara had not even thought about the concept and phones didn't revolve as far as she knew.

Soon the long descriptive prose was forgotten, much to Ciara's dismay and Karl seemed happy to race forward sending racy images of himself; maybe he thought she would follow suit and do the same. He had mentioned getting creative with a web-cam but she had ignored this suggestion. She wasn't sure that she wanted this. It seemed that he wanted her to comment about his bathroom with shower curtain offering, but he had sent her his back, was this impolite? Was he flexing his muscles to entice or repel her?

A few weeks later after they had met she opened the image again and examined it. Could this be a show of strength or was he just a show off? Was this voyeuristic or fun? He had mirrors everywhere; maybe he did this sort of thing regularly. In fairness, on closer inspection there were just two mirrors and he proudly held his phone, like the lost biblical tablet of old. Was he saying that his back was his most attractive feature, more attractive than his face? "Thou must worship my back" as the eleventh commandment may state. Well he may have been a little disappointed by the lack of skin she displayed in her image, tough!

'I am sitting at my desk now after a very fruitful foosball game, still exhilarated from the buzz and I wish to get buzzed up with you. Are you free to chat?' asked Karl the next day at work. He was a week back from Norway and in great form.

'Briefly I am very busy in work today,' you barefaced liar you Ciara.

'Oh I will be as brief as…When I think of you it is always outdoors. Maybe it is the Wellington (Quay) affect. Did you know that Arthur Wellesley was the first and only Irish born PM of Britain?' Their discussion of Quays had lead as far as Wellington Quay being the most important Quay in Dublin due to their marvellous kiss.

'I may have heard that somewhere before,' said Ciara modestly, she had been doing her homework but didn't want to seem boastful. Since they had been talking about Napoleon so much she had of course revised his Irish nemesis. 'His being born in a stable not making him a horse did not greatly endear Wellington to the Irish people.' "I bet he is going to look this up and get the witty response. Was it Daniel O'Connell who responded or some other notable Irishman in London?"

'Ah I seem to remember this from school, there was an interesting response but I am not going to Google it just to prove the deftness of my fingers.'

Ciara was a bit put out, so she decided to give him a little test, 'I know your fairly bright so, do you know which War the Ha'penny Bridge commemorates?' It was a typical "A LITTLE KNOWLEDGE IS A DANGEROUS PHENOMENOM."

'Waterloo of course, hope we are not meeting ours soon.'

'Hope not.' He was still e-mailing. This was unusual, were e-mails going to take over from text?

****

The next Monday he e-mailed again, 'I am sitting at a new desk!'

'Oh,' what does it look like?'

'It's big its shiny and it is very near you' said Karl. He snapped a photo of his desk and sent it to her.

'Near me? Did you get another promotion?' her heart began to race. 'Ps yes your desk is very shiny."

'I got a new job Ciara. The company are quite well known.'

'Congratulations Karl. In this climate you have had a promotion and now a new job, well done.'

'Thank you.'

She remained e-mailing him as she would generally respond in whichever mode of communication Karl initiated. The day was bright and the sun was shining on the Liffey.

'The promotion I was celebrating on the night we met gave me good experience and the exposure I needed to move up to a more senior position,' Karl continued.

'That is kind of impressive,' said Ciara as she thought it was unusual to be promoted in such a time as the property industry was in more than the doldrums it was on its knees.

'You are either very lucky or very bright ;)' she sent what she hoped was a wink. Either way it somehow excited Ciara, maybe as it was the antithesis of her career and its inglorious achievements.

'So this new role will hopefully give me the international experience I need to develop as an architect.' It really was a coup in light of the disastrous job market.

'How are you feeling on your first day on the job?' she said.

'Ah Ciara it's amazing here, I now, like you have a window view. I never knew there was so much activity on the river.'

'Generally the more activity you notice the less the activity on your desk!' She said. Then she thought it best to qualify her remark by supplementing it with this, 'mine is a desk of window activity. I like to think of it as environmental scanning it helps to enhance my creativity.' She had given him a rather fuzzy explanation of her work so she could imply creative aspects without actually lying. He also had not specifically asked her so it was fair enough really.

'It is my first day so I don't think they expect me to do anything yet,' said Karl.

'You're right Karl you could probably avoid work for a good month!'

'Ciara I will spank you when I see you. You can be really cheeky.'

'Chance would be a fine thing.'

'So Ciara by typing to you I do appear to be busy.' Could he be teasing her by copying her use of words? Surely not!

'So you have a window seat also,' she ignored his gibe as he had ignored her previous comment.

'I do, floor to ceiling windows, with a green tint to reduce the glare if the sun ever shines. I would say normally unnecessary in our usual climate but today I am happy to have it.'

'It *is* lovely and sunny today. The light is glistening on the water and high tide is close I presume.'

'Ciara, I look out onto this water and think about the generations of people who used it.'

'Yes I know, it is so cool,' she smiled and wondered how close he was to her. He hadn't said which side of the river but with the light shining in he must be on the north side.

'Even before our time, the time of Napoleon, there were the medieval traders, the Vikings, the Celts, all using this same waterway.'

'No wonder it's so dirty!' she joked back.

'Maybe you have become used to the view, but for me it is the first day.'

'I wouldn't say that Karl, after ever difficult client meeting, or after a run in with the boss I sit and gaze and dream then get my thoughts on track. So what else is nice about the new offie?'

'Ciara, it isn't an off licence. I am a bit important now!' was Karl indignant?

'Sorry!!' but she wasn't really. 'What about the canteen?'

Good, great in fact. There is a free canteen which does cooked breakfast. I might avail of it some hungry mornings.'

'Are you going to ask me what I had for breakfast?' he added after a moment.

'No, is there any foosball?'

'No it's a bit more serious here Ciara,' he was using her name a lot. Could this be significant? 'But the cooked breakfast would be good on the mornings I am hungry after rowing.'

'That is good,' then she added for a bit of fun 'could you row to work?'

'I will have to see if I can berth my canoe!'

'Mooring rights?' she wondered if there were any up in the financial bit of Dublin.

'Yes. It would be ok rowing from the club to work but going back there is a weir. So that makes things a bit tough.'

'Hmm and I suppose it would be too far to row the whole way from Celbridge to the rowing club?'

'Not necessarily too far, but my daily commute would take about 4 hours.'

'There would be no text time then.'

'Yes obviously that would be a huge disadvantage,' he said. 'I would have to get a waterproof phone and use my voice recognition activation function.'

'It's a bit hit and miss, that function.' He could always use that underactive call function she grunted.

'Yes you mentioned somewhere that you start with Anna and end up with a bit of a boob!' So he had received that text, she was sure she had deleted it rather than sending it.

'Have you looked at the lunch menu yet?' She thought it was a good idea to change the subject. Also since their offices were so close now he may ask to meet her.

'Are you on the menu?'

She thought about this one, maybe his mind was rowing down the river into e-mail-dirt and she wanted a polite and if at all possible humorous response. 'Maybe if you were one of my customers, they never fail to eat me alive.' No that was leading to brothel banter but she had sent it, she wasn't going to agonise about the content any more.

'Could I be one of your clients?'

She left it a while as she didn't want to think of Karl in a work context.

'Shall we meet and discuss construction; it's a lot cleaner than you think?' He was e-mailing again after lunch which they, surprisingly enough didn't eat together.

'Is it cleaner than the Liffey? Do you have a proposed location for these complex and detailed discussions?' she asked.

'Yes certainly cleaner, I don't have a location right now but we can arrange something X x.'

'Thought you were consumed by a pile of "uncool" plans,' she knew he had no work excuses so she thought she would annoy him a little.

'Ah Ciara, be nice to me, you know it's only day one.' She well knew he was quiet as she had never had pre and post lunch text with him before or rather e-mails this was progress. However there was not the same ring to an e-mail, to have e-mail sounded a bit PC in the computer sense.

'Any particular construction?' she enquired.

'Well the Liffey, what it looked like 1000 years ago. Also maybe what the houses looked like, how the fishwives smelled that sort of thing. Could you call it the un-construction or even pre-construction?'

It was true she was interested but she didn't want to say yes in case he teased her and said something important had come up.

'I could send you a lock of my hair by courier! You could examine the DNA, X'

'That would be nice, definitely better than toe nail cuttings! Haa Haa.'

'Yuck, is that one of your usual dating tactics?'

'Yes I do it all the time,' he joked hopefully. 'Sometimes I even paint them, cappuccino colour or racing green.'

'Have you spent a long time thinking about this?'

'Noooooo, I just want to see you,' he said.

'Good,' she said.

'When?' he asked

'Now! Do you not think I'm worth it?'

'Now? Yes of course you are worth it miss bouncy hair' he said. Then he asked, 'which side of the river are you on?'

'The South and I presume you are on the North.'

'That is correct' he confirmed.

'Well your building is probably opposite mine so why not stand at your window with a big colourful card and see if I can see you.'

'How will I see you?'

'I will pull my green burka out from under my desk, its racing green to be precise, just like your car hee hee.'

'You are such a live wire it wouldn't surprise me if you had one!'

'Ah an electrician as well as an architect!' she said.

'Yes, I am a man of many talents, right I'm off to find the colour cards' he said.

Ciara was a bit afraid to meet Karl again face to face. She was being polite but diverting the focus on an actual meeting. Emotions had run so high in the little tea shop in Temple Bar and he had said so much which she could not compute at the time or since that this removed meeting with the river Liffey as a divide would suffice for a second meeting. Yes it would mean seeing him without meeting him as safe as if they ran into each other on Dublin Bus. She smiled "this will be fun."

'Ciara, can you come with me for a moment?' asked Anna her boss.

"Oh, drat," thought Ciara. "He will be standing there at his tall green window and I will miss him." 'Ok Anna, but just for a minute if you don't mind as I am working on a strategy.'

'I know it's not a work strategy but it will only take a second.'

The task was a relatively quick one and luckily Anna didn't need to detain her too long. Reality was a nuisance when it tried to compete with fantasy.

'So Ciara, how is the romance going with Mr. Texter?' Anna was hovering around Ciara's desk so Ciara was going to have to be honest and tell her what she was waiting for.

'Well he just got a job in a firm at the other side of the Quays and he is getting a colour card to hold at the window to see whether I can see him.' Ciara hadn't realised that Anna cared about her non-existent, well virtual love life. Had people nothing to talk about in this office?

'Ah, interesting, I have to see this.'

'No please Anna, it would be embarrassing!'

'You do enough environmental scanning as it is, so at least this is gazing with intent.' Ciara thought she was the only one to use this term but maybe it was widely used. Or could it be that she had used it so widely that it had become a commonly used term on their floor? Woops.

'Ok' Ciara reluctantly sighed, 'if you must.' Anna was a happily married lady who fortunately didn't feel the need to have children, or so she told everyone. Ciara generally considered that when people were so emphatic they usually were finding it hard to conceive. Maybe this was a bit mean or a myth as Ciara knew nothing about marriage, but Anna seemed content Adam was cool and she was able to put her whole effort into work. This may not be possible with small children and sleepless nights.

They both got into position and looked at the buildings across the water. Whilst the buildings were very clear the people were just tiny specks. They scanned, and scanned but to no avail. Then suddenly Anna said.

'Look to the green building on the right, third window from the left two floors down.'

'Ah, yes I think I see a large racing green card stuck in the window. Could it be him?'

There was someone waving, it was very far away but she could just about see an arm poking out from behind then card moving from left to right and back again in a wave motion. The thrill, her heart started racing and she imagined him as close as he had been that day in the tea shop. The sun was on his Aryan hair and glinting from his eyes. This she only imagined, but it seemed real, she was light headed with elation, he had got to her. He was her every waking thought and unfortunately he knew it.

If Ciara had been able to reply "yes you are the one for me too," would they be still looking at each other from across the water? Or would she be with him now? Meeting for lunch arranging to take the same bus home, going for breakfast to his new office, who knows? It was a few months ago since they met, maybe it wasn't a memory but a construct of her very fertile mind.

'Yep its him, it is kind of thrilling this.'

'Are you serious Anna?'

'Yes, the dashing stranger who keeps your attention through his exciting life and interesting texts. I can see how you have got hung up on him.'

'You can?' asked Ciara. "So not everyone thinks I am a somnolent idiot, that is good."

'Does he have large hands?'

'Yes, very large.'

'Oh. You know what that means!'

'Yes it means he is about 6' 5" and is in proportion with the rest of his body.'

'It means he is manly.'

'Anna do you mean well endowed?'

'Probably,' Anna blushed a tiny bit and Ciara was delighted.

'Well I will have to wait and see about that one.' This was more than a little uncomfortable the speculation about the manliness of one's object of interest with one's boss, whilst standing at the window idling away work time. In other words it was much more fun than work surfing.

'Well let me know,' continued Anna.

'I will do, I only got as far as kissing him.'

'Yes I heard! Was it nice?' said Anna. Ciara couldn't believe her ears, her boss on work time at 3 pm in the afternoon nearly talking about, could she say it? Sex!

'It was soooo romantic, the snow was falling, we were on Wellington Quay, that's why I call him the tall Napoleon and he took the cap from my head and kissed me. It was soft at first but definitely finished firm. I had to lean on his arm my knees went so weak. I was dizzy, freezing, light headed but most of all happy. The happiest I have ever been.'

Anna smiled, 'it was like that the first time I kissed Adam. I knew he was the one I was going to marry.'

'That certain, wow, if I got to know Karl maybe I could feel like that but the distance he keeps is confusing. I think he would be the sort of person I would look up to if I were going out with him, someone I would be proud to introduce to my friends. However to marry him, I am not certain.'

'And you met him again?' were there no secrets in this office?

'I did but I didn't tell anyone, it was a special day.'

'Ciara you buzzed into work that afternoon. It was as if you had won the lotto, of course everyone knew.'

'I even took a taxi back to work so as not to be too late,' Ciara added, yes she really was as transparent as a drop of Liffey water.

'You must have been seriously late' said Anna as she knew Ciara never took a taxi alone if she could help it.

They stood there for a while, Ciara feeling embarrassed and Anna seemed to be contemplating something.

'It is lovely to be in love and you have delayed the courting process. This though, the start is where all the excitement is. I think this evening Adam and I will have a bit of romance and you have re-ignited the flame in me to do romantic things. I would never think of getting a guy to hold up a colour card. He is so excited his arm is almost falling off with all that waving.'

'Thanks, he is quite enthusiastic though. That is funny; he lost his cool for a moment.' Anna was opening up so Ciara thought she should ask her something. 'So what are you going to do to make this evening romantic, dinner, lingerie, what?' Was this really happening? It was surreal, or was Anna? Ciara didn't know, she couldn't work out the what, or why could it be boredom? Even Anna the amazing was getting bored and de-motivated in this very idle work environment. However anything to be away from her computer was good, so she wasn't ready to ask why.

'You are creative so can you think of something unusual?'

'I will get back to you just before 5 pm.' Ah this was the worst, mating or at least helping her boss to court her husband, please may the economy recover quickly. There was mischief and mischief and this was definitely the second type of mischief.

'Grand so,' said Anna ready to leave now as maybe she had said a little too much.

The board was lowered. Then it was gone. The moment had passed but the memory would keep her warm the whole way home.

'Did you see me?' he e-mailed.

'Well I saw the board from a distance and your hand waving.'

'Cool, talk soon.' He was also gone.

'Yes, you were great,' she wanted to encourage him.

What to tell your boss to improve her sex live? Send a picture of your cleavage and say you have bought Belgian chocolate to melt and rub in later? Wow this was a quandary could she get fired if she got the answer wrong? And if she was right would this become a regular occurrence? Which would be worse? Considering it was particularly awkward especially as Ciara couldn't remember when it was that she had actually been known by anyone, in the biblical sense that was, so she was probably the last one in the office to ask. Sophie was your woman for this job, the French were experts apparently. The closest she had been to body chocolating was when the marshmallow and chocolate fondue had spilt all over her and burnt her cleavage. Hot, scaldingly hot, actually and not sexy or romantic in the least.

'Thank you x' e-mailed Karl.

Advice for Anna, how was she going to get her boss to have a romantic night with her husband? "Get a Chinese chief to cook you dinner in your own home?" This may be difficult at short notice. It would have to be simple, underwear, music, a bath full of rose petals. Hell she hadn't a clue she didn't know Adam well and the last thing she wanted to think about was her bosses sex-life. Sugar, why was life so tough.

'If you were getting romantic, where would you start?' she e-mailed Karl.

'Ding dong! Did the sight of my forearm get you going?'

She had to think about this one, if she said yes would he think she were easy? And if she said no well he wouldn't

281

inadvertently help her out. Could she say "it got my boss so excited that she is going to seduce her husband later?"

'It was nice to see the real you in the flesh rather than images. I seem to have imagined meeting you as it seems like ages ago now.' Two "seems" she was on shaky ground.

'So Ciara Creed I would take you to somewhere you like to go, such as a Museum, hopefully with lots of military history, pictures of the Duke of Wellington and Napoleon so you would be relaxed, interested and talkative. Then on the way home I would knock you into a hedgerow and jump you.'

'Ha, you are such a romantic.' He completely ignored her mention of their meeting or his signs of commitment. Maybe he was still euphoric from his first day in his new job. "Did we meet, I am uncertain. He is always so non-committal how on earth could he have said something as definite as "you're the one for me"? It doesn't make sense."

'I can but try!' he e-mailed back.

She would have to think this one out on her own, her Boss and her love life, so much for outsourcing! He was an architect not a consultant after all.

At around 5 pm Ciara had still not come up with anything, she popped over to Anna's desk to see whether she could squirm her way out without sounding too weak. 'Hi Anna, how has the afternoon been,' she began slightly uncertainly.

'Great, busy and so did you have any ideas?' Anna was cutting to the chase!

'Well, have you ever sent him a picture of your cleavage and then a picture of body chocolate? Then said you run the bath I will run the rest? Or something to that affect.' Ciara was blushing and her words hurried out tripping over each other as she tried to finish the embarrassing sentence as quickly as possible.

'That might work but I was actually thinking underwear.'

'Do you want me to come and help you shop?' Ciara was hoping that she would say no.

'Absolutely, I can see this is a bit of a strange work situation but I have been trying so hard to conceive that the romance has been taken out of our love life. It has become our procreation time rather than fun time.'

'I know, well I don't know but I can imagine.' Yes she was right she had got her boss totally wrong, she knew absolutely nothing about human behaviour.

They chatted the whole way to the shops non-stop and Ciara thought again she really had the coolest boss in the world. It made work very easy, yes boring but definitely easy.

"Ciara, I have always liked you,' said Anna.

'Really?' said Ciara. 'And obviously I have always liked you.' She thought she should really get the reply in.

'You don't squirm, I'm going to use a phrase I don't like because I can't think of another one, its brown nose.'

'Yuck, yes I see what you mean.'

'You are not strategic with your friends in work,' continued Anna. 'You are straight forward and tell it as you see it. I appreciate your honesty.'

'Thanks Anna,' she smiled.

'So I'm going to tell you we have a window of about three months to conceive and if it doesn't work I am going to have to try IVF.'

'I'm sorry, is there anything I can do?' she really hoped Anna would say no to this.

'Well your virtual relationship has helped my fantasy life and today, I don't know why but Karl putting up that card at the window was so sweet. Romantic almost and I thought this is it, I am going to put the romance back into my marriage for the next while.'

'Yep and see what happens dash dash dash!!' said Ciara.

They headed out to a very expensive shop, bought some slinky undies, they were stylish and silky. Anna convinced Ciara to look at them even though they were both really uncomfortable with the situation. 'Is this what they call work bonding activities?' said Ciara.

'Right we are way past the embarrassment point now so why don't we go all out and you take a photo.'

'Are you sure?'

'Yep' said Anna.

'Who will you say to Adam took the photo?'

'One of the assistants!'

'Oh you bad thing. So now you just need to entitle it LATER!

They fell out of the changing rooms with silly laughter and double entendres. Ciara thought her social life was on the up.

The big one!

A few weeks later Karl was off on his first work trip. He had a conference outside Europe and he told Ciara the name of the city but it didn't mean anything to her. As she hadn't seen him since the arm across the river moment she felt it wasn't worth checking where he was. In other words she didn't know which country he had visited he sent lots of texts and he sent something rather large to her. Or rather he sent an image of something rather large to her. He was always pushing the boundaries of propriety and this time he went way over the edge as if he had stuck his hand, head and most of his body out that shiny green window. He probably would have fallen into the murky green waters of the river in his breach of good taste.

'Did you get it?' asked Karl excitedly some seconds later. He had sent a picture of his manhood from a hotel room at the Architects conference. Just in case there was any ambiguity he sent it twice!

'Pardon?' she was playing dumb. She had received his e-mail but wasn't happy with what she had received.

'Me and my excitement for you. Did you get it?'

"Could this be Karl's crux? It is a bit scary really, too big for my liking," Some say size is everything, but Ciara begged to differ. "Maybe it is a different kind of skyscraper on display here. Why did boys think 'the bigger the better?' He sent this one twice! Does that mean something? It was a slightly different angle. Could he have been a bit tiddly as he forgot that he had sent the first one?"

She was affronted. She was aghast and turned her computer off. She went out to the kitchen and shook the bag of coffee. "Empty" she would just have to have a glass of wine instead.

Ciara sat and thought and sipped, "silly boy was getting a bit carried away with the big tablet of a telephone. He was completely naked, most likely out of the shower as his hair was still wet and the droplets glistened on his very white muscular frame."

Off she hopped back to the living room, cranked up the machine and reopened the image. She looked at the detail this time and the hotel room was fairly plush. It had deep pile carpets and a large bed. She zoomed in to the bed and the bedding had been pulled back and duvets and cushions were scattered everywhere. It appeared that he had been seeking the perfect angle. She ignored the Karl part of the picture for as long as possible but her zoom went a bit wonky and it went back to him and his camera. His camera was close to his right thigh and he was clenching his leg to accentuate his muscles.

Use your imagination guys! Ciara had no intention of sharing everything!

'Ah, that, yes lovely pillows, is that you there or your room-mate?' she sent after some consideration.

'Me!! Of course!!!'

'Oh. Nice room, the bed looks so big you would need to sleep diagonally in it.' The plush room looked like the 5 Star variety. It was the kind that Karl wouldn't pay for out of his own pocket, well not for Ciara anyway.

'And?' Karl asked.

'And!'

'I wanted to give you something nice to think about if you couldn't fall asleep.' Maybe his version of nice differed from hers.

'Oh' she said.

'Oh?' he enquired.

'Was the conference that uninspiring?'

'No it is great,' he said. 'I sent the image before the gala dinner, now I'm back, all alone and wishing you were here.'

The man was a stranger to her still yet he was sending very intimate pictures of himself. Was this the reason she wasn't so excited about the eyeful of an image? The angle on his large and erect member was exactly the same as the previous image the only difference was the bed was at different side. Otherwise she would have thought it was the same image sent twice.

'Are you still over exposed?' she enquired, there was a harshness of the light which washed his skin to a luminous white.

'I want you,' affirmed Karl.

'No I mean the light is very bright and,'

'No I think the glaring lighting is suitably subtle!'

'I mean you sent the image or very similar images twice.'

'Oops, sorry, I forgot I sent that before. If you ever feel like sending me something personal, no matter how many times then I won't mind!!!'

'What I mean is, that if you want my company is this a SHARE issue?' she said in a pedantic vein which was loosely business like.

'Ah, well I am certainly happy for a share of you it will reap dividends!!'

'Hmm,' sent Ciara. She had no intention of a return of the same to the absent company in question.

So she painted her toes and tried to make a video of her feet walking across the kitchen floor. The nail varnish matched the colour of his pillows!! It took ages and she was being pedantic or at least podiatric. The trans-Atlantic communication ceased for a while.

'I'm back!!!' he sent a few days later, maybe he thought he could receive another image or video, from somewhere above the ankles. 'Just realised I have a limited liability company so you can send less safe photos if you wish,' Karl added a few moments later, 'lovely colour and I like the candles you are walking through.' Well he was taking time to look at the video clip anyway.

'So you're back in Europe? Or are you planning to send me an image of your back again?' Sent Ciara, so he was angling for her to increase her visual output, she surmised.

'Would you like to see the back of me twice?' he asked.

'No.'

'Good'

'I didn't think share issues had a back catalogue,' she said trying to develop the business theme.

'So shall we meet up again? I thought you might like to discuss the creative design process, intimately ;-)' He had sent an emoticon, was he complying with convention finally?

"Did you now" thought Ciara, was he talking of buildings here or other types of creation as in conception? Why had he moved from companies to construction? She had been on solid ground there and now she felt uncertain.

'Any particular stage in the process which piques your interest?' she asked. She had ignored his "wanting you" emotion feeling that it was more likely an emoticon.

'Yes important stages such as inception.'

'Is this the head stage?' "Woops he is going to take that in an oral manner," thought Ciara the premature sender, or excessive tooth-brusher.

'It would relate to your preferred position on, or under, as in foundation or super-structure.'

'Hmm, well is not the foundation always the starting point?' She was likening the foundation to a drink such as coffee or tea. Hopefully he was too.

'Actually there are many ways to build a skyscraper. One can start in the middle and just bore in deeply to the soft receptive soil!'

Uh he was feeling fruity! "Let's think on this one."

During her contemplation time there was another ping! 'It is important to prepare the soil clear away rubble and barbed wire. To ensure surfaces are smooth for long, strong steel rods!'

'Too high a building can unsettle the foundations unless correctly prepared.' She sagely stated.

'Yes certain load bearing capacities need to be worked out or additional supports attained.' He said.

'So what would you suggest?'

'For the said skyscraper a very close shave is required for the deep rods to correctly enter the prepared narrow ground work'.

"He is getting a bit personal" Ciara was not comfortable. 'Close shaves depend on which side of the river you are at. When your office is that far away....' "That sounds awful what else can I put though? It's kinda insulting this dialogue."

'Discussing whether shaved is better than unshaved could be important (I think shaven is best). As all steel rod receptors are different! I think an oral discussion on this for starters would prove mutually rewarding.' He was racing away without her even responding. The offie was slow today!

"Does he now! Is this fun or crude? Am I really interested or just playing along in the vain hope that it will lead to more? It is true that my curiosity has been aroused but someone who expects stuff done on the grooming front is asking a lot. Does he know that I only shave my legs once a week and only if they really need it?"

She thought something playful would be good, so 'are these fundamental issues such as the required skirt length suitable to work for an MNC?'

'It could be a starting point, definitely a talking point.'

So he had retracted a little bit, this was a good thing, how to keep things racy but not too fruity? It was a difficult balance.

'Could our texts be like a ghost development? Then maybe our interactions would be like a ghost estate?' Maybe a bit of social conscience on the plight of the wronged thousands in the property world would stem his flow. Also his building was just down the road from the head quarters of a bank which bankrupt Ireland, property is all about location.

'Well they are the phantoms of poor design and planning unfortunately. This gives us space to explore the built environment with abandon.' Was he a bit callous? Karl sent another large smiley face which was gleefully grinning and to Ciara it almost seemed menacing. Maybe she was reading into it too much but it irked her somewhat.

Nope she really didn't like this line he was taking. She had decided. So she closed of her personal e-mail and opened her work one. Hopefully there would be something to do to keep her occupied until lunch time.

Over lunch she realised that this was the first time that she had left a conversation mid flow, especially when he had been in the mood for more. It felt good. She was in control for a change.

Stephens Birthday

It was coming up to a very important time of the year Stephens Birthday was rapidly approaching. Ciara usually organised this event and he usually organised hers'. This year was going to be different however and Ciara was off the hook. Her naturally slovenly nature which longed to take the back seat could be gratified once more as Sophie had volunteered to take on the task. Sophie was so tactful, she hadn't wanted to hurt Ciara's feelings by taking over but it was clear that she wanted to do a bit more than help out! Thus Ciara happily abdicated but said if Sophie needed any help sourcing stuff she would gladly assist.

Ciara was able to focus on an interesting present. Generally they, Ciara and Stephen had decided not to buy expensive presents for each other, but unusual ones instead. Ciara decided to buy Stephen an 'I want MY-tunes' t-shirt and looked all over Dublin. There were none to be seen so she had to commission one herself. She headed for the exclusive national chain of stores where the average t-shirt was €8. She scoured through the men's section, feeling a bit inspired, as there were plenty of good looking guys and her interest was piqued. Was she supposed to be grieving for the other guy? He had dumped her by text. That was mean. However he had been her only meaningful relationship in the past two years. Maybe she should retract the word meaningful and use real or actual. Yet she was Karlified and seeing his arm, then a bit more then well the full line up meant that

Mr. Chippy was a distant memory. Yet why was she thinking about him now? Could it be that there were real life guys, male's other than Mr. Chippy and Karl the Creative? Grief could be brief, if it was grief as she was being otherwise distracted.

Wow she had never thought of seeking eye candy in a department store. The talent was talented and she was a woman in the male T-shirt department. Did the budget of the store reflect the particular male's purchasing power and whether he would buy you a Nescafe or a Mocha and pastry on the first date? Would dinner comprise fast food? Would they become the Supermac's and Stout brigade by the time they could afford to shop in Brown Thomas? Yes her thoughts were racing ahead and she had almost forgotten what she was in the men's department for. Ah that was it, male apparel! Best not look in the extra-large sizes, the compact male, neat of frame, this is what Ciara sought and would achieve. A trophy must be won this lunch-time. "Forget distractions."

"Focus on the purchase." Deep blue was Stephen's favourite colour so this was the colour to aim for; she found the right size eventually. He was also an avid Dublin supporter for both hurling and football and Blue was their colour. Ciara and Stephen had been complicit in not joining the 'I-pod generation.' They had many conversations about market dominance and the resultant costs of monopoly positions. It was fair to say that Stephen was not exactly into gadgets as they were so popular and Ciara didn't understand them. In fact Stephen had convinced Ciara to buy an Android phone.

This was mostly because the title reminded him of silly science fiction television shows from their childhood.

Stephen could not see the point of buying something where one started with zero and had to do all the work one's self. The customer in his mind was a user not an operator. So having to go to a website, browse for a few weeks then pay for the privilege of downloading something just seemed a bit silly to him.

Ciara once achieving the t-shirt find, buy, wrap and exit realised she was out of time, she dumped the garment into the nearest printing shop. The guy in the t-shirt printing shop liked the idea so much that Ciara informed him that she had actually patented 'My-tunes' and he believed her, or maybe he was trying to flirt!

'Hello, is that Anna?' after their recent bonding moment and hopefully Anna's subsequently enjoyable evening Ciara thought she should let her know that she was running a bit late and hopefully get some extra lunch time.

'Yes, hi Ciara, how are you?'

'I'm good thanks, I just wanted to say I was buying Stephen a present and I am running a bit late.'

'Ah that's ok, what did you get him?'

'I got a personalised T-shirt for the anti-I-tunes generation. Hopefully he will like it.'

'Yes, sounds like an interesting idea he was always an independent thinker. How much longer will you be?'

'Well I couldn't see what I wanted so I have brought a plain T-shirt into a print shop. Sorry, I am on my way back right now. I will have to collect it this evening as the printing is going to take another half an hour.'

'Why don't you wait and see how it turns out and come back when you are finished. It is not as if we are rushed off our feet!' said Anna.

'Thank you Anna that is really kind, I will show you when I get back!' exclaimed Ciara. This left her a bit de-motivated; there was no hurry, no objective in the office nay in the company. No wonder she was bored and a bit unfulfilled at work. Was this a reflection of her entire life? No definitely not, she just had an unexpected half an hour free in the middle of the day and this was her time to enjoy. So she got a take away coffee and sat in St Stephen's Green, thinking of the real Stephen, enjoying the ducks whiling away the time until the t-shirt was ready.

When she got back to the office she slyly showed the finished garment to Anna, who thought it was a great idea and said she would get one for her aunt who couldn't understand the i-pod gadget anyway. That suggestion made Ciara feel really up with her generation.

At the same time the party preparations were underway. Sophie's theme was 1798- the year of the French! Ok technically the year of the French was a bit before but Stephen really liked battles. She was so thoughtful; there was the Napoleon thing for Ciara, the History for Stephen, France for her and the introduction of the tri-colour taking over from the Blue as the National flag of an island which was not yet a nation. Ciara was unsure whether Napoleon actually brought the tri-colour to Ireland but thought best not to dampen Sophie's' enthusiasm.

The dressing up would be the usual for fancy dress, the girls would put in huge efforts and the boys wouldn't. The boys wouldn't have to do anything to their hair as true revolutionaries, the Croppies, were short haired men who were anti-aristocratic and distained wigs and fops. They could always wear military style jackets and look dashing. Ciara wasn't sure they would invest so much effort. Someone mentioned that they should put a bit of gold into the theme to highlight the backlash against the Golden Circle. However everyone wanted to forget the present banking crisis and do the Wolfe Tone ideals, United Irishmen and women for a night anyway.

It was going to be in the French Centre on Kildare St, an expensive location but Sophie had negotiated the price down quite a lot. It would be a big change for the office crowd, of whom most of the guests comprised. The crowd were used to Stephen's birthday being a boozy affair. They were willing to try the new format but not much enthusiasm pervaded.

The day arrived and Ciara was walking to Kildare St with Sophie and Stephen. Sophie had not quite got the hang of crossing the road with Stephen. She was used to jay-walking which with a wheel chair can be difficult. Not for the reasons of the speed or the safety needed to get out of the way of traffic as Stephen's chair was motorised and very fast. The issue was pavement depression or the ability of the chair to mount pavements of any great height which was something which took Sophie some time to gain a handle upon. They were on the far side of the road from the French centre and Sophie saw no traffic and hopped off the footpath and onto the street. Stephen diplomatically stated 'Sophs, I am going to go up a bit and wait for the lights.'

'Ah, Stephen, please forgive me I was distracted with the other things I have to do. No of course I will walk back and to the pedestrian lights with you.'

'Let's just about face and get the lights on the corner of Molesworth St. They are much closer than here' suggested Ciara helpfully. She spotted a very tall blond male striding down Kildare St about to turn right onto Molesworth St. This is the location of the Norwegian Embassy, could it be Karl? Her heart began to beat rapidly almost pound, her breath became shorter as trepidation rose. He was some distance away, what should she do? Drop everything and run up, to verify if it were him? Scream at the top of her voice and wave hysterically, very attractive. Had he really said, "you're the one for me?" She could pull his trousers down and check whether he had photo-shopped the hotel room image!! Or maybe she had just imagined it all. It was all too surreal it couldn't really have happened, they hadn't met, like most events in her life it had been more or less a direct projection of her imagination. These words were what she wanted to hear rather than what he had actually said.

No it was Stephen's day, she would not see if he were Karl, her errant texter. Karl would have to take second place in her thoughts for just one evening. On the other hand, there was a Norwegian Embassy, this could mean that there were other Norsemen in Dublin. "Why couldn't I have chosen someone in the Italian department?" she thought, "I even speak a bit of the language, love the food, the opera and of course the shoes. At least I would be able to see him when he tried to avoid me!"

She was still not certain whether it was him or not but the thought of meeting him again made her face flush with excitement. If only she could run into him in a casual non-contrived manner she could be satisfied, well she could see him again. She would be able to say that he was the one for her also. "If only I had said that, that he was the one he would be here now, coming to this party and he could be dressed up as Napoleon. Then I wouldn't think that every tall blond was him from a distance." Ciara did have a tendency to torment herself.

'That sounds like a plan matey,' said Stephen bringing her back to reality of crossing the street, he wheeled past her with the rapidity which a F1 driver would be proud and beat her and to the pedestrian lights. They were all going to cross the road safely. His chair had several speeds similar to a car and 5th gear went almost as fast as a Moped or Vespa. Ciara bemoaned the loss of his speed as pacemaker on her power walk lunches. He had been her personal trainer cajoling her to go faster. And now she was out there alone, dawdling and browsing the cafe menus.

'That is some boy!' exclaimed Sophie and the look she gave him, that look was filled with awe and admiration.

Ciara smiled at the look and was gladdened that someone else finally appreciated Stephen in the way that she did. A fleeting thought flashed through her mind, "if only Karl would look at me that way. Well I suppose "if" rather than "when" we ever meet again. What did he mean by 'I want you?' Was he just lonely?" A visual image of scattered pillows haunted her and she tried to bash it away nearly hitting Stephen on the back of the head. She felt a bit sorry for herself once more and then had to snap out of it.

'Sophie?'

'Yes Ciara.'

'Do you see what I see in Stephen?'

'I think so' smiled Sophie.

'It's just, well you're a fine-looking thing who could have anyone and Stephen is one of my closest friends so I don't want him getting hurt. You know.'

'I know your fears Ciara but he is the funniest, most honest, warm person I have ever met. The Irish male has always held an interest for me as well as many foreign girls.' Sophie stopped and looked wistfully away maybe to gather her thoughts. 'Ciara, I never considered disability, I never thought I would be in love with a person who I so recently met. It doesn't matter what shape, size or form the person takes, but the purity of their heart and the warmth of their thoughts.'

"Opps" thought Ciara "and all I seek is 6' 5" great cheekbones, a big career, flashing bright eyes, a complete all-rounder in sports."

'That's great but if you ever do anything to hurt him I will run you over in his sports-chair!!'

Sophie half laughed as she knew Ciara was half serious.

'I don't know where Irish guys get this romantic, witty image from, it must be all the films,' Ciara wanted to soften the conversation as she knew Sophie would be busy.

'Maybe it's because we don't understand what they say,' joked Sophie and they both laughed.

The party was interesting and all the women had made an effort as predicted and were dressed in empire line gowns. The lads being lads had not made much of an effort. The odd one had a military style Adamant jacket and there was lots of hair gel on show. Many had worn their Dublin shirts as they were blue, big effort the females had thought.

Everyone had brought whatever champagne or crement was on offer at their local supermarket, lots of wine and the odd bottle of Napoleon's brandy was on show. Baguette and brie was consumed by the basket and someone had bought a cheap replica guillotine for affect even though this was supposed to be Wolfe Tone and Ireland. Well it didn't matter so much it was of the time rather than the place. Stephen wanted to sing Boolavogue but since no one knew more than the first verse they decided against it. Someone piped up that the Fields of Athenry was an easy one. No one was sure though if this was a true '98-er song or from the famine so no singing was done.

Racy Texts

Maybe it was a case that Karl was emboldened by meeting Ciara after so many months or maybe it was the image he had sent but the tone of the text changed. There was a lot less subtly and the content tended towards a more visceral nature. Many men focus on just one organ in the wooing process and it is rarely the heart. He was s-texting more often and from Ciara's research this was commonplace.

Late one evening Karl texted her, 'Hi Ciara, are you at home?'

'Yes Karl I am.'

'Alone?' he said.

'All on my lonesome,' was she walking herself into something?

'Would you like me to be there too?' said Karl.

'Would you like to be here?' she replied.

'Definitely!!!' Well he was certainly being clear.

"It's very late he's probably thinking about one thing" she thinks to herself. 'Maybe it could be nice but it is late, earlier another day would be better' she sent.

'Ah, but later is now!'

'Now is always now Karl' Ciara sagely observed.

'How right you are Miss Guillotine dodger. However I would like to see you in this now and not another now!'

'Now, this now is gone and I am tired after my Bastille days and waiting to be carted Place de la Guillotine. Adieu to my intrepid Napoleon.'

'Don't go just yet, what you up to?' he asks.

'Watching True Blood,' it was all the rage and everyone in the office was talking about it.

'You like Vampires?'

'Yes' she said.

'I could get free with your neck. It is superiorly long, lean and with fresh veins throbbing.'

'The shows just over now' she texts after ten minutes, there had been a pretty racy scene with the two main characters. She was knackered just from watching it.

'So Ciara do you like Bill or Eric?' was Karl trying anything even a feigned interest in the two love interests to keep the texts going.

'What do you think Karl?'

'Eric I presume'. He said, 'as he's more like me'.

'Hey egomania, are you a smelly Norseman?' could she have been getting a bit cranky now? Then again Eric was a Dane.

'Touché, my hygiene routine has improved in the last millennium.'

'I know you have good oral hygiene, you have told me about it. Anyway, talk soon I'm off to bed.'

Twenty minutes later as she is tucked up in bed. 'Without me!' he texted insistently, he was not giving up. What had got into him?

She picked up her "Josephine a Biography," deeply intellectual and relating to her love of shoes and scarves. Ciara decided to read at least a chapter before responding to the text. This was historical fluff after TV fluff, what a fun evening and Karl pretending that he wanted to be there, topped it all off! Now the world was looking good. Maybe the longer he waited for the text the more he would want it.

'What you wearing?' he asks halfway through her first chapter.

'You will have to work harder than that to snuggle into my scratcher' she texts after she finished two chapters in blatant defiance of his question.

She didn't hear from him for a few days.

The next time he was on he asked, 'what has been your favourite part of our texting so far?'

She was on the bus home so she had lots of time to think. The long johns it was definitely the long johns. It had been the idea of having colour coordinated long johns and thermals which had made her smile.

'It was the long john affair' she replied after ten minutes of contemplation time.

'Really! Interesting, not, was the array of colours?'

'I think it had something to do with the olden days and wooden houses and wilderness. Or maybe it was your quick-thinking reply.'

'Ah!' He sent then a few moments later, 'yes, something to do with what I wear in bed being a personal matter which I am happy to share with you.' Had he been looking at his back catalogue of texts or did he just have a good memory?

'Exactly' said Ciara then wished she hadn't. She was in the door now and kicking off her shoes. Home at last was bliss.

'Well Miss creative story teller what about being lost in the wilderness? Tell me a tale to sweeten my evening.'

'It was a freezing cold night on the rocky mountain so he had his long johns on.'

'You can do better than that!' said Karl.

'Ok, "he was alone on a rocky mountain he pulled on his white long johns and unlocked the cabin door." How's that' she asked.

'There are other types of underwear apart from long johns Ciara, maybe lacy type underwear!'

'Ok he pulled on his lacy long johns and unlocked the cabin door.'

'Ciara! Where are you going with this?'

'It's all your fault really, with your coordinating colours in long johns! Bear with me though as I am thinking of log cabins and prospectors building the USA so I am inhabiting my character.'

'Ok, on you go.... will there be any cowboys and Wild West style saloon girls?' said Karl.

'Maybe, so "he pulled on his very long lacy long johns and had difficulty with the last bit. He had been living in his prospectors' cabin, alone for far too long. Just the motion of material touching his skin and rubbing up along his leg was enough to get him into a rather excited manner." That any better?'

'Ok that's a good start, where is it going.'

'He is going on a journey,' she said.

'He unbolted the cabin door and saw his neighbour bathing naked in the stream,' Karl thought he would help.

'No Karl we need more drama, a slower build up, he decided to take a journey to the town along the Rocky Mountain trail. There was one other passenger.'

'She had long ringlets and big eyes which smiled at him. He blushed and smiled back bashfully. Is that slow enough for you?' asked Karl.

'The journey was bumpy enough and they were thrown about the wagon.'

'He nearly landed on her a few times but she didn't seem to mind,' said Karl.

'"A storm blew up and the driver could not keep control of the horses. They brayed and broke loose of their restraints."'

'The horses ran off and the driver raced after them. She looked up excitedly but somewhat nervously,' said Karl happy to assist.

'"The wind howled and the hatches were battened down. They were safe but stranded. The woods were wild with the wind violently shaking all the branches. The rivers were full of melted snow, enlarged and swollen in the spring thaw. Buttons, belts, boots and bonnets. The wagon shook dangerously,"' she sent feeling rather pleased with her creative output.

'Now it is your turn to slow down. "She was frightened but he reassured her that the hatches were battened down. "Don't worry, I will keep you safe" he relaxed her by placing his large hand underneath her two very prettily gloved hands. Once he had touched them he felt the soft velvet material"....'

'With lacy bits at the end,'

'Very good Ciara,' she could sense a hint of cynicism in the tone of his text, '"he removed the gloves gently and her breathing quickened, she looked down to where his long johns were and got a bit frightened. Maybe also a little excited, she was lonely too and had lost her husband recently. However her late husband was the last thing on his mind. "Are you alright?" he asked her and she nodded her head. They looked deep into each others' eyes..." Your turn.'

Ciara was a bit excited herself but really unsure what to say. Could she leave him hang for a moment, maybe get a vodka to lubricate the brain? This was hard work.

'Ciara, you are taking some time on your creative output?' Texted Karl after about twenty minutes as it was getting late and maybe he was a bit impatient.

'Yes super speedy scribbler!'

'Are you having a drink?' was he psychic?

'Did she smile?' Ciara asked ignoring his question totally.

'Who? Are you back to the story?'

'Yep, the lady in the carriage' she said. 'Right I am nearly there on my creation!'

'Finally, I mean brilliant!!' He was getting impertinent.

'Back on the rocky mountain... "and the wagon was shaking dangerously in the wind, but there was a little action taking place inside as well. The gloves had come off and she was moaning very gently under her breath. It was almost inaudible but since he was so close he could just detect it. She had I high collared lacy top," I AM OVER DOING THE LACE A BIT AMN'T I?'

'I don't care, KEEP GOING, I'm getting aroused!!' said Karl.

'"He started unfastening the myriad of tiny buttons at the side of her throat and her breast began to heave, he was feeling more excited now, more than just the sensation of long johns passing up the broad tree trunks of his legs." SORRY!'

'Really good Ciara, please don't stop...'

'Finally "after what seemed like an eternity he had finished unfastening the buttons and her corset was revealed, beneath it her ample and visibly heaving breast."'

'Please continue, I am so hard...'

'" He couldn't be bothered removing the corset so just focused on the skirts, there were a lot of them! How the multitude excited him. Her eyes were wide with excitement and anticipation."' She pressed send to assess the reaction.

'Ahhh Ciara, keep going, I'm going, pleeease keep going!!!!'

'"He moved on top of her to get closer and kissed her, a long hard kiss firmly on her lips. Her lips parted and he went further. His hand went down and touched her boot, a hard well worn leather boot, she had lovely firm ankles and he looked at her stockings. They were patterned and he looked at more of the design as more of the stockings were exposed. His hand raised her skirts higher and higher he was nearly there. Her legs were long and shapely and the stockings ended mid-thigh. At this point her skin was exposed, pink, young, soft, supple, fresh thigh."' She sent to see what he would have to say.

'Ahhh,' was returned two moments later. Wow had she caused this?

'"He rubbed his large rough hands against her soft pink skin; she leaned into him and touched his long johns, then under his long johns. Their eyes focused on each other's' and were locked together like positive and negative ions. He shimmied off to somehow work out the hooks of the skirts, as he wished to possess her and make her is own."' She sent this to see what Karl thought. The hard bit was definitely his turn, it was well, too hard to do.

'Ahhhhhhh,' then a few moments later, 'Ciara you could go on but I couldn't. Wow, that was sex text if I ever saw it!! Come back to me tomorrow when I get my strength back.'

"Shit" she thought and she didn't ever curse, even to herself. "I thought there was more to do in the wagon. Is this painting your wagon red or what?"

'Were you a little premature with your creative outputs?' Ciara asked a few minutes later when the first flush of success had worn off and she thought he may have been acting or even faking!

'You needed a bit of encouragement, but it was a very good first effort.'

'Thanks your compliments are overwhelming!!' It was hard to tell if he was fibbing or telling the truth, he was a bit complex that Karl.

'Bye Ciara, until tomorrow...' and he was gone.

The next day she felt unfulfilled, he had, she decided after hours of analysis and a bit more "Josephine the shoes and scarves biography" that yes, Karl was prematurely texting and she wanted a bit more from him as her hormones were running cold. She began the next day by e-mail she fancied using more words than is usual on text. However she wondered about how to get him to be a bit more involved so she got him to go first as she formed her thoughts.

'Give me something Venetian in this late summer season.' It was a very lame rhyme but her creative skills were well exhausted from the truncated texts of the night before.

'Are we not going to do Napoleon?' Karl asked.

'Ok Josephine is in Venice and they have just conquered Italy.'

'Right, just a moment then,' replied Karl.

'Take your time' said Ciara but she really meant HURRY UP I'M WAITING!

'"Venice had just submitted. Napoleon was victorious and he disguised himself as a lowly gondolier. He punted along the narrow canals and could hear voices above. He was hidden below and paused beneath a low canal

313

bridge. The warm waters were lapping gently onto the shores. The sixteenth century masonry was crumbling before him. Whose were those voices,"' he began.

"'I Josephine, am listening to operatic airs drifting from a nearby balcony, they seem to call a lusty melody. I am sitting on the banks of a canal allowing my satin slippers to dip into the warm waters. A Gondolier floats gently nearby in his gondola. He has a nice three pointed cap and I see it is you. He is enchanted by the rhapsody of the music. He splashes some water, wetting my satin slippers and I smile. He moves closer, andante, the music quickens as does his breath. He opens his mouth to speak but the sound is taken by the rise of the music."' She thought "no crap, must do better." Unfortunately she couldn't think of anything better. Ideas had been flowing freely in her head as she power walked from the bus stop, but once she opened her netbook they vanished like a gondola in the mist. Maybe she should have written them down as she was walking. She would use them as ammunition to fire at the Norwegian Napoleon. She would do this the next time.

'R u complicating things?' he asked.

She opened a bottle of wine and thought, "maybe I could be the opera singer instead of Josephine?"

'No they are both listening to opera singing from differing vantage points' said Ciara.

'Ok, so he is under a bridge and she is sitting on the side of a canal.'

'Exactly, simple really!' she said. 'Your turn.'

'"He thinks they could be a couple. Are they to be taken over by their senses? The warm air, the warm water, the opera is romance in motion,"' sent Karl.

'"Napoleon takes out his little mandolin and begins to strum in tune with the song. The tempo of the music quickens and his dexterous fingers move faster, picking up the pace. He can feel her breath through the music and feels close to her. Her dress is made of fine materials it is as thin as a negligee and billows about her in the gentle breeze,"' Ciara was doing much better.

'"She hears music, an accompanier below on the waters and begins to hum quietly and slowly to the music. She is focused but likes his brazenness; she becomes the star singer a Diva he sounds like a lowly gondolier paddler. The other sounds are forgotten by Napoleon the punter. She tries to ignore him but he is talented, the difficulty of the piece is easily mastered by his lithe little fingers. She imagines however that they are long and narrow, like a pianist. She imagines their pizzicato; the rapidity of their movement creates a desire in her to see them. She falters a moment almost losing concentration then gets lost once more in a musical trance. This time though she is not alone, she is accompanied by the dashing mysterious man below,"' Karl was getting into the rhythm of things.

'"He hears her falter and knows she is thinking of him, he crosses the narrow divide of canal and they are making music together. Should he increase his volume or stay as he is? He sees her in her flowing dress with creamy décolletage her long hair is billowing on the bank in the gentle breeze. Her eyes are sparkling, he is sure and they have connected. He will know her but then..."' Ciara was also.

'Your turn,' she sent a short while later, fairly happy with the output.

'Hmmm, I don't know where to start.' The time was nearly midnight and maybe the dawn punter, sorry rower was running out of creative juice. 'I am imagining the music and presume it was Italian Opera, Verdi or Puccini.'

'Maybe, you can use your Napoleonic licence.'

'I can imagine you there, all willowy and billowy and all I can think is "are you not freezing in your nightie?" Ha ha.'

She left it at that.

Stories

They had sent e-mails, military texts, racy texts and she wanted more depth. Now, she felt, it was time for a creative writing exchange. Karl encouraged Ciara to give him something sexy. However Karl was still a mystery to her so whenever she thought of him it was not in the present. It was always distant; it was far away so she thought of Europe at the time of Napoleon, still undiscovered. She wanted though to lock her thoughts into the present. She opened her "images file" drew inspiration from his first image, his back image and what she would do if she were there with him, looking in the mirror. Maybe this would help him materialise as quickly as the condensation was disappearing from the mirror.

Ciara's Contribution

"He gazed at his reflection resplendent in the bathroom mirror. A light mist was clearing from the surface of the glass and the view became visible. Water was glistening over his large muscular frame and the recessed lighting of this rather expensive hotel room accentuated each undulation. To have reached one's destination was rather rewarding a deep breath was inhaled and blown out fogging up the mirror once again.

"He heard nothing of the intruder's entrance, she moved as silently as a cat; she was upon him in a flash. "How did you get here?" he asked but she did not reply. Instead she made as if to grasp something on the green glass shelf in front of him. However her rapid hand moved up and grabbed his hair and pulled his head back. He could only see her large tiger eyes under a huge Russian furred hat. She moved her mouth to his neck and kissed it gliding her lips down to his shoulders, teeth, tongue and he moaned. He pulled his hand over to her hat and dragged it from her head. Her long, dark hair fell out across his wet back, tickled and aroused.

"She continued to kiss him moving down his back. Her gloved hands lightly touched his arms and rapidly caressed the crevasses of his shoulders. They moved along his sides and to his front. He held her hat in his hand uncertain what his next move would be. Should he stand rigid and receive or should he take action? He grabbed her hands and removed her gloves, they were soft and silken but her ungloved hands were white, fine and trembling with intent.

"He turned around to her and stared deeply into her eyes, she looked away and leaned forward, and she kissed his torso and ran her tongue along his front. He struggled to remove her heavy winter coat still speckled with the snow of this cold day. She would not hold still, he was excited, frustrated and longed for more..."

She wasn't sure whether she was confident enough to be a temptress yet there was a contrary feeling spurring her on. The detached nature of their contact heightened a sense of zero consequence. All she thought was play and fun and creativity. She could be totally different to her real self, could this be the benefit of fantasy?

His response was different but gave her some insight into his thoughts and his inner world, well the inner world he wished to portray anyway. This was something really important to Ciara as she had only hazy ideas of what motivated him. Ambition was so two dimensional.

"She disappeared. She was but an apparition, merely a vision of his imagination, the actualisation of his desires. He wished she were real, hoped she would reappear, but she wouldn't, couldn't, shouldn't. He was far away in another land, dreaming of her and his dreams were impure.

"What could he do to make this dream real? What would convert this desire into reality? How could he cross over without losing himself? Without subsuming his whole being into another, one who was equal but stronger, she was in control as he could not control his desire.

"Should he call her? If he did would this fantasy evaporate? Would they become a boring couple who went shopping on Thursday evenings to avail of late night Supermarket offers? When mystique is dead what remains? All is open when a shopping trolley is wheeled before them exposing half price cans of beans.

"He would think on it," Karl sent.

Ciara's thoughts when she received this email were interesting! She had now her insight into Karl's world however shallow. He allowed her glimpse into his mind for the briefest moment. The question was, was he telling the truth? Maybe he was appearing vulnerable, frail even in an attempt to draw her in. Why was he submissive in fantasy and her dominant? Was it role play? Did he really think they would become a boring couple?

'You forgot the love letters they would be texting in their fifties x' she smiled as she sent it.

Her thoughts rolled on. "Is he trying to make me believe he is thinking of calling me but unsure what sort of response he would get after all he is seeking the perfect life and had not reached it yet? He seems unsure of when or how to proceed. However we have met, it was great so is a phone call not the logical progression from a meeting. The meeting was so perfect I almost think I imagined it. Was it real as he had said exactly what I had hoped?" Maybe she should get a lock of his hair to prove to, he was real as he was fading again from her reality back into fantasy. Her imagination was such a powerful force in her life though that she couldn't actually remember a few sprigs of blond brown hair peeking out from his open necked polo shirt, could she have dreamt it all? It was confusing.

'Yes we will be as we are, decades from now,' Karl said.

Was it a ruse his story, to keep her interested, keep her writing so he could keep being enthralled with himself? Make him feel desired, an object of affection.

She would think on it too. Did she want to text forever?

Napoleon KARL

Karl had got a taste for this type of creative writing, maybe he would not have veered towards the bodice-ripping genre if she were willing but he certainly seemed to be enjoying himself. It was he who came back with the next submission. Ciara had expected him to take a few weeks to think up something new but two days later here he was.

'Hey Ciara, I have thought up one on our mutual theme, Napoleon and Josephine. Do you want to hear it?'

'Yes I would love to, fire ahead!'

"It was Italy, I was on the assent and the Principalities were giving up easily, just as easily as the Dukedoms had. Just as they had ceded to Charles of France a few hundred years before and I used the same tactics, heavy bombardment on the first town and heavy booty from the next. The French coffers were bare and soldiers had not been paid in years, their uniforms were ragged as the aristocrats of old had not taken it upon themselves to look after them. I did not partake of the pillage I spent my time writing to you. Every day I wrote to you twice or three times. There were rumours of another object of your affections, my dear, my sweet Josephine, but I knew they were not true. I knew you were true.

"The spoils from the Planes of Northern Italy helped to replenish the French finances, they filled the galleries and museums and fine houses of the new elite. Italy was being denuded of her cultural heritage. The enormity of the costs involved in the Revolution could finally be paid for. This was good, but for me though all that mattered was you. What did it matter that I was youngest general if I didn't have you by my side?

"I called for you time and again and eventually you came. When my patience had run out, when my hope was gone, when my confidence had been beaten against the walls of Milan. You came even though you feared carriages, you came even though you almost died crossing the Alps. You came even though you didn't wish to leave France. You were my everything. You were tiny boned, you were brightly powdered you were lively and stately in your daring dresses. You were there to share my victory, host my banquets and flatter the Italians. You were a reflection of me and my success. If you had not come there would have been no point in victory." He sent this for dramatic effect.

'I know, I never see you these days' said Ciara trying to lighten the mood. How many times had she been doing some rudimentary task and turned to share this with Karl and he wasn't there? He was never there.

"You were mine." He concluded. 'Do you like it?'

'Very much, except that Josephine **was** having an affair.'

'Well I know that but you need tension to make a relationship passionate, as passionate as theirs' was.'

'Maybe' said Ciara. 'So have you any hunky friends you could introduce me to in order to make you, well passionate?' She thought of a great line from a song, boys only seem to appreciate things when they are jealous. "I would rather get with your best friend as he is so much fitter" but she didn't want to pass it on. She thought of the Lily Allen song and smiled.

'What have you got for me?' he asked a little later.

So maybe he had no handsome friends, or he didn't think sharing was caring. Pity.

'I think I need a day or two of contemplation time.'

'I know how quick you can be when you want something,' said Karl. Was he trying to imply that she was under-inspired?

Josephine - Ciara

Ciara's submission also had drama but there was a strong undercurrent of loss. It was set in the cold. How could one feel loss if the dream guy had never been possessed, or really had never been yours? It was a mystery to Ciara.

'Check your e-mail,' she said.

"Moscow was burning, how could Muscovites burn their own city? Burn everything they owned just to prevent you taking it. What a waste, what a wasteland. It made no sense to you, Napoleon. It was mid-autumn and a chill was forming in the air. All had been a success, a glorious success until then, well apart from Egypt, maybe we shouldn't mention Egypt.

"Europe was at your feet, everything had fallen to the might of your superior forces. From the Northern Lights of Scandinavia to the Southern suns of Iberia and the Leg of Italy were now in your dominion. All that remained was Britain which was essentially a floating army and

Russia a big sleeping dog. Or was it a bear, anyway it should be left to lie.

"You were the strategist and I was expelled from your life, but I knew we were not over, would never be over. Yes you wanted an heir, but you wanted me more, more now than ever before as fortunes were turning. Your new wife had performed her duties and now you were restless, keen to move forward and with me the movement and direction you were famed for, was always forward. I am a woman who changes her destiny, a woman who has survived nay cheated death on many occasions. I could live without you and content myself with my fabulous shoe collection, my young admirers, my expansive property portfolio and did I mention the scarves? By and by I would be fine. Yes I would miss you and do miss you, off across the continent in a very cold inhospitable place, but then you wrote. You needed me again and I had power once more in this crazy Empire of France. Not that I needed you to need me, but it was nice to know you thought of me.

"I was the one you wrote to not your wife, it was I you called upon to come to you. I had been put away and disregarded like a dirty pair of silk stockings in your mind. Yet then I was rejuvenated in your eyes, the mythical phoenix rising from the ashes of your defeat to be desired once more. The personification of your desire lived and breathed and would cross the tundra for you. I would lose a fur or two to allow the carriage to get to you sooner. The trials I suffered! What would I find? I would see an amassed carcass of an army which represented the walking dead. It would be late November by the time

I would arrive and by then, your men would be waist deep in snow, freezing temperatures, with their boots wearing thin allowing the cold to get in. Clothing designed for France would not suffice for a long hard Russian winter.

"Did I go? Or did I only imagine I was there, with you, feeling the cold, sharing the hardship, living the defeat."

'What do you think?' she asked.

She had ignored all historical facts everything she knew of their interaction, Josephine and Napoleon was by and large forgotten as she wished to display her independence. Her lack of need for Karl, all that she desired or wished for was him to miss her. Maybe Russia represented Norway to her, the far off unknown land where Karl seemed to reside, frozen and distant.

'Did that really happen?' asked Karl.

'I haven't a breeze, this is historical fantasy not real life history!!'

Karl's Northern Advances of Napoleon

'Ok Ciara, this may not be historically accurate either and I will defer to your superior knowledge in these matters. However this is where I would like to see us.' He was also canon balling the history books apparently but in a more positive light.

"It was getting on for the Summer solstice and the days were bright, everyone wore their lightest clothes and we had installed one of our relatives in the Kingdom of Sweden. It was a key strategic site on the Baltic Sea controlling trade into and out of Russia. My aim was to cut off the British, outmanoeuvre them and gain key ports in order to take over the rest of Europe.

"You came with me, North in a large cushioned carriage which provided both luxury and privacy. It was the first time since Italy that we had travelled together and I wanted to show you the World, My World. We left Paris and took the road North through Belgium, onto Holland and over into Denmark. We were entertained by all our subjects, welcomed as the heroes we were. All were dazzled by your wit, by your charm, your beauty and your dresses. Nothing had been worn so low since the seventeenth century. We were a triumph.

"Then we crossed the Seas to Sweden, you had not been on a boat since leaving Martinique. It had not been a pleasant experience then and you were not looking forward to this crossing now. It was rough but luckily brief. You showed no fear even though the mast nearly split in two. I could see worry and wild anxiety in your eyes, but you remained firm, resolute in your strength, determined to appear brave. To ensure all our subjects knew their Emperor and Empress were superior, sturdier and nobler in self than all others you were strong.

"When we landed in Sweden I felt at home even though the height of the people dwarfed us, but it is always the same the brightest star is small, perfect and surrounded by large star fragments to protect the white light. We travelled up from Malmo, a few days it took to get to the Capital. Then into the Imperial Palace to see our cousin, we were creating a new Imperial network. No more Valois, Bourbon, Stuarts and Hapsburgs, it would be Bonaparte all the way. Every nation would have a Bonaparte leader be it regal, imperial or civic. It would not matter the form only the structure.

"You encouraged me in my ambitions, you were behind me and you were at my side supporting me then ahead, always leading me on. Now we were entering the beautiful palace of Stockholm and there was a heightened sense of excitement. It was our first time and maybe our last time to this fair city of the North. Wonderful! Daylight Conquests, no robbery needed." He sent.

'Is it finished? It that it then?' said Ciara. There was no warmth between them.

'My thoughts got cold.'

'Glad I inspire you, great man of the North!!'

'Will you help me?'

'I thought this was your fantasy?' This was his first show of weakness, had he just got bored or was it that Ciara spent a lot longer on her scribbles than Karl did. 'I will see if I get some free time over lunch, I'm busy today.'

'Looking forward to it, have a good lunch.'

Ciara's Secret

Ciara went flat hunting. Or rather one day she logged onto a property site, not that she was particularly looking to change anything but she wanted to see what was out there. So if she did at some point wish to change some aspect of her life she would know what to aim for. She looked at the apartment's bracket and in central locations. How nice would it be to be able to walk to work? She looked and could not believe the prices, they were so affordable. The prices had dropped so much that they were within her reach. It was amazing. For a reasonably sized two bedroom apartment in the city centre the asking price was less than what her house was worth, theoretically. She discovered this when she keyed in her street instead of where she wanted to buy and saw a house for sale. She wondered which number it was, who the owners were and if they knew her. "Ciara don't get distracted." Also this made life nice and easy for her though as she had a ready comparable.

This meant that if she wanted to, she could move in, she was not stuck with her commuter lifestyle until the day she died as she had long-times thought. Then something caught her eye, it was an attic flat, or rather a top floor apartment as the building was modern. It was expensive in relation to everything else. It had great big windows south facing and an oblique view of some interesting Dublin buildings. She looked at it, then looked at the location on the map attached she looked at the living room again then, then the bedrooms. It was expensive. Finally she looked at pictures of the street. The street was more of a lane, it was cute and it was pedestrian with lots of cafes and impractical shops. This was the one but it was expensive. She e-mailed the agent to see if she could get a lunch time viewing. Maybe she was being hasty.

No one batted an eyelid when Ciara sneakily hauled her runners from under her desk 'I'm off power walking' she lied. She felt though that everyone was watching her, she felt guilty lying. 'See you all later' she added and remembered to shut down her computer. No one looked up. They didn't care or maybe notice. She was expecting everyone to ask her where she was going, but they didn't. Ciara felt like a loner now, power walking on her own, going to sandwich shops alone even sometimes going to cafes alone. This could have been because there were less and less people to go with these days.

She strode out of the office area with its shiny green glass and underutilised employees working on tasks she didn't understand and into the long straight street linking this new area to the main City. The journey was long nearly half an hour and she was late for the auctioneer. She apologised profusely. 'I'm really sorry; I thought it was much closer.'

He looked relieved that she had turned up at all. He brought her through some smart metal gates off   the lane with its jewellery shops, antique fairs and pretty cafes. She felt at home.

'This is one of the newest streets in Dublin in the oldest area' the auctioneer informed her. 'Just down there is a watchtower from Norman Dublin.'

Ciara was impressed and couldn't help the 'wow' which left her lips. There even was a Charles II connection as the oldest theatre in the City was located here. 'I'm not so hot on Norman history but I love this theatre,' she said. She had a thing for Charles II, she wasn't sure why but he was very sexy.

The auctioneer unlocked a smart high chrome set of gates. 'So as we climb up these steps on the left is the Spa and courtyard,' he continued.

'Lovely, are there res rates?'

He looked quizzically at Ciara and then caught her line of thinking. 'You mean discounts for the occupiers, maybe. You would have to check it out.'

'I will' she said. They climbed another stair's and she thought she would get fit living here. They travelled through two further doors and Ciara felt a definite prison sensation.

'Is there a high crime rate around here? She asked.'

'No' he said, 'but it's good to be safe, to be sure.' Maybe he was attempting to joke. They walked through the third security door then through a fire door and a lift faced them.

They whizzed up to the top floor in the very fast lift, and then entered a corridor with a large window. The window had a wonderful view it was facing east and she could almost see her office block. That may not be a good thing. The entire low-rise City spread out at her feet. The auctioneer brought her out to the flat roof on the right which was shared with the apartment next door. It had views to the west and they were lovely also. She was sold before she even opened the front door. They went back inside and down a short hall with two entrance doors hers was the one on the right. He opened the door to a lovely wide hall and it felt welcoming. To the left was one bedroom and to the right a large bathroom with a big bath. Again on the right was the main bedroom facing north with interesting views of Georgian Dublin, a view from every aspect, Ciara was falling in love. Then, straight ahead was the last door into the large living room cum kitchen cum dining room come where she would spend the rest of her life. The windows were as large as advertised on line and the light was streaming in, even on this dark overcast day the room was extremely bright. She was doubly sold. The condition of the apartment was poor but Ciara was no perfectionist.

'I love it' escaped her lips before she could think.

The auctioneer smiled, he knew that look and the inability to restrain words he had seen it before. So it would just be a matter of time before she would be able to do the deal.

'It is early days' Ciara attempted to qualify her previous remark. 'I have a house to sell.'

'I know, but in this market there is really no rush,' he explained.

She smiled, relieved, this was going to be hers. This is where she would live her life. It was love at first sight.

They stepped out onto the small balcony and looked down the street over the roof tops and could see College Green. 'It is a very narrow balcony' he said.

'More like an elevated smoking platform' said Ciara as she looked down six stories to a lane below. She felt a little woozy staring down at the ground so to steady herself she took hold of the balcony railings and her sleeve pulled itself up. Her watch was exposed She looked at the time realised she had spent far longer than she had intended she needed to get back to work. 'Just give me some time, I really like it' was her parting remark.

They shook hands and she was gone hailing a taxi in expectation of getting an update on the news events from the informative driver who was listening to a popular day-time-opinionated radio show. He began conversation but she wasn't engaging.

'Sugar why is this flat the only one I love, maybe I should start looking about!' the taxi driver stopped his chatter as he realised Ciara was not answering him but was thinking out loud. 'It is perfect I love it more than Karl, no I don't love Karl but it is the only example I have at the moment. Yes I finally have perspective, I don't love Karl but I do love this apartment. Wow my life is clear finally.'

They drove on and Ciara spoke all of her thoughts aloud to the quiet amusement of the taxi driver. It was fairly likely he had heard people talk to themselves before but maybe not for the entire journey.

'I will look around, research and see what else was there on the property market. This is the first property I have ever viewed on my own. Maybe I am getting over excited. Maybe it is too soon am I ready? I have not even decided that I want to sell my house. I was just bored and browsing the internet. Do I want to move? I will be far away from my Mum and Dad, that maybe a good thing I would be a little more independent. I will look around in a while. It was all happening too quickly!'

Fantasies

They spent a considerable amount of time writing fantasies to each other. They were stories and more stories and were a continuation in some respects however the difference was a lack of reality and a wishful overtone. They were some racy texts but the aim was freedom. Whilst Ciara had a strong sense of imagination she wasn't used to or comfortable exploring her physical self, she preferred fantasies which lots of art, architecture and history where the costumes most definitely stayed on. She did not send him her driving fantasy it was very personal and a whimsical stream of conscious thoughts. She thought back to their meeting in Temple Bar and it seemed more like a dream than a fact, she wondered had she imagined it as the strong contained Karl would never expose himself so much as to say "you are the one for me." Then before, him embracing her in the snow with the wind whirling around them, that was beautiful. There were no taxis and as if summoned up by magic one appeared and he held the door open for her, that was like a fantasy and then he hopped in. Reality seemed to jar when a large hand was placed on her knee, no wonder she was imagining wagons of old. It was a very dangerous journey home and thankfully the driver was from Europe where they get snow and was very confident about the driving conditions.

Show-house

Karl e-mailed her one day and said 'wow, Ciara, I was just at my dream development and I thought of you.'

'Well of course you would Karl. Am I not the gal of your dreams? Hee hee.'

'Oh, but of course you are. So I had a little fantasy there.' He was lying, definitely lying.

'Did you now' she replied.

'Would you like me to share it with you?'

'If you really want to' she said teasingly. Karl wanted to lead the way as always, Ciara was curious to hear what he had to say but also apprehensive if he went too far.

'Your enthusiasm is overwhelming but I will go on.'

'No please do, I am only messing, I would love to hear your thoughts on me.'

'So I was on-site completing a beautiful housing and office complex in a really cool part of the City. I was inspecting the job in order to sign off on the work. Unusually this luxury development didn't get completed due to the down-turn and NAMA (national asset management agency). Apparently you're nothing if you are not in NAMA these days, a small fry in developer terms! Sorry I had to get that in Ciara, but some of these developers are, well they are individuals!!

'We took over the site a few months ago when the developer got some outside, read Russian funding and is now back on track.' He presses send.

'Very romantic introduction there Karl, I hope this gets better.'

'Thanks for your vote of confidence and yes it does get better, a lot better!'

'I have every confidence in your writing skills,' she said.

'The house is low rise which if Dublin architects are famous for anything, it would be this. The exterior walls are stone facing. The windows are large to allow the usually cloud covered sun the maximum chance of transferring light into the house. See I am getting your light and metrological features in. I know this bit is a little boring but I am trying to set the scene!'

'Thank you, you are very considerate' she replied. "Get on with it," she thought.

'They, the windows, are also triple-glazed as we have twice as much damp as the rest of the world. The front lawn has been manicured excessively into a Disney type Fantasyland. So now I am getting into character...

"He walks into the kitchen to get a glass of water from the American style fridge. It's not an ice-breaker but an ice-maker!

"She is perched on the counter top with impossibly long hair and arched dark eyebrows. She smiles demurely. He sighs intently, "would you like some water?" he enquires. "It's all I can offer."

"She smiles again to assent and to indicate that is not ALL he has to offer. He pours the water and forgoes the ice, it is a bit cold atmospherically. He takes her hand and begins to lead her about the lower level of the house. She is remarkably quiet, yep this is Fantasyland. They sip their lightly carbonated water as if it is vintage champagne which is meant to be savoured. She has worn her alluring clothing for the tall Napoleon. Comprising high heels with swirly patterned tights a short dress. Her long hair and short dress are inversely proportioned to accentuate the narrowness of her ankles and length of her legs. 'Apparently the Greeks judged beauty by the turn of the ankle but with long flowing gowns there may not have been much else to go by. I remember you are fascinated by the Greeks.' Her hosiery is opaque and swirls have a dappled affect when she moves. Her movements are light, almost gliding, ethereal. He notices the heels of her shoes are not spindles so he won't have to worry about marking the perfect wooden floors. They are constructed of Perspex and have a playing card motif engraved on them. The club symbol is the most prominent feature on the left heel and the diamond on the right. "Game on" the youthful architect thinks to himself.

"He explains the rational for each design feature in the house and she listens attentively, nodding and smiling to ensure he knows he has her complete attention. Whilst she is there she is also elusive, there is fragility to her or maybe a sense of impermanence. She admires the fittings as well as the features, the low sofas in muted colours, the dining table and chairs, the media unit with sliding doors which exposes and then conceals the TV and other gadgets.

"He drinks it in, someone admiring and praising his work without a hint of scepticism or irony, with no agenda except to be there with him, for him. He does not want to move too quickly or the moment will pass. He takes her to the cantilever staircase with steps floating out from the wall, suspension hidden behind panelling. The handrail is hanging from the ceiling, firm but malleable. She takes the lead. He watches how her garment is belted to fit snugly to her lean frame. She walks slowly, gradually moving away from him releasing the grip of his hand. She mounts each step with a gentle sashay. Her feet do not appear to touch the stairs. 'This does sound like a bit of meta-physical prose, maybe we need to insert a bit of Shakespeare and recite "my mistress eyes are nothing like the sun!"' he pressed send as the e-mail was getting quite long.

"Show off" she thinks, but sent, 'I always listen to you and you seem good at listening to me too. I do love the Greeks.'

'Thank you Ciara.' He continued..."She is at the top of the stairs and surveys the affect of the large domed skylight. The sun is streaking in through a weak and watery sky. It is autumn and the sun has passed the verticality of high summer. "Find me" she says and darts off. The sun emerges from a cloud and he is a bit dazzled for a moment, which is enough to give her a head start.

"He goes to the master bedroom first and there is no sign of her, the designer bed is so low that even she couldn't hide beneath it. He crosses the room, feet sinking into the deep pile Donegal woven carpet; it feels warm and lush beneath his kid leather shoes. To the en-suite bathroom he searches, not there either. Maybe he should check the wardrobe but why would she be there? On to the next room he trots excitement and frustration coursing through him in equal measure, one room then the next and the next. Finally he goes to the family bathroom hoping to see her in the Jacuzzi or running the water for a long hot bath they can both share. Alas no, still not there.

"His phone rings "drat" 'yes he really is that polite!' "I'm viewing the show-house with a prospective client. May I call you back momentarily?" On with the search, there is still the hot press. This was one element which he felt was superfluous to requirements, but which the developer –wherever she was gone, was determined to retain. On opening the door he spies lots of fluffy towels and expensive chi-chi lavender sachets to fragrance the space and to hide the damp smell. No not there either. Back to the master bedroom and into the walk in wardrobe. Well this was actually a walk in and get lost and need GPS to find one's way out. There are a few choice charcoal suits for him and impracticable flouncy frocks with teetering heels for her. All are aspirational brands with the logos sewn into well cut high street garments. God bless interior designers! The light is movement activated and switches on as he opens the door. "Its bit dark in here" she states profoundly.

"Energy saving," he sagely states, "it's a very green house."

"Don't throw stones then," she quips.

"So" he smiles, it is definitely her, his elusive tauntress as her jokes are always terrible. She is real again, he is reaching out... His phone rings in real life, double drat! He wouldn't mind but things had not even been interesting up until this point. "Hello" it is his boss speaking. "I am just about to go out to a viewing of a show house with a prospective client. May I call you back in due course?"

"I think you have moved into that show house. Would people not contact the auctioneer?" the boss asks in his fantasy.

'It's for another location but the details of their specification seem similar to the show house.' "That fantasy has been too frustrating to let go. Can I get back in the zone? Rats." Karl sends this part of his submission with a small note, 'I am trying to infuse a bit of reality into the fantasy just to show how dedicated I am.'

'Does this mean you are always chasing the dream Karl? She asked.

'I will catch you Ciara, don't worry. You are very real to me and sure I talk to you more than I do my boss.'

'Oh really,' even though she does not want to she believes what Karl is saying. It is true they do communicate a lot.

'Your turn, what can you give me? Karl said.

She thought about this and if Karl were to live with her it would be in a penthouse not in a house in the suburbs. Maybe he was ever so slightly more grounded than her as in his house was touching the ground where as her fantasy was going to be fantastic, so it was not really going to be a poky attic and it would have to be romantic. It would have to have a massive balcony where she would make him breakfast after his two hours out rowing, he would be starving with a voracious appetite for more than just eggs Benedict. What would happen, would it make for interesting lunch hours, or just the end of the road of wishful thinking. "Is that just too much reality for a rainy Wednesday?" she thought. "As once you get whatever it is you were longing for it is not unattainable anymore. Yes that may be obvious but it has deep resonance for the psyche. Can't imagine why though, there is always something else to gain, knowledge, attention, kindness, the care and maybe the affection of the object one desires'."

'Ok, are you stalling on your fantasy?'

'We are living in a penthouse with a wrap-around balcony I am cooking eggs Benedict and you have just got in the door from rowing. You are starving. It is raining, the end.'

'Ah Ciara, there is no build up, no sense of drama or conquest. If I were your teacher I would mark "must try harder" on your copy book.'

Fair enough, it had not exactly been the most evocative piece she had ever written but the one she had drafted out a few weeks ago was a bit out there.

"The rain is dashing the windows and the wind is howling on the flat roof, it is bouncing and hopping and jumping around. I have the coffee brewed and am sitting by the window reading. I feel a drip of water and look up hoping that the roof isn't leaking. I am thinking to myself "these Celtic-tiger-cowboy-builders have a lot to answer for." There is no leak, so I return to my book and I feel it again a cold drip of water down my back and I shiver. Maybe the non-triple glazed windows are letting in the buckets of rain which are falling out of the heavens. I hear a little (but deep) giggle. I look around and you are wetting me with your wringing wet hair. You begin to shake your thick blond mop of wholly saturated hair into my lovely fresh coffee.

"'Ah, Karl, your eggs will be burnt,' I say." She sent her submission.

'You would not be saying the eggs are burnt, you would say "AH JASUS KARL, YOURE WETTIN' ME" or maybe I would draw you into a passionate embrace and ...'

'And I would spill a hot cup of coffee on you by accident.'

'No I was thinking I would drag you into the shower and you could clean me up,' said Karl.

'Go on..'

'I thought this was your story.'

'I thought you didn't like my story Karl!'

'I like this one better,' he said. "I was freezing and filthy, the water had been icy cold and no matter how fast I paddled my fingers were still frozen. My knees were red raw and I was dreaming of a hot cup of coffee. I crept into the apartment as silent as a mouse. I knew you were reading your favourite book, 'Josephine and her 5000 scarves,' there were even pictures in it. I saw your lips move when you were thinking and your eyes flicker with amusement. You were engrossed. I tip toed up behind you and I dripped a rain drop from my hair onto your book. Then I bent my knees as quickly as I could so you would not see me. You looked up, I smiled trying not to laugh. Then you settled yourself down again and I stood up once more inhaled the coffee wafting around and shook my whole self over you. I drenched you and you were annoyed but amused."

'What do you think?' Karl asked.

'Yes you are right I hadn't started the eggs. Ha!!'

'Meanie!!'

'Yes I liked it, it was real somehow. Not fantasy like your show house. In the show house you are trying to make things real by having your boss ring you. And whilst that is interesting I don't know whether there should be a conversation.' Ciara liked this fantasy/real life story and was going to develop it. However Karl's next text was a bit out there.

'Ciara, can you do me one of you're really whacky ones?' he asked. 'I think I am a bit more reality based than you.'

'Ahem! Is that a Karl-like compliment?'

'Probably, but I know you have it in you. Like who else would jump from Helen of Troy to a horse outside in two texts??' so maybe Karl did like a bit of quirkiness. 'That was a compliment, just in case you didn't notice it.'

She smiled and she thought. Karl wanted a bit of Ciara's individuality or maybe something out there. So far out there that it could be an island off the coast of East Africa. Hopefully Anna wouldn't read this piece of prose, or she would be fired straight away. It was fair to say that this was not on the Napoleonic theme or the property theme as used by Karl. However if Napoleon had set his sights on India and failed maybe he would have chosen this spice island of delight. He could have chosen it if he had been aware of it.

An exotic adventure or a dream

'I'm a bit afraid to send this one Karl.' It was a few days later and she had been composing on the bus, at home and again at work. It was a big one, very different. She really didn't know how he would take it.

'Don't worry Ciara.' He was trying to reassure her and possibly was slightly impatient after three days of a wait.

'Oh but I do.' She really shouldn't be sending this he would never speak to her again. What would she do with all the extra skin on her thumbs and no one to text to? Her typing was getting really fast.

'May I be the judge of your piece, please?'

'Just to let you know,' a short introduction was necessary. She wanted to put things in a small bit of context, 'this tale was inspired by the scarves and Georgian doors photograph which I sent. It was my first image and you didn't reply.'

'I don't think I got it, maybe you could send the image again.'

'I was in Mayfair and the streets were full of Arabs, so I automatically thought East Africa. Well more specifically Zanzibar as this was formally part of Oman.'

'Yes a logical thought process, not!'

'Well Napoleon was in Arabia, mostly Egypt so I am sticking to the script.'

'Ciara you are always original' said Karl, 'this should be interesting.'

'You asked for interesting so here goes,

"He is wandering through the Zanzibarian jungle in his lilac thobe. He arrives in Stone Town rather abruptly and happens upon the old slave markets, which bring a tear to his eyes. The cruelty, the noises and the smells still resonate deep within all his senses. They are an engrained memory which has become part of his psyche. He moves on rapidly and disdainfully, glad that this brutal era is long since passed. He strolls through the town and finds the English house a bastion of Colonialism and quickens his pace. Then rather suddenly he sees Dr Livingstone's house and is drawn in by an almost primal compulsion.

"He enters and climbs the stairs slowly, as this is only way in. The steps are dilapidated and begin to crumble gently beneath his feet. The stairs narrow as he ascends and then finally he reaches the top. A room opens out and has four large walls each with a beautiful Omani window. There is no glass but rather elegant ironmongery.

"He has a Stanley moment 'Dr Livingstone I presume' and almost expects to see the great explorer himself. This was the man who was impervious to malaria and who discovered the source of the Nile. (This maybe a bit too lecturing sorry)" she sends to assess the effect.

'No, I am enjoying, please continue,' said Karl.

"Then he looks over to the corner of the room and notices the shape of a woman in full Hijab. She is crouching down attending to some detail. There is an object in the corner of the room, which is disordered in some way or for some reason. It seems to be only a tiny speck of dust but it is lilac exactly the same shade as his own Thobe.

"He walks over slowly to ascertain why this minute speck is actually lilac, could it be angel dust? The veiled woman turns and he sees for the first time her large pale green, kohl lined eyes. This is the only part of her form, which is un-masked, he can see her eyes and is enthralled. The gown is so long that he cannot even discern the shape of her ankle to ascertain whether she is weighty. The turn of the ankle is the only means to tell beauty when a woman is veiled and the Greeks judged beauty by this measure." 'See I am following your lead!' She sent as she wanted him to think she listened.

'Yes very interesting, I am smelling the spices and feeling the heat and tropical rain,' Karl said I'm liking this tale so far, what else have you got?'

"She looks at him and her eyes widen a fraction into what he believes is a light smile. He is transfixed by the subtle change of expression. The dilation of the pupils and the briefest flutter of the eyelashes have him enthralled. She rises from her knees and even through her abaya he can tell she has a voluptuous and sensual form. Well of course she would, she is an Arabic lady after all. What is she doing in Stonetown, Zanzibar? Where is her husband? Her hands are gloved in the smoothest, sheerest, blackest fabric and as he stares at them. He cannot detect the bump of a ring on her wedding finger. There is a chance, is there a chance, he muses confusing himself.

"It seems that time is moving both extremely slowly yet she seems to be propelled forward at a dizzying accelerating speed. She is within a-hairs reach now. His breath is on her facial veil. He can see his breath move like a wind over the sands of the Sahara. The material on her veil is very finely woven and so sheer it is almost translucent. It is the most erotic experience he has ever known. She again flutters her long, curled and incredibly black eye lashes at him and he feels his knees weaken. Should he reach out and touch the tip of her finger. However it is haram as he is not in his hareem. What to do Yanni, what to do!

"It is frustrating but she is so pure she is irresistible. He leans forward but then recoils in terror. He changes his tact and brings his hand very slowly towards his face. He reaches out with his index finger to touch the very tip of her nose.

"He feels something delving and hears the splash of water. His senses are awoken to a vivid and exciting sight. He is in his own Roman style bath, in his very own hareem, with his very own wives flanking him front back and sides. Wow it is good to be home. They are unveiled and their brilliance is resplendent. Their long luscious hair billows in the warm steam and is offset by the rich Arabic mosaics which frame each wife in her own individual likeness. Ah what a frustrating dream, thank goodness he moved to Manama, manna from Heaven. And yet, the dream felt real."

'You like?' she typed just after she had sent the piece.

'Yes I do very much. It is a bit confusing, where do you fit in?' he replied in a few minutes.

'Can you not tell?' She texted back hoping his imagination will fill in the gaps.

'Yep Ciara you are out there!'

'Like the horse outside?'

'Maybe, probably but it least it is not as cold as Norway.'

'Am I out there on my own?' She enquired.

'No, of course not I'm right there with you,' came back in a flash. That was heartening even if a bit disingenuous, did he even care where Zanzibar was?

A few moments later he said 'Ciara did you make all that up yourself?'

'I did' so maybe he did like it as he was questioning its authenticity.

'Did you spend ages composing it?'

'Not much longer than yours took. It just flowed,' she was laughing, that was a big black fib. She had written a small bit on the bus in the rain one day and had been tweaking it for the last two. It had taken her a good twenty minutes then when she got into work she typed it up as quickly as she could in order to look busy but also to keep the flow of the heat and the drying lemongrass on the sides of the dusty roads. She left out lots of it as she thought even Karl would think it boring but she had needed pages and pages of details to get the feel right in her head.

'Unfortunately I don't think so fluidly but I type a bit quicker than you so I will have to work on this reply on the way home. It is a challenge but as you have seen I always rise to a challenge!!'

'Looking forward to your story' she said.

'I'm looking forward to writing it,' said Karl.

His Response

So the next day true to his word Karl e-mailed over his version of the hot and exotic, he may have done a bit of research as he seemed to know a bit more about it than the day before.

"How had I got to this place? I had never been to Africa before never mind the exotic island of Zanzibar, the former colony of the Sultanate of Oman (was he googling on work time?) Yet I felt that I belonged. I was fascinated with the Sultans Palace and the size of my harem. Whilst wishing to have a large horde of beauties for my personal entertainment it astonished and unnerved me. I feared my own virility would be tested, but never 'texted' too much. What would be required of me? Primary research could be interesting though, in fact it was necessary. Once I paced myself I could, in time thoroughly know my harem.

"I was apprehensive, yes, yet I was excited, very excited. It was a challenge to become the new Sultan, but I belonged here, this was the destination for which I had spent my life until this moment, in preparation for. Hey a King has to perform and so forth. I needed to produce heirs. And so I entered my harem, the bounty of beauty would all be for my benefit. I felt greedy with lust and desire and so I paused to regain my composure. The building has straw roofing and a wattle wall. There were brightly woven motifs binding parts of the outer wall together. The air was hot and filled with spices, cloves mostly, pungent with restorative powers. I dallied no longer and crossed the threshold. It was dark inside, drat! I had hoped all would be open for me, immediately but maybe good things are worth waiting for.

"Yes, dark was good, I would have to rely on my wits until my eyes caught up, sound and touch would compensate for the momentarily failing sight. I had to await sight readjustment, I could not wait I was impatient. I hastened forwards and fell on a nubile figure, warm and perfumed. Her skin was smooth as silk, woops that was a scarf. Was there something beneath it? It was just a carving. My eyes were adjusting, finally. I could see the room now and there was no lighting. The central area was clear and empty with the perimeter encircled by cushions, large, rectangular hand woven cushions. There were wall hangings in hessian, brightly coloured, covering the wattle, handing from the sparsely beamed ceiling. No women, ah, maybe I should clap my hands or say "open" no not sesame, maybe I should say "come here cloves" would I end up with a nubile with cloven feet? Allah forbid! 'Can you say Allah Forbid?' "Without the help of Allah," 'maybe –I digress.'

"Clap, clap – first began the sound of percussions, the loud shrill voices with distinctive clicking of tongues. I was a bit scared, they sounded quite frightening. However I was Sultan, the King of my Sultanate so I should not be scared merely seeking my sultana. I was and had been the heir presumptive the first of my late fathers' 52 sons – 40 of which I slayed by secretive means. The other 11 I only castrated so there would be no competition. My coronation was but yesterday" 'am I beginning to sound regal Ciara?'

'Yes Karl very regal!!!'

"Not yet a day to inhabit my lofty status and this is now why I am reluctant. Maybe it is the masculine pressures which cloud the mind. They come, my concubines, I am ready. I am ready now, I will now choose, now ready to choose.

"Two hundred women and girls walk in front of me, of all ethnicities and nationalities, enslaved from every corner of the known world. Wow where do I start. Supposedly begin at the beginning and then there is you. 'You are about 130th but I cannot be exactly sure' as I commenced my gaze with slow pleasing glances. My eyes then quickened as I wished to get through this line of lovelies. By number 90 they begin to look similar, all alluring, desirable and luscious and one would be as wonderful as the next. But then I see you and I differentiate lust from desire."

'What do you think?' he asked.

'Good research' said Ciara. 'You have really got a feel for the place so to speak. Did you enjoy writing it?'

'Yes it was fun, it took ages though, to get into the colouring of the piece. Then though it is funny it just sort of writes itself.'

'I know the feeling that happens' me if I am doing something I enjoy.'

'Well enjoy the day and we can share fantasies another time.'

'Sounds good, bye Karl.' He had tried and that really pleased Ciara and things were going so well on line or on ether.

Office
He sent a quick piece to Ciara over lunch.

'This will help keep you company on your power walk.'

'I won't have a free hand to read the piece' she pinged as she hoofed, un-cloven on her walking shoes.

He sent it anyway and she took a-quick-breather-five minutes into her stride to read the text.

"He is in his office and has a complicated project to finish. He looks at his screen then she is sitting on his desk top and ruffling his plans. Everything is done on desktops these days and palm tops are even closer to hand. She is there she hurriedly moves closer, onto him and unbuttons his trousers. He looks up she smiles and they are away in his mind it is as easy as this. Quick, abandonments and onto the next building! Not very creative but maybe that's the point!'

'Is this what will brighten your day? Better than foosball at the offie?' maybe she shouldn't have objectivised herself by introducing a harem theme, drat!

Was he trying to say that he didn't want children with her? She wasn't sure, creative probably referred to the lack of drama and build up to the piece. Maybe he was merely attempting to compare technology to body parts in an attempt to get frisky without her getting offended and blanking him.

'You would always be better than foosball at the offie,' Karl replied.

'Your compliments are excessive!!'

Banks, Mortgages and Grown-up Stuff
OR No financial strings attached?

Ciara was gazing out the office window, thinking, there was no seagull today but she remembered the moment of freedom. That moment when she had locked eyes and her ties, cares and worries had fluttered out through the thick green glass caught for an instant under the feathers of the bird and then floated away. She wanted freedom in reality, not just a fleeting feeling. The only way to achieve this was to change her life and leave her job. As usual Ciara's thoughts began in the middle then flapped forwards then backwards in eccentric circles. Her job was an emotional drain. She hated it. The only thing which was good was her friends; her friends were more than work colleagues.

That light filled apartment would make her happy, make her feel less tied to the past. The idea of living there would be heaven. It would be certainly closer to heaven all those floors up and she wistfully hummed that old Fred and Ginger song. How could she actualise this fantasy, change it into reality? Was the flat a Karl substitute or a representation of their future life together? She, they had already had a fantasy there, why could she not live reality instead.

The first step would be to get a mortgage arranged then after this she could leave her job. She would be refused a loan if she did things the other way around. Then she may well be financially sound, viable and afloat, adrift more likely. She would be floating on a lightly suspended platform way above the Dublin streets. This could well be her seagull moment. She would be a good loan candidate after seven years of service. Also on leaving work she would be rewarded with a strong severance package, wouldn't she? Maybe in the new apartment she could rent out a room that would surely help with the bills.

The thoughts occupied her all day and in the evening also. She sat in her kitchen looking at the mug of coffee and stared. She couldn't reach out and pick up the mug, why? Maybe it was fear of change which paralysed her. What if she couldn't handle the changes? What if she couldn't sell her house? What if the apartment block collapsed and there was no insurance? These were merely fears; resistance to change and her mother constantly noted 'change is the only constant.' If only there were some small changes in her life, then she would feel less adrift and more purposeful. She had been drifting for five years well treading water anyway and Karl was rowing past her with all of his changes and advancements, she needed to decide a direction.

The most important change was leaving her job, it paralysed her with boredom. Obviously it was not sensible to leave a permanent job in these financial times but if she could see no way out she would not be able to get up in the mornings. It was a huge struggle facing the cold mornings, the long bus journey and the grey grimness of each day. This paralysis inhabited her body, she felt like a victim of a car crash and she could not move. Every limb and ligament would resist getting out of bed and could only be coaxed by a really nice coffee at the start and even sometimes at the end of her journey.

If she did get a redundancy package maybe she could pay off the old mortgage with massive negative equity and get a tiny new one. "Maybe I should volunteer for redundancy; it always sounds better to offer rather than be pushed. Best check the figures first though!" Caution was the name of the game after her large financial mishap which was the result of her last property deal. She was paralysed once more, redundancy or seek new mortgage, which was the right step to take? Realistically any redundancy would be minimal as she was one of the few remaining workers in the company, chances all the best severance packages had already been give out.

"Work time equals surf time, things are so quiet." She decided to get motivated and stop dreaming, so much. So the next morning her task would be to look up the banks and mortgage terms. It was interesting that this was supposed to be work but all Ciara could think about was how to finish up her job. In many respects she was happy that she had not been fired, not yet anyway as if she left what would she do? The work situation in Dublin was likened to the depression in the 1930s she may not ever work again. Relief! She could watch all the Fred and Ginger films again and again and have them word perfect, maybe she would even set up that reality TV show to recruit the new Noughties (or the pre-teens, the two thousand's as the beginning of this decade was being known as) Fred and Ginger. The participants would dance classical jazz routines and half way through the performance the screen would be cut and Fred and Ginger would be dancing to the same song. The reality couple would try to follow their steps, syncopation and all. Now that was just dreaming.

Ciara wondered whether she wanted to be distracted just a little bit, without totally unsettling in her life? Usually that distraction was someone, his name was Karl. Karl means to guard as Ciara had found out in old Norse or at least one of the Viking languages. It was easy to complain to herself about being unfulfilled but it was harder to do something about it. Was this the extent of the relationship she sought and actually wanted? A distraction from the day to day doldrums or was it a case of what she was prepared to accept from Karl? Was she guarding herself from a relationship or was he guarding her from his life? A few, well many, many texts and e-mails were a pleasant way to while away the long day in between getting out of bed, waiting for a bus, trundling up the road to work and sitting at her desk gazing out the window until it was time for lunch and then home time.

Maybe she needed another occupation apart from Karl and gazing out the window. Will it be that my new occupation is house hunting? This new distraction would reduce the number of texts I sent." Her new occupation would stop her spending days writing fantasy and stories and the effort would result in eventually selling her house rather than worn out thumbs. Organising viewings with auctioneers to sell her house was one way to productively spend her time.

"Or maybe I could sell my own house," now that was an idea. How hard could it be as there were many 'sell your shack' sites? She felt pretty confident about doing it herself and so she did consider advertising it herself. She would review the implications and obligations that evening. She had a very pressing text. She had to answer it.

'Ciara, you may be 130 in that story but you are only number three or four to me!!' Karl was texting about his Zanzibar story, the Sultan of Stonetown.

'Karl the ROMANCE!!' she replied.

"I have to conclude this sale quickly, as time is of the essence." Ciara was back on productive thoughts not reminiscing un-happened fantasies. There was a strong chance of repossession. Ciara was in arrears on her house mortgage and the value of her house was decreasing by the day. If the bank sold her home they would pocket all proceeds from the sale, great! Obviously this would be the worst-case scenario as many years of repayments and her deposit would be lost. Things had been especially tough for the last two years when 'Sean the slitherer' had emigrated his responsibility.

The deposit had been her own money and she had borne the majority share of repayments all along. However no matter how meagre his contribution was it made a difference. The problem with Ciara was fantasy. Every time a negative event happened to her she bought a pair of shoes. As if she could just walk out of the problem with her new footwear, as if the new soles had no imprint and she was starting afresh new shoes were new Ciara. It was silly, this behavioural pattern but it was her weakness, her crutch. She couldn't be perfect all the time! She needed some light relief, but unfortunately retail therapy would equate to repo-therapy soon.

She was going to get the debt by the horns and blast one credit card bill at a time with very small cannon balls. Now this meant that she would have to shop at cost reduction stores so it was lucky that bargain supermarkets were fashionable. It was interesting that even the more upmarket supermarkets were offering deals. Deals were the name of the game. It wasn't that she had chosen the posh-nosh gastro-markets regularly, but sometimes it was a treat or maybe a regular treat, she wasn't sure. Would this new frugality feel a little like a financial refugee who hadn't left her shores shopping in the bargain supermarkets? Would she have to pull the product out of its container of cardboard and plastic from a height of about 6 feet 5 inches? She was going to become an economic migrant, migrating to the stack them high and charge cheap food outlets. The crazy thing was everyone was there, even people who didn't have to be. Her Mum had been to one and she had got lots of bargains.

Wine, her main staple would not be trolley-ed, well added to her trolley if the bottle was not reduced by at least 50% and she would seek 60% or more off Vodka and it would be drunk only on special occasions. She was also going to forego lunches and bring in her own sandwiches. Nobody would see the cucumber on white bread sandwiches anyway as she was power walking at lunch time.

Yes times were tight but there were services available to assist one to renegotiate the terms of their mortgage thus reduce one's monthly repayments. This would mean however that total interest would be much greater as the term would be longer. She could be saddled with debt for forty years instead of twenty, she wanted to spur it like the devices strapped onto Napoleon's black shiny boots. And the banks were broke!

Barristers had offered their services pro-bono which was admirable, worthy even a token gesture to redeem the reputation of the legal profession potentially. They had taken a bit of a beating recently according to Aoife. However the majority of agreements carried the mortgage over to the new property. This she did not want to do. She definitely did not want to have a millstone around her neck in perpetuity. It would be ardours nay defeatist to continue in such a manner, if she could she would just cut her losses and move on. You can only lose twice right? Then maybe the xy chromosomes, of selling high buying low could conceive a flat like the loft she envisioned inhabiting. The one she salivated, well almost, at the thought of, when she had first viewed and had made an appointment for that lunch break. It was her one and only secret, from everyone and she relished the thought of having one, a something sacred, only for herself. It was do-able, the acquisition, well just about manageable; she would have to make a very low offer and to stick to it no matter what. She was not being mean, or even stingy to the vendor she had to be frugal and sensible for once in her life to finally become debt free.

She was on the bus home now, tired after a day of thinking and she focused her imaginings onto the apartment, she would forget about moving jobs for at least two days and work out the practicalities of moving. Given the decorative state of her dream pad she would have to make friends with the various home and interior stores. Firstly though she needed to make her own home saleable, this would take a lot of work. Befriend the enemy in the home stores of West Dublin so to speak as her mantra had been "I would rather get penalty points on my driving licence than spend time in decorating superstores." It was like decoding hieroglyphics trying to find anything in a space so large. Now who did she know who was good at that, decoding hieroglyphics that is? She had an Egypt moment, she thought back to the Museum in Cairo, her Mum and Dad had visited it. Her Mother got the symbols. Needs must and so she would engage in the necessary visits and be self-sufficient. Or rather self-decorating was more the right term. In other words call your Mum the hieroglyphics expert.

'Hi Mum, do you want to come to Woodies with me?'

There seemed to be a thud, as if something was falling on her Mum's side of the line. A long silence ensued, then 'Ciara?'

'Yes Mum, you did hear me correctly I was wondering if you would like to go to Woodies with me. I think there is a 10% discount on a Thursday.'

'Are you ok?'

'Perfectly well, thanks' said Ciara.

'Will you hop off the bus outside my house? I am a bit worried.'

'Yep, no problem I will be there in less than ten minutes.'

'And you will have a bite to eat here?' asked her Mum.

'That would be lovely, see you in a while.'

A short while later she rang on the door, 'hi Mum, I'm home!' but she wasn't really home, it was her parent's house. It was funny though it always felt more like home than her own place.

'So Ciara! What is the big news?'

'Nothing Mum,'

'Nothing?' asked her Mum.

'Well I was thinking of buying a flat and it is in poor condition.'

'Oh, how exciting, will it be a flat or an apartment?'

'I am not sure of the difference but this is purpose built, so maybe an apartment?' said Ciara who had not intended to tell her Mum anything. "Why can I never keep anything to myself? I am such an open book."

Her Mum gave her a bit of a look which Ciara both completely knew but didn't understand. 'I know you are not happy in that house.' There it was out her Mum knew it too.

'No I'm not, it was Sean's decision and his home I went along with it as it was close to our home.'

'I hated Sean, sorry Ciara but I had to get it out.' Her Mum had seen Ciara change from a fun sometimes scatty but confident young lady to a worn down emotionally dependent woman. Ciara hopefully still had her core inner strength but Sean's actions towards her were always so subtle that her Mum could never fault him. There was no particular incident which she could pin point, unfortunately but like a very faintly painted canvass the evidence was just about visible and the outcome unmistakable.

'So do I' said Ciara very simply. 'I am finally coming back to me Mum and it feels good.'

They would have hugged if they had been a demonstrative family but instead Mum opened a bottle of red and half-filled the glasses. This was really pushing the limits as normally the glasses would only be one quarter full.

Her Mum whipped up a marvellous feast in less than an hour just as her Dad was walking in the door, yes her Mum was definitely the Minister of Internal Affairs. The large house was immaculately clean and the place felt like home.

'Do you want to stay?' asked her Dad.

'Ah' Ciara thought, 'Maybe, I have stuff in my room.' She was easily persuaded as tonight was a night for home comforts.

'Yes probably more than you have in your own house' said her Mum.

After dinner Mum said, 'Ciara is thinking of buying a flat and selling her house.'

'It is very early days in the decision,' qualified Ciara. 'I have only recently viewed the flat or apartment.'

'Well I will crank up the old computer and maybe you can show us what it looks like,' said her Dad knowing that Ciara would never be practical enough to have a brochure with her, especially since this was an impromptu visit.

Ciara opened up the website and they did a virtual tour, 'It is lovely' said her Mum. 'I can see why you like it.'

'Love, if you need a hand getting it I would gladly help you out,' her Dad said kindly.

Ciara bristled, one thing she was not but hoping to be in the near future was financially dependent on her parents. Independence in all aspects of her life was her goal, 'thank you Dad, but this purchase I will manage on my own. The aim is to be debt free.'

'It is a nice way to be' agreed her father. 'Well in a hands-on way, decorating maybe, or whatever you need.'

'Thanks Dad,' she smiled. She thought to herself "once I have the mortgage paid off, let the bank's collapse around me as I will survive, in their rubble my fate would no longer be linked. I will be my own financial entity no longer a figure on a balance sheet." She would not need to worry about interest rate increases or bank bail outs ever again.

She started surfing that new-ish foreign superstore which had such complicated assembly processes for its products, that one would need a master's degree in process engineering just to understand the instructions. Good that she wasn't in a relationship as purchasing one of these products was a sure way to conclude any fledgling romantic flight of fancy! From a brief viewing of the website Ciara found the prospect too overwhelming.

'Does the apartment come with parking?' her father asked while Ciara browsed.

'No it doesn't but I'm thinking of selling my car and that will help the funds.'

'You can always park it here' said her Mother. 'That is if you don't want to part with your green angel just yet.'

'Thanks' said Ciara, her Mum had remembered the name she had given her car, it made Ciara feel special. 'Maybe I will wait to sell her as its better not to make too many changes at once. Don't worry though the process is all going to take ages.'

'Just as well,' said her father, 'you can tend towards the all or nothing and we wouldn't like you to feel stranded by too many changes.'

Ciara didn't inform them that she was thinking of leaving her job as well. That would have been too much information.

She looked at the computer again after discounting the large self-assembly store and assessed the options locally. She knew one, the one she had called her Mum about but there were others. She would use the car to get out in the evenings and hunt, be a predator on the home front! Attack like the British did to Napoleon. That was what she would do over the next while.

Her Mother saw her worried look and said, 'Ciara I will help you going around those big stores. They can be scary places if you don't know what you are doing.'

'Thanks Mum, this is REALLY the area where I need help.'

She got out her note book, yes some people still use them, generally those who when trying to add tasks on their phone without deleting those already stored. Task one was to make her property presentable. She would start with the wall colour decision one made.

Work

A four-letter work but a bit more palatable than Dole, "if you got a bit of potato and leek soup doled out while you were queuing, well it would be so much more pleasant. Like building the famine walls of the west in the nineteenth century would that be kind or insulting? Stop being fanciful, there is no shame in unemployment," soon she could well be joining the ranks if there were to be another round of redundancies in the offing. Yippee!! She was glad to live nowadays when there was social welfare and didn't have to go into a poor house if she lost her job. She was also glad that there were no longer debtors' prisons as she would be an inmate trading her shoes for the doled-out soup, thinking were these Ferragamo's really worth the months of internment? Or worse running into her ex in Oz the emigrant's new debtors prison.

Anyway enough about serious stuff, Ciara had achieved her aim. The most important thing to Ciara was a window seat or rather a work station by the river, she was really sad to see so many people leave to give her this space and maybe it was a glint of guilt to make the pleasure more acute, illicit even when she realised that the workspace was only available due to someone else's departure, why did they leave? Did it matter? Did she care? Yes of course she did, this was a guilty pleasure, but she could do nothing about the financial state of the World economy. They all knew, each person had their own reason for quitting or being made redundant, but she didn't wish to consider too deeply as it was out of her control. She had not been selected for the recent round of redundancies and she was glad as she was not yet ready. Not ready to go just yet.

She looked out the window. A traffic bollard was gently flowing down the Liffey, its semi-conical shape being buoyed along on the currents, bobbing now left then right as the water flowed under the three bridges within her view. The sun glinted upon it reflecting the red warning stripes. It seemed to dance in the current as it was an irregular shape and gave more resistance depending on which direction it faced. It would get caught in a barrier which had been flung in by a caring Dubliner to unblock and free the pedestrian strides along the busy City streets. The bollard would then release itself again and float freely along. At low tide it was amazing to see how successful the Dublin bike scheme had become by counting the carcasses of discarded bicycles. Their remains were art in motion to a certain eye. The sniffy Liffey, coursing through the heart of the city as rivers generally do when towns are built upon them, especially when buildings were constructed on either side.

She was gazing out the window, again as she had done so many times before, on this day of days, this day of window triumph. She had been edging towards this window for months now and finally she was here. It was a special day, as the newest bridge, the harp shaped bridge the Samuel Beckett Bridge was to open, open today. She was expectant, happy and excited. The bridge was a spectacle. Truly it was a sight to be seen. Especially as it would not open vertically but tilt to the right, more than tilt. It would fully open, almost 90 degrees. Wow! "Bet Karl would be interested to see this! Mr Architect, the design guru" maybe he knew but he hadn't text about it yet today. And what would enter through this bridge? What indeed? Tall ships were to arrive, replica ships majestically sailing through with their mast heights almost equalling that of the bridge. Was that all a bit regal for a republic, probably but with this level of excitement she didn't really care.

She heard a beeping noise, alerting her to the fact that the cars were to stop, all traffic indeed, even the bicycles which usually ignore all traffic signs. The pedestrian too, he or she would also have to wait, not gingerly cross lane by lane. Could she actually hear the beeping of the bridge opening or was she just imagining it? She looked at her desk. Ring. Ring. Ring.

"The phone" why was it ringing? 'Hello Zzzz Company, Ciara speaking, how may I assist you today?'

'Are you sitting on the fifth floor, looking out over the river?'

'Why do you ask?'

'I think I see you' strange, this wasn't Karl, it wasn't the other guy, so who could it be, she hadn't exactly grown super popular with the expansive male population of Dublin.

'No Actually I am on the sixth floor. Who is this?'

'It's Sean; remember we used to live together!'

'Vaguely, why are you calling?' Ciara was a bit of a romantic, she hadn't wanted to move in with someone just because they had a meeting of direct debits. Sean was a practical type and his views varied somewhat from Ciara's. He was always concerned who had paid for what last. Ciara equated economy in the outlay of funds with economy of emotions. He was always holding back a little in case there was a big purchase or maybe another person. That would mean a lifetime purchase probably.

'I was looking on the web and I saw our house on the market. So I think you owe me.' He had seen the same house as Ciara, the one down the road.

He had not given himself to Ciara, he has merely been there, always there and now in retrospect she felt, well a little short changed! At least he was short winded and had cut to the chase. She was thankful for the small change.

'Incorrect, ex, there is a house on the road for sale, but it isn't mine' "it's internet you Dumbo, no wonder I was glad you left. The web is just the wires the internet is actually the database which can be accessed via search engines. Wow though, check out the nerve and the stupidity." She was really angry and hadn't a clue whether it was internet or web, actually she didn't care. It was just that Sean had said this that she wanted to correct him, to be right. What was most annoying was that she couldn't even say it to him; she could only think it to herself. Even still she could not stand up to him. How long can someone be angry for? Maybe there were reasons but they were ages ago. "Move on Ciara, let it go Dumbo and stop calling his girlfriend's phone."

'Actually Sean the property, if I choose to sell it, will sell for less than the value of the mortgage so you owe me.'

'What!' he exclaimed incredulously, probably from Australia. Could he not be aware that everyone in Ireland was in negative equity?

'Yes, you contracted to buy the house with me and left reneging on your obligations both legal and financial not to mention moral. You have forfeited your right to receive anything as you are in excess of two years in arrears on your repayments.' "So there, you scrounger!" She had managed to speak in an even tone, not shout, not stick her tongue out at him which wouldn't make sense as they were on the telephone, nor make a noise that any 5-year-old would laugh at, the last had been the most difficult. Mature, that is what she was trying to convey. Hopefully it was coming off. That was Sean though talking millions and borrowing fivers. It had always annoyed her that he was so mean with his money.

'Oh' he swallowed with a gulp. 'But I want to buy something in Melbourne.'

'If you contact me again I will let the Aussie banks know what a poor loan candidate you are and reduce your credit rating to zero. Stay in your debtor's prison down under!' There she had at least been able to say something a bit annoyed even if it was totally out of context and a rather obtuse reference that she had shared with Aoife.

'You couldn't it's a different jurisdiction. Anyway what do you mean debtor prison?'

'Well people were transported to Oz in the nineteenth century for wrong doings and now they are choosing to go for financial wrongdoings.'

'You mean economic migrants,' said Sean trying to catch her drift.

'Yes so it is a twenty first century debtors' prison.'

'Yes but you are not locked in a cell, the sun shines and there are no financial repercussions.'

'My tentacles spread wide, there will be financial repercussions and I have more digits than an octopus. Sean you are a slither-err and a bit of a silly slitherer at that. Cop on mate, or whatever is said Down Under! Get your girlfriend to bail you out, AGAIN. So long!'

She was gone, yes it wasn't all men who were idiots it was just him! He was silly. She had got it out though and some of the anger had been released. Now however she began to feel a bit shaky and lightheaded. Some men were nice it was true, but generally only because they had spent their teens and twenties working on their personalities to compensate for their looks. Ouch, was she really that bitter? She was almost acerbic, sucking on the bitter lemon at the end of her vodka. Yep she should stick to normal fizzy lemon and keep her thoughts sweet. She thought back on Sean, silly Sean, sweet Sean, strange Sean, strung-out Sean. Where did he get off calling her after over two years? Ok she was pestering his girlfriend but that was different. No it was just Sean she was bitter about she could never feel like that about Karl. Karl had so much life in him she felt regenerated after a textual exchange with him. Nor the other guy for that matter, he was not right for her but he was not bad. He was a romantic, Mr. Chippy and into poetry and had said some really nice things, he had tried with her. He had tried really hard. Sean was bad, a really mean guy. He must have been work-surfing too, Sean that is.

Maybe he would invest in this relationship in Australia but he most certainly hadn't in their long term common law co-habitation. Ciara did feel a bit bad for calling his girlfriend, it only happened when she was drunk, very late at night and really it was to warn her about Sean. It definitely had no hint of jealously, none whatsoever; it was completely out of kindness. Sean had given her the number after all, he had called her on it so it was ok. Negative thoughts were swirling about Ciara's overheated brain.

'Hey Ciara', Stephen popped his head around the side of his cubicle. He was also edging closer to the window. 'Are you ok, matey?'

'Yep I will be after a quick smoke break. I really need it. Will you join me?'

'I can't. I'm just in the middle of my French homework.' Oh he had restarted French lessons and had not even told Ciara. Well at least she wouldn't have to go to the classes as languages were not her strong point. It was interesting though that Ciara didn't know every aspect of Stephens' life anymore. Yes that was actually a good thing, but in this moment she felt a little left out.

'It was my ex, Sean calling from Australia.'

'Silly Sean.'

'The very one,' said Ciara confirming Stephen's assertion.

'Ah well in that case I will have to come out.' They went out to the fresh air and to the front of the building. There was lots of commotion with all the tall ship activity and it felt good to be among action which had nothing to do with Ciara's long lost private life. The sun was shining even though there was a chill in the air. People were waving from and to the ships and some of the vessels looked really old. She couldn't tell which ships were original and which were replicas' but it didn't matter.

'Thanks, it's been a while since I spoke to him.'

'I know, are you feeling a bit unsettled?' asked Stephen.

'No it's not that it is just that he is so mean. He called me because he had seen my neighbour's house for sale on the internet. He thought it was ours or rather mine. So he decided to call up and ask for money or whatever proceeds he feels are owing to him from the sale of the property.'

'What a scrounger, that is low.'

'Yes a silly scrounger,' said Ciara agreeing.

'Are you okay now?'

'I need a few moments.' Ciara was still feeling shaky and her legs were wobbly.

'Of course you do. You are looking a bit pale. Anyway' Stephen thought he should change the subject, 'thinking selfishly, that new French class is tough. I much preferred it when we were doing the colours and the numbers.'

'Le ciel est bleu!'

'No il est gris,' he returned.

'I think you are right on that one usually but today il ya du soleil!' confirmed Ciara.

'Ta raison.'

'Actually I'm good,' Ciara said after a few moments of silent contemplation about her colours and seeing a bit of sunshine. 'Sean leaving was the best decision I ever made. And the best thing about it was that I didn't have to make it.'

'That is good,' said Stephen not quite knowing what to say.

Bus Musings

Later that day she was on her way home she tried to distract herself from the after-Sean shock. Karl was her usual distraction and she wondered had she merely been using Karl as a thought bouncer to avoid anything of Sean getting in. She was not a victim. She thought about buses a nice safe area for thoughts when one's world is black and when there are no metrological signs in the sky to inspire. All feelings were going to be externalised and projected onto Dublin Bus, buses don't have feelings, they are very big and so they were a good target to aim all her overheated emotions on. So that would have to do.

There are many reasons to take the bus; firstly the light is better than a taxi which facilitated make-up application. In fact it is de-rigueur to publicly apply ones public face, on public transport. What are lights for anyway? It made no odds that she was on her way home, as generally each morning she practiced her beauty regime on a bus. "There is no better buzz than a Dublin Bus", she thought, maybe she should enter the advertising industry.

The next advantage of taking the bus, was that one does not have to listen to taxi drivers received opinions, generally originating from day time radio shows (yes usually Joe Duffy). On a more serious note if one enters a taxi alone, then one is at the mercy of the taxi driver. She harked back to a time when visiting London she was attacked by a taxi driver. It was the most unsettling experience of her life. She had taken a taxi to be safe and the driver had told her to ride in the front seat with him as the main cab doors didn't lock. She had agreed following doe-like his advice. She didn't want some drunken people to hop in at the traffic lights in a large City which she didn't know. Unfortunately it was the taxi driver who was the aggressor and he put his hand on her leg and tried to pull her over to him at the third set of traffic lights. She commanded all her strength had told him in no uncertain terms to stop, put both hands on the steering wheel and drive her straight to her friend's house. She also said this was a free fair and she had taken down his ID number. He assented and she got to her destination without any further molestation. After the attack "never take a cab alone" became her mantra from that day forth. Well except for that special meeting with Karl and the even more special meeting of her new, or nearly new flat.

So buses were safer and potentially this is why she had felt so threatened when taking the cab home with Karl. Probably it could well have been why she told him of her grandmother dying and ruining her chances with him. Or maybe it was the 21st of December, the anniversary of her grandmother's death, yes it was and there was always some point in the day in which she thought of her. Why couldn't she have had a nice normal first memory like red lemonade and Tayto's or orange squash and banana sandwiches on white bread?

Finally the best reason for taking public transport was that it was a bit cheaper. This was always a good thing undoubtedly. Ciara was on her economy drive today was day one and every cent made sense to her new frugality, she was going to be in the black financially speaking.

QBC – standing for a quality bus corridor, or a snobbish pneumonic for a bus lane. Quality is a relative term and something relating to meeting the customer's expectations. If a customer has absolutely no expectation that the bus will come to take the commuter home from work then this expectation cannot be met. And the customer is waiting out in the rain with only a vague hope that a bus will come sometime before it is time to go to work again. This would make the journey worthless and the value of a sleeping bag under the desk a worthwhile option to be considered. When one does arrive, a bus that is, there is such a feeling of relief and joy that the rain sodden shoes are barely noticed, that pair of delicates which were only worn as there was a strong promise of a dry day are ruined. "I will have to lobby for a parking place at work." She considered, "my car is really more of an ornament than a vehicle."

These thoughts were distracting her and she really was not thinking about Sean, silly Sean who had been such a sweet Sean at one time. He had listened, he had such great ideas he was going places. Nope she was not going to think about the nice things.

Real time information at bus stops could be likened to Microsoft time. It begins with one minute to download one's file and ends up being about ten times longer as there are files within files. So the bus would be due in three minutes, then because of forces outside the bus company's control, all of a sudden the bus is due in eight minutes. Then it will disappear from the screen entirely as if there is a big black bus hole in the universe like one gigantic pothole that that takes the bus off the radar. Then all of a sudden it will re-appear and the expected arrival time now will be due, here right now. Then the bus arrives as if it's a mirage and all the passengers board delighted that it is here. It was not as if there was seriously heavy traffic at 5.30 pm on that Tuesday evening to cause these delays. Could this lack of timetable certainty disprove the rational for having a QBC? Or could that be QED?

What had happened to the sweet things? Why had he stopped listening? He had started on a business plan which didn't go well, but no one expects to succeed the first time right? He had lost all his savings, the savings which were supposed to go into the house. They had already decided to buy and Ciara was sure he would make back the money very quickly. So she put all her savings in which amounted to about 25 Cent and they got a bigger mortgage, a much bigger mortgage. It was okay though, everything was going to be ok.

"Green issues, well why pay a carbon tax if one creates no carbon. A weekly trip to the shops is hardly going to ruin all the trees in Brazil. Is it worth paying road tax, insurance and a subsidy to very wealthy oil producing nations oh and of course the Irish Government?

"Why do I need a semi in the suburbs? It was a good idea when I was considering marrying my ex and we succumbed to the purchasing frenzy which epitomised the Noughties. However now, it is just me, not a house mate in sight to justify all the space and a Mum who can pop by whenever. That's not a bad thing mind you as she is a great cook and sometimes even good company. Yet it is a bit settled, an unsettling thought all the same when I am not planning to settle down with any architects in the next decade." Home purchasing and selling thoughts entered the frame and consumed her mind, but it was so difficult to push herself, motivate herself as she had no deadline, no one to answer to. She realised she was thinking concentric thoughts and this was a regular thing.

Things were not ok, the next business venture didn't work out and Sean could not find work. He tried a third time and Ciara took any equity they had in the house out so now they were at 100% loan to value ratio and Ciara was bearing all of the costs. After the third failure Sean gave up. He sat about and watched day time television and got depressed. Ciara understood but when he began taking his frustrations out on her she could no longer understand or forgive. He chipped, he moaned and he accused her of every neurotic thought which entered his head. Then Ciara shut down. She stayed shut down for nearly four years.

Usually Ciara's thoughts were fluffy, mostly centred around other centuries and always in the past. Often she was wearing big skirts and lots of people were helping her in and out of them. So she got an idea, a new career idea. She loved history so why not to show people about the history of Dublin, maybe she could be a tour guide. Anything was better than thinking about Sean and it was nice to be thinking again. She fantasised about being a tour guide in Dublin, walking about the streets making stuff up as she went along. What was new as she regularly toured the City on her work outings with her colleagues she had already driven them demented with the aborted Georgian tour of Dublin? There had been others though, many others. The Georgian doors had been cancelled by the snows at Christmas and Karl, Karl. Well maybe she should reorganise it. The next social outing with work was long overdue. Well it was overdue in her mind anyway and she had worked really hard on that research. Did the significance of colour in Georgian Doors have a good ring to it? Maybe she would try to explain the colours of the Greeks, or would that be too complicated a tour?

'I do have one other great love,' Karl texted. He had saved her from her own thoughts, thank goodness. She must be getting him into texting out of context. 'Other than architecture that is,' grr he had clarified.

'Ah yes, pray tell!' So he was a man who loved rowing, show houses and there was more. He had depth and he understood ankles.

'Look @ u & yr C18th terms! Thought we were in the romantic period. My other great love is cross country skiing, a bit like your city walking with the rhythm but a lot lower impact!' He was getting colloquial with his texts!

Ciara sometimes liked the relationship with Karl because it was virtual she didn't have to engage with him in the real world and get hurt. Other times it really annoyed her and she wanted it to be real. Well maybe not really real, like Sean, but fantasy real and perfect. She has been scalded by Sean and was still reeling from the phone call earlier and a mess ever since. Her knees were still shaking so Ciara didn't feel she was ready to put herself out there again. On the dating scene, that is. Not yet, not for a long while yet.

Then on the other hand this was Karl, she was crazy about him, they were electric together. It would be different with him. It had to be. They could talk about everything and anything at any time of the day. He was the best. It was fair to say things were moving a bit slowly but it was definitely good to know someone first.

She had now cooled after a burning pain had shot through nearly two years of celibacy and self-protection. Sean did that to her. This self-protection felt like a large black hole of frozen ice which had consumed her internally. It meant that her life was on ice, her emotions, her job, her motivation and her home situation were static and had not moved forward since the day Sean left. She thought that she was Norway she was the frozen wasteland of wonder and distance removed from the reality of rain and unpredictable buses. Neither Ciara nor anyone she knew had actually been there, so it could be true. She didn't know Karl well so he didn't count.

She looked at Karl's text.

'Maybe hard to pursue in snowless Dublin, yes you're right the romantic period was early 19th century,' she said in reply to his update on the loves of his life, the new addition was cross country skiing.

'Well I was thinking of improvising on the night we met and using my scarf as a ski to take us home, That would have been romantic, but then a taxi came along. You are correct skiing is easier to do in the snow.' Karl was a bit quicker at typing on his tablet than Ciara on her phone.

'Have you ever been to the dry slopes here? I think there are some in South County Dublin.'

'Yes I have' he said, 'but they are a poor relation to the real thing. The aspect which makes skiing, everything interesting is the space. The expanse of space, of a frozen landscape is beautiful. In some respects indomitable, but I try! I can but try, not necessarily to dominate but to cross as much as possible, to reach the point on the horizon which was my starting view. It is freedom!' Karl continued, it sounded as if he were thinking wistfully maybe he was a bit of a dreamer too.

Ciara almost said "I have never been able to be this open or had someone open up so much to me" but she restrained herself. Instead she said, 'wow, that must be cool. Does the colour of thermal underwear determine the distance you can travel?'

'Yes Ciara I wear my long, sheer lacy long johns which I have to pull up over my tree trunk legs!! You are funny sometime. I wear orange for mountains of course, white for the flats and black for the forests. It is very important to get the colour combination right, ha ha!'

Before Ciara pressed reply she had second thoughts, he was being really open before, she did not wish him to freeze up again. So she decided to go back to the cross-country skiing and sent 'that sensation must be amazing, all that snow all that space, what does freedom feel like?'

'It feels like nothing is restraining you, you can go and go. Would you like to see a picture?'

'I would love to.'

The Snow picture in photos.

'You are in control and no one is telling you what to do' was its caption.

'That is beautiful Karl,' smiled Ciara from her 1/3 of a seat on the very busy bus.

'It feels like I don't have a meeting in five minutes.'

"He is going to go back to the present, drat. How can I stop him? Do I want to? I like that he is free even if it frustrates me."

'I am happy for you, to have something you love' she said. He was still at work and had a meeting still. Everyone worked harder than her, she was such a slacker. She would do longer hours if there was the work to do, she attempted to justify why she was well on the way to her home whilst he was still in the office. She was feeling guilty for being nearly home. She was guilty to be working in a company which was barely surviving where so many people had had to leave and had not enough business to retain its' employees. She was really feeling guilty for having a job when she wished she didn't as she wanted to be free.

'What is freedom for you?' he asked.

'I don't know, maybe I should take up sky-diving or heli-skiing before I can answer that.' "How can he know my thoughts so well? Or I probably am predictable like the words which pop up with my predictive texting." Maybe she already had too much freedom; she had no obligations, no deadlines, with a nice boss who never gave out to her and no boyfriend nagging her. Yes she probably had more freedom than most people. Her only tie or worry was financial, her overspending and her large monthly mortgage repayment. This was the reality of her life, she considered yet she didn't feel free, it was odd. "I am free," she thought and was about to send, but she held back, her mind was not free. She was still tied in her thoughts and in her self-belief. She could not fly just yet and sometime walking was a bit of a problem too.

'It does not have to be extreme, Ciara, maybe you get it when you are doing your lunch time walks.' She was surprised he was still texting, maybe there was a delay in the meeting.

'Maybe, this is my stop, talk to you later.' She almost gloatingly got off the bus. Hers had been the Expresso bus and had only taken twenty minutes to get from door to door. It took the Chapelizod by-pass and sped the journey up by fifteen minutes. Maybe she shouldn't grumble about Dublin Bus, she would be home before 6 pm, how many other Dubliners could be home this early? It was the ideal job to be home in time for the child minder. No wonder it suited Don so well and he had a parking space. "Must lobby Anna and use the photo in the changing booth lever." The she thought "if I did drive, when would I have time to text? Morning texts are the best part of the day." She smiled for the first time since she had hung up on Sean, "yes I need Karl."

'Sure slacker x' he had sent her a kiss. He was still texting progress. She would examine the photograph and read through the threads of the conversation later it was lovely. He had joked racy but kept clean. It was the right balance. Even though she had not said it, she really felt close to him again, he was opening up more and more to her. He had a dynamism to him and depth which attracted her. He could change subjects and tones with ease and grace. It was almost as if he were skiing over the subjects.

Still Not thinking about Sean

The next day was really cold, she had not slept well. Every time she woke her sleepy words were reliving fights she was having with Sean. She was freezing at a bus stop fantasying about a nice warm bus and a whole seat free. Sean had changed from sweet and understanding to a complete nightmare and her days had turned into the blackest nights. He never cleaned, he was always asking her for money and he was constantly watching soccer. When they had met he had been into Gaelic football, what had happened? Ciara tried distraction, it usually worked for her, "why I am a CIE VIP?" inserting an air of positivity into the air. "Well generally I get a seat, especially when those without beady eyes give up too quickly. Usually some hefa-lump sits in the middle of a seat and I being on the scrawny side can suffice with just a third of a seat. In fact hanging in the aisle has the advantage of more leg room! Its' how you frame the solution as all those self-help books tell one." Yes there were many self-help books on a shelf waiting patiently to be read. Wait they must as it's kinda hard to read on only one third of a seat.

'Hey Ciara, are you sloping in late again?' asked Karl.

Is reality always grim, always old or always the dole line? Her thoughts were not remaining positive. Restraint in response to Karl, this is what she would do. He would have to wait at least ten minutes these days before Ciara returned his texts, she was being strong she was becoming controlled. She had her fingers stuffed in her pockets and as it was only September didn't want to start wearing gloves just yet. She could read Karl's text quickly, but to type out a response would mean that her finger tips would be really cold so she would wait until she was on the bus.

Could reality merely be the absence of fantasy, the here and now? This could be ok, even good sometimes? Her reality was a lot better than most, she had a job and warm house with no screaming children actually it was not so bad at all. Maybe this was why she didn't go around reading those self-help books. Yes she had thought this thought on her last bus musing, was she over-analysing?

'Yep, I am on the bus. Are you out inspecting your play houses I mean show houses?' yes she had waited until a bus arrived and it took seven and a half minutes, that was good enough, controlling her response time to Karl was a major advancement in her texting career. Also time was relative to the amount of space available on the seat.

"Why can't I walk to work?" she thought but she was still not on the bus, she had lied to boast her flexible work hours and she was still shivering at the bus stop and a particularly windy bus stop at that. "Why am I constantly waiting for public transport? Why not sell the ornament, Anna will never give me a parking space. Sell the negative equity house and buy something small centrally? I will only lose on paper with property. Maybe I can buy a wreck of a place, a repossession of a flat with no doors, no windows but a cool view out those glassless window frames. Then I **can** walk to work or even cycle. I will start today looking at auction sites and get a valuation on my house. Then I will know how much money I have to play with." Her thoughts were verging on concentric again. She had ruminated excessively about the loft apartment but the asking price was too high for her. She had talked to her parents but they didn't know quite how bad her financial plight was and she was too proud to enlighten them.

'No I'm at my desk, I was thinking of showing you a red colour card this time, but you are not here so there is no point. BTW I don't play house in the show house, I'm, no auctioneer' texted Karl.

'No, no point, oh diligent and hard-working skyscraper-builder. What does it smell like?' Ciara asked putting aside her motivational thoughts for another moment of delving into fantasy. 'The tundra, the North, the....snow,' "I want to smell anything other than this bus stop. I seem to spend my life here."

"Phew," the bus came finally; she shook her hands, took out her travel pass and waited for the herd of other passengers to climb aboard. Then she hopped on and felt the instant blast of heat, relief.

'Pardon, I hope the paint is dry on the card' Karl texted back, a bit confused at the second part of her text was completely out of context and a few days after their text conversation about cross country skiing and snow and freedom. He should be used to her thinking at this stage!

'The tundra you great big colour card, where you go cross country skiing, is there a scent and if there is what does it smell like?' "Would I really like to be there or is it that I would like to do something with Karl that he likes? Or maybe just do something with Karl whether he likes it or not."

'Ah, yes, the frozen landscape, nothing, it smells of nothing,' he texted back.

'Really, apart from temperature reducing the survival chances of animals' "wait Ciara that sounds a bit scientific, or maybe clinical." 'Apart from the cold & there being fewer animals, is there really no scent, smell or fragrance?' "Scent is so evocative I wonder does he remember my scent on that lunch date well enforced meeting, eau de Ciara glow!"

'Well, when you are close to the sea, you can smell the freshly caught fish. If you are near a town there are human type smells, cooking, washing, and the waste and so on. In the thaw you can begin to smell the flora but ever so faintly, like the leaves, they have a fresh smell after the rain washes them. The main thing you are inhaling is fresh, then cold.' It seems as if he were there again, his thoughts so fresh and crisp they could almost carry Ciara away with them. He was really thinking about what he was saying, Ciara was so grateful.

'You will have to show me someday.' Ciara had sent the tread before she had thought and now could not retract it. There could be consequences, whilst he was open and giving with his thoughts he was not about his space, nor his time. In other words she felt he wasn't going to meet her again so he was selfish with his real time but generous with his virtual time. Was this a bit opposite to Dublin Bus? "Telephone company or Ethernet or whatever it is, please fail, knock yourself out and loose that tread, please. I don't want to seem needy or clingy or force him to lie."

'Definitely, chat later?' he was gone.

"See he just lied, how easily he does it. Or maybe he does really want to get to know me. Maybe he will introduce me to his grandfather and I can have a Heidi moment. Wait no, Heidi was in Switzerland. Maybe he will show me how to make a boat. I like physical work if it is fun, with the chance to work up a good appetite for...FISH! Well they will have sushi, they must have. Hell there is oil in Norway so there has to be everything else also. Would he ever take me?"

Ciara got back on track and started thinking about her own life again, real life, her meaning of freedom and how to attain it. Whilst things had stopped once Sean moved out she had space. She had not done a lot with this space but it could be a means for her to be alone and away, non-functioning in secret. Floating in an inert liquid some would call vodka others would choose wine, but whatever it was it gave Ciara the space to just be. She did nothing and could do nothing but maybe now was the time to start. So it was not exactly a wheel she had to re-invent but maybe herself, all of those quiet niggles which had been bugging her for so long finally came together and she had a plan. Now was the ideal time to move, so do it. Change and cut out the dead wood. Woops that may not leave much in the world of Ciara. There had not been fresh shoots of growth for quite some time. It may be a bit frightening to change and change so much of herself and her life, it meant changing everything.

She logged onto a property website once she got into work and began to get excited. There were some new options out there and not as expensive as the last one, the perfect place.

"Wow a first-floor period conversion on Fitzwilliam Square could be just the thing," she thought she was browsing the internet and surfing with intent! It was so exhilarating she thought the phone would blow out of her hand, but she didn't care, her imagination was sparking. "Or maybe a cool studio off Baggot Street, a duplex studio, with just enough space for a guest to feel comfortable for two days but then like a fish the guest would go off! Very Oscar Wilde" maybe that was a bit mean.

****

Again at the bus stop and she was waiting, and waiting and waiting. There was an advert for the company on the bus shelter, "we meet most of our customers on-line." Ciara smiled a wry smile, "but not on-time!" as a gust of wind almost swept her spindly, matchstick like legs from under her. Finally it arrived, the bus to the 'burbs. On the bus again and passing the rowing club. Ciara had a quick flash back of Karl in his kit, way too much lycra on show. She checked the photograph again to refresh her memory. It was out of focus, so it was really hard to see his face. The river was high; the ripples of his biceps dominated the ripples of the water. The tautness of his quadriceps, they were broad and well defined, she inhaled sharply. She could not actually see them but the fact that they were there and she almost could make him out made him tantalising close. Her imagination was left to fill in the rest and hers was a powerful imagination. "His loss really! Or maybe not, his strength is so powerful, almost mighty, but he *is* vain to have sent such a picture. Maybe he thinks I am vain considering the ones I have sent him. Oops."

'Hey Ciara, how is life?' sent Karl. Think of him and then he was there, he seemed to text her at this time every day. Did he know she would be on the bus?

'Life..' she said.

Things to do to keep the seat to yourself, once you have the seat that is; "firstly work one's voice recognition software function to draft inane texts. Could this be construed as on bus anti-social behaviour? Would this make it more likely that someone wouldn't take the seat next to one? Making complaints to shops is another good one. This idea could stretch to solicitors and other random miscellaneous companies merely to get a reaction from other passengers it could be a bit mean, but sometimes a lot of fun!"

'I had a bit of a demotivating day,' she added to Karl. This meant that she had only one task the whole day and had lots of spare capacity for challenges or at least challenging texts.

"How to assert one's right to the whole seat?" Ciara thought this would make a fitting title to her wedding speech to whichever mystery man she would finally betroth herself to. If it were Karl she would be marrying him in a snow kissed village with lots of log cabins, made for her guests by his grandfather. "Well as a regular public transport user. I know that it is considered a bit mean to occupy the whole seat if the bus is completely full. However should there be spare capacity there are options, that construes alternative seating arrangements so why not? Requirements necessary to achieve this state of bliss include lots of baggage such as lap-top bag, umbrella or if not completely prepared a large bulky overcoat or anorak which will broaden the visual and make one look like they really need the whole seat. It is helpful to sit in the very middle of the seat which assists the bulky look.

"Then sigh loudly when someone makes moves to encroach your space! If someone persists in wishing to take your space, move slowly and lugubriously whilst scowling, a lot. Chances are they will move on. If they decide not to move down the aisle, then it is necessary to scowl some more. I don't advocate the 'pick and flick' method personally but I have seen it work on numerous occasions. It however may well attract those of an unsavoury nature to choose to sit beside one.

"One can always revert to an earlier step of composing an outrageously inappropriate text via voice activation. It often works unless the hopeful seat companion is also really nosy. Always save these texts to draft for a rainy day!" Then she considered her reasoning for such unsocial behaviour, it was the perfect counter balance of the bland "I'm on de bus Mum, pick me up in Liffey Valley" something had to be done. She was doing well not thinking about Sean, the days were passing and she was letting the thoughts of him slide. Keeping a seat free was one strategy but texting a cute guy was a more distracting one.

'Are you fishing for a compliment cool Ciara?' said Karl after a while. Could he be practicing the ten-minute response time rule also?

"The best place to sit in the rain is generally upstairs" her romantic wedding speech would continue, as there are less people on the 'upper salon' as there is no standing" thought Ciara. "Wet bodies giving out steam are still about but there are less of them and they haze out the windows so you don't have to see the grey rainy sky. Could I have a drearier wedding speech? Who am I kidding?"

'Do you have a rod on your oar Mr. Rower-man?' ok this may have been slightly bizarre but she still had the memory of him rowing, or rather the memory of the image of him rowing fresh in her mind. Didn't he know she hated fishing, it was a pet hate, even though she didn't hate pets.

'You know Ciara I have a grand big rod,' he returned in a flash. He would wouldn't he, the boaster!

There was one rather unusual occurrence or maybe it was a phenomenon that evening which made all the wind, the rain and the cramped bus conditions bearable, no more, things were great and special for Ciara. It even made unpalatable images of Karl palatable. The true reason she liked buses and it was happening right in front of her was phone Tai Chi. She often talked of it and had driven her friends demented with her enthusiasm, it was a theoretical possibility. Then finally it happened, more than one person unlocked their smart phone with a wave and a swipe. It had nearly happened once before in her many years of bussing it home, but then at the last moment one of the participants had changed their mind. This time though as she put her mobile into her pocket she looked up. And there it was, three people unlocking their phones. Their motion was in perfect synchronisation with each other. It was random, unrehearsed, functional and yet utterly beautiful. Unconsciously these three passengers were in sync for a moment and the fleetingness of the rapid motion made it all the more special because it was transient. Things were going to change for Ciara, this was her sign. "So long Sean, even though I am not thinking about you. And so long negative equity I am moving on." Essentially she was looking for any positive signs and even if this sign was not explicitly for her she would make it her own. Motion Tai Chi was she and she was going to move her life forward.

It was like the moment in American Beauty when there was a plastic bag dancing in the wind. It spoke to Ciara; the effort was unnoticed but actually very conscious as people were trying to remember the shape they had chosen. Some people were highly skilled like a Chinese master others were rather hesitant and slow. When it came together though three or more people swiping the air at a time, it was almost an art form, beautiful. Yes we are all individuals but there are only a certain amount of movements permitted to achieve the unlocking of one's phone and so this gives for the synchronised affect which so delighted Ciara.

'Hmm, yes so I've seen!!!' She responded to his fishing rod response ages later. At least 10 minutes she was sure. He seemed to be fishing for a reply. She had sat still after the occurrence, breathed slowly and hadn't consciously made an effort to delay her response time to Karl. It was a natural delay for once, it was genuine and she had given herself pause.

All of these things, distractions were easier than reading heavy history books about Napoleon. Ciara had finished her Josephine reading and was now onto Napoleon, the subject was a bit more serious. She however wished to ensure each vague historical reference when texting Karl was accurate. Whilst most of their texts hadn't been and the conversations were maturing, Ciara felt it was time for a bit of historical correctness! It was not her period, Napoleon and the early Nineteenth Century. Her favourite time had been the Restoration Period and she used have rather odd fantasies about Charles the Second. This could have been sparked by a TV series and a dishy actor who had played him, Charles II. The Power and the Passion had been the name. Now however she was decidedly stuck in the early nineteenth century, a time before telegrams and steam trains which would hasten the progress of her rather Austenian romance.

Home

At lunch, she compiled a works appraisal of her house, it was too rainy to go walking so she didn't feel guilty about not power walking. Once she arrived home she just needed to see if there were still three bedrooms as she only ever used one. They most likely were still there but it could be a good idea to check, just in case.

She got through the front door she kicked off her shoes, this was the new Ciara, the Ciara who had clean carpets. Soon! The Ciara who cared about her home environment, the Ciara who was house proud, nope that was going too far! Her Mother called, checking whether she was still alive. She patted about her person and confirmed 'yep I'm still here. I'm breathing, moving and contemplating cleaning my house.'

'Well good luck with that dear,' said her Mum. 'It may take you sometime.'

'Thanks Mum.'

'Ciara, do you want to go to the home-store?' asked her Mum.

'Yes, lets tomorrow.'

'Tomorrow is fine with me.'

'Once I clean then I will decide on the paint colour,' said Ciara.

'We can see what is in the shops and get little samples.'

'Ok, sounds good,' said Ciara. 'See you tomorrow, thanks Mum.'

'See you love.'

Where had she left off before the phone rang rudely disturbing her renovation contemplation? Her bathrooms, yes she had tiles on the floor, they had come with the house, but for the life of her she could not remember what colour, they were. She ran upstairs, off white, so neutral, neutral must be going out of fashion soon it was so ubiquitous. Anyway they were neutral, stuck to the floor and around the bath so no need to change.

'Hey Ciara, how are you?' Karl was texting. It was nice to hear from him but she was a bit busy. She would ignore him for a while and get the en-suite bathroom appraised.

She looked at the sink and saw her toothbrush and new tube of toothpaste. It hadn't been opened; she picked it up and examined it. It was long and conically shaped in her hands and she twisted off the cap slowly, there was a thin film of sliver to preserve hygiene which she quickly ripped off. The tube felt firm and substantial to the touch and she got her toothbrush. She pressed the paste slowly and it didn't spurt but flowed in a thick viscous mass nearly a solid. She placed a long thick quantity onto her brush and brought her brush to her mouth slowly looking at herself in the bathroom mirror as she did. She imagined Karl was behind her, looking at her, drinking her in with his eyes and shaking his wet hair on top of her. She rubbed the brush around her mouth and felt its sensation in every area of this oral orifice. She half glanced to the tube of paste and it seemed to turn into Karl's phallus. She looked at herself again and thought maybe she could be into oral if he tasted as nice as toothpaste. "Karl's crux will be the death of me!"

'I'm good how are you?' she replied.

She finished her tooth brushing and looked about the room, she was going to focus and finish her house checks. The wall colour it was something off white, tick that box, thus the bathroom inventory was finished. She would go onto the next room. She forgot that she had intended to clean the room.

'Same, what are you up to tonight?' he asked.

'I'm thinking of painting.'

'Painting really? Portraits, landscapes or home deco?'

'Home decoration unfortunately and I have to decide on a colour,' replied Ciara. She was unsure that she wanted to talk about home decoration with Karl.

'What's your favourite colour?' Karl texted, rudely disturbing her momentum. She felt a delayed twinge of guilt as if he knew what she had just been thinking about, or doing. At least he wasn't interested in talking about interior decoration either.

'Well not beige anyway,' she considered beige to be the interior decorators version of the silver car. In other words grey on the move.

'Me neither, so what is it?'

'Purple.' This was definitely not neutral; maybe she should paint her house purple! "Could he sense that I had a fantasy about him? Did his teeth tingle as I brushed mine? That is silly." At least there could not be a quiver heard in her voice through text.

She got back to the task in hand "Purple is a strong statement, it is not liiliaac which is a bit wishy washy. I think the house would look too individual if it were all painted purple."

The next area to be surveyed was the kitchen; she could not remember the colour of the presses or cupboards as they were called in any other English-speaking country. Could they be wooden or plastic, if someone were to offer her, well lots of money she really couldn't hazard a guess. She had been to the kitchen occasionally usually to make beans on toast. Were there other appliances apart from the toaster and the microwave? Ah yes there was a rather smart coffee machine which was used some Saturdays. Usually this thriftiness of brewing her own coffee coincided with the arrival of a monthly VISA bill, brunch with friends was then suspended for a week or two until finances had been rebalanced, well sort of rebalanced.

"He must be thinking of a witty answer as he is taking ages to reply," her thoughts were being distracted.

'Purple is a good colour it represents the power, not the persuasion' he texted in reply to her favourite colour. It was an interesting response, even if it had taken him ages to think up.

'So Mr Architect, what is your opinion on painting the whole house purple?'

'It would be good if you were trying to make an impression,' he said much quicker in response this time.

'The byzantine, born in the purple,' she liked the Byzantine Empire since her school days and that poem 'Sailing to Byzantium.' It was the East Roman Empire and the language which had very quickly changed from Latin to Greek. The main colour was purple and it was from this that the church established the importance of the colour purple. Only the great rulers wore purple. They were on the same line of thinking.

'Is that the sort of impression you wish to give?'

'Well I know my house is large, but I don't want to brag that it is on Byzantine scale,' she replied.

'Oh Ciara, did I ever tell you how beautiful your eyes were?' he said.

'No I don't think that form of compliment will get you my property!!'

'Purple is a Bishops colour, I'm getting back to the western faiths before the great schism. Or the Western colour view being the man with the colour cards. Now that I am thinking about it you would need a bit more-light to paint your pad entirely in purple.'

'I know I will paint it red, the colour of a Cardinal!!' Cardinal red was definitely not a colour to paint for the feint of veins. One would have to come from the Caribbean like Josephine to pull off that colour.'

'Why' he asked, although she wondered why he asked as she thought he may well know the answer.

'I don't know, why not?'

'It would look like you had killed lots of beetles and pasted them along the living room walls, one at a time.'

'As you have to spill your blood for Christ,' she texted. She had been watching the Borgia family recently and preferred when Cesare was a Bishop than a Cardinal.

So if she were to have viewings of her house, should she put loo paper in the main bathroom and the downstairs toilet? Would people notice? Her thoughts returned to the domestic front and how best to sell her house. It may make the house look inhabited. She only ever used her en-suite. Should she set the table before the auctioneers came around or that may be going too far!

'Yes, red is the colour of passion,' he seemed to be enjoying this.

"If only, all this talk and no action." Could Karl be a man of passion? He seemed to spend a lot of time talking about it but not actually doing anything about it.

She went into the main bathroom and it was so dusty, it looked like a plain in Northern Africa before the Sirocco blew in and gave it a good dusting. She liked when cars were named after real life winds or towns or something other than the manufacturers imagination. The Sirocco was a cool car even if it were a harsh wind. The taps were scoured with stale water and the shower door was opaque from lack of attention. She looked again and there was a tube of tooth paste on the sink. It must have been Aoife's as she was the only person who stayed over and used this bathroom.

'Red is certainly the colour of my bank balance! Especially now as my mortgage has just been direct debited.'

'Ah, so you own your own house. Good for you,' texted Karl.

'Do you not?'

'No I'm just renting, but I am saving hard!!'

She picked up the tube and examined, the same Karl's crux thoughts began to fill her head, swirling about like the river water under his oar. Her mind was turning to filth after all of these salacious texts. She put it down quickly and ran out of the room in search of cleaning products.

'And what is your fave colour?' she asked after not coming to any conclusion on the presentation of her house or whether she liked the shape of Karl's thing.

'Blue,' he said. 'I'm not into the off whites either. They remind me too much of show houses.'

'The ocean' she said. 'Why do most boys like blue?'

'It is the infinity of calm then the storm, melting ice on fire!'

"Wow he has illusions of himself," she thought. 'Steady on!' she sent.

She eventually got to the living room and switched on the computer to look at floor coverings. At least she could be acquainted with ranges, colours and prices before the homeware store visit with her Mum. Solid hard wood floors, whoa, who could believe trees were so expensive, no wonder Brazil was turning to football. The next option was laminate wood, Ciara had an aversion to these in the past, but as she looked at the display some were really nice. She just had to look harder. Laminate floors of now were what wood chip was to the 80s and flock wall paper was to her parent's generation. Well price it the first factor of demand, it depended on how deep the planks were, a cm or so as deep as Ciara herself!

A flat in town, again this was what was driving the effort. Ciara returned to the fantasy of a new life, a new start, to begin again. It reminded her of what all the practicality was for and wow if felt great to be there. They were too many ideas, too many decisions to be made, she felt overwhelmed. Maybe it was one of Karl's blue ocean waves crashing over her. She looked at her hands and there was a mild tremor, only noticeable with a cup coffee in her hand. Maybe she had done too much. It was time to rest. She walked slowly to the kitchen as her legs were ever so slightly weak and found a bottle of 60% off wine. She went back into the living room poured a glass of merlot, rhyming with charlotte. She smiled one of her favourite escapisms was beginning. True Blood, and the lively southern states of the USA music was belting out from the screen. A lot of the action happened around Merlottes and the barman cum owner Sam Merlotte. All the characters were pretty easy on the eye but Mr Merlotte wasn't as cute as the cardinal in the Borgia's. She should not really be comparing TV series but it was in the pursuit of colour thus happiness. Neither the cardinal nor Sam Merlotte were Vampires like many of the characters such as the very handsome but very scary Eric. It was good to be easily distractible. She sat on the couch and watched.

'Blue is such a natural colour,' Karl continued. 'That is probably why I like it.' Karl was still contemplating colours, or he might just have wanted to disturb her from her favourite TV show. He regularly texted her during it, the meanie!

'No more natural than green.' She replied at an ad break. Was she being contrary or merely observant? Green was as natural as blue. It was the Earth while blue was the Ocean. Maybe blue was a more dominant colour as 4/5 of the planet was covered by water. She wondered whether Karl was dominant. "Yes he sure is!"

'For the Emerald Isle,' he suggested.

"He is only half green" she thought, "he is only half-Irish." She looked up the Norwegian flag to see what his other colours were. Red, blue and white so he only had a tiny bit of green in him, maybe he was only Irish on St Patrick's Day.

Reality returned with the closing credits of True Blood. Now her thoughts returned to the house inventory. A decision had been made after all these colour texts and she settled on white walls. That was a productive evening. The texting was slow going and her bargain basket wine was bad. After two sips Ciara decided that frugality was fine only if it tasted fine. She was motivated again now that she had rested and had a clear head.

She had been learning whilst work surfing about how to sell her house on the internet! How much fun it could be, taking photos and learning how to up load them, that may take some time. Then by writing a description of her property using lots of floral tones and exaggerating local amenities many buyers would be enticed to view. She would have a few viewings and someone would like the house and ultimately buy it. It would be a hoot. She would definitely understand the process. However the Dublin Property Market had not experienced such a price reduction in living history, it may be a tough time to sell.

'Maybe loose the Emerald Isle. I quite like the gem stone,' she replied to Karl's text ages later. 'Some say diamonds are a girls' best friend but I have always preferred emeralds.'

'Ciara, the trails gone cold!' complained Karl.

'It was only an hour since you sent that text.' Her house was a diamond in the emerald setting of a large art deco bracelet. It would definitely sell.

'Over two' he sulked 'but anyway back into colours! Ah, a lady of quality!' he was replying almost instantaneously there must be poor viewing this evening on the television now that True Blood was over. Had he been watching it too, should she ask?

Shampooing of the carpets would be essential to freshen up the stale smell of un-vacuumed floors, hey if that worked she may not have to buy wooden floors. One less expense, one less decision, one step closer to getting this house on the market but then Ciara thought "the last time these carpets had attention was when Sean lived there. They may well be beyond the beyond. I can rent a carpet cleaner and see how they clean up." Right there, was another tick, she was powering ahead with all this progress.

There were special things or tricks sellers used to make a house appetising, like sprinkling cinnamon in the oven to give the homely smell of baking. That was crucial to make an idle kitchen look lived in but working out how to turn on the oven would be hard. Remembering to turn the oven off after a viewing would also be useful but probably way too practical. She would nearly buy her own house it would look so good if it were not situated in the last road of Leinster before the Galway exit!!

'Well if you're going to talk quality,' she said. 'Maybe you should qualify quality.'

'It is relative as in related to ones expectations or one's relations!' Wow go Karl, he must have been asked this question before.

'Good answer,' said Ciara. "Go on you ya Einstein!!" she thought to herself cynically. 'Green is for virtue not envy, it is the colour of bounty not barren, as in earth. La Costa Smerelda for example,' she continued. This was the only part of Sardinia she had visited so it sounded good.

'You and your Sardinia, just because Napoleon was from Corsica,' he said after maybe a minute of Googling. 'I thought Josephine was from the Caribbean.'

'There is an emerald coast on Martinique as far as I know.'

'Maybe green is your favourite colour,' he said so he wasn't going to take the bait.

'No it's purple,' she said confirming her first position.

'Do you also like rubies? Actually I think I prefer rubies to emeralds,' he said.

'They are beautiful. Rubies remind me of my eyes on a Saturday morning.'

'After a boozy Friday feast?' he asked.

'No generally fatigue from the weeks work,' she lied blatantly. Her screen staring time was more likely to be social than work related these days.

'Boring!'

'Unfortunately my office isn't an offie' she gibed again.

'Touché Ms, it is true that in the last place we had a great off-licence across the road. However now that I am in a serious company it is a lot less fun. I have to go out to have fun' Ok so maybe he was moving on in his career and becoming a bit serious but there was still a lightness in his thumbs which was nice.

'So any other colours you like?'

'Pink, I wear it well (smiley face).'

'It takes a certain type of blond to carry it off,' she said.

'Do I?'

'Of course,' but she had never seen him do so she couldn't be sure. Pity there wasn't a voice accentuation facility to text; she would be able to ascertain whether he was serious, enquiring, joking or just insecure! Or maybe just as well as she has an image flash across her brain of him in a pink tie and well not much else.

There was one mode of communication which would assist in distinguishing the tone of the other's voice and give it some colour be it purple, green or blue, but unfortunately it was called a telephone call. It was something he didn't do, call her that was, or receive her calls.

'Well that's good. I can now reclaim pink from the Barbie brigade (see I'm using your alliterative style as a weak attempt at flattery). Why should plastic toys had monopoly on a colour?'

'Why indeed. Could it be a marketing phenomenon?' Ciara liked the symbolism behind colours; many great thinkers had idled away years on them whilst ignoring their main theories. So if it was good enough for the ancients it was good enough for her.

'I think if I ever have children I will dress the boys in pink,' Karl was taking a radical stance.

'Yes a clear sign of manliness to wear pink. I will bid you adieu.' Ciara said delighted that she had finished the texting first for a change. He had mentioned children, his children, not theirs but she decided to ignore it. Ciara thought often guys talk of children as a hook to reel the female in. However generally it helped to meet the person if you wanted to have children, there was something a bit clinical about sending a vial for insemination. Something Ciara likened to the bovine industry and AI in the non computing sense.

'A thousand times goodnight,' he attempted a Romeo moment or was it Juliet who had said it from the balcony. It didn't matter, it was romantic and sweet. Could he have been thinking of Sopranos and Venice or Verona or somewhere from one of their racy texts? Who knows?

She had had a good evening and that was all that counted, she had made lots of practical decision and she was finally putting fantasy into reality. She would sell her house.

The Auctioneers

Ciara spent the entire journey into work thinking about how she would advertise her house. She thought about what she would say when people visited and that she probably would say really negative things about her house and this would put people off. By the time she reached her destination Ciara had decided against selling her house on her own. Her first task of the day was to research local auctioneers and she made three appointments with local agents the for the next weekend day. She realised that she was no estate agent she would make a bag's, of the sale should she try to sell her house herself. This was another example of how to optimise ones work time and the following Saturday she had them in one after the other. She was preparing to give each property consultant (as the websites described them) a drilling in order to drive down their fees as every cent would make the difference between being able to move or not. The house was an average three-bedroom semi-detached home in a small estate close to transport links. This was a great way to get away from suburb-land and into the country.

Logic dictated that if she had bought this house well signed as silly Sean had wanted to buy it; someone else would, buy it too. Luckily she wasn't in a ghost estate, unfinished and un-inhabited, there were an unlucky group of people whom had purchased off plan for a 'discount'. Very inverted commas as prices were being discounted now by about 60%. They had bought and moved into new developments with an expectation that others would join them over time and a new community would form. Then things had changed. "Those poor people must be sick," she thought, but she was too, she had to take a huge price cut. "Ah well cut the losses." In Ciara's case she would lose on the purchase price and clear a big mortgage, but hopefully she could buy an apartment for cash and it was all paper loss in the end if she could be mortgage free.

The first agent came on Saturday morning, looked around and when asked gave lots of tips on what to do. Obviously these were just opinions but as the lady worked in property hopefully they were informed opinions. Her valuation was quite high in Ciara's un-informed opinion. What she did know, and she only had "Daft" evidence, a house on her street in better condition was selling for less. Or maybe this high price was a tactic; make the competition look cheaper or something. This auctioneer was also selling the house on Ciara's road so maybe her loyalties were a bit divided.

'Hey Ciara, what the craic?' Karl was texting early on Saturday afternoon. Was he back from rowing she wondered?

'Rien bouche ou pas beaucoup,' she wasn't going to tell him she was in the middle of the most important decision of her life. Getting her house valued was a huge step to making the new Ciara.

'Pauvre toi!' it looked as if he was using his Google translate well he was Nordic so French may not flow like some of his other gushing's or outputs!

'Life is good though.'

'Nice to hear it, I'm off to Norway next week.'

'Ah that's nice, any boat building with your grandpa.'

'Unfortunately he is a bit sick at the moment.'

'Ah Karl, I am sorry to hear that. I really hope it isn't serious.'

'He is very old, over 90. He had a wild life and only married in his forties.'

'Did he tell you interesting stories of his miss-spent youth?'

'Actually he did, we are very close. He had to be serious with my father to ensure he didn't turn out as wild as he was, but with me he could be himself. He wasn't responsible for me, I will really miss him.'

Ciara wasn't quite sure what to say, "sure he's having a good innings" may have been a bit insensitive. 'It sounds like you have had a really good relationship and I truly hope it continues.'

'Thanks, I like you sometimes.'

'Wow, what can I say, sometimes, I can be likeable.'

'And sometimes you can even be funny.' Karl must really be upset if he was complimenting her!

'Careful, I might get a big head,' what was she going to do with him at all, at all!

There was a ring at the door and it was the second auctioneer. She was going to have to put a hold to the texts for the next half an hour. The next lady was middle aged, inspired confidence and was very professional. She gave sound advice and cited the recent sale as evidence of the rational for her valuation. Ciara went with her and forgot to negotiate down the fees. Ah well most battles one loses!

If the Auctioneer was as professional as she had seemed at the outset she would sell the house and all that Ciara would have to do was keep her house in order. In other words she would just sleep there and eat out every morning noon and night. Not a big change really. The lady advised her that there was a narrow window of opportunity which would last a good three weeks. If the price was low enough Ciara would not need to paint, tile, sand floors, re-light or in any other way engage with home decoration. This was probably the main reason Ciara chose her. Ultimately price was the primary factor of demand but lack of hassle came a very near second.

The third auctioneer didn't show up. It was probably a good thing too.

Karl didn't text back, maybe he had said too much. Ciara was thinking again that she definitely imagined that meeting. Like would Karl really have lost his cool and said, "you are the one for me?"

****

Ciara kept her side of the bargain and checked her e-mails regularly over the next few weeks to ensure she wouldn't be at home during viewings. She also regularly slept over at her parents' house to avoid any cleaning, tidying or household tasks. And it worked the Auctioneer was true to her word. Then there was an offer on her house. It was at a good level actually higher than she was expecting. She thought she should accept it. It was all happening very quickly but after years of inactivity this was exactly what she needed. A solicitor was sought to act on her behalf. She asked some friends and family who they could recommend and decided on one fairly close to her office. She would be able to walk over on her lunch breaks if the solicitor didn't perform and loiter with intent on the pavement. Also, eventually when the process came to a close signing conveyance papers would be easy.

Next the second half of the process began, to browse and buy a new place and this is where the fun really started. She could not believe it but in this day and age one had to pay for a brochure at the auction house. Everyone was talking about very cheap properties being sold at auction and Ciara wanted to see what all the fuss was about. Brochures had been the raison d'être of rainy Saturday afternoons where it was the national habit for women to browse show houses in new developments getting ideas for their own houses. This was in the good times when you couldn't see the sky between all of the cranes. The brochure was the trophy showing the endurance a woman had by visiting at least three developments on that same rainy Saturday, well some women. They were displayed proudly on coffee tables like glossy hard back design books or pictures from great artists of works never seen in real life but known intimately from friend's coffee tables. No wonder she was interested in Karl, he must have so many show houses and apartments available to him, it could occupy her for a whole weekend!

The auction house route was focusing on repossessions but seemed to derive most of its income from selling brochures or auction lists. There was no gloss, just an address and one viewing time, then the auction. She tried the method once but it was too hard work. It seemed too cruel to buy from someone in distress; ethically Ciara couldn't have done it. The online site Daft was the new way to go. It was the Google of property. She looked about for apartments in the city centre but couldn't forget the loft or attic as she liked to call it. She could imagine taking up painting and pretending she lived in Paris as she sketched the cityscape. So she viewed it again and it was all she remembered. Bright, airy with lovely views, central yet quiet if that was possible. It was in terrible condition and so she made a really low offer and asked to be kept in the running. She didn't really mind the condition, it had a bath and would have a bed what else did she need, she would be in town for goodness sake.

The auctioneer, Irish for estate agent or realtor laughed at her low offer and she felt a little insulted. Maybe this was why the profession had tarnished its own image and likeness during the boom. Ciara stayed calm and confirmed her offer. 'I am serious, I am in a strong position and I would like to hear your clients' thoughts on my offer,' she said in an authoritative tone in her voice. 'On the first viewing if you remember I had to sell my property but now I have a firm offer and it is in solicitors hands.'

'I will do,' said he, the unhelpful auctioneer. 'Can you come up a bit as I think there is a chance that she would accept a higher level?'

'Put it to her and let me know. Thank you.'

Ciara put down the phone confidently she really didn't like this guys' attitude but hey he was just a gate keeper. She needed to get past him and it was a process. It was a bit like a clip-board-blond outside your favourite club. That was all, a bit of patience would be required but she was in a strong position. Her position would be strengthened though by having contracts signed on her own house. She could let the purchasing side drift a few weeks, seem nice and laid back and also fish for what other opportunities may lay out there on the Dublin property market. It was a buyers' market according to every media comment so she was in the drivers' seat. "I'm in no hurry."

It was all action today as 'R u in 2 power play?' Karl texted a few moments after she put down the phone. There was no "hey Ciara," or "how are you?" He was straight into it; could this be to do with the colour blue and its plans for world dominance? Maybe he was already away in Norway or on the plane with the doors about to close and trying to look important? Although he couldn't have been that upset if he were in a naughty mood. His grandfather must be doing ok.

On the other hand then news may be really bad and he was distracting himself through text. Had his grandfather passed away and this was grief related texting. Maybe she should give him some slack just in case. He was using text speech so he probably was abroad saving words it had been a while since she had heard from him.

'R u ok?' "Two can text-speak." He must be into power play if he had asked, that was the only conclusion she reached. It was interesting timing for this question as she had been confirmed into a position of power. She was directing her own property affairs and that was something powerful.

'Yep, so r u?' he repeated.

'No, well only if I'm in control,' it was a joke of course, it was not as if she were really career focused, she was not. She never played competitive sport the only thing she was good at was History, could this be similar to being competitive in a past life? Oh and day dreaming and her special skill, environmental scanning. There had not been any exciting environments to scan recently as she hadn't seen Karl again, hanging out his window with a green colour card but she lived in hope. Any large hand would do.

'Control, is that not the result of power play?'

'Well maybe it depends on where the starting point is' she said. Karl was dominant and dominated the ice and melted Ciara's inertia, her frozen will to live and her automaton state. Whether he realised this or not was immaterial as he was a catalyst. It was his activity level which was restarting Ciara's life.

'Sounds a bit like Irish directions' he said. 'If I were going there I wouldn't be starting from here, ha ha.' Was that a non-confrontational dominance?

'True,'

Her attention was distracted for a moment as she imagined a phone call where her offer, would be accepted. Wow could the vendor be as desperate as herself. She had strong pangs of desire for something other than Karl, how novel. It was a cheekily low offer but all that she could afford. She looked up the location of it on the attached map. Wow the flat in town had the same postal district as Aras án Uachtarain, if that wasn't coming up in the world she didn't know what was! Granted it also had the Central Criminal Courts and one of the highest rates of crime in the sleepy city. Well she would just have to take the bad with the good. It was just as well she was planning to buy an attic, if anyone clambered up six floors then they were welcome to steal something it was a just reward. Conversely if someone robbed one's bag should they not pick up ones credit card debt, it's only fair! It may be the best deterrent ever. It may however encourage irresponsible spending which would inadvertently lead to economic recovery, and they say crime doesn't pay. "Focus Ciara, are you going to text him back? Or is it his turn, yes it is his turn." She could happily idle away days at a time with happy thoughts in her head, if people only knew what went on in her brain she would be most likely put on anti-psychotic tablets.

So a loft apartment in the New York sense was way too aspirational a term, but there were cool roof top views, oblique they may be from a narrow railed, floating platform not quite wide enough to be a balcony. No work was being done this morning and she wished she was busy enough to be distracted. However the views were there and so would she be given time. She was very rarely certain of anything or wanted anything but she wanted this and she knew it would be hers. God bless Daft, the one stop shop for a flat. "Please may the vendor come back soon" she crossed her fingers and closed her eyes tightly.

'Yes the weaker has all to gain and the stronger everything to lose.' He texted again and she looked down to see his offering. Karl was back on his power-play again.

'I have felt that we were fairly equally balanced.' This was really the main draw for her, the brain, there did seem to be a bit of tension maybe even friction through their texts but she thought this was more a sign of sexual tension than power play. Maybe she was wrong or she just had a different view of things to Karl.

'As you said it depends on the situation. If it were Napoleon he had all of Europe to gain.' Karl was stressing his point.

'Yes but eventually he lost his freedom,' she said.

'Elba would be a nice place to be exiled.'

'I suppose it was less remote than St Helena.' Ciara thought that her house was like St Helena and her nearly-flat was as central as Elba Island, you could be in Pisa by speed boat in about twenty minutes and on the Dublin scale that was like a twenty-minute walk to the Phoenix Park to visit Wellington's Monument.

'To be there with you now, under blue sky not grey,' he said.

"Chance would be a fine thing you complete chancer!" She thought she should not get cheeky with him as he generally ignored her for an interminable amount of time like a few days sometimes and up to a couple of weeks on other occasions so she thought a jokey directive would work best. 'Check out the tickets! Or could you row me there?'

Ciara focused her mind on the business in hand. There was a small snag; she had a good €25 in her bank account. This was not enough to put a deposit down on the attic if her offer was accepted. So she decided to use Aoife's advice and take in tenants as an interim step. This would ensure that when her offer were acceptable that nasty holding deposit which, much as she wished it to be waived, which had to be paid, could be paid. She had already asked her solicitor to transfer her holding deposit but the answer had been no.

Her creative idea was that the deposits the future tenants would be her holding deposit. This would alleviate the cash flow issues also. Their rent would mean nicer wine as frugality was not her strong point. She could work the details out later but this was a good start. She would advertise for short term tenants and fill the house. It would be like a grow house, actually no, that meant weed, a student house with at least one person in each bedroom. However this would mean that her space would not be her own. She would be sharing in her own house and that would be weird. This place which even though she always cribbed about it was her home, it may not be the cool pad of her dreams but it was quiet, warm, bright and spacious relatively. It would feel very strange sharing again after all this time. "It is only for a few months until the deals are tied up. It will be worth it in the long run." Long term gain is one thing but when you have to actually live through the short-term discomfort, it is very different.

'Rowing may take a long time Ciara, but you're light' said Karl, he was answering her text about getting to Elba.

She would wait until the evening and then research room to rent rates, assess what sort of photographs she would need to take and get her head around it. A lot was happening and after a half a decade of inactivity it was a bit too much for Ciara. She switched on her computer and tried to answer some work email. They were hum drum regular problems so she copied and pasted her standard answers, changed the titles and brands and sent them off. 'Phew, twenty minutes work, I'm exhausted' she yawned to nobody in particular.

'I'm the same' said Stephen. 'Ten emails and I'm done in!'

'Fancy a break?' she asked.

'A sneaky smoke break?' Stephen suggested.

'Let's do it' so they popped outside into the freezing cold air and clogged their lungs whilst clearing their heads.

Back at the desk Ciara's thoughts reverted to renting out rooms, how would she take decent photographs when she couldn't use the camera on her phone? "Maybe I could 'borrow' the photos from the sale of my house. I do have a legal right to them, well hopefully." Yes she would think about it later, at home as she tried to finish that yucky bottle of merlot.

'Could a speed boat be easier than rowing?' said Ciara to Karl. 'You could check out the prices.'

'Will do,' replied Karl a good hour later. She had forgotten what he was "will doing" to. So she scrolled up through her texts and discovered Karl was into world domination and power play and was checking out the cost of renting a speed boat or maybe flight tickets. It would be the top of   his   to   do   list   of   course.

The Sean Affect

It was some time later, weeks in fact after that traumatic phone call from her terrible ex that Ciara could contemplate what had happened and her reactions to it. Ciara was not being dramatic the relationship had been more than a little difficult for her. Now though as she was moving forward in her life she could analyse things rationally, well nearly rationally.

Ciara had one serious relationship in her relatively short life and it had been with a guy called Sean. On the outside he had seemed wonderful, a few years older, a good bit taller, good cheek bones and a nice warm smile, yep she was as deep as a puddle that a toddler had just splashed in. They were going out a few years before they moved in together. Ciara was paid more than Sean but only marginally and actually she had more disposable income as she had been living at home at the time. As luck would have it her mother encouraged her to save what she would be paying in rent. So when Sean wanted to buy a house Ciara was able to fund the deposit. Not that Ciara minded as Sean always had big plans, he was going to start his own business, the business plan changed regularly but she believed in him. However what he did to her was harsh, when one business after the next failed he blamed Ciara, he accused her of sabotaging the concept and distracting him from his work.

He often worked from home and became well acquainted with day time television. His earnings sunk so low that

Ciara bore the lions' share of the mortgage. As his confidence diminished he turned his frustrations on Ciara degrading her to a point which verged on mental abuse. As Sean's career was floundering in a time of unprecedented economic success, his sense of failure was heightened by his friends earning huge money. They went on extravagant holidays with their girlfriends and he was barely surviving, he blamed Ciara for all these problems and wore her down. As his confidence dipped he began to accuse Ciara of flirting with other guys then he began accusing her of seeing other people. It got so bad that when Ciara walked along the street her head would point to the pavement. Ciara did not tell anyone about this and felt guilty for behaviour patterns which she had not committed. She sunk lower and lower into herself and became unsure of who she was and what she was capable of.

Sean was incapable of meeting Ciara's needs as he denied that she had any, in fact he was unaware she had any. He never listened, was never interested in her life, activities and achievements denigrated them so low that Ciara didn't think they mattered.

All of these thoughts came rushing back to her and she needed to talk to someone. Stephen knew a little bit but not the extent of the character undermining but she really needed to tell Aoife. Now that Aoife and she were closer she should not keep this secret from her. She called her, the dial tone connected.

'Aoife?' she asked, 'It's Ciara, are you free.'

'I'm just about to go out but I'm yours for five!'

'I may need about six minutes or even seven minutes,' Ciara was trying to joke but she was so out of sorts that humour glands or those areas of her brain were disconnected.

'Are you alright?' Aoife could hear in her tone of voice that something was very wrong.

'You know I had a call from Sean a while back and it has really upset me.'

'Ciara I am sorry to hear that but he left over two years ago.'

'Yes I know that, but Aoife how do I say this without sounding to emotional or dramatic.'

'Just tell me straight.'

Ciara felt this information was too personal to say over the phone so she was silent for a few moments. Should she arrange to meet Aoife and tell her of the deep dark secret which had been lurking inside her for far too long? She couldn't wait, now was the moment and she may not have to courage to say it another time. She started intending to explain slowly and give Aoife some time to consider what she was saying but in the end it was like the valve of a very hot industrial revolution machine. It had become loose and all of the hot, burning contents gushed out the top.

'Sean abused me emotionally and completely undermined my confidence. He criticised me, how I look, how I dress, my job, my friends everything. He tore down my confidence one layer at a time until I was a shaking shell like a big glossy advert for new apartments on an unfinished concrete block. Unfortunately the wind and rain had damaged the glossy exterior and large ugly steel rods were visible out at the sides and top. There was just a hollow ugly core remaining.' There were definite signs of dramatic and emotional feelings with the symbolism in Ciara's' speech.

'Glossy exterior' said Aoife. She was silent and then said without knowing 'And you seem so normal.' She seemed shocked, stuck for words and all the wrong things were coming out of her mouth.

'Amazing what you can project,' said Ciara. Was she talking about the steel rods or the sham of a happy person as displayed on the wafer thing adverts curtaining those unfinished carcasses of apartment blocks?

'Sorry Ciara, really I don't know what to say. I am stunned.'

Ciara was silent for a moment then said, 'you don't have to say anything. I just wanted you to know.'

'Of course, but I have to say something. I never knew this, yes Sean could be difficult at times and he and Brian hung out in the looser club as far as I was concerned, but I always thought you were the boss of that relationship.'

'No I was never the boss, Sean was a control freak.'

'I am skipping the gym,' said Aoife. 'Actually I am in shock.'

'Sorry!' said Ciara but not quite sure what she was apologising for. Maybe it was the gym, that guy she never got to know, "Jim" she preferred slim Jim.

'You were such a together person that you seemed to carry him. I have always felt I needed to put my best foot forward with you as I was always a bit threatened by you and your ability to cope with everything life throws at you.' Aoife was incredulous.

'Well I feel the same about you. You are a superwoman and a free woman now. Sometimes I thought you would laugh if I told you little things about me. Laugh the way Sean used to do, but I tell you anyway, well in the past few months as I have to tell someone. You can't bottle everything up or there wouldn't be room inside.' Ciara had finally got it all out and maybe it was better to say such hurt over the phone. She didn't have to see Aoife's face.

'We really hid ourselves from each other, why were we so silly?'

'Maybe we are or were fixated on perfection' said Ciara, 'we have such high ideals of each other we don't want to let down or else we have to face the reality about ourselves.'

'Who knows but let's be a bit more honest from now on,' said Aoife.

This was their BFF moment but they were much too embarrassed to say it to each other, so like many feelings in Ireland it was left unsaid. However this conversation solidified the healing process of their friendship, Aoife became more open and Ciara saw her has human rather than angelic.

Life and friends

Ciara had not heard back from the Auctioneer about her offer, still. It was her main day dream and had transposed Karl from her every waking thought. If only the vendor would answer and the apartment would be hers. So she decided to distract herself. Since her chat with Aoife she thought it could be good, sometimes to live in the present as Sean was in the past and that was where he was going to stay. She didn't live in the early nineteenth century all the time, only in text times. Whilst focusing on the good things in her life, she realised she had lots of friends and work colleagues. She had collected friends since her first day at nursery school and had kept hold of them till the present. Here and now was good. It was true that now she didn't see her friends as much as she had done in the past but contact was retained through text, a quick and unobtrusive method. Texts could be sent at any time, responded to whenever and were a testament to the amount of people she knew. At the end of each week she did have a full inbox, but not in the way Karl had intended it.

To be able to leave a text a few days before responding was a sign of a mature friendship, in Ciara's eyes at least. If you have known someone since preschool they wouldn't think that you were blanking them if the response was not instant. Even a delay of a week was considered completely acceptable. As some of her friends were now endowed with children the likelihood of seeing them from one end of the year to the next was remote. Thus humorous or memorable responses were appreciated and a bit of contemplation time was good. Drafts were often generated on busses, at work or wherever and left for a few days in order that the spark of creativity would enliven the message and hopefully brighten up at least a little the receivers day. Ciara was now remembering to send her draft texts, which was definitely a sign that her life was beginning to come together.

'Hey Ciara, what's up,' said Karl on what's app. He was enjoying using this medium as he could send lots of photographs of himself doing lots of activities such as rowing. Was he more into his body than she was? He had also referred to the scarves photograph on many occasions in the hope that she would send more of the same.

'Apart from the sky, and that isn't very far up today, not much.'

Her two friends Aoife and Stephen were her rocks. They were the ones Ciara saw most, Stephen because was working with her and Aoife because she worked nearby. That however was not the reason why she saw them the most; really it was because she felt closest to them. It had absolutely nothing to do with laziness.

Don was lost to Ciara, unfortunately he had been given notice of redundancy and had been feeling low. Whilst he liked his job as little as Ciara did, he had an ego which seemed greater than his family man bravado and his great financial responsibilities. This job had been convenient for him as he could have flexi time and family time. If his children were sick he could allegedly work from home. However the company was failing financially and there was not enough work to go around.

He wasn't responding to Ciara's motivating texts and she had decided to leave things for a while and give him some space. Maybe he was blaming her as her contract hadn't been terminated or told that it was no longer there, if that was what redundant meant. He had always said that his work was better than Ciara's. She had never challenged him on this as she thought he was only joking.

She had been thinking of inviting them all to her unusually clean house, as in all of Don's family, for dinner with Stephen and Sophie but as there was no response from Don she had to put plans on ice. Definitely she wouldn't have invited Anna and Adam as she knew that would be insensitive and wrong. Anna after all had given the notice of redundancy to Don. "Do people normally get notice?" Ciara thought that Anna was being particularly kind giving Don time to leave.

Stephen felt that he was still working for the company purely for diversity monitoring or a sign of positive discrimination. He enjoyed his job more than Ciara but he was feeling really guilty at not being sacked. He was quite sensitive and was concerned for Don's situation especially as he had a family and a large mortgage. Stephen had been single for most of his friendship with Ciara but now that he was seeing Sophie things were looking up. He was feeling fulfilled and cherished in this relationship and

Ciara if she was truly honest with herself was feeling a bit left out. So maybe life and friends were not as strong a point as Ciara had thought before she started examining.

Things were not rosy in the international department of their company either. Sophie was preparing herself for a move to hopefully a better company. One of the few growth areas in the Irish economy was international software. Companies were locating in Dublin and needed language skills to access the European market. Sophie was extremely capable and got a job at a social networking company only a short walk from the office. It was a real step up the career ladder which heightened Ciara's sense of her career wallowing in the doldrums. This meant that most of Stephen's lunch breaks were spent with Sophie and Ciara had to power-walk alone. No pace-maker with a five-gear wheelchair. She was to be on her own for a while now, well apart from the odd text from Karl to keep her company.

It was Don's final day so Ciara went over to him to bid him good bye. He had barely lifted his eyes to her all week. She wanted to encourage him to stay in touch and continue attending the employee nights out.

'Hi' she tried to chirp.

'So Ciara this is it' said Don.

'It is.'

'This is the end of my long and inglorious career in customer infrequent-service. How many times have we joked about this term and changed it about?'

434

'I know Don, the dis-service-ers, so many times, but you have a lucky out.'

'Is that so? You don't have responsibilities' he said. She didn't think it the right time to highlight the fact that his wife bore the lion's share of financial responsibilities and that by being at home he would be able to nurture his children even more than he already did. His was the homemakers' side of the marital relations and from all evidence Ciara had seen it was a role in which he excelled.

'Ah but I have an extensive shoe collection, most of which still has to be paid for' she said trying to placate the situation.

'Don't be flippant Ciara; I have a mortgage, two children and a wife who wants more shoes than you do.'

'I know but you will be still able to enjoy our nights out,' Ciara didn't want to mention the large severance payment which would more than likely clear Don's mortgage and put his two children through boarding school. Also his wife the highly organised and successful banker must be doing fairly well so what was the problem, his ego? He was feeling hurt and she wished to keep the mood light as she always found reality difficult to deal with.

'Come on Ciara what interest would I have meeting up with people I used to work for and with?'

'To have fun,' she said, she didn't want to say it would maybe help to keep his spirits up by keeping in contact with former employees many of whom were already unemployed.

'It was only a networking exercise for me' he replied rather harshly.

Ciara was hurt she had thought people, well Don enjoyed the social events; they were almost a relationship substitute for her. It was fair to say that she ideated and Stephen and Sophie organised these outings but she had felt the creative process was key to the success of social gatherings!

'You only organise them because you have an empty life,' said Don.

It felt as if a dagger were entering her side and was heading for the kidney or was it the liver? 'Don thank you, I know where I stand.'

'Ciara you live vicariously, through the families of other people, their relationships and their children.' The said dagger was definitely twisting. 'We are all sick of your virtual relationship. It will be one thing I won't miss from here.' Was he referring to her virtual relationship? That was the sacred Karl or rather cow, the elephant in the room, the tiger who came to tea. Everyone knew how much this virtual relationship meant to Ciara, they had blow by blow accounts and some of the better, funnier e-mails and texts had been circulated around the office. Some of this had been to the embarrassment then later a source of pride to Ciara as she felt she had banged out some interesting creative writing. Actually she was thinking sometimes it was the opposite way, many of her co-workers who were in happy but sometimes dull marriages and relationships enjoyed the spark of the unknown. Anna was certainly one, not that her marriage was boring or anything.

'I thought we were friends Don.'

'You were never a friend, you self-absorbed so and so!'

She was thinking Ferragamo's now, shoes were the usual escape from daggers aimed at the vital organs.

A bit of reflection

Meta, could this be to induce a change? Ciara had always thought that there were three stabilisers in life, home, work and relationships. As she didn't have a relationship she had 2/3 and in the lines of a 1980's song two out of three ain't bad! She had all of the above however as relationships need not be just with a guy or a gal but friendship, family, nieces and nephews and if she were really honest she did like her brothers children. These were all rewarding and fulfilling relationships and whilst to be with someone one loves is important there are many types of love. So therefore she had lost none of these components which balance life but was trying to change all three. She was trying to start a relationship, she was attempting to move-house and also to change jobs. Generally doing one major change at a time was good enough for most people, but doing one thing at a time generally bored Ciara. It wasn't as if she were capable of multi-tasking but it tended to be all or nothing with her. It seemed to Ciara that she had to endure struggle and strife to become, well a little less bored. Is the journey demeaned a little as it is a choice rather than a necessity? She wasn't sitting on a rooftop with the seagull when she saw the wings flap and their eyes lock. She had a nice warm office she was not a victim of a war a flood, a typhoon or an epidemic. "Would a natural disaster make Karl feel for me? Would he row across the

Liffey to save me if the building was burning? I am not really the damsel in distress type."

In this case however nothing has actually been thrust upon her. She has found herself to be unfulfilled and so decided to make a change. Does this make one more or less sympathetic for her and her plight? Is boredom really the greatest torture? We slowly sink under it out of fear of change, of the unknown; we might not make it out of our comfort zone.

And then it happened, her phone rang, she almost jumped as it was so rare for the phones to ring in the office.

'Hello?'

'Is that Ciara?' came a jovial upbeat voice over the phone.

'It is,' who could this be, she didn't know anyone who was this friendly?

'It's Miles and I was calling to let you know about your offer.'

'Oh Miles, nice to hear from you,' her voice echoed his joviality.

'Yes I want to let you know that your offer has been accepted.'

'Ahhhhhhh,' she screamed down the phone. 'Pardon me!' She composed herself. 'Thank God in heaven, really and truly? I can't believe it? I am sooooo happy.' This was better than kissing Karl, the sweetest moment of her life.

'I take it that you would like to proceed.'

'Yes, definitely, ah thank you, thank you so much.'

Lots of giggling was happening around her, Ciara was not normally the most restrained worker but this was her best example of boisterous outbursts in a while. Since Don had left all the office fun, was over. He seemed to have taken the lightness with him. Even Stephen was concentrating on his ten e-mails a day and learning French the other 97% of the time and it seemed that everyone else was getting serious also. By staring at their computers they tried to look busy, everyone that was but Ciara.

She was hopping out of her seat and gave a big wave across the Liffey, 'here's to you, you great big colour card!' she exclaimed vaguely in the direction of Karl's office block. 'And if you called me now, I would say you were the nearly the one for me. Except I have found my ONE and it has four walls and a roof.'

She thought she had better sit down. She composed her thoughts and thought.

The things which were important to her, back to thinking and calming down, friends, home and job in that order. Ciara was classifying her friends as romantic relationship substitutes, in the strictest sense of the word. Although her friends were better in many respects than a romantic relationship, as they constituted all the fun with less of the fuss, yet she would always be on the outside when someone romantic came along for them. She was not envious of Stephen and Sophie as they didn't have her penthouse, ha! Actually at this particular moment home was number one in her triangle of life and stability.

She had many work friends, yes she was looking around the room at the lessening number of desks but not all her work friends were current work friend. In general work friends were circumstantial but on reflection did not all life's interactions rely on circumstance? School, many years sitting beside the same person, eventually you would have to make friends. Or a train journey across Russia, weeks in a carriage with strangers who would tell you only the interesting aspects of their lives, okay she was not going to think of Napoleon now. No more sieges and long trundles back to France losing boots and furs. Many, many years working together had given depth to formal work interactions. Losing colleagues, winning clients, sometimes, had brought her closer to people like Stephen, Anna and even Don. Ciara didn't want to state the obvious but one had to be there to experience the circumstance. It was only after one moved on that a friendship was really defined. With all these leavers or depart-ers at work would there be anyone with whom Ciara would stay in touch?

Would they still come to her social nights? With employee numbers reducing so rapidly it was important to keep a social outlet in order to avoid survivor syndrome.

'I can't believe it' somehow escaped her lips. No one asked her what her excitement was about, not just yet anyway. Mostly they thought she was mad. Could they be thinking she had got a new job, fat chance she hadn't even started that part of her life changing exercise.

Ciara tried some calming thoughts, social nights out now this was the line of thinking. She should organise another one and encouraged ex-colleagues like Don to come along. "Who am I kidding?" she managed under her breath. "There is no way in the world Don would come along, he had said no, no and another no for good measure. How mean of him." In Ciara's mind attending social night was an important attempt to increase people's morale and to retain links as they were now colleagues no more. The success rate varied. They were not quite friends, these colleagues but more than acquaintances. It was a good opportunity for people to network. "Network, yuck, pseudo intellectual conversation whilst swilling Chablis around a peculiarly shaped wine glass." Networking was Ciara's most hated topic she really disliked pushing herself forward. "It is good all the same for those forward thinkers to see what is out there, beyond our company, I suppose. Some people especially those with, IT skills have been fortunate enough to find new jobs and are happy to help others as much as they can. That is kind."

It was time for a smoke break, she couldn't stay quietly in her head, her head was ready to explode with happiness she didn't think she had ever been this happy in her whole entire life. She closed her text file and she took one last look at the property web site which had already marked 'Under Offer' on her apartment and she walked away from her desk. Ciara went to the lifts but decided to take the stairs. By running down the six flights of steps she attempted to release some excited energy and nearly knocked over two people on her way. 'Sorry!'

She was outside now and calming down. She was thinking of nothing. She was looking at nothing except the water when she crossed the road a car screeched to a standstill as she walked straight in front of it. 'Sorry' she said to the white-faced driver who looked in shock.

'For goodness sake misses, you didn't even look.'

'I am sorry' said Ciara. 'My mind was elsewhere.'

'You would have been on the tarmac if my brakes were not good.' The driver started his car and drove off slowly.

'Woops!' Ciara went to a seating area beside the river and felt the sun on her face. She didn't feel shaken up, in fact she felt completely alive and happy to be. She looked to the left to the Samuel Beckett Bridge and watched the sun glinting on all of the components which made up the white suspension frame and admired the length and elegance of its design. "It is said that you can play the bridge like a harp" she said to herself. She forgot to take out her cigarettes as she watched the bicycles avoid the walkers and the riders ringing their gingili bells on the newly rented Dublin blue bikes.

"Meta, I had been thinking of stability versus change. These were my thoughts for the day before the offer was accepted. Maybe Karl was my Meta, or is that catalyst or something. Karl is someone who is doing his own thing irrespective of me so I have to get my thing on. He is like my friends who are married and busy with their nuclear lives. To meet me they have to worry who will mind the offspring? Do they arrange to leave those children at home just to make me feel good? Or could the reality be that these friends are using our meetings as an excuse to leave children with their respective partners. Maybe I am an opportunity to these friends rather than an excuse. I can enjoy my role of singleton without guilt whilst being able to provide for them with singles times again."

She was thinking these were nice thoughts. Ciara was the time to be in the moment for her friends, and generally they were mothers. Ciara was the time and space to recollect past moments of fun and abandon without always having to watch for dangers. To constantly need to scan the floor, walls, and doors to the outside world where tiny tots would roam, in other words the opportunity to relax. Ciara couldn't claim a lot but being good fun she always was. 'Wow we can have an all-night house warming party, hit the clubs and then back for bubbly at mine and we can walk. It may be economy-finest bubbly but I will serve it in nice glasses and even put in a bit of juice to hide the taste.' She was getting excited again, a house warming or flat warming would be something to get her over the E5,000 holding deposit quandary. She was still in a positive state of shock that her offer had been accepted.

The sun continued to shine glistening the waters of the Liffey, the tide was turning and there was a strong smell of salty sea water rushing in. She should really be going back in but she looked beyond the water to the shiny green buildings at the far side, Karl could be looking out right at this moment on these very same waters.

"You are the one for me," she had actually not said this aloud, this was progress. Ciara relived the meeting arranged in her head. Karl, she was the one for Karl. Karl and Ciara, Ciara and Karl like graffiti written on the back of a ladies room door. Or maybe it could be sprayed from a gaudy coloured canister of purple and blue on a wall. Karl she felt the letters of his name flow around the undulations of her mouth. Monosyllabic names are a bit premature, over before they have begun, difficult to know where to stress the importance. Especially in English where there are no clues such as fadas. Is it at the beginning, stress the K, it could be a bit too harsh and front-loaded. As there is no middle the end was the only logical place. It however sounded too Nordic to stress the L as if she were attempting to mimic his very light accent. Generally he had no accent at all, except on certain words, which words were they? Assimilating his sounds in order to feel closer to him, maybe even get to know him. That was not logical. Actually she really hadn't a clue how Karl was pronounced in Norway and her pseudo intellectual terms lead her to consider that the name was a bit Germanic.

If she were really honest she couldn't remember his voice, how it sounded but she had imagined it many times when she read his texts and e-mails. Why could she forget his voice but not him, she really wished she could. To be free from texts, yes she was the one who was over-text.

"I am ready to go back in."

As she was walking the stairs she tried to resume her friend theme. Yes friends were a good substitute for relationships with boys because boys were just incorrigible whatever that means. Karl was worse, he was desultory she thought, she should look up the word just incase, ambling, aimless, here then there then no-where. Yes it was the right word for him or maybe just his interactions with her.

Once in a while she would lose one of her male friends to a relationship or the big one, marriage. Never to be seen again. It was like a void a veritable precipice over which people stepped. As if the new wife or partner wanted to take him off the market and keep him there, like a bag of boiled sweets. He would only be viewed or brought out with other couples. That would never happen to Stephen. However this situation did not make sense to Ciara, she didn't fancy her male friends; ergo they were friends and not to her partner or boyfriend or marriageable material. So now they were in boring tied down type of relationships generally they really needed her friendship, but what difference was it to her if that was their choosing and they didn't make an effort to keep in touch. Nothing was getting her down today. It wasn't as if the wife was jealous Jesus Weeps!

'Anna' Ciara said later on in the afternoon. They were in the break room having coffee. 'Is there any point in me seeking voluntary redundancy?'

'Ciara, goodness no, God forbid that you would ever leave us.' Where were all these religious references coming from? It must be the texting, word being made text and sent among us.

'Pardon?' Ciara was taken aback.

'In spite of your best efforts to pretend never to do any work, when you finally get down to it you are very good at what you do.'

'Anna you are my best friend forever! You are joking right?'

'No, I'm not. You are really helpful. Our clients ask for you.' Anna looked at Ciara's face and her mouth was wide open. 'Often' she added.

Ciara giggled.

'We get customers from all walks of life who have quite complex problems but want simple solutions and that is what you deliver' Anna continued. 'Obviously these days we call problems issues, you listen, sometimes patiently but you let the customer air their grievances as if it is hot air passing down the phone lines. Then you make four or five points and hey presto, problem solved.'

'Do I?' said Ciara incredulously. This was not true, she was a slacker, she was useless at her job, she was a dis- servicer.

'Yep it is just hot air travelling down the phone line to you Ciara. You don't take personally what people say and then when they have said it you start to solve it.'

Obviously Anna had been on the batter and was still drunk today. With a bit of lubrication Anna could be a wind up artist. Ciara was still incredulous.

'Yes if the firm had been performing better you would have been promoted ages ago,' said Anna.

'You would. I mean I would?' Ciara could have been blown over by a pink feather; she was so taken aback by this incredible news that was the only word for it, incredible news, even though that was two words. Since forever Ciara had felt her performance was so below par that she was going to be dismissed on grounds of incompetence and if boredom was a legal ground for dismissal, well that too. To hear the total opposite to the belief she had held to be true for about half a decade was beyond belief. Someone actually had confidence in her ability and didn't want her to voluntarily resign. She was confused. She really valued Anna's opinion and she had always been a fair and reasonable boss, so her confidence in Ciara reinforced this sense of disorientation.

'I think I need a cigarette' Ciara was about to leave when Anna decided to continue. She sat down again hoping no one else would come in.

'No its fine, go. Will you come to my office afterwards and we can have a chat in private?'

'Definitely' Ciara bolted out the door. Actually she didn't want a cigarette, she wanted to sit at her desk a moment and wag her finger across the watery divide and say 'Nah, nah, nah, nah, nah' over to Karl. What a day, two out of three life stabilizers were going well, who knew.

A few of her colleagues looked out the window also just to see if there were any other fortune telling seagulls who would whisk away all of their troubles also.

They reconvened in Anna's office a few minutes later and Ciara smiled expectantly yet very nervously, was this a rouse or was it real?

'Firstly I wish to tell you that I am expecting.'

'Expecting?' said Ciara, then she realised to what Anna was referring when she repeatedly tapped her tummy. 'Oh, sorry, yes, congratulations.' She wasn't sure whether she should hug her boss as it was work time. However since she had taken a photo of her boss's boobs she decided to forgo protocol!

'Thank you,' smiled Anna. 'You are the first to know.'

'Wow, that's cool. How are you feeling?'

'I am ok actually, still a bit green in the face.'

'You look great' said Ciara hoping she didn't sound like a lick.

'Just for the moment I want to keep it quiet around the office.'

'Of course, did the green colour card have something to do with it?'

'That and your racy text file!' said Anna and they both giggled as it was such poor work practice for Ciara to have opened a text file and then for Anna to have read it. However sometimes we need some inspiration in the creation process. Her husband was Adam but she was Anna!!

'Is he delighted?'

'Over the veritable moon,' said Anna.

'Ah that is great, I'm so happy for you both. My lips are sealed, I promise.'

'I was thinking' said Anna, 'on the work front maybe with a bit of training in public speaking you could give some in-house talks on your technique.'

Ciara giggled, she couldn't suppress it.

'Seriously Ciara, you have it in you. You know how to motivate people in a work context as well as a social context. I will not be able to work as hard over the next few months and you will really help me.'

She swallowed a second round of giggles and there was a definite excitement within her which is rarely experienced by those over nine years of age.

'REALLY!' she exclaimed.

'Yes Ciara, really, that is so, I believe if we had been a productive company you would have thrived. You have no confidence in your ability. That is true because this is a demotivating office environment and you have no means to gauge your success but that doesn't mean you can't do good work.'

'It is difficult to stay positive here,' Ciara agreed.

'Really Ciara, you have done it and you have managed to encourage your colleagues as well. Your social outings have been really important for people here. You have really helped to keep up morale.'

'But it is Stephen who does the organising.'

'Yes he does the bookings and checks peoples' dates, but you are the creative driver.'

'Creative driver,' Ciara repeated the words with relish, with pride and almost with a small inkling of confidence. What a compliment! She had never had such like or was that such positive affirmation of her efforts before.

'Thank you so much Anna.' Ciara almost had tears in her eyes, how she had needed good news? And for so long, then when it finally came it was from someone Ciara not only liked but respected. Some people say fortune comes in threes but like a modern nuclear family two would do for Ciara. 'Thank you again.'

Anna was blushing; maybe there is something in the Irish psyche which is unused to compliments and positive feedback that the automatic outcome is embarrassment. 'I will look into courses and maybe you can get you to the head office in Scandinavia.'

Anna had said the magic word, Scandinavia! Ciara may go to Karl-land. Ok fortune in threes was good and Irish people have larger families than the average European. She was so excited she needed a real cigarette; she had only had three all week, she was great at deceiving herself. This would be a well deserved treat. If treats were truly treats, they had to be unhealthy?

'I know you are thinking of Karl,' said Anna.

'I was but I was also thinking ours was an American company.'

'Ciara, I don't think you listened at our interview!' Anna was laughing. 'Nor at any of the meetings we have had over the past seven years.'

'I never told you but day dreaming is one of my strong points.'

Anna laughed, 'Ciara your honesty is one of your strong points. It is probably also the main reason why you haven't progressed up the career ladder.'

'It could be my key selling point,' Ciara joked.

Corporate Ciara

"Wow this is cool" said Ciara to herself as she was packing her trolley-dolly sized wheelie bag with lots of things she really didn't need and trying to keep it under 10Kg. "To travel and get paid for it. What a result!" She had no idea what training meant or necessarily entailed. Her only experience of training dated to a time when she was a child and had received a puppy for Christmas. The training was to ensure there were no puddles in the living-room, especially on the new carpet which had also been acquired for Christmas.

This type of travelling would mean that she would get a chance to see Scandinavia without seeming like she was stalking Karl. Of course she wasn't stalking Karl but merely by being in the Nordic vicinity felt made her feel closer to him. It was great. It wasn't Norway but one cold northern country looked much like the next at this time of the year. She would get somewhat acquainted with Nordic ideology and maybe she would be able to understand Karl a little more. Maybe eventually she would gain an insight into what motivated him apart from rowing, world domination and cross-country skiing.

Anna had promised her a bonus for the extra work at the end of the period and if she chose to leave with the next programme of redundancies. In addition Anna would give her an excellent reference. Ciara was not generally money motivated but at this particular moment a cash injection was enough to get her the holding deposit on her dream attic. She wouldn't have to make her home a grow house of renters.

There would be so many Aryan types at the airport, on the plane and at the other airport. The thought was so exciting. Her dream had come true. There would be so much eye candy that her pupils' would pop out of her head. She flung some extra party dresses into her case, a few more pairs of high heels, lots of cosmetics and she was done.

She arrived at the very plush hotel, checked in quickly due to Nordic efficiency and went to her room. She looked out the window to assess her new vantage point. It wasn't exactly a landscape as she was in an urban area. So it was difficult to envisage the land, it was an urban-scape, no that was not the word. She who purported to be so wordy could get the exact word, any moment now. Cityscape, this was the word and an attractive historical City at that. She scanned the streets and there was talent to be seen walking up and down. She would have to stand outside the hotel door and ask for directions later on. Wow the thrill of it. It was not the capital but a small city which had not expanded much since the sixteenth century.

When she got to the conference, there were employees from all over the world and this training session was a bit too serious for Ciara's liking. There were meetings morning, noon and night, everyone was in business attire. Everyone but Ciara, hers had been a casual office, mostly jeans, pjs and t-shirts woops, she felt inadequate. If only Anna had given her a briefing on clothes. Her confidence was at a low ebb, she decided to text Karl. It was her last refuge.

'In Northern Europe, beginning to understand why everyone has left.'

'Now Ciara,' he texted back shortly. 'Don't be disparaging, people can be dour, but it is just the climate. In the summer everyone is really happy. Which country are you in?'

'No it isn't the people, it is the conference. Everyone is sooooo serious. Is it always like this?' "MYOB, I didn't tell you which company I worked for so why should I tell you where I am?" She was already giving too much away, she didn't care, she was feeling lonely and Karl was a great refuge for loneliness.

'Ah, your first conference?' he asked.

She didn't want to sound like a complete novice 'yep' but what else could she say.

'You will have fun. Have you checked out the gym yet?'

'No but I have booked myself into the spa. I'm exhausted from all the brain activity.' She was really looking forward to her Wata or was it water massage with specially prepared South Indian food for her skin type, flaky supposedly, like her personality.

'It can be trying but you are bright, I know you will get through,' Karl was being kind.

'Thanks.'

She got through the next day just about.

The city was compact but very pretty she did some exploring and had fun. However the sun had set by about 3 pm so this could be a reason why suicide statistics were so high. They were even higher than Ireland which was almost impossible.

She was lying in bed when there was a ping. She should really ignore it and leave the text until the morning. However she couldn't resist checking.

'Hey, my beautiful Josephine, are you still surveying our Northern territories?' Karl said.

'Nope I have just conquered them all!'

'Are you lying in bed dreaming of me? Karl asked.

'Tall Napoleon I believe you fancy yourself' he could be quite cheeky sometimes.

'So you are in bed.' Then some moments later, 'you know I fancy you.'

That was not what she said, she was feeling, what was it that she feeling? 'I know!!' she replied, a bit of aloofness was required.

'Fancy having texts?'

She was going to reply but she fell asleep with the phone in her hand. Exhaustion was a good restraint method.

Cool Ciara

Ciara was to give a number of motivational talks and she was taking some of Anna's workload especially the travelling aspect. The subject of the talks was customer services, essentially the path of least resistance. After these talks Ciara could get her bonus and then secure the attic. Now if that wasn't cause and affect she didn't know what was.

Ciara considered that life was most unfair. Even though she received a holding deposit on the house she was selling this deposit could not be transferred onto the flat she was buying. It wasn't as if her solicitor was doing anything with the money was it?

The talks were not just in Dublin Ciara would go to lots of places around the country and explain the simple formula to lots of people. These people were generally employees for the companies her firm represented. In other words the talks would comprise of the best method to take a call or an e-mail from a disgruntled customer. Then she would describe how to most efficiently deal with the call by saying hmm and yes a few times whilst holding the phone or handset at arm's length until the frustration had been talked out. After that she would have to recap, the customers' issue X, her or his problem Y and so the solution would be a combination of X, Y & Z. Simple as that. It would be a doddle.

The next part of the talk would deal with emails. For e-mail requests all that was needed was a problem identification sheet and Ciara had already drafted a very simple yet comprehensive response sheet. This sheet would identify the problem, classify the issue, ascertain the response time required and remedial steps which should be taken and could be taken. In other words what had to be done to solve the problem and then was there anything above and beyond what the customer was looking for which was simple to deliver, not very costly and would give the customer a warm fuzzy feeling of satisfaction at the end of the interaction. There were an expansive six points on this sheet and more than comprehensive in Ciara's view.

It was a formula which worked in every scenario because after all this time Ciara had listened to all situations, issues and complaints in. Well she had listened to a little bit of the problem, sorry issue. From experience all she needed were the facts, all the hot air would be either talked out or typed out and then the solution could be generated fairly speedily.

Anna felt it would be a good idea to see what Ciara had planned to talk about so Ciara was to conduct a dry run with her colleagues in the office the next day and luckily it was not the whole building but merely her department. It was so obvious and simple a method of customer service to her but Anna hoped it would be an A-ha (the only Norwegian band she knew) moment to everyone else. That concept really confused Ciara, if she understood something how come everyone else didn't and this could have been one reason why Anna was the manager not her.

It was going to be fun. Ciara took her notes home and practiced on Aoife. She was very nervous speaking in front of her friend, how peculiar. Aoife brought over pizza and red wine in preparation for a long night in. Ciara drank a full glass before she began.

'Yes Ciara, you Italian aficionado I know one is supposed to have beer with pizza but I don't really like beer,' Aoife announced. Her brain was still in top speed and Ciara could really not remember making such a profound statement.

'Hey I am no pizza purist and you know my preference for wine.'

'Well this is certainly wine time, great to calm the nerves when you are about to launch yourself outside the comfort zone.'

Ciara nodded mid-gulp.

Elaborate displays and explanations were not exactly necessary as the message was so simple. Ciara wasn't comfortable multi-tasking anyway. So she drew a smiley face on a piece of paper and said, 'this is what we want.'

'Yes,' said Aoife, 'we want lots of smiley faces. Especially from Anna as she seems to have invested a lot in you.' Aoife was glugging the wine also.

'Come on now, don't distract me. I am really not used to doing this.'

'Ok, sorry, keep going.'

Then she drew an emoticon style sad face and say, 'this is what we have. How do we marry the two?' Ciara was getting to grips with emoticon faces and was texting them regularly, sometimes inappropriately to all her phone contacts. It had only taken her about nine months to work out.

Aoife was silent, for a moment. 'Am I supposed to say something?'

'Ah maybe you could say "I don't know?" or "how can we do this?"'

'How do we get a happy customer?'

'That's a good one. Well we listen, and listen and listen,' Ciara noticed Aoife making a face then grinning unconsciously. 'I sometimes listen Aoife I do for at least 10% of the conversation!!'

'Ok, sorry go on again,' smiled Aoife.

'So you take note of the key points and generally there will be six. You let the customer talk themselves out by giving them words of encouragement like, "I understand" or "yes that must have been trying," and so on. Then when they have off loaded all their emotional baggage onto you, you feedback these six key points. Then you ask them to agree, well obviously you say do you agree, but you try not to give them any wriggle room or else they will start blaming you for ancillary things. These things will have nothing to do with you e.g. their washing machine doesn't work or their partner has left them. So the aim here is to close off the dialogue and focus on the issue in hand.

'Sometimes older people need a bit of time to think about things so you give them your direct line and also a deadline as to when they can call you back by or else the complaint will be null and void. However the wording is crucial here. "Could you call me back by 4 pm this evening?" would be good for an early call anything up to 11 am in the day. "Could you get back to me by 10 am tomorrow?" This would be a suitable response time for an afternoon call. This will give people time to consider what has been said and not feel under pressure. The key point is empowerment the customer feels in control of the situation. Then when the conclusion is reached she or he feels happy with the outcome.

'Then you close the call by repeating their purpose for the call, explaining the course of action and the time period in which the remedy will roll out or come into effect. Then finally there is an add-on, the nice thing that will make them happy and come back to you again. Well not the individual but the company from whom they have purchased the product or service. I digress, so if it is a product, say a tumble dryer, you offer them an extra six months on their warranty free of charge. Generally they are delighted and when someone from the tumble dryer company calls them they say, "your nice girl in customer services was really helpful." This means our company keeps the contract.'

'That sounds great!' said Aoife, 'now let's have some fun.' It seemed like Aoife was really bored.

'That sounds like a plan.' So they drank, chatted about everything and nothing and ate really unhealthy pizza. A while later Ciara said, 'do you know I was tidying the house for the viewings and I found something.'

'Oh, what was it?'

'It was a poem, from the other guy!' Ciara could never be brought to say his name. She didn't know why.

'Do you have it there?'

'I will get it from upstairs,' which she did and passed it to Aoife.

Ciara, Ciara (so hard to rhyme your name),
Wish you were my Dera,
You're so far, it could be Madeira,
Yet you are as sweet as cake,
Sometimes you thoughts are half-bake (d),
An enigma is what you make.
If your heart were mine to take,
But to get to you, re-enforced glass I must break.

'So he liked you' was all the comment that Aoife made.

'I don't know he was really into poetry so maybe he wrote something for every lady he met!' Maybe she had not let him in as her head space was already occupied by someone else.

****

The next day silence reigned supreme after Ciara's presentation. The silence may have been out of politeness or confusion. Ciara just delivered her first talk the next day and it had lasted approximately seven minutes. The duration had seemed interminable whilst speaking. The meeting room was small and bright with about 20 people in the audience. Anna looked at her watch and said, 'well it was certainly succinct.'

'Is that a good thing?' asked Ciara.

'Can you expand a little?'

'On which points please?'

'All of them' said Anna.

So she said, 'usually the answer to a customer query is in the question. Yes it is obvious and we all know this but the customer already knows what they want. So as I said before listen until they are talked out and then give them what they asked for. Well within reason.' Then she added, 'as we know most people are reasonable so this simple solution works for 80% of our customers. For the rest we just need to let them talk a bit longer, until they have talked themselves out. Then ask them one more time, "What do you want?" at that point they will usually tell you. And that's it.'

It was going to take a bit of time getting used to public speaking.

'Ciara, that is a bit obvious,' said one of the lads. He possibly had thought that he would get guidance on best practice, a manual of some sort. This however was Ciara she didn't even have power point up and running as she had forgotten how to use it. Why were emoticons never enough?

'It's simple when its right!' she blushed as this was the first question ever.

The lads joked with her, 'the cool Ciara,' they called her when the meeting broke up. She came out with whitened face and shaking hands. It was so difficult standing up in front of her peers explaining something which they did every day. She felt more like the overheated rather than the cool Ciara.

'Ciara' it was Anna calling her into her office.

'Yes,'

'Is that all you learned from your trip away?'

'I thought that was all that was necessary to give in the lecture as I thought I was to keep it simple.'

'Right well, it's not, draw me a thirty-minute presentation, with PowerPoint for tomorrow and I will review it in the afternoon.'

Anna had said the scary word PowerPoint; she would have to get some help. 'Ok, I will Anna. Sorry I am only learning.' Ciara shuffled away feeling un-cool, deflated in fact.

The guys in the office said she was cool because she travelled to the North. It was a myth that there was an office in the North, as no one had ever been there. Just as

Vikings in the dark ages were not sure that there was land to the west like Ireland and Britain so the idle employees felt civilisation ended at the northern shores of Germany and Holland and anything further north was just out there, ideologically, geographically and climatically. Why Ciara had this strange fascination with the North it was bizarre and they didn't understand it. Why think of Norway when there was Spain? Why have Sweden when Italy was so much warmer. So the cool was not exactly hip, with it and trendy but cool as in liking a cooler climate. She was almost on the way to being cold Ciara but they still liked her even though they thought she was daft.

'The corporate Ciara,' they jibed as she wore a city dress into work the next day and had actually brushed her hair for the first time that week. She wanted to impress Anna after all her help, Ciara was going to get it right. She ignored them.

'Ciara the caring,' was the one which really annoyed her the most as it was the least true. Well maybe she cared about receiving texts from the tall Napoleon. Oh and she really cared that Anna's secret pregnancy was going well, she was seven weeks gone already.

People stopped her in the corridor and asked if she was going to a job interview. She never looked this groomed.

'No I am going to give a presentation to one of our clients' she replied. They knew she was lying she was having a second or fifth dry run with Anna. Ciara was not ready to be client facing yet, if that the term. It was going to be a tough few weeks.

Mornings

It was a dark, cold autumnal morning; the rain was spitting sleet, too damp to snow. Yet the damp permeated deeper than the cold, seeping through anoraks, gloves and fleece boots to attack the bones. How grim to catch the 'express' bus from the side of the motorway. She felt like the rubbish about to be collected and dropped into the back of a dirty lorry. The spray from passing trucks was gently saturating, nearly freezing on impact through un-water-proofed trousers and boots.

Even the bus shelter would have frozen if the humidity levels had not been so high. The temperature was hovering at freezing. The water droplets moved only slightly as the wind gusted this way and that, then they lay on the glass of the shelter, blocking any view of the long-expected bus.

She leaned against the rear of the shelter and drifted in and out of sleepy thoughts trying very hard not to wake up fully. The moon was full and high fleetingly glimpsed through the rapidly moving clouds. Apparently there had been flood warnings due to spring tides. How interesting a spring tide in what felt like the depths of winter, yes it was a lunar controlled cycle but was this spring tide washing away any hope of a mild winter. Could it all be perpetual winter or was this just the eternal week. It was only Tuesday but there was definitely a late Thursday feel to the morning.

Then an apparition, the bus was here, mood lifted, seat to be acquired as sleep zone awaited. She boarded almost expecting to see Karl, yet there was no reason for this expectation only a vague hope. It was true that he lived just a hop or two away so it was not inconceivable that he could be there. He took one of the three buses which were available to Ciara, so there was a one third chance that he would take her bus one morning. The expectation was vague but it did not fade over time, each morning in fact her heart skipped a beat when his bus number arrived before the others. She climbed the stairs, as she always took the upper salon, slowly as the bus jerked off in a hurried acceleration. She held the rail as she mounted; the steps were damp and slippery, still not wanting to wake fully but wishing to be alert enough to spot him if he were there. It reminded her of the thrill of taking the bus home from school as a teenager when there would be boys, one boy in particular was nice but boys in general were fine, just to look at, from a distance of a about three seats and dream about whilst attempting to get through 3 hours of homework in fifteen minutes.

She scanned the seats, eyes darting left and right, but there was no sign of him. In fact it had been so long now since they met that he may be there, sitting just in front of her and she would not recognise him. She had softened his looks so all angles were smoothed to perfection. In her mind's eye he was different to what she may see if she were to behold him now. It was a dream she had not met him since December, that summer encounter was only a dream. It must have been as he had said such definite things. She took her seat, the first behind the stairs, with the most legroom and allowed herself to drift off. Not quite sleep as the air was too damp with wet coats and umbrellas. Yet she could doze, daze, and gaze at nothing in particular but the blank grey beyond the window. He may well be doing the very same thing on a bus very near, maybe just ahead, or just behind. He was after all heading in the same direction, destined to arrive at more or less the same time. Oh the trials of life when circumstances were left to random chance rather than chosen, by her, or in her power to arrange. She wasn't into control but it was annoying when things were so out of her control. "Maybe I'm a little bit into power play but only on the bus front."

At this stage she was almost afraid to meet him. Invariably she would be let down, as, he was after all just a man, a person with frailties and imperfections. He may have a sneering face, or a self-satisfied jaw line. Maybe he had moles all along the side of his body which she didn't see. It was hard to tell as the light had been, well yes it was glaring, there was no doubt, he had good skin, just a few spots. When he walked into the small tea shop the light was behind him and his frame swallowed it all up in an instant. She could just about remember his polo top and his long arms reaching out to her.

He could be cross-eyed, it was dark, no she could remember that much, he had light piercing eyes, like an arctic fox. What would it matter that he had imperfections, she had. It would make him less distant, less alien and maybe more personable. It was the flaws which made one human, the foibles to which one was drawn and the idiosyncrasies which differentiated one person from the next, to make him an individual, whole and complete. She would have to contend however with the distant Karl, therefore the perfect Karl. The Napoleon of the North, striding across the tundra after taking a burning Moscow, but before the long defeating march back to camp. He was the 1811 and a ½ Napoleon, the pre-Elba, pre-divorce where he chased, courted and incessantly flirted with Josephine.

She was the lithe Josephine, distinctly taller without the blackened teeth and reputation Josephine. Hopefully! The sometimes risqué in dress but adroit in property acquisitions type of Josephine was what she emulated. Not the 200 odd pairs of gloves, stockings and shawls Josephine whose love of glitzy artefacts, furniture and objet d'art, but the garden creator with a host of helpers type Josephine. Ciara would need an army of assistants as hers were ashen rather than green fingers and would rather shoes to gloves.

Ping, there was a text 'Just thinking of you my Josephine, with your perfect décolletage on a beach. I have just been looking at you in your blue and white bathing suit, two-piece at that! It is true that the image is somewhat out of focus, but it gives for imagination and all that sand before you represents my imaginative possibilities.'

She may, obviously she was not admitting to anything until there was evidence to prove it, have sent a very blurry photo of herself on a beach to Karl. If she had done so it would have been at a time when he was really annoying her by, well doing nothing, doing nothing at all. Therefore the image would have been to show him what he was missing! Alternatively it could have been by accident when getting used to technology or apps or whatever they were called this week. There were many mishaps when habituating or learning how to use new technology.

'On this cold and rainy morning you bring sunshine to my day,' he continued.

'We need a bit of sunshine on this abysmal and dismal day,' she replied with a big smile on her face. She didn't send him a smiley face, as he had already had an eyeful and so didn't need any more encouragements.

'I am on the bus the windows are fogged up and all I can think of is you. Your bikini is an escape from grey.'

'Oh,' she said.

'It is the rhythm of motion which propels us forward,' Karl texted. 'Whether it is rowing or skiing the exhilaration motivates us to achieve more in work and are more driven in life.'

'Ah that's a nice thought as it is indeed a freezing cold morning. Have you just finished rowing? Janey you're hardcore if you're out in this weather' "You may well be motivated for other pursuits Karl of Norway." How early did he rise in the morning to be finished rowing now? Really, it was still the middle of the night.

'Yes and have just had pancakes at my favourite cafe. Now back on the bus.'

'Yummy.'

'Are you on the bus?' he asked.

'Yes I am, feeling really lucky to have found a seat, this morning we are packed like sardines. People are even standing upstairs.'

'Oh, that's not nice. You will have to join me someday, we can breakfast together.'

'Someday, as long as you don't expect me to row over icy water' Ciara replied then she thought wistfully, "if only."

Why had she not chosen Count Vronsky from Anna Karenina or some dour Nordic God instead of a squat Corsican as an object of desire? He would have called, as in telephoned, Vronsky that is. Well he would have if the telephone had got to Russia in Tolstoy's time. Any icon or hero of yesteryears would do when it was only fantasy to which this contact amounted. He could even have been Roman there would be lots of food for thought there. Maybe it was the romantic character, the active and far off air which he emitted that night. She had met him on Wellington Quay so maybe she wasn't as creative as she thought she was after all.

More bus musings ensued whilst she waited for his reply.

'I will meet you for breakfast if you wear that bikini.'

'Then it would have to be on a Napoleonic exile island,' she said in return.

'Yes I was looking into the tickets, maybe Elba might be easier for pancakes!'

'I could always wear it underneath my work clothes.'

'I would have to be able to see it,' he said.

'Well maybe you could see the ties about my neck.'

'Meany,' he said.

She felt good. She always felt good when they had a fun exchange. When she was in a good mood she felt a bit less frugal, so for example she would throw out the old tube of toothpaste before it has been completely squeezed out.

She was not stressing about the nearly thirty-minute presentation which was about to be delivered to Anna. Nor was she worried about how much her colleagues would joke with her calling her an eejet, a doozy or lots of other pejoratives. This is why a strong sense of imagination was Ciara's forte; she could escape reality for weeks on end and live a very happy fantasy life. Now she was imagining she was sitting on a beach in Elba that is if there was a beach on Elba, watching the speed boats come in from mainland Italy. Then watching as a tall pasty stranger with rapidly developing sunburn hopped off the boat and asked for her SPF 50, now that was a beautiful image.

'This bus terminates at Bachelors Walk," announced the bus driver. 'Final stop.'

'Sugar' muttered Ciara under her breath, she would have a really long walk into work and she had wanted to be relaxed before the day ahead rather than windswept and bothered.

Ages After or 30 minutes later

Ciara arrived in with a slightly more prepared presentation. Anna said she would get better at public speaking and she would, eventually. You can only fall over so many times before you eventually hit the table and walk, isn't that what every toddler discovers? Ciara's first audience were the IT or techie department. They were a tough audience as she had blamed them for most of the clients' problems for the past seven years and they knew. "It's a technical issue" explained away a multitude. She knew most people had a fear of the technological void that happened between I and T so they would take this statement verbatim, the C which was supposed to fit in the middle was generally missing. This talk was a bit more interactive as Ciara got to see the consequences of such sweeping statements. It was difficult to talk to brainy people about stuff which they knew inside out but which she barely understood, but it was an eye opener. Gradually Ciara realised that Anna wanted a facilitator not an arbitrator. At the end of the day Ciara was exhausted but rewarded as she finally understood what the company did just as she was considering leaving it.

So the weeks passed slowly and eventually Ciara had completed her serious work, she had given her customer service formula talk to all the groups, both internal and external clients that Anna had asked and as a result she was getting her bonus.

473

She dropped the E5,000 into the Auctioneers office and apologised for the delay citing legal reasons. The Auctioneer, Miles sniffed, thanked Ciara and informed her the pack or legal documents were ready and awaiting order to be sent. 'Send them, my solicitor is waiting,' she said and left rapidly.

Anna as promised wrote a sterling reference and even helped her with her many job applications. Was it that Anna was expecting her first child that she was in particularly nurturing form? It was a gruelling process. Ciara started looking about and spotted some roles which she might like. She felt intimidated though with the application process. Some application forms were like examinations, at Masters Level. Anna explained that this was to reduce the number of applicants and so make the process easier for the recruiter. This person was generally a human resources administrator, who would have pile upon pile of forms to decipher and administrate before selecting a short list for interview. The process was tough ant it went on and on and on.

'Ciara, be patient and don't get down hearted,' said Anna one day when Ciara had had another rejection letter. At least she had had a reply on this occasion sometimes she got an automated response to say that her e-mailed application had been received other times not even that. After completing a ten-page application Ciara expected at least an automated response that would prove that she had got the e-mail address correct.

'Thank goodness you persuaded me not to resign until I had got something else.'

'I heard, but it isn't confirmed yet that there will be a new round of redundancies at the end of the month. So that gives you something to aim for, a deadline.'

'I will be dead before I pass that line,' said Ciara despondently.

'You are such a drama Queen!' Anna was nurturing but she didn't suffer fools.

Yet through all these rejection letters the loft had been the goal which got her through, it was the "feel" in feel good. It had given her a spring in her step as she stepped out on her lunchtime strut. Her route did not consist of Brown Thomas, arguably the most expensive store in the City, but she went east, to the sea some days and the distance that she travelled meant that she had to sprint back. She really didn't want to be late as Anna was so much on her side. Inadvertently she was getting fit, fit out of frustration, fit out of a desire to make a change in her life, fit for a new job, a new home and a new Ciara. She was going to be scrawny no more! Maybe she would even start protein smoothies, build up some muscle mass, but it was hard to walk and slurp.

 She was going to be able to pay off the Banks, hopefully. The ball and chain of a mortgage would be gone never to be heard of again and she could begin again.

On one of her walks she started fantasizing about living in her new place, how bright it would be, how central and maybe a flatmate, "why not share with a stealthy s-texter? It could be fun, best of both worlds and all that.

He works close so commute time would be about twenty minutes.

"Even if he was emotionally unavailable my natural joie de vie and warmth would melt his austere frozen remoteness. How could he possibly resist? Impossible!" She marched on looking intent and maybe a bit mad as she was talking out loud without realising. She was a scout on a military endeavour, to subdue Napoleon. She passed a Martello Tower, an anti-Napoleon device. She drew an imaginary sword and swished her arms about pretending to duel.

"Would it be a disaster to have someone you fancy live with you? Could things develop slowly? Would you be hurt beyond the point of devastation if he were to arrive home with someone else?" Phrasing the question in that manner gave Ciara a clear answer. She chose to ignore reality and ran on with her fantasies. "Maybe it would be possible get to know him as a person since he is a complete stranger really. We have only actually met twice. That feeling of knowing someone virtually is not necessarily virtuous it can be vicious, can I think of any other V's? Could it be dangerous as I feel I know him in some ways but am actually only seeing the bits that he wants to show me, that is, figuratively, oh yes and literally speaking? Yes I am in oscillation mode, great. I don't even know who he lives with, a sister or a landlady. There is definitely female influence judging by the bathroom photo, that shower curtain is most definitely not a male feature". She remembered first looking through her images file in her phone gallery his first image was a bit egotistical but the more she looked at it and then the others as she did on many rainy days the more familiar each became and the less judgemental she became. It was such an ostentatious Word gallery; it reminded her of a large room with high ceiling and lots of pictures. Maybe by the arrangement of the photographs in an easily viewable manner this was a mobile gallery. Who could tell? Getting back to the image in her head thought, that shower curtain was feminine, large colourful circles would a man have chosen them? Maybe they were on offer in a shop.

"So how would I broach the issue? Send a casual text 'Hey Karl, fancy moving in as a flatmate?' Yeah, perfect! Or maybe 'So crazy Karl, you wanna reduce your commute and shack up with me?' Or 'Fancy prolonging your phone credit by living with your textee?'

"Naw it would have to be face to face and chance is a fine thing.

"Should I advertise 'desperate and lonely female in eyrie looking for a knight in shining armour to pay my bills. Hair almost as long as Rapunzel's as unable to afford coiffure!' Yes that should do it; I would be committed and have free rent for months! If I were locked up the whole flat would be rented out but to someone else. No I should be sensible as my hair would never grow that fast."

She went back to more practical issues and was considering retraining in another industry, discipline or field before she was redundant. Human Resources that had been the buzz word when she had been finishing her primary degree, and only degree, but by saying primary it kind of implied that there had been further studies. Was

HR now what a commercial course had been when her mother was finishing school? This discipline seemed to comprise lots of women getting busy. They were making decisions that were about feelings in an organisation, but decidedly not talking about their feelings in the organisation as they were involved in, serious business. It was driving business forward, talent managing as if employees were performing in a circus or a musical and the HR function was their manager. Ciara had been doing a bit of reading on the subject and key phrases stood out. On reflection the field seemed way too competitive for Ciara and she had zero response to applications for even the lowliest roles so she decided against.

Maybe she would try extras work, very unreliable but with free tea and coffee on film sets, chatting to lots of people, having a break for lunch and then doing a bit of walking. It would be a stress free life and she could read up so she would be a Napoleonic expert after a few months. The money would be just about manageable, but she would get fed, watered and paid for it.

Or maybe tour guiding, taking people about historic properties and making up lots of interesting stories. That sounded like great fun, she would do some research. The British had built so many beautiful Houses and Palaces in Ireland there was bound to be a need for guides, even if it were just for the short term. Anything to tide her over would be good.

How to get into this line of work? Could it be construed as a career? If someone asked, 'what do you do' in a general line of introduction, such as speed dating she would reply. 'I show people around other people's houses, look into all the rooms and answer questions.' Would they think she was an auctioneer, a thief or just plain nosy? Well if she were speed dating she wouldn't get a chance to find out as she would be onto the next person and the 'what do you do for a living'. Answer, I'm nosy. Definitely wouldn't get a tick beside her in the want to meet again category!!

More surfing would be required to see how to go about this as touring sounded interesting.

Anna after an inane amount of Ciara's concerns found one very large government web site which was a portal to another life. There was a link to may historic sites around the country and a clear yet difficult application process.

'Hey,' said Ciara, 'all the questions are about customer service. I am the expert apparently in this field, hee hee.'

'Yes Ciara, after the amount of time you have been doing this job if you were not an expert there would be something wrong.'

'Point taken, let's see what has to be done. This is exciting Anna, it is the only thing I am remotely interested in.'

The application form needed to be returned by the end of the week so they were lucky, well Ciara was lucky that Anna had been resourceful enough to be able to find this website. The form was very long and cited situations where the applicant showed examples of customer services practice. It demanded concentration, creative thinking and well composed answers. Ciara printed out the application form to work on overnight and Anna promised to correct the answers the next day.

That evening Ciara got out her pencil and rubber or eraser as polite company requires. She thought, she scribbled, she rubbed out or erased away and started again. On the next day Anna noted that 'this is not an exercise in creative writing. It has to be fact.'

'Oh!' said Ciara and she started again. She looked at what she had done and what the question required and somehow merged the two together. It wasn't going to fit but she tried to reduce the imagination or creative writing factor.

'That isn't too bad,' said Anna the day after 'but if you could just focus here a little and then on page 37 say this, then on page 49 give an example of that I think you will be finished.'

This was hard work! What an ordeal just to show people around one crummy stately home, like would she not be given a script to learn off. This was too much like hard graft. Finally the application was ready and sent off. One automated e-mail was received so at least the job existed and had been sent to the correct address.

The wait was long it seemed to take ages but eventually Ciara was called for an interview. It was two weeks later but as Ciara was obsessing the wait seemed like two months. The interview went well. It seemed too easy after the really difficult application or maybe Ciara had prepared herself well during her anxious wait. It was so strange, as every barrier had been blocking her before but now they seemed to fall away and her path was clear. The interview was informal and relaxed and the lady conducting it was very warm. She was almost as personable as Anna but Ciara could not be disloyal to Anna the awesome. The lady really put Ciara at her ease and the process only took forty minutes. It was as if Ciara had only begun talking and then it was over, there were so many more things to say but Ciara for once in her life managed not to over-talk.

Walking out of the large house over to the car park Ciara realised this was only the second interview of her whole life. Wow she was lucky that her life had been a sheltered one on the career front. She reflected that this lady, the interviewer would provide a very nice work environment. If Ciara were to be fortunate enough to be offered the job she would gladly accept, she would be really happy here. She considered running back and letting the interviewer know this but managed to restrain herself.

A few days later she was offered the job, it was supposed to be Anna who had morning sickness but it was Ciara who fainted in Anna's office. She realised she had inadvertently put the work address instead of her own and Anna had been sent the contract, genius Ciara! The next round of redundancies for which Ciara volunteered came up as planned very soon after and she was free to leave. She was now, finally free, as free as that bird which had flown outside her window. The feeling was wonderful, complete and blissful.

She was two thirds of the way to "the new Ciara" the interested and efficient Ciara, the Ciara who changed her work clothes every other day and brought them to the dry cleaners. The kind of Ciara Karl would like or maybe more importantly the kind of Ciara she really wanted to be. Not boring but a bit more organised, more capable and living her life rather than wishing it away.

The last third of the three-part remake of Ciara was to find a relationship but at this point she would focus on the tasks in hand as they were quite overwhelming, whilst she had been bored in her job it had been a real comfort zone. It was her only serious job, ever and she felt really lucky that Anna was giving her such a good reference, not just for her job prospects in the future but as an acknowledgement that all her years there were not wasted. It showed in hard copy that she had been appreciated and had contributed to the office the environment and the people and that she would move forward with something to show for this.

Maybe she would still attend the social nights out so she didn't get too lonely and keep a link with the old when everything was new. It was exhilarating but also quite daunting. She was more than a little frightened, but at least she was feeling. It seemed as if her senses which had been dulled into a grey haze, soggy and damp were now bright the sun was finally shining and she felt like an Egyptian cotton sheet drying on the line. Or rather, a pair of power-walking runners airing in front of the fire.

'Ciara,' it was Stephen. 'You weren't going to leave without saying good bye?'

'Ah you know me Stevo, I hate goodbyes.' She smiled at him unsure whether to reach over and give him a big hug this was her last day and it had come around too quickly. It wasn't as if she wasn't going to see him again, he had moved in with Sophie and they were to have Ciara over for dinner in two days.

'I know we will see each other soon, but you are leaving the building for the last time as an employee, it has to be recognised. Your departure that is; I, we have been working here for as long as we both can remember it is a monumental step you are about to take crossing the threshold.'

'One small step for me but a giant, huge step in my life.' She didn't exactly want to say to Stephen that she had wished to be alone when leaving, but now that he was here it felt good. 'This is what I always wanted.'

'Don't pull my leg you never knew what you wanted. Also you might knock me over,' said Stephen in a self-deprecating manner.

'Don't worry, I won't, I'm not covered on the insurance anymore.' Ciara couldn't resist a little joke back. 'So you will come and visit me.'

'You are having dinner with us.'

'I know that and I will but I want you and Sophie to visit me at my new work. It would mean a lot if you would visit. Stephen you were right though, all I knew was what I didn't want and it was called customer service. It took me far too long to work out what I did want and you never know how things work out; I may be equally terrible at tour guiding.'

That was it she left the building.

'You will love it I know how nosy you are' he followed her into the lift and they went down to the ground floor.

'Ta Stevo, you always know the right thing to say.'

They gave each other an awkward hug in the lobby. It was a good bye to a whole life time of work friendship and there would be a bit of readjustment before they were more than circumstantial friends. Ciara was sure they would be real friends they had too much in common and got on too well to not keep up. Also Ciara needed to keep her disability monitoring street credentials, she was even joking in her head this was definitely the right thing to do. "I am happy in my head, how nice."

Return of the Texter

It seemed like ages later when there was a wicked wand waved! Well actually it was a stepping stone tone as she had finally worked out how to change the noises on her smart phone. There was no techie-talent to fiddle around with Ciara's phone so she was working out how to do things for herself. She had this sound, the stepping stone for Karl and just for Karl so she would know when he was on. It would give her some time to prepare, mentally and tread cautiously across the rapids of the river Liffey and any overextended oars. She had to word her responses carefully or he would blank her for another few weeks.

'Hey,' said Karl.

She was on a week's break in between the old Ciara and the new. Her Mum had asked her whether she would like to get some sun abroad in somewhere warm, but for once Ciara was happy to stay in wintery Dublin. She was busy and her productivity level was higher than it had ever been working. She was property focused, the sale of a house was still not concluded and therefore the purchase of a loft was delayed. She wanted to organise her belongings and sell what she didn't need as she was buying less space than she had.

It was sad not getting up like everyone else, not going out in the dark cold morning to wait to be collected with the pre-dawn refuse, honestly. Ciara set her alarm for the same time each morning and knew in the luxurious heated, calm pleasure of her own bed that she didn't have to get up. It was brilliant, she would roll over, snooze her alarm for twenty minutes, pad her pillows and dream of the lovely day ahead, bliss!

'Hey back, Mr. Early-Morninger,' she replied.

She also had to prepare mentally for the new role ahead as it would be a huge change. However as she didn't have a clue what it entailed thus preparing was merely a technicality. She had given up the window view and was to become something that was on view, an entirely decorative role. Very front of house in one of the finest houses in Dublin, the official state residence for guests of the Nation! That would be fun work and not too taxing for her after the stress of boredom.

'It's been a long time! How are you? It's that Napoleon guy...' he texted after this interminable silence, ok it had been four weeks but it seemed like an eternity. Time was relative, and as always the determining factor was the frequency with which she checked her phone. She had deleted his number, in her Winter-clean of all that was the old Ciara, but not got around to blocking him. She really hadn't thought that she would hear from him again. Really!

At least an hour passed but she couldn't really hold out as curiosity is an additive bug. 'I'm great thanks. Trust your creative writing is going well. Are you looking for new material?'

'I am good and in Norway at the minute. Writing going well but cannot compare to your creative output obviously. It was hard imaging myself as a Sultan. I could never have thought up that Zanzibar Dream. Have you finished your job? What are your plans?' He typed, politely as if nothing had happened. Well nothing had actually happened so he was right.

'Yes a few plans in motion and starting to resemble progress,' she replied a while later. Hopefully his Grandfather was ok, was that the reason he was back in Norway? She had absolutely no knowledge of his family life the only person he had ever talked of was his grandfather. So Ciara felt strangely attached to him. It was an odd attachment as this man had only been referred to in passing remarks about his health or boatbuilding skills, yet he was the only person to whom Karl had referred. Therefore he was or must be important. She couldn't remember telling him that she was leaving her job, she thought she had kept at least one secret from him, apparently not. Why was he so smart?

'Ah that's good,' said Karl.

'How is your grandfather?'

'He is well thanks; he got over his turn and is now feeling back to himself.'

 'Great, so all recovered?' she enquired.

'I told my grandfather about you (smiley face)'

'Not your parents,'

'They are dead.'

'Oh, I'm sorry Karl, I didn't know' flip what could she say "recently?" That may be more than a little insensitive. Maybe she had been too judgemental of him after all and maybe he was as delicate as her.

'No it was years ago,' he said 'a car crash in Ireland when I was still at school. So me and my sister went back to Norway and finished our studies there.'

Ciara was really stuck for words. She hopped out of bed and went to the kitchen to make a large pot of coffee. For someone she had only met twice she knew a lot about him but just when she thought she knew him he would completely surprise her and she would feel like he was a stranger all over again.

'Is that why you have a very light accent? Which I find endearing by the way,' was the best she could come up with when she was half way through her cheap and cheerless bargain basement coffee.

'Maybe sometimes, but I thought I had a Dublin accent!' said Karl.

'Most of the time you do, but at the tea house when you saw me it wasn't Dublin-English you were speaking but something much older!!'

'Huh? Something breathy like old Norse?' he asked.

'You big Viking!!'

'Desire that is what I was speaking!'

'Oh!!' she said.

'Desire is an old feeling Ciara, raw and primal. It can do strange things to the breath!!!'

'It is very strong' then she thought, she would quantify this thought. 'It has wreaked cities and civilisations.'

'Yes and built new ones by architects like me!! It has also provided the drive to re-populate the lands and begin anew.'

'A bit scary really' she said.

'You're not scared of me, are you?'

'Only sometimes (wink)' then she continued, 'other times I want to slash and burn and destroy civilisations all on my own!'

'Now YOU are scary (wink back).'

 She left it a while as she had some errands to run. She had also scared herself a lot, to think she had all of this desire in her was a frightening thought. To realise she could do something with it was nerve-wracking. She was powerful, yet she had never felt this until now, she had the ability to do lots of things, well like everyone really, but to realise it at this point in time, with all her life changing decisions was freaky.

A few hours later she was still thinking of the same thing, him and couldn't resist pinging Karl. He had no parents, was he showing emotional vulnerability to draw her in or was she getting harsh with all of her decisiveness? He only had his sister and his grandfather. That was nice but limited, handy maybe for a guest list at a wedding! His reduced family would be easy to remember, not so many names. "Focus Ciara, he has worked his wand over you or stepping all over you and you are worrying for him."

'I want to change characters' now this was her decision made for the day, tick. A decision a day was the motto for this week.

'Pardon?' he asked. 'Do you want to be Napoleon?'

'No and I don't want to be Josephine. I was something Russian!'

'Can't Count on a Ciara!'

'Ha, ha! Were there not more Princes than Counts?'

'I don't know I'm only from Corsica!'

'You can be Count Vronsky and I will be Anna Karenina.'

She didn't hear from him for a while and for the first time she didn't notice the passing of time, then...

'I was thinking of having the Emperors Suite playing on the background of this text as I don't want this to be the 1812 Overture, not yet anyway. I really like Napoleon, I may be a good foot taller than him with less to prove but it is fun. It has been really diverting, when I'm down you're there. You are the perfect Josephine, you are lively, changeable, distracting, sometimes I can't get you out of my head and you are discrete. You always give me space, you never text me when I am not free and don't give out to me when I am distant for a while.'

'Josephine complained and had a relationship with Napoleon, we have texts.' It may have been direct but these thoughts were confirming and then by default solidifying a situation which Ciara was not happy with. It was hard to grasp what he was actually saying but the meaning seemed to lead to Ciara being a peripheral part of Karl's life. She didn't want this. She wanted at least a chance to get to know him.

'Don't go Tchaikovsky on me' she continued in an 1812 Overture Vein. Maybe he should have been sending that when he was talking about her but she did always want the upper hand with her.

'We have regular texts.' Well maybe regular is a relative term. 'And I prefer Beethoven to Tchaikovsky!!'

Their texts crossed over so the con-text was confusing, she was referring to them being stuck at the overture and he meant, well maybe it was that he was happy as things were.

Ciara thought her Russian Novel analogy was true. Theirs was a novel or a series of short or long texts which went on and on with no action, for once in her life she really wanted the bodice ripping, page turning fluff, she had waited too long and maybe if she hadn't been so hung up on Karl she would have been open to meeting someone else. Yes she had closed herself off to other potential interest, hopefully love interest. The other guy had written her a poem, for goodness sakes. Maybe it wasn't his best work but he had thought about it and spent time on and then given it to her. He had actually handed it to her during one of the times which they had met. It was something special a poem, to keep maybe, how often does it happen that someone writes you a one. It was lovely. He wanted to get to know her. On the other hand Karl had written his Sultan Suite, well story and he had invested a year of his life texting her, showing her colour cards and opening up the fantasies of his head to her. Maybe this was enough.

'But you are always running from me,' Ciara texted him with this assertion which she believed to be true.

'I am he.' Karl texted and she couldn't believe her eyes. The timing was uncanny, as if he had read her internal monologue. Weird!

'Pardon?'

'Just as Josephine wanted Napoleon, you want me.'

Ciara thought about this, Josephine had been an inconstant lover, did he want this? Did he want to terrorise her the way Napoleon had? What would she say? Or should she leave it? Could the statement be inverted?

'At least they met. We are stuck in the Overture.' That was what she sent, as that was all she could say. Well when she had a good thought or phrase she had to use it, they didn't come into her head very often.

New U

So there had been a lot of change and Ciara, for the first time in her life was enjoying her job. She took the bus only sometimes as there was training in the City Centre. She could drive to work which was bliss and she often ate dinner with her parents. Her new work was guiding. However there was a lot of research to do in this job to ensure she would know what to guide about. Ciara could put her creative ideation to good use. The house, her new place of work was vast and dated originally to the Eighteenth Century when it had been built as a hunting lodge. It had been extended in the Nineteenth Century and was owned for a large part of its life by the best known brewers in Dublin. Or rather they were the most successful brewers in Dublin, the stout family. How interesting a turn of fate that the result of too much stout was a paunch Ciara's pet hate and now the paunch or the stout which produced it was the main part of her job.

As the family had rights to the waters of the river Liffey this was one if the first electrified houses in Dublin. There was still evidence of a mill race down on the Strawberry Beds, near one of her favourite watering holes.

She had not decided what to do with her car once she completed on her loft and moved in to the City. There was no parking with the apartment unfortunately. As the sale and purchase were rapidly drawing to a conclusion she needed to make a decision. However Ciara had made enough decisions for one year. Her car may well become an early Christmas ornament in her parent's driveway.

It was such a luxury to driving though, waking up later, hopping into her lovely low mileage car, with its soft bucket seats and drive. She would zip out at about 9.40 and arrive promptly at work for ten. What a life. She was even blow-drying her hair twice a week as she had more time. This was a client facing role and for once she wanted to make an effort and erase the fuzz which her mother so strongly disliked.

The tours were supposed to last for 45 minutes and Ciara was so nerve-racked in the beginning that she spoke really quickly and her tours generally finished within 30 minutes. The knowledge gained from her public speaking training was useless as Ciara could not remember any of it. Luckily however there was a safety blanket in the form of a lovely conservatory where she could invite visitors to ask as many questions as possible to kill at least ten minutes. So by the time she dawdled back to the greeting desk she had made up the necessary 45-minute tour. The best bit about the conservatory was the unusual plants. The foliage of one of the creepers had once been a drug in the nineteenth century. At this time ladies didn't drink much alcohol so to compensate they would put their tea cups beneath the branches and drops of this drug would drip in. Apparently there were very happy and relaxed ladies in the house. Gardening had generally been considered a female pursuit. Ciara hoped some resin may still be in the air and calm her too.

The more she learned about the house the more her interest was sparked and she even took to researching at night when she got home. She realised that she didn't dislike people as much as she had originally thought. Her boss was cool, seriously cool and so funny. She could recant stories of the house and its visitors as this was more than just a West Brit pile. Whenever heads of State visited they would stay there. The Queen of England had even stayed she was the first British Monarch to visit and stay in the Republic since the inception of Ireland. When Ciara heard this she couldn't believe it.

Should the day be quiet she was allowed, actually encouraged to browse about the rooms to inspect the art work and architectural features. The average auctioneer would have been green with envy. Maybe even an errant architect could have been interested, who knows.

There were lovely grounds in which to walk and Ciara brought her runners with her every day to survey the gardens at lunch time. Then she began to explore the woodlands and should she eventually tire she would be able to leave the grounds and wander into the Phoenix Park. The on-site cafe was formally a boating house on a little lake, man-made but picturesque all the same. The ducks were loud and lively, really diverting and provided a rural backdrop in which to re-read the picture filled novel-like guide book which was the manual on the house. This gave Ciara a chance to memorise the parts of the tour which she kept forgetting. Aspects like the full name for the Camino or the way of St James. It was slightly amusing to Ciara that one of the families who had owned the house had their headquarters at St. James Gate in Dublin. Was this stout religion?

She was in her element, an over-heated electrical element at times likely to fuse and spark just as the first electrification of the house had been. Basic words tended to elude her whilst giving tours, words such as 'like', 'the' and 'if.' Sometimes this could give for a slightly disjointed tour! On her days off which were oftentimes during the week she intended to tour the National Gallery to see examples of other art by artists whose work was on display at the house. She would also visit sites of cultural interest to steal touring tips from more experienced guides. Could she now be construed as a committed employee? A swat even! One thing at a time though as she didn't want to confuse her overloaded little head just yet.

Maybe there was something to texting after all. Karl the Crusader, fighting for diversions and against the plight of the boring life. It was true that he was dynamic this was one of the greatest draws which Ciara fancied. He had been promoted during one of the deepest World Recessions, if he had been telling the truth. Then he had been virtually head hunted to the best, well the only architects firm which Ciara had ever heard of in Dublin. Did he admire her move? Would he like it if she got a really high-powered job? Something where she would earn the same amount of money as him, or more maybe? Maybe she was thinking of Don again and she was sad that they had not spoken since that falling out. His brainy corporate wife had a more prestigious role than him.

Maybe she was just extrapolating one situation and assuming it to be true for all guys. But hey, if that were the case, if guys wanted a gal to work in a fluffy role she would have been a lot more successful with them in the past, as she had never had a threatening role which could in any way emasculate them.

Maybe she should move to China and be a tour guide there. There was such a male dominance in the population that she would be bound to meet a husband there. "Do they have lofts in China?"

'Hey Ciara, have you started your new job yet?' texted Karl.

'Yes I have and I am playing tour guide, it's quite fun' she answered. She had definitely made the right decision in her new job; she didn't dread getting up every morning. Generally something new gives one the motivation to get out of bed on the first chime of the alarm but she felt even more and so far she was happy.

'That is nice' said Karl.

'It seems you need a PHD just to make coffee in a barista these days in Dublin' she added. Maybe she was giving the game away on the job hunt front. If she had realised quite how difficult the market was she probably would have settled for boredom. Well that's why it is said that ignorance is bliss.

'The jobs market is tough. Is it good?' asked Karl. So he must be aware of the difficulties also.

'Yes really good, I have landed a job showing people about historical sites.' As Dubliners say jammy, most of the time she would be based in the Phoenix Park, near the deer which were brought over for Charles the Second to shoot if he ever got over to Dublin to visit a mistress or two. He must have missed a few, of the deer, as there were still about 400 left in the Park. One particularly nice feature was that she could drive through the Park to get to work and see them grazing. It was not a permanent job but that was fine, it would tide her over while she waited for her redundancy payment to come through and the sale to complete on her own house before she purchased her loft. Ah that lovely loft, in fact the loft was her object of affection now. It had replaced even Karl as her favourite musing!

'Tour guide sounds fun. Where and what?' he delved.

'It's near the Taoiseach's house. Spouting spurious stories is really fun! Most people believe me surprisingly.'

'That sounds great! You can be convincing, haa haa. Can you do individual tours? You know how to string together phrases in the no strings context!' It was curious, he still harked back to no strings attached when all she had said was "you'll be back." He had a predictive memory or remembered things the way he had wanted them said?

'I will have to see what my boss says,' replied Ciara in regards to the one to one tours.

'Is it Casino Marino you are at? The move to a corporate firm has been a good thing, selling my soul for a new cityscape!'

Was he thinking of a previous Taoiseach, Mr Bertie Buzz and the 'Ps I owe u' saga as Marino was nowhere near the Taoiseach's house? This joke was probably older than the daughter who wrote the novel. Unknown to many people, there is an official residence for the Taoiseach it is a bit smaller than the president's house and only up the road just outside the Phoenix Park.

'No sale (as in selling your soul) if you like the job, I thought you were creating a new Dublin.' Then she added, 'thought you were good a research.' As if the current Taoiseach's house is near Marino she thought.

'I am' and then he added, 'definitely would like a private tour, for sure! I could be a visiting dignitary! When can I get the Grand Tour?!'

(Karl's Crux Ha) she thought about the very indiscrete image he had sent, was this the type of grand tour he wanted? Then she reverted to the formal Ciara, the on-show Ciara.

'Forgive me but I thought you were an avid researcher!' She sent after a number of hours. He had not worked out where the house was. Ciara didn't want to be too open with him at such an early stage in the relationship!

'I am you are well informed' he pinged. 'Ok smarty pants, give me some other clues' he said.

So she let him hang for a while as she did actually have to give a tour. It was fun tour guiding, with loads to do. The house had been considered a country house but only a few miles to ride or later drive to the brewing head quarters. Country may only need trees in some descriptions. The hours were great and she could do things in the evenings. No more bus musings for her!

'What is your tour?!' He asked again, he was obviously bored she would like to believe interested but let's not stretch the truth.

It was nice to return to the desk and have a fresh text waiting to be picked up. Hot off the thumbs anyway. She popped out to chat to some of the wildlife in this somewhat rural idyll style. Sub text was a sneaky smoke and a salacious text.

'Think of a big walled garden with the Presidents' House anatomically speaking near the knees'. She sent.

'That's a pretty esoteric clue!' He replied.

'If you think about it then it's clear. What's the largest Park in Dublin?' "Oh he of size and aggrandisement" she thought. 'Or maybe I know the answer. CLUE the walls keep the deer in.'

'Oh well now I feel like a fool!! For some reason I thought Drumcondra area because you said Taoiseach's House! That's great I cycle past the Phoenix Park every day. (Two smiley faces) maybe some evening we can do some deer watching.'

"Get off your Bertie buzz, silly boy" she smiled to herself. It felt good to know something which he did not, it didn't happen very often, but maybe that was what she liked about him. His knowledge, then she thought he cycles too, crazy adrenaline seeking boy.

'The Taoiseach's official residence is Stewards Lodge beside the Park, but it isn't used much. Deer watching is only nice on a fine eve'. She returned. Maybe the tone was a bit gloating and maybe even mean, but she couldn't help it.

No response came back. She waited for several days and there was still nothing so she thought she should send a smoother.

'Were you thinking of a tour of the whole park or just watching the deer? What's your usual cycling attire?' She asked. She knew he rowed, he cross country skied and now he was cycling, what a man of action she thought once more, no wonder he wanted to show himself off to her after all that effort.

Still nothing from that trying texter, then a long while later he sent a despondent e-mail. Why did it always seem so long until he got back to her, was it a control thing, he of power play and dominating frozen landscapes?

'So how are the tours going? Pity you can't give me a personal tour. Pity the weather is so rainy x' He made no apology for the delay, with no reintroduction or preface, just straight in. It was rather perplexing really.

A few days later, she had managed to restrain her thumbs, twitching as they were, she sent off a longer e-mail which may have been a bit cutting but she was kind of annoyed with the lack of carry on and texting activity.

'Well the weather has taken a turn for the better! Truly I am doubtful of your investigative skills as if you had bothered your handsome little head you could have been on one of my 1-2-1 pedal in the park tours today. It was a bit windy for a wrap over dress but I was going less for speed than style.' She was lying but whatever; never let the truth get in the way of a fun text.

'It is uncertain whether you wish to actually locate me as your efforts leave me somewhere between the walls, 1752 acres and some fallow deer! Hope you're having a good weekend,' she continued as she was looking forward to the weekend, it was going to be busy.

And so he didn't respond. It was all dead, blank, nothing, like the trees now that it was winter or the culled deer as the population was getting too great. Maybe she could have said "you're the one for me too," back in the cafe in high summer. If she had gushed back all the things she had been thinking and feeling would things be different now? Would he be more reliable? Would they know each other? Would they be meeting? She thought on the word "discrete" why this word? It was odd.

****

The next day was Saturday and Aoife had promised to come and visit the house and site. The plan was that Ciara would give her a tour and then they would go to the boat-house for lunch and after stroll around the grounds. As the festive season was well underway the house was festooned with decorations.

Noon approached and Ciara sat at the desk in trepidation. She was beginning to know what she was doing and talking about. She was quite confident with certain aspects of the tour but it was the fact that she would be taking a friend about which unsettled her. This was the friend whose opinion she truly valued and she didn't want to mess up. Aoife was such a success at everything she did that Ciara was in some ways in awe of her. She knew that Aoife could remember dates, facts and figures easily and was never wrong in a quote. Whereas Ciara had to learn a subject, forgot and re-learn in an iterative process until the penny eventually dropped. Or maybe that was that it eventually made cents (sense). She couldn't resist the pun. One of the lads in her old job had joked that inflation was so rife in Dublin that one couldn't spend a penny after the € change over, one had to Euro-nate, yuck that was just off.

After a little silly humour she smiled and tuned into the chatter at the desk and relaxed a bit more. Christmas plans were being discussed and choirs were to visit by the bus load to sing in the main hall or ballroom.

Aoife came at 12.15 as arranged for the tour and Ciara introduced her to her boss and the other guides. They exchanged niceties and Aoife said, 'what a great place it must be to work.'

'Yes' said Ciara's boss, 'there is always something new happening here,'

'Ah that's nice I wish I could say the same for my place of work.'

503

The tour began and there were a lot of visitors almost the maximum 25 guests. Ciara brought her guide book manual and papers as she felt having something in her hands made her look officious and in control, two things she really didn't feel. The first room they visited was the study, the gentleman's private room. Ciara started with an overview of the house, its context, the history and the main protagonist who lived there. She explained what he contributed to Irish history and how he made all his money.

There was a quiver in her voice which she could not suppress. She tried to breathe deeply, in through her nose and out through her mouth. However she began to sound like she was in an ante-natal class preparing for childbirth. Whoops! So she tried to speak slower, there may be a chance that one in twenty would understand her. Hopefully that one would be Aoife.

'So why did he decide to leave his Irish town house to the Government?'

Ciara looked about her; it was Aoife asking the question, a really hard question at that. Ciara paused, collected her thoughts and said 'Edward Cecil (He) had left his London house to the people of Britain and he realised the Irish State did not have a great deal of money. So he decided to leave his town house in St Stephens Green to what is now the Department of Foreign Affairs. This is fitting as his product was one of the largest Irish exports at the time.'

"Phew, hope that was ok!" The group nodded and seemed to be contented with the answer and the extent of this gentleman's philanthropy. The rest of the tour proceeded well but there were lots of questions as once the politeness factor had been overcome people felt free to ask questions and the group's interest could not be sated. At the Conservatory Ciara received some tips, as in money rather than gardening advice. What a result!

'That was passable,' said Aoife and then she burst out laughing at Ciara's grimace. 'You were great, I mean it you were great. I am so happy for you. This is your thing.'

'Thanks, I love it Aoife. I have never in my life thought of work as more than a four-letter word which gets you pregnant but with money.'

'Hmm, all that research has meant quite a lot of time at home then, over-thinking.'

'You could say that, but it is no chore, actually I think I am turning into a teachers' pet.' Aoife was referring to her analogy Ciara supposed, maybe she had been thinking too much about this job. However it meant she was thinking a lot less about Karl, even if he was an orphan he wasn't getting her sympathy texts.

'Don't be silly, it is really important to be enthusiastic about work in the beginning and this is a super cushy number.'

They strolled out the back of the house and across the gardens down to the cafe. 'You will have to see my ducks,' said Ciara. 'They are so cute and there are also moorhens and a heron.'

'I didn't know you were into nature.'

'No I wasn't before but it is just so accessible here.'

'So how is Stephen doing without you?' Aoife asked, this was almost a Pavlovian response. Ciara was more than a little taken aback at this automatic word association, to Stephen and disability. In her mind Aoife was quite PC, maybe nothing was meant by it but Stephen was her piece of precious. Never to be undervalued and accessible had more than one meaning in her mind. It also meant someone not being accessible to you, such as the intermittent texter.

'Actually he is doing really well for himself. Remember Anna my old boss well she is going on maternity leave soon and Stephen will be doing the cover for her, it is a semi-promotion. I mean it is a great promotion but it is not permanent. He was really suffering survivors' syndrome with Don gone, then as you know Sophie got a new job and now me. However since he got this promotion he is in his element. Anna is training him up for it.'

'Ah, that is good to hear.'

'Also and most importantly to Stephen he is in-charge of the social calendar. He is chief organiser and has even got a few career coaches in to mentor people on options for work and stuff.'

'Yes I can see your eyes glazing over there Ciara the corporate ladder didn't really appeal.'

'No not one bit,' Ciara was cultural not corporate she was sure that Tourism and Culture would be the means of

Irelands recovery programme. Well obviously it would now that she was involved, she smiled to herself.

'So will Stephen visit you here?'

'He and Sophie will pop out but I don't want him here just yet.'

Aoife gave a knowing smile, 'yes he is such a history boffin.'

'He is that.' Ciara stopped a moment and smiled, breathed in slowly and Aoife knew one of her over-thinking and profound statements was about to be unleashed. 'You know Aoife, life is very simple,' Ciara said sagaciously.

'Yes, let me know your pontifications, oh wise and bookish Ciara!'

'Well change the things which are not good in your life and keep those which are. That's all.'

'True, but easier said than done. Have you changed texts?'

'Ahem, no there is a third part to my tome which I describe as the "waiting at the bus stop bit." That is, if things are ok, just tipping along, sure just let them rattle on until something better comes along.'

'Are you saying this in the context of you and your imaginary friend Karl?' said Anna.

'He is something to have but not something to hold.'

'Whatever makes you happy,' said Aoife.

Ciara smiled and for a change said nothing.

'No Ciara, I worry that you live in your head not on Earth. Reality can be too fun to switch off.'

'I do live on Earth and interface with reality sometimes,' said Ciara. 'I am content here.'

'So you are happy.'

'You know since that phone call with Sean I have been able to let go. Sean doesn't have power over me anymore, I am well and I realise that I am emotionally independent.'

'Oh' said Aoife.

'I know Karl has been playing with my emotions, but until I was able to extricate myself from Sean I would not have been able to have a relationship with him or anyone. Finally I feel strong again. If Karl wants to meet me again I will be able to say to him that I can now be available to him.'

'Would you really like that? He is a bit of a meanie,' said Aoife.

'What Karl has done, probably unintentionally is to provide a safe and removed space where I can reawaken my emotional and maybe sexual side.'

'Well, keep that space safe. I think he has been playing with you,' said Aoife.

'Maybe I have been playing him!'

Aoife looked puzzled but said nothing.

At the end of the day when Ciara was on her countryside commute she thought "is it true? Have I been playing Karl too? Have I been using him as an emotional crutch until I was strong enough to stand alone?" Had she been leading him through her own emotional battlefields just as Josephine had thrust her children on Napoleon and expected him to secure them in powerful positions or good marriages? There could have been mutual benefits he had certainly told her so. Yes she was in control.

The End

It is debatable that if something never existed then how could it end? Actuality and fact can be rather different to fantasy and emotion. If it is felt internally can an emotion form a synoptic path which is strong, but just like pain it is difficult to quantify? Could this path be traced back in memory? Does something have to be real to be measured as feelings are felt; maybe their depth is the measuring tool.

Every day for nearly a year, Ciara had been hoping to see Karl on the bus. She had now reconciled herself to the fact that she was never going to see him. That was ok, more than ok it was fine, she was getting on with her life and things were going really well. Karl did not actually exist he was just a remote response unit or computer in other words projecting her emotions and fantasies and keeping her busy. It was good to be busy. She thought back to their first meeting, it was in the snow but had she imagined it. Now it seemed like a dream, another world and another person. Then the next meeting was in the heat as hot as Dublin ever gets, it was such a contrast. No that meeting was not true either, her brain was too suggestive.

Now he was here, what, was that possible? He was on the bus. She turned her head to the left at Wellington Quay, as she always did, the special part of the Quays where they had spoken, smiled and first kissed. A year to the day of that first time she fell over in the snow. She looked down to the exact spot to reminisce and saw a large figure bend his head and climb on board. Ah, reality was about to clash with fantasy and she wasn't ready for the confrontation. Why was he getting on here anyway? He worked opposite her, or rather where she used to work. This was her first bus journey in weeks and here he was. She had been at the head office training for the day and had enjoyed the buzz of town after her rural working location.

Her hands trembled and her breathing became very shallow and fast, he was here. It was a wet winter evening and the bus was full-with people. Their coats, umbrellas and hair were wet. Some windows were open on the bus to ensure they didn't fog up and the rain had just stopped. Now the clouds were clearing and a weak sun would begin to shine from a far off but very hot place. Ciara pulled out a mirror and some lipstick from her bag to tidy her face and make the most of a bad lot. Maybe he would come and sit near the front and she could nonchalantly say "hey Karl, how are you! What a surprise." For once, unlike in her fantasies it would be true. He trawled up the stairs and as there were not many seats available he bent over his head and headed for a space but he kept walking head down away from her, he would never see her at this rate. Maybe that was a good thing.

The seat Karl chose was on the very end row and he would be able to stretch out his long limbs. Ciara discretely observed all this action through her compact mirror. It appeared he hadn't noticed her yet, maybe because her face was obscured by the mirror. She was also at the far end of the bus, facing the other way.

She took several deep breaths to gather her courage and calm her nerves. He was here. She looked around to catch his eye, it was a long way away, but she had to try. The clouds continued to roll back and the sun temporarily shone illuminating a large platinum ring on his wedding finger. It seemed to be huge and encompass the rear third of the bus, this ring, this physical symbol of his emotional and legal tie to another.

She gulped deeply and turned away facing the front again. Her disappointment was acute, tears stung her eyes and she felt cheated. It was not just a feeling of disappointment but a sickening sense of being deceived which hurt her to the core. Every atom of her being had been deceived. "He's married! Of course it makes sense now. The emotionally unavailable male is unavailable for a reason. I have to confront him. He has been playing me along." Her thoughts of emotional independence, her playing with him and her being in control vanished as quickly as her dreams of meeting his Norwegian grandfather and getting married in a longboat! She was not in control, it was his game and it always had been.

Ciara hyperventilated several times and if the passenger next to her were looking he would have observed her turning many colours ranging from ashen grey to bright red boiling with anger. Then finally she composed herself. It seemed like this sense of composure had taken hours. What to do? Could she confront him, should she wait until she was home and e-mail him from a safe distance?

He would not have to see her crying and know how much he had hurt her.

"The con-texter and his textual relationship and I played the willing victim. He didn't have to lead me on I was already saddled up and ready to go!" She could not leave this rest, she had deluded herself and she had to know why. He had said she was the one for him. It was lies, all lies and she had meant nothing to him.

She had to see his facial reactions, his real life, real time reactions and make him squirm. That what she wanted, she wanted to see how he looked caught out! Let him know there were consequences for excessive texting, excessive complimenting, excessive, what else had he done? He had led her on. She had been his emotional boost like Berocca for the ego.

'I'm on de bus, look up!' she texted as she could not yet face getting off her seat. It is said that necessity is the mother of invention, but to Ciara it was the mother of anxiety. She wondered were there any Greek Goddesses called Anxiety or was this concept too modern to be personified. She had likened him to feckin Napoleon, no wonder his ego was had big as a skyscraper. She had been building him up one compliment at a time so he was able to reach for Moscow and win. Or in other words she was why he was able to aim, achieve and succeed at such a high-powered job. What was more stinging was that this recession was primarily property-based. Behind every great man maybe these days there is a great texter!

Karl read the text and looked up. As he did so he automatically removed his wedding ring and slipped it in a pocket. She observed him stealthily between the many heads. Was it too large for him or had he just married the wrong gal? His head motioned from side to side in an attempt to see her. He looked down at his phone as if a sign would appear. Well supposedly it had, she had sent him a message. Her already crucified heart was being hung drawn and quartered, he was a cad. He really was a cad.

'Hi Ciara, are you on the 67X?'

'Of course, would I joke with you?' Joviality always leaves us when we need it most. It is a nuisance that Jupiter was funnier than Zeus. These Roman Gods were more developed than the Greek ones. If she could only think of a pithy response, pithy yet cutting she would feel a bit better. None came to mind unfortunately. If only Thor were with her now, but he had been, he was the weather god after all. It was he who had allowed the sun to shine through the clouds and let Ciara know the truth. "Thor I knew you were the cool God, I didn't have a weather obsession for nothing." With this diversion she finally calmed herself.

'Should I come up to you?' he asked.

She thought about this. Did she want him coming up to her where, maybe a melodramatic scene would be created? Would she feel embarrassed in front of all these strangers on the bus? Only a few moments ago she had been boiling mad and had to know why. Now though she was unsure whether she really wanted the whole story it would be a harsh truth. She knew the reason for his unavailability, it was a long bus journey he could wait five minutes.

'Are you near the front, I cannot see my Josephine from the rear guard.' He repeated hopefully, getting in to character.

Where was this man of action who had escaped from Elba, who had Europe on its knees? Well sitting at the back of the bus, playing with his phone, spreading out his long legs and hiding his wedding ring. She was disappointed, not just that he was married but that he could hide this so quickly. By hiding his ring he could be available to her and unavailable to his wife. The duplicity of it began to anger her again. His action had been automatic, not considered, not questioned but enacted at the first opportunity of a diversion. Had he done this before? Did she care if he had? Now that she knew what else was there to say?

Up she hopped and stormed down to the aisle of the bus. She was propelled forwards with such self righteous vigour that she lost her sense of space. Knapsacks and laptop bags were hurriedly cleared from her narrow path and she was a woman on a mission. Determination burned in her eyes. Her face was set in a stern grimace. She had no idea what she would say but now she was unthinking, propelled forward with outrage and indignation. She reached the back of the bus.

'You're married!' it was out there and there was no point in mincing words. Whilst seated she had intended to begin humorously, slowly and then catch him out. However her anger had resulted in her going to the crux of the matter, straight away. This wasn't the photographic type of crux either.

He squirmed, inhaled deeply, gulped several times and eventually said, 'what do you mean?' In an unconfident tone this statement was expressed.

'Karl! Karl, Karl' she shouted the first Karl, spoke the second and the third was almost a whisper.

A few people in the second last row, where she was standing, shifted uncomfortably and politely looked out the windows. They were pretending not to be there, most likely wishing they had not been.

'Would you like to sit down?' He asked.

She was unsure. She had the moral high ground and by standing was actually physically higher. If she were to sit they would be on the same level and this may diminish some of the affect. She may feel less dominant, powerful and in control. Her ire had been vented and now she didn't really know what to do.

'Please sit,' he repeated, more gently this time. He gave her a half smile maybe in an attempt to give off warmth and encouragement.

'Ok' she collapsed into a tight space in the back row beside him. She squashed into a large bearded man who was pretending to be asleep.

'Ciara, you are right I am married.'

'Why did you pursue me then?'

'I was not married when I met you. I was engaged but I seriously thought of breaking off my obligations when I met you. That night you were a vision.'

A passenger along the row snorted under her breath.

Ciara was almost going to say, "Am I not a vision now?" A diversion from the facts so thought better of it bit her tongue and kept quiet.

'That night, the night we met was perfect.' He continued, 'it seemed as if all the planets were aligned for us on one snowy night. We were star crossed strangers, destined to be lovers.

'That kiss,' he went on 'in the snow on Wellington Quay was perfect. Nobody was about, all sound was muffled and I knew you missed your very last bus to be with me. You may not have got home that night but you were prepared to risk it as you felt this too.'

The rather squashed bearded male's left eyebrow raised at the thought.

'I took off your hat and your hair billowed down your back and across your face. I had almost got the memory out of my head until you wrote me the bathroom fantasy. Now it is scorched in my brain and can never be removed. I tell you if I had been in the country when I received that e-mail, I would have run to you and made love to you there and then.'

Ciara sensed slight movements of uncomfortable passengers who were embarrassed to hear a flawed love story enfolding in front of them.

'Go back to the Quays, we have a long journey yet,' directed Ciara. She was going to make him talk about their arranged meeting but she wanted to hear his story in sequence.

'You laid your hand gently on me, so lightly that I could not quite feel you. Yet I sensed your gloved hand must be there. I knew it was. We had talked as equals that night, intellectually, socially, economically and when I kissed you I knew we would be equals intimately. My knees weakened and I felt light headed for a long moment. You were about to leave but I couldn't let you go. I hopped into the taxi after you as I knew if it ended there I would never see you again.'

'Well you nearly never did. You went to Norway, I said you'll be back!' he didn't take up the theme of no strings attached and as his story was unfolding Ciara really wanted to know why. Understanding was the only thing to be gained at this point; hopefully this would give her solace when she reflected later.

'Yes I went to Norway, my fiancée was, is Norwegian. I snuck out in the freezing cold to text you at Christmas but at New Year she wouldn't leave me alone. Not for one second. She would say "you are distant" or "are you having second thoughts?"'

'I remember that night I checked my phone so many times, again and again and again. I felt so let down, the most romantic night of the year. I was away from you and you never called. No word of poetry or prose not even a text was sent!'

'I am sorry,' he stated with a deep undertone of pathos in his voice and she understood this to be true. There was sadness in his arctic blue eyes and he lowered his head in shame.

"Good" thought Ciara "he is finally feeling some shame at his actions and maybe a sense of loss!"

'I was going to tell her that night,' Karl continued. 'Tell her that I was having second thoughts, but she kept so close to me all night. She was so kind, so caring and kept visualising how great our life would be together, in the future. Being married was all she wanted I just couldn't let her down. So I told myself I would text you the next day and then the next.'

'But you didn't' Ciara was hoping that he wouldn't confirm this. Hope is a curious emotion, when all of one's being logically indicates a certain course, the most likely outcome, based on all the evidence, hope pops along and gives a completely different version of events. It also comes up with very idealised and oftentimes silly conclusions. Ciara realised she had hoped, had ignored all evidence to the contrary as she had really wanted to be with Karl, so very much.

'No, I didn't,' Karl went on. 'I rationalised this meeting we had had and wondered was it worth changing my whole life for...for...for something which I was uncertain of.'

'Karl, when we met you confirmed your feelings. It was months later but when we touched we must have shorted all the electricity in the tea shop. We sucked it in and threw it out into a handshake.'

'Yes' he said, 'how could I forget.'

'I offered to be a flower girl at your **FAMILY WEDDING**!"

'I know and I am ashamed to say I was on my way to get married.'

'Yes and I am a gullible fool who believed what I wanted to hear.'

'You would make a nice flower girl or even brides-made,' he tried to smile. 'I did imagine winding daisies through your hair.'

'Yes it is true there were only two meetings. It was real though, the time together, intense and moving, it was amazing,' she was restraining the tears which were proving as undisciplined as Austrian soldiers at Austerlitz.

'It was' he said quickly. 'It was amazing.'

'I was sick of the coffee references which had been going on for months. I felt your resolve had frozen like an iced coffee.'

He smiled and relaxed into his seat. 'Is that why you chose a tea shop to meet in?'

'Yes and I wanted to blast your inertia away with Gun Powder tea,' said Ciara in her dramatic voice.

'Well Ciara, you do have a way with words,' he assured her and in-spite of herself she grinned. 'You were at a safe distance, but I was addicted to the buzz. That meeting was great, I meant what I said. You are so alive.'

'Come on Karl, I have heard enough compliments. Now I would like to hear some reality.'

'I meant you are the one for me,' he was emphatic.

'Bastard' the bearded man interjected unable it seemed to restrain himself any longer.

'I saw you in the tea house, it was a bit scary. I lost control.'

'Yes actually you are right I have a great way with words' confirmed Ciara she may as well big herself up. 'Keep going, I want to know.' She was going to add "you big blue-eyed liar you were off to get married in Norway" but she somehow managed to restrain herself.

'I went into the tea house and I couldn't see you as you had ducked under the table!' He was continuing the story.

'Feck, did you notice?'

He was silent.

'Yep, but I did it with such grace,' she smiled feeling very embarrassed.

'Of course you did,' in a rather unconvinced tone, 'but I had the same feelings, dread and fear but with an equal compulsion which propelled me forward with an almost preternatural speed. Then before I knew it I was there beside you, at your table and our lives merged again.'

'Yes they did, but you were on your way to your wedding.' Sugar she always fired her cannons to soon.

Maybe one could not keep powder dry on a damp evening such as this.

'I was. I had my suit pressed, my mind resolved to do it, I was seeing you...'

Ciara listened she did not want to interrupt him again and remembered the electricity generated from that look, from him standing beside her it could have powered the whole of Dublin for that evening.

'I touched your hand and I went blank' Karl continued. 'I forgot about my fiancée my wedding the next day, all I wanted was you. I said it, I said you are the one for me. I knew you felt this too but you said nothing.'

'How was I to know you were getting married, it could have been your Grandfathers' wedding for all I knew, he was a player.'

'Yes you are right. I was not completely open,' said Karl. My, that was an understatement.

'No you were not. I knew there was something very strong, but I wanted to get to know you. I didn't want to simply mimic you and repeat the line you had given me.'

'Yes, but I felt that you were not prepared to commit to me.'

Ciara was silent, was this true? If she had made a declaration would he be sitting beside her on the bus because they were married?

'I have never had so much contact with someone I didn't meet again,' agreed Karl. 'They were stolen moments, you haunted my dreams and inspired me on, to achieve. You were like a Josephine always there whenever I needed you. Ciara I felt you were not serious about me, I felt you would always be elusive that there was a part of you I could never reach.'

Ciara thought about this, could it be true that her core had been an iced-coffee and he didn't have enough boiling water to melt it? No he was wriggling out of it, she would have been his if he had let her and that was the truth, she was not going to accept his denials!

'Is she beautiful?' why did Ciara have to torture herself?

'My wife?' he stopped a moment and Ciara nodded. 'Yes she is the perfect Scandinavian look, blond straight hair, total contrast to you...'

He would have gone on but Ciara stopped him by glaring in his face. She was boiling mad again, it was like swallowing that damp powder for the cannon and somehow it dried out in her throat and set all her organs on fire, was this fight and fight syndrome? They had been through enough imaginary battles that this one was finally for real. She had advanced, attacked and there was not retreating until she had said her piece.

'You are a cad, because you chose the safe option, you craved the fantasy of an exciting life. You fantasised about illicit meetings in the Phoenix Park or pretending to be a visiting dignitary at my work place. Or any grand house in which mischief may ensue, these fantasies were all compensation for a safe life. You however did not have the courage to actualise this. So you are a coward.'

Karl looked down at his hands and said nothing.

'The less exciting but more certain option was the one you chose back on New Years' Eve. You didn't follow the Napoleon trail of adventure, bravery and battle. You have a rented house and you rent your dreams from me!'

'Well said,' agreed the bearded male who was actively participating in the goings on.

'It's obvious you are not fulfilled in your life, with your boring blond wife' Ciara went on but really she should be stopping. 'However it was your choice to marry her and let me say that life with me would have been fun. Always seeking new adventure! I live my life to excess, follow my dreams and it is always mine. Borrow, beg or rent your dreams elsewhere.' With that she hopped up quickly and skipped up the aisle, down the stairs and off the bus. All the resettled back-packs and lap-top cases which had been carefully left in the aisle again were hastily lifted out of her storm path. She was way too early for her stop, but today, in spite of the wind, the dark and winter she wanted to walk. Nay she needed to walk.

'Zoom, zoom, zoom, zoom, the World is in a mess. The politics and taxes, people grinding axes, there's no happiness....Zoom zoom the rhythm eases my aches. The future won't beget me, if I can only get me someone to slap that base...Happiness is not a riddle, when I listen to that big base fiddle.' Fred Astaire always had a song for every mood, an escape from every escapade.

'Actually this is the time for "no strings no connections, no ties to my affections," that is more apt. "I'm fancy free and free for anything fancy..."

Printed in Great Britain
by Amazon